THE
WEAVING
OF LIFE

THE
WEAVING
OF LIFE

NEW DIRECTIONS
BOOK ONE
AN AMISH ROMANCE

LINDA BYLER

Good Books

New York, New York

THE WEAVING OF LIFE

Good Books books may be purchased in bulk at special discounts for sales promotion, corporate gifts, fund-raising, or educational purposes. Special editions can also be created to specifications. For details, contact the Special Sales Department, Good Books, 307 West 36th Street, 11th Floor, New York, NY 10018 or info@skyhorsepublishing.com.

Good Books is an imprint of Skyhorse Publishing, Inc.®, a Delaware corporation.

Visit our website at www.goodbooks.com.

10 9 8 7 6 5 4 3 2 1

Library of Congress Cataloging-in-Publication Data
Names: Byler, Linda, author.
Title: The weaving of life : an Amish romance / Linda Byler.
Description: New York : Good Books, 2023. | Series: New Directions ; book 1
| Summary: "The first in a captivating series about an independent Amish woman and her struggles in career and romance"-- Provided by publisher.
Identifiers: LCCN 2023000816 (print) | LCCN 2023000817 (ebook) | ISBN 9781680998603 (paperback) | ISBN 9781680998757 (epub)
Subjects: LCSH: Amish--Fiction. | LCGFT: Romance fiction. | Christian fiction. | Novels.
Classification: LCC PS3602.Y53 W47 2023 (print) | LCC PS3602.Y53 (ebook) | DDC 813/.6--dc23/eng/20230109
LC record available at https://lccn.loc.gov/2023000816
LC ebook record available at https://lccn.loc.gov/2023000817

Print ISBN: 978-1-68099-860-3
eBook ISBN: 978-1-68099-875-7

Cover design by Create Design Publish LLC

Printed in the United States of America

CHAPTER 1

THE DAY WAS SIZZLING HOT, THE MERCURY IN THE THERMOMETER outside the kitchen window showing almost ninety-five degrees. The white impatiens in the moss basket appeared wilted and despondent in the filtered sunlight from the leaves of the oak tree. The neighbors' black-and-white house cat prowled the flower bed, watching for stray birds from the feeder.

Susan sighed, turning off the faucet to stop the flow of water before lifting the plastic bucket of hot water out of the kitchen sink, grateful for the cool air blowing from the vents. Central air conditioning was a wonder, as was the central vacuum cleaner she plied from room to room as she cleaned the entire house: five bedrooms, four bathrooms, large family room, huge kitchen, and living room.

She was the maid. The house cleaner. The help. Call it whatever you wanted, she was a servant to the Klausers, a well-to-do couple in their sixties who spent most of their time at work or on vacation in various locations throughout the country. She'd cleaned this house to perfection for seven years, starting when she was fifteen years old, so she knew the whims of her employer, Carol. She knew when the bathroom vanity needed to be wiped underneath, knew to check the toaster oven to see if it had an accumulation of burnt cream cheese frosting on the racks.

Eight hours of hard work. She took a fifteen-minute break to eat a granola bar for lunch and drink a cold Pepsi if she had time. Working alone, her thoughts had free rein as she snapped clean sheets on king-sized beds, smoothed luxurious bedspreads and duvets, dusted, swept, wiped, and polished.

The money was nice, the roll of cash in her pocket book a testament to her hard work. She'd slump in the front seat of the black Infiniti, glad to relax and listen to Carol's monologue, which was usually about the absolute stupidity of her yard man, plumber, builder, or husband, and not always in that order.

Carol was smart, informed, well read. She was a lawyer in Lancaster and viewed the world with cynical contempt. She had seen too much of a world seething with divorce, bitterly contested wills, human beings scrabbling and fighting for ownership, for power and greed. But there was a soft side to her, a side Susan saw when Carol told her about certain cases like the one she won on behalf of two orphan children, her eyes filling with tears of compassion. And when Susan tired of the hard work of housekeeping, there was always the loyalty she felt for Bill and Carol, her employers. What would they do without her?

And so she was picked up and driven to the house every week to clean and polish the inside of the microwave, the Italian coffee maker, the endless round of showers and commodes. She had been taught to work and to give her parents her paycheck until she turned twenty-one, which had been last year. She had been allowed to keep about a third of the money for herself.

This was Susan's life, the life of an Amish girl at twenty-two years of age, unmarried and unattached, now with a balanced checkbook of her own and a significant amount of money in her savings account. Most of the time she liked her life. A slacker husband and a passel of runny-nosed kids were not for her.

She bent over the new Kohler commode, wiped the seat, the lid, and the outside of the bowl with Clorox water, then brushed the inside of the bowl. Then she got down on her hands and knees to do the ceramic tile floor. Her sister Kate had married at nineteen, small and dark-haired and radiant the day of her wedding. Dan, her husband-to-be, was just as short and as dark-haired and radiant. The perfect couple.

Except Dan turned out to be a very troubled person. His emotional turmoil had been hidden well. He was a favorite in the family, on all accounts seeming to be the kind of man who would make a good Christian father and husband.

It was when yet another baby was born and her mother noticed that there were hardly any groceries in the house, the refrigerator and pantry alarming, that suspicions were aroused. Kate's mother began asking questions. Kate cried, admitted the sadness of her existence, the self-blame, the hopelessness for a better life. She told how often Dan missed work, how their finances were in disarray, bills unable to be paid.

Their mother took charge, insisting no one outside the immediate family needed to know. Dan was a good man. If Kate tried hard enough, she could change him. Books were bought and distributed, showing Kate how to be the perfect helpmeet, one who would win him over in Christian love. And Kate had rallied. She put her all into accomplishing the impossible. Susan watched the deterioration of her happy, glowing sister into one who was like a waxen doll, one who neither laughed nor cried, who cared for her babies mechanically. When she came for sisters' day, a day to bake together and catch up on all the family news, she went home crushed. Their mother always told Kate to brace up, to try harder to be a better wife and mother, which left her feeling even heavier, like the whole mess was her own fault.

And there was her sister Rose. She had married into a large, close-knit family considered far superior to hers and who had no qualms about correcting her way of doing almost everything. Her mother-in-law blamed her for things gone even slightly awry, but of course her husband could do no wrong. And so Rose had turned into a snorting, disenchanted wife who couldn't stand her in-laws.

If that wasn't enough reason to avoid any relationship with a man, then Susan didn't know what was. She figured marriage was just a trap—the men put on airs to impress the girls, but after they were legally and spiritually in their clutches, look out.

Nope, no boyfriend for her. Absolutely not.

She opened the sliding glass door and threw the Clorox water over the railing of the back patio, watching it drip off the shrubs. She had been told to take it down the steps to the mulch beneath the patio, but no one was home—they'd never know the difference. A bit of Clorox would not hurt those shrubs, and she was tired. Her feet hurt.

Liz, the sister closest to Susan in age, had done alright, she guessed. Married at twenty-one to Dave. He was a decent fellow, if you could put up with that big stomach and the trousers pulled up over it, the suspenders frightfully short. He was a good provider, a talkative, jolly soul who loved Liz and the children the way a father should. Liz had a pretty good life with Dave. But then, Dave's father had Alzheimer's now, and since his mother had passed away from kidney failure, it was up to the children to care for him. He made his rounds among the children; eight of them had to take their turn, caring for this poor, babbling soul who had no idea where he was and was prone to bursts of anger. Liz dreaded her two weeks, but inevitably he'd arrive and be shepherded into the house, inadvertently terrorizing the children and setting Liz's teeth on edge.

So there you were.

Susan stepped up on the ledge of the large stone fireplace in the family room, lifting the glass vases and a battery-operated candle and dusting the mantel.

Then there was this whole thing about having babies. It was just one big misery. She watched her sisters become fat and grouchy, unable to bend down to wipe their toddlers' noses. And then they'd be delivered of a squalling red-faced infant who refused to nurse, and tears would roll down the young mother's face while the good husband stood there with a stupid grin. Babies were not all they were cracked up to be. There was a whole lot of suffering involved, the way she saw it.

Susan had always been there for her sisters when they had new babies. She did the laundry, cleaned, tried to keep order with confused two-year-olds who were throwing fits or getting into trouble. Susan had her own opinions about how the children should be disciplined, but it wasn't her place to make those decisions. So she usually managed to restore some semblance of order by cajoling them with a storybook or a handful of Lucky Charms on the highchair tray. She didn't always agree with her sisters' choices, but she admired their patience, their perseverance in the face of so much against them. They always seemed to manage a smile despite their lack of sleep as their husbands came in smelling like manure, dumping their lunch boxes on the counter and leaving a trail of dried, caked mud on the floor.

Good for them.

Marriage and motherhood were overrated. Why put yourself through all that if you didn't have to? Susan planned to remain free and independent with money in the bank from jobs she enjoyed.

She pulled the sweeper hose out from the opening in the wall, inserted it into the one in the dining room, and began vacuuming the brown, blue, and burnt orange patterned carpet. She loved the feel of the dense plush on her bare feet. It was difficult to imagine having such luxury in her own house. She wiped down leather chairs, dusted end tables, removed an array of pottery bowls and dusted underneath, then grabbed the Windex and paper towels to do the French doors.

Carol often told Susan, with a good-natured laugh, that windows were not her thing, she always left streaks. Susan blamed it on the Windex. She should be using the new *fenschta loompa* (window cloths), the single best invention ever. One to wash and one to wipe dry. Zero streaks. But there was no persuading Carol, who insisted Windex was best. Every TV commercial told you that.

She thought of Kate's children's threadbare sleepwear. The yard sale hand-me-downs, the too-small shoes Nathan had worn to church. She thought of her own growing savings account and felt raw guilt. But then, the last time she'd tried pressing two twenty-dollar bills into Kate's hand, she'd refused, flouncing away with a sort of belligerence and leaving Susan ashamed of trying.

Susan had no idea how Kate managed to feed her children, make the house payment on the small ranch house, and keep up with the other bills. She had three children already, and one due in September. Micah was not yet two. A sizzling rebellion against all of it caused

Susan to wipe ferociously at the small panes. How had the rosy dreams of girlhood turned into such a dismal reality?

Liz and Rose saw things differently. They told Susan she was like an old car rusting away in the weeds, being eaten away by her own negativity. No marriage is perfect, they said, but you take the good with the bad and the love you have for your man carries you through.

The door to the garage opened and Carol breezed in, her car keys jangling as she threw them on the table.

"Did you get some lunch?" she called out.

"I had a granola bar."

"Good."

As if there was anything else to eat, Susan thought wryly. They had a huge Sub-Zero refrigerator filled with salad greens, lemon water, wine, and orange juice. Not much else. They both cooked but were committed to an all-organic, plant-based diet, so the refrigerator held no real food, not the kind Susan was used to. She was always ravenous when she arrived home, her mother's good supper foremost on her mind.

"I'm back here on the computer. Yell when you're done."

"I will."

She wiped down the hardwood floor with Murphy's Oil Soap, emptied the bucket (down the steps this time since Carol was home), and hung up the vacuum hose. She cleaned the stainless steel sink with Bar Keeper's Friend, put the rag with the other used ones in the dishpan by the washer, and she was ready to go.

As Carol backed the car expertly into the L-shaped drive, she told Susan she wouldn't need her next week since they were spending a few days in the Outer Banks. *Good*, Susan thought. *I'll help Kate a few days.* This time of year she'd be busy in her garden, canning and freezing things for winter use.

"Oh, I'll tell you. I get so sick of Lowe's. Whoever heard of charging twelve ninety-nine for perennials? They're all half dead. I'm going to have to go south if I want anything decent. All I wanted was one rugosa. You think they'd have one healthy rugosa? No, of course not. It just burns me up the way these megastores operate."

Susan agreed at appropriate times but wasn't really listening to the usual battering of people or places. Tomorrow was Thursday, the first market day, the day she would be preparing salads and sandwiches at the deli. She looked forward to working with the usual crew, among them her best friend Beth.

As they pulled up to Susan's house Carol handed over the usual roll of bills, thanked her, and turned to her phone, as if to speed up Susan's exit.

"Thank you, Carol. I'll see you in a couple weeks then."

There was barely an acknowledgment, Carol's attention on her phone, so Susan shut the door and was thrown into the suffocating heat from the macadam drive.

Her mother greeted her from the kitchen stove, her face red from the heat and the cooking. The table was set for five: Susan, her two brothers, and her parents. The clock chimed five, first the one in the kitchen followed by the strains of "Amazing Grace" from the battery-operated one in the living room.

"How was your day?"

"The usual. Glad for central air."

"I bet."

"What's for supper? Any mail?"

"Fried chicken, rice, and BLT salad. Too hot to go to a lot of trouble."

"That sounds like work to me."

Susan found the mail, riffled through it, found her check from the market, then took it upstairs to her room. Even the shade of the maple tree did nothing to cool the house; her room was stifling, the curtains hanging straight without a breeze. She looked around, appreciating the cool white of her bedspread, the white walls, the grayish-white hue of her furniture. The tall fig tree in the corner and the floral prints on the wall came together to create a room that was her own personal space, her haven.

Her home was a vinyl-sided two-story along busy Philadelphia Pike, the 340, the main road through the heart of Lancaster County. It had a macadam drive, a barn-shop combination in the back, a large garden, a pasture, and a line of pine trees along the side of their property. Her father, David Lapp, worked at a furniture shop. He managed fifteen employees and loved it. Her parents were always low key, in unison, merry and talkative, keeping the atmosphere of the home alive with the oxygen of love and moderation.

Sometimes, when her two single brothers became a bit boisterous or had too many late nights, her father would become stern, the air around him thick with disapproval, and the boys would know they had overstepped their boundaries. Her mother would agree to the words of rebuke, doubling the effect of his words, helping curtail the reach for a more liberal lifestyle.

Tonight the kitchen was too hot to enjoy their supper, so the boys persuaded their proper mother to carry everything to the shaded back patio. She complained, said they never ate their supper on a porch when she was a girl at home, but Mark told her times change, and they might as well go along for the ride.

The leaves on the maple tree hung still and dusty, no breeze to riffle them at all. The dull sound of traffic along the front of the property was not bothersome, everyone so accustomed to hearing the usual sounds of motors, an occasional rumble of steel wheels, and the clopping of horse's hooves.

The fried chicken was crispy, the meat falling off the bones, just the way Susan liked it. The salad was fresh, with tomatoes from the garden, the rice fluffy and flavored with chicken base and butter. Her mother was an outstanding cook, her pies and cakes renowned through the neighborhood, which she said had everything to do with her father's liberal praise of her cooking. They drank a gallon of meadow tea, that delicious minty concoction made of freshly cut spearmint, peppermint, apple tea, sugar, water, and ice cubes.

"Another wonderful supper," her father said quietly.

"It was great, Mom. Thanks," Elmer echoed, running a large, tanned hand through his closely cropped hair.

"You're a good cook, Mom," Mark chimed in, leaning back in his chair, mimicking his brother. Susan smiled at him, and he grinned back at her.

"Come on, Susan. Tell Mom how good that was."

So Susan praised her mother's cooking and meant it, which pleased her mother so much she told her family they spoiled her, they really did. Not every mother was blessed to have an appreciative husband and children.

"Yup. We're good kids. Hear that, Dat? Next time you wanna tear us out, think about what Mom said."

Her father grinned slowly, his eyes twinkling.

It was too hot to sleep that night, so Susan set up the battery-operated fan by her window, one in Elmer's room, and one in Mark's. There was immediate relief as the cool night air was blown into her room, and Susan wondered how folks got along without these fans in summer. Times did change. Susan was grateful for the lamps that used DeWalt rechargeable batteries instead of the heat-producing propane lamps. The new lighting options meant Susan could read in bed even on the hottest nights.

The attic was stuffed with heavy cardboard boxes of her books. Bookshelves lined one wall of her bedroom, and still she had nothing to read. She'd read all of the children's classics repeatedly, then moved on to novels, literature, history, romance, anything and everything that held her interest. She simply loved to be borne away into other worlds, places she could only learn about through books. As long as she had her books, her work, her best friend Beth, and her happy home, what more could she want?

The market was a huge brick building in the heart of a thriving city, filled with vendors of every race and ethnicity. Amish women baked Dutch pies and cakes and whoopee pies, Amish produce farmers piled the fresh fruits and vegetables in colorful displays. There was Indian food, Asian restaurants, artisanal leather goods, candies, doughnuts, soft pretzels, smoothies, and coffee shops. The busiest place was the deli. There were always long lines of folks eager for the hoagies and rolls fresh from the oven, stuffed with their favorite deli meats and veggies.

Susan was dressed in a cool lime green dress with a white apron. Tall and businesslike, her tanned face brought more than one appreciative glance from the men, her large green eyes startling, her thick auburn hair with the natural wave rolled and sprayed into submission. Beth, who worked with her, was blond and blue-eyed, a bit rounded, but as sweet and fresh as a summer morning in her sky-blue dress.

Thankfully, the market was cooled with enormous, clattering central air units, but the bake ovens and the barbeque pits all took their toll on the cooling units' efficiency, so they were already beginning to perspire at ten o'clock in the morning.

"Yessir. May I help you?" Susan asked, addressing an enormous man who was mopping his face with a camouflage cloth.

"Are those rolls fresh?"

"Yes. Just out of the oven."

"When?"

"This morning."

"When this morning? Three, four o'clock?"

"No. Probably like seven."

"Okay. Then I'll take a sub. Extra mayonnaise, but not on both sides."

Susan applied it liberally on one side.

"More."

She added more mayonnaise.

"Now, I want two slices of the roast beef, two of honey ham, no not that one, the other ham. Two chicken breast slices and pepperoni, bacon, Swiss cheese, sweet peppers, hot pepper relish, onion, horseradish, and that's all. Oh, oil and vinegar."

Susan listened attentively, finished the sandwich, and wrapped it up expertly. She taped it and handed it over.

"May I help the next person?"

"Ma'am. Hey, I know what I forgot. Salt and pepper."

Susan took back the sandwich, unrolled it, and added both, mindful of the disgruntled customer behind him sighing heavily, shooting angry glances at the big man ahead.

"There you go."

"I thank you."

"Have a good day."

"And you the same, ma'am."

"There oughta be a law against that. I have been waiting," snapped the small thin man, obviously angered even more than she'd thought.

"How may I help you?" Susan asked, choosing to ignore his comment.

"By refusing to put on that salt and pepper. He can do it in his own kitchen."

"Shut up, man." This came from the next man in line.

Susan shrugged, thinking this was going to be a winner of a day. She needed a glass of icy lemonade, but there was no hope for one anytime soon. The line extended well past the doughnut bakery.

She knew many of the regular men and women who appeared every weekend, greeted them with recognition and a few words about their families, the weather. Her hands flew, as did Beth's beside her, forming foot-long hoagies, flat bread sandwiches, some made with rolls or wraps, always fresh.

She loved feeling industrious, yet she could not shake the feeling of being a servant to the whims of the public. A servant cleaning Carol's house, a servant to anyone who ordered a sandwich. Or demanded one. Or disapproved of one.

Her pay was fair, the owner easy to work for, the deli itself clean and pleasant. So why did she let herself feel so gloomy about it sometimes? Perhaps it was merely the repetition, the mind-numbing groove of making sandwiches over and over. Or she had fallen down the steep slope of boredom and self-pity. A lethal combination, a sure way to eliminate happiness.

"Tomatoes."

Beth poked her chin in the direction of the sliced tomato tray, now containing only a few. Susan wrinkled her nose but hurried to the cooler for more, accidentally running into Steve, the owner.

"Whoa there, Susan. Sorry."

He was always running, always in a hurry.

"Ran into Steve," Susan hissed to Beth.

"Like, literally?" Beth asked, her eyebrows raised.

No time to answer with customers waiting, so Beth returned to her work and Susan to yet another customer.

IT WAS EIGHT o'clock before she came home, finding her parents asleep in their recliners, side by side beneath the battery lamp, their magazines opened on their chests. The house was stifling in spite of the fan whir-ring at the window, the fading sunlight casting a tired evening glow over everything.

They started awake, both of them, scrambling to pick up their mag-azines, apologizing for having fallen asleep. They had meant to stay awake, they said. They really had.

Susan waved them off, said it was fine, she was a big girl now, but why wouldn't they sit in the evening breeze on the back patio?

"Too many mosquitoes," her father said, grinning mischievously at her mother, who burst out laughing.

"What? I don't get the joke," Susan said.

"Oh, it's Sylvie," her mom said, referring to their elderly neighbor. "As soon as she sees us out back she comes wandering over, and Dat isn't in the mood to watch her maneuver that toothpick around her mouth. *Ach*, you know how she is."

Susan smiled, then pointed an accusing finger at her father. "Way to model kindness," she mocked.

"Oh, I put up with Sylvie a lot. She's lonely, and I will gladly visit with her. Just not every evening."

Susan smiled at her parents, then headed upstairs to the shower. She loved them both, bless their hearts, and felt undeserving of being raised in such a happy home. Her childhood had been good, her days lived in security and trust. She would shake off this melancholy, these depressing thoughts of existing to serve the whims of her employers and customers.

But the night was oppressive, the heat unrelenting. She tried to read but found she could not concentrate. Finally, laying her book aside, she turned off the lamp. It took a long time before a deep, restful sleep claimed her.

CHAPTER 2

Susan's sister Kate took after her mother's side of the family, short, petite, and dark-haired, dark-eyed. She was the cute one, Rose and Liz would say, the one who could have had the most boys asking her for a date, the sought-after one.

But Davey King's Dan had claimed her heart, thoroughly, with all the efficiency of a hurricane, leveling every surrounding suitor.

She had left her own youth group to join the liberal one he belonged to. They rode around in fast cars and dressed in worldly clothes behind her parents' backs. There was always alcohol and cigarettes, the two vices of the wild groups, the *ungehorsam*, the ones with easygoing parents who winked at the drinking, said they had to sow their wild oats sometime before they settled down. It had been done for generations, but it never ceased to cause a furor among the ones dead set against these untamed heathen youth. The more conservative folks were appalled that youth were allowed to carry on the way they did, driving cars in and out of parents' homes, dressed in English clothes. It was *schantlich* (scandalous). They vowed, with God's help, to put a stop to this foolishness, the shameful youth casting a dark cloud over the light of the Amish.

But there were always those who would not conform. Some would later shed the sins of the past and become steadfast followers of Christ—even ordained ministers and deacons in some cases. Others would sink into dependency on alcohol or drugs, perhaps trying to hide the deep despair of depression or other undiagnosed mental health problems.

Susan suspected that in those teenage years, Dan fell into this latter category, learning to use alcohol to deal with deeper issues. Kate, still in love with Dan, did the best she could, trying not to speak of the unthinkable times when he chose to lock himself away when life became too demanding to deal with. Kate and Dan both loved their children, but it was a lot to handle and the responsibility threatened to squeeze the life out of Dan. And so he withdrew from his wife and children into his own deep, dark pit of resentment.

Susan drove the horse and buggy along 340, keeping well to the side, the constant stream of traffic never bothering her at all. She was so used to vehicles as a way of life. She turned off to the right on Salem Road, then enjoyed a quieter ride past Amish homes and places of business, palatial English homes with three-car garages and well-kept lawns.

At the end of Salem Road she turned left, and there was Dan and Kate's house, a cute brick rancher with a small barn on the right side of the gravel drive. The two oldest children, ages four and five, burst through the back door, waving their arms and calling her name. Susan smiled, then swung out of the buggy and unhooked the horse's reins. She attached the driving reins to a ring on the harness before bending for hugs from them both.

"Susan, Mam said you were coming, and you did." Emily, the oldest, was as sweet and winsome as any child could be, her dark hair and eyes unusual among the Amish community.

Her brother, Nathan, had even darker skin. "When I'm bigger, I'll help unhitch your horse, okay?"

"You sure can, Nathan. But I can manage by myself now."

"Hi there, Suze!"

There was Kate, holding the baby, her slim form rounded by the promise of another child who would soon be added to the growing family.

"Kate!"

"Put your horse away, if you can find room. I think Buster is out."

Susan led her horse into the only box stall, which was piled high with manure, old and dry from the previous winter. She managed to step around the worst and tied the horse loosely so he could stand comfortably.

Kate smiled when she returned. Susan reached for one-year-old Micah in her arms.

"Come here, sweetie. Seriously, Kate, he just gets more adorable every time I see him."

She squeezed him, kissed his tanned cheeks, then looked into his eyes as he laughed happily, reaching up to touch her face. Emily and Nathan tugged at the hem of her bib apron, vying for attention.

"Suze. Suze. We might get a cat. Dat said. Henrys have kitties."

"Really? A real kitten. What color are they?"

"Yellow and white and gray and black. All different colors," Emily said proudly.

The small brick one-story house was so warm on the inside, Suze could hardly see how they could live there in summer. There were no fans, only the windows providing small amounts of moving air.

"Sorry, Suze. The house is warm in summer. These bricks seem to hold the heat overnight."

"It's okay, Kate," Susan called over her shoulder as she bent to wash her hands at the bathroom sink. She enjoyed driving a horse, but you could never get the horse smell off your hands without soap and water.

"It's so good to be here," she said, looking around at the cozy home Kate had made for her family.

Kate was clever with thrift store finds and bargains at yard sales. The living room floor still had the original brown carpeting, but she worked around it, placing her furniture at strategic spots and decorating in neutral shades of beige and white. Healthy houseplants with large waxen leaves gave the room a real sense of beauty. Everything was spotless, if showing signs of wear after six years of marriage. On the surface, the home appeared to be a beautiful example of young parents and children living in Christian harmony.

It had been a long time before Kate had confided in Susan the sad story of a husband who retreated into days of sullen silence, the ensuing air of disapproval of everything she said or did. The children weren't oblivious to these pockets of depression, the cloud enveloping their existence as well as Kate's.

Workdays were often missed and there was never a raise from his employer, who was known to be tightfisted with his wages. Kate slowly took on the responsibility of managing the finances, as Dan was unable to shoulder the stark, glaring load of providing for his wife and children. Kate soldiered on, the fear of being a failed wife and helpmeet keeping her afloat, the pride of keeping up appearances the oars and the tiller that navigated the choppy waters of her existence.

Once, Susan had mentioned getting Dan some help, perhaps taking him to one of the houses the Amish had constructed to help troubled souls in need. But before she had finished, Kate shook her head.

"No, don't ever mention it to him. Never. He's not a nut case. We're fine. If I'd straighten myself out, he could do better."

This had been like an arrow into Susan's heart, but when she brought it up to her mother, she disagreed. She brought up how Kate had always been flighty, anxious, sometimes driving her to distraction. She had to change her ways. Dan needed calm, untroubled days. Kate had to take care of him. It was a sore point with Susan, who took up fiercely for Kate but was completely outnumbered, with Rose and Liz siding with Mam.

The children ran outside to play. As the sisters sipped ice cold mint tea, Kate began to talk, wiping the perspiration from her forehead, her pregnancy making the heat even more uncomfortable.

"Susan, if you only knew how much it means to me to have you come over by yourself. I can talk to you. But you have to promise to stay quiet. Please don't tell the others, OK?"

"You have my word."

"It . . . the situation is getting worse with Dan. I honestly don't know what to do anymore." She raised a hand in protest as Susan opened her mouth to speak. "Don't. He's taken to paddling the children for no reason at all. Well, in my opinion. But if I as much as open my mouth to protest, I am in serious trouble."

Susan listened with increasing distress, amazed at how matter-of-factly her sister was talking.

"Kate, you just sit there and say this stuff like you weren't even here in flesh and blood. Do you ever cry?"

"Oh, I'm here, alright. I have to stay strong for all of us. If I started to cry I would never stop."

"Kate!"

"It's true. Don't pity me, Susan. This is my life, and I made it for myself. I was blind, completely head over heels, without a shred of common sense when we dated. You know that."

Susan didn't disagree.

"It's just that I try so hard, but I never know when or what will trigger an episode, when he turns quiet and . . . well, he's mad. He's angry at me, at the children, his boss, his foreman. It's not fair to the children. But I do believe a lot of it is my fault."

"How? How can any of this be your fault?"

"Well, our finances, for one thing. We can barely survive. I am determined to make the house payment every month to his father. You know, if it wasn't for him we wouldn't have this place. And some weeks, it leaves nothing for groceries or the gas bill or anything else. And I say something to him, and not always calmly. I'm not perfect, Susan."

All this was spoken with measured words, without emotion. Her eyes showed no spark of tears or frustration, merely a stating of facts, an acceptance of a world containing events completely out of her control.

"I'm determined to do better."

"But . . ."

"Don't. It's in me. If I learn how to handle him, my life will change. Rose gave me this book."

She held up yet another self-help book, the one everyone was talking about, the latest instrument in achieving the perfect union.

"Rose gave you that?"

"Yes. She's trying to help, Susan."

There was a long silence. Susan knew if she opened her mouth to speak, her indignation would come spewing out. She wanted Kate to continue to feel safe telling her things, but she also felt desperate to get through to her that she was not responsible for Dan's issues. It was a tricky balance.

"I'm not going to sisters' day anymore." Kate said this in the same flat monotone she said everything else.

"Why? Kate, come on. This is our family. You can't do this to us."

"You don't understand."

"No, I don't."

Emily and Nathan came through the back door, their faces shining with the heat of the day. They needed a drink, which put the heavy conversation on pause. After they were settled at the child's table in the playroom with their pretzels and tea, the atmosphere at the kitchen table turned uncomfortable again.

"Kate," Susan began. "You know we only want what is best for you."

"Oh, I know. And we're fine. We really are. Once I get my act together, things will be different."

"But what about Dan?"

Kate's eyes turned into narrow slits as she refused to meet Susan's caring ones.

"What about him?"

"Well, where's the blame for him? Why can he retreat into his shell without shouldering any of the responsibility?"

"He doesn't feel well. And besides, he's right—I have a lot of problems, too. I'm far from perfect. But I just can't deal with all the questions from Mam and Rose and Liz."

"What can we do then? What should we do?"

"Nothing. We're fine."

There was a determined set to her chin, an evasion in her eyes, and Susan knew she had lost her. This would be the last of this conversation, the last of being able to hear how hard Kate struggled to keep her head above water. And so the subject went on to Susan's work, her hilarious customers at market. Kate laughted at appropriate moments and listening attentively at others. But the real Kate—the bubbly, funny girl who always thought up the best zingers—simply wasn't there. She was a shell of her former self.

When Susan asked to use the phone to call Beth about Friday night, a strange expression settled over her features, and she turned her head away.

"You can't use it. It's . . . something's wrong with it."

"Kate."

"What?"

"You couldn't pay the bill, right?"

Kate sniffed, averting her eyes.

Susan grasped the edge of the table, leaned forward, and lost all composure.

"Stop this, Kate. Stop it. You know I can help, and it's just foolish pride not to let me."

"Susan, what am I to do? If you pay this bill, and I'd be ashamed to tell you how much it is, what about the next month, and the one after that? And what would I tell Dan? He can't know anyone else knows we're struggling."

"But you can't do without a phone." Susan brought down the palm of her hand for emphasis, hitting the tabletop hard.

"I have to."

"You mean there's no money at all?"

"No. I had a choice: gas, food, or phone."

"Did you pay it last month?"

"No. Or the month before that."

"Well, I'm writing a check. Or no, give me a deposit slip, and I'll put money in your account. You have to pay that bill."

"I can't tell Dan."

"He's not going to know."

Was it Kate being so close to tears that made her act so strange, or was she really so displeased at the thought of taking any help from her sister? At any rate, Susan barely knew the stony-faced person handing her the white deposit slip, her eyes red-rimmed, expressionless.

"Kate . . ."

"Just go. Don't say anything. I mean it."

THE RIDE HOME was full of conflicting emotions and unanswered questions. What could she do? Nothing, except deposit money, which she had done at her bank, tying the horse along the line of teams at the hitching rack. But that was a Band-Aid on a festering sore. She was mad at Dan, her sisters and mother, herself, anyone who had ever blamed Kate. Or was it really the job of a wife to "fix" her husband?

She ground her teeth in frustration. She wanted her sister back, the sister she knew, not the one battered and scarred by the unfairness of life. She wondered briefly if Kate could get a job she could do from home. But there was a baby due in September, and she already had her hands full with the other children. Well, she would at least have a talk with Rose to tell her to stop waving all those stupid books in her sister's face.

And Susan vowed to remain free and unattached.

There had been a time, not too long ago, when she would have taken the chance to date the dashing stranger from Lititz who joined their group of youth. Indeed, she would have. She welcomed his glances, was not slow to respond. But when she was told he had moved out West, she figured it was a good thing. Every weekend she continued to have a good time with the guys she knew, and had even contemplated dating a few she knew she could have. But she always lost interest the minute they became too familiar. And now, more than ever, she'd be cautious, committing to the life of a spinster in all sincerity.

Susan thought back to Kate's whirling weekends of fun and pleasure, the glowing faces the day she and Dan were pronounced man and wife. Why had God allowed things to go so downhill? Susan felt so helpless.

Well, there was always prayer, and this she would certainly try. Sometimes, her faith was a fluttering little bird, a fledgling who was only learning to fly on its own. Many nights she closed her book and snapped off the battery lamp, immediately falling into a deep sleep, prayers forgotten. She'd wake in the morning feeling guilty for her lack of a good solid prayer life, but there was never much time before she had to be on her way to work.

She brought the reins down on the lagging horse's back and thought she might as well turn right to go see her sister Rose. Her heart leaped uncomfortably, her breath coming faster. Rose was a formidable person, smart, opinions like cast iron, but Susan knew she had a solid case. Things had to change. Her love for Kate spurred her on as she pulled on the right rein with firm determination.

THE FARM WAS lovely, a huge newly renovated house, the trees and shrubs clipped to perfection, the barn newly sided with white steel siding. The house was white with black shutters, colorful flowers spilling out of hanging baskets along the porch. Amos inherited the farm, with barely any payments to speak of, so with his good management, dealing in horses with famous bloodlines, they were able to keep the cows in the dairy in spite of declining profits.

She tied her horse to the hitching rack after loosening the rein, then was halfway into the house before her sister came sheepishly from the bedroom, holding her covering, her hair in disarray, clearly woken from an afternoon nap. Susan could hear the whirring of the fan in the window.

"Susan, what's going on? Popping in on me like this."

"Caught you," Susan said, smiling.

"I was tired; the baby didn't sleep well last night. Even with the fan going, it's just so hot."

"Tell me about it. I'm still stuck upstairs, and you know how hot it gets up there."

"We didn't even have fans when we were kids."

Susan laughed. She looked around at the unwashed dishes, the baby's bib lying across the messy highchair tray, the kitchen floor littered with toys, a basket of unfolded laundry. This was a problem the mother-in-law nagged Rose about—the relaxed attitude about housekeeping and lawn care, and especially the garden.

Rose waved a hand at her kitchen. "Excuse the mess."

"You always say that."

"Do I? Well, you know why. I'm always under conviction, knowing I should have washed my dishes before a nap, or never had the nap in the first place."

Susan nodded, noticing the widening of Rose's hips, the solid roundness of her arms in short sleeves. The style had changed from puffy sleeves with lots of gathers to fitted, tight sleeves with no gathers. It worked for thinner girls and women but wasn't flattering on those with thicker arms. Rose would sacrifice anything to be in style, highly conscious of things such as who wore the latest fabric and whose coverings were as neat as a pin, snow white and fitting to perfection. In spite of being dressed plain, there were always new styles, new ways of creating differences in subtle ways to stand out from the ordinary.

Susan watched her sister lift the bib and swipe halfheartedly at the caked-on food on the highchair tray before going to the refrigerator for the tea pitcher.

"Tea or Mountain Dew?" she called back over her shoulder.

"Tea. Seriously, you drink that stuff?"

"What? Mountain Dew? Of course. I love it. No more sugar in it than that tea."

"You should drink Lipton peach tea. Zero sugar. No calories."

"Okay, Miss High-and-Mighty. I hate all diet drinks. They have that stuff in them that's hard on your heart, forget what it's called."

Susan swallowed her opinion, knowing too well there would be a stronger one to knock hers right out of the air. Combat. That was Rose. Her opinions were conceived in righteousness and flown from mountaintops of her own making for the whole world to see and admire.

Susan shook her head.

"Go ahead. Shake your head. You know I'm right. Sugar's not nearly as bad as that other stuff."

"Mark asleep too?"

"Yes, and let him sleep. My word, what a grouch he is in hot weather. I told Amos we need to go on vacation. To the beach or a lake, anywhere near the water. An air-conditioned house would be great."

"What did he say?"

"Oh, you know Amos. He'd never do anything his parents disapproved of, doesn't matter what I want. Calvin and Lena are going to Cape May. I'm so jealous."

"I guess living on a farm is different."

"No, it's not. His two brothers could live here, do the feeding and milking. Nothing wrong with that."

"Guess not."

The afternoon slid by and gradually Susan abandoned the idea of approaching Rose about Kate. She drove home wondering how Rose managed to make her feel like she had absolutely no backbone.

CHAPTER 3

THE WEEKEND WAS HOT AND SULTRY, THE AIR DEAD AND STILL. Ominous clouds hung low to the west. Church was held in Dave and Fannie King's basement, which was small and airless. The benches were set too close so that knees poked into backsides. The Kings were by far the most conservative family in the community, which meant there were no fans or battery lamps. You had to hold the *Ausbund* (hymnal) up to your nose to see it in the dim light. Fathers bent to wipe the perspiration from their sleeping babies' faces, then used the white handkerchiefs on their own.

After the first prayer, the benches started to empty out as folks went to seek a bit of comfort upstairs, glasses of water, a visit to the ladies' room. Babies cried, mothers scuttled to rocking chairs to feed them and change diapers as they visited with other mothers doing the same.

Susan was perspiring freely, uncomfortable on the hard bench as the minister droned on in his quiet, level voice. There was so little emotion in his sermon that it could easily lull a person to sleep. His message was scattered with bits of wisdom, though, as Susan knew well, so she kept her eyes on him, trying to appreciate the effort he put into teaching the congregation about God's way.

There was a loud clunk and the startled cry of a child who had fallen off a bench, then the hurried motion to retrieve the frightened one from his place on the floor. Heads swiveled and necks craned until order was restored.

The last song was rousing, relief flooding the congregation as the words were sung in true praise that services were over. Old Sarah Stoltzfus had to be helped out of the basement, concerned ladies bringing her a cold drink as soon as she was settled upstairs where there was more air flow. She stayed up there the remainder of the time, along with a few others who couldn't tolerate the heat. Someone brought lunch and another cold drink up to her.

Susan stayed downstairs, helping with bringing dishes and food to the tables the men hurriedly set up, rearranging the benches they had used for services. There were plates of sliced homemade bread, sliced lunch meat, cheese spread, peanut butter and marshmallow spread, butter, jelly, pickles and red beets, seasoned pretzels, and schnitz pie. Coffee was served and water glasses refilled.

The more conscientious among them did not mention the heat, but merely smiled as they wiped their faces discreetly. Meanwhile, the fancy young girls flapped their aprons and waved their hands, rolling their eyes as they exclaimed how hot it was.

"Hey, Susan."

She stopped and turned to find Roy Stoltzfus with a smile on his face. A middle-aged father of ten and a member of the school board, he was well liked and respected by everyone.

"I think it's time we come see you."

"We?"

"Yeah, the school board."

"Whatever for?"

Roy laughed, which drew her father nearer to see what was being said.

"To ask if you'd be interested in teaching school. Clark's Run needs a teacher, and it's the beginning of July."

"What's wrong with Clark's Run?"

"Nothing. We just can't find a teacher."

"You'll find one."

"What's that supposed to mean?"

"I'm sure someone will be happy to teach."

Roy dismissed her with a wave, then turned to her father, who laughed aloud at some comment that Susan didn't quite hear. Susan smiled, knowing her father would be on her side. He knew she'd never teach school, no matter how often the school board came to ask her. All those children. All the repetitive days, the cape and apron, covering tied. Sunday clothes every day. No, it simply wasn't her thing. They surely should have gotten the message by now.

LATER IN THE afternoon she took a cool shower and waited for Beth to arrive, her brother Mark transporting her with his new pony and four-wheeled cart. Susan was happy to see her, having had little or no time to talk at work. It would be good to have the afternoon to catch up on news of their group of youth. Beth was quite pretty, with her fair complexion and blond hair, the kindest, sweetest person, a very close friend and confidante. Today she wore a cool, thin dress in light pink, making her appear like a hothouse flower, a hibiscus. She was hardly her usual bubbly self, though. She trudged up the stairs to Susan's bed-room, exchanging the usual pleasantries with little enthusiasm.

Beth sat down on the small sofa, turned the fan to get more air, kicked her legs out, and viewed her bare feet below the hem of her black apron.

"I'm so tired of running around."

"What? Beth, come on. Where did you sprout that idea?"

"Everything is always the same. Suppers. Stupid Saturday night vol-leyball games. Adults acting like kids. I'm just sick of it."

"You're two years younger than me. What about me?" Susan asked.

"You don't want anyone. I do."

Susan lowered herself to the sofa and draped an arm across her shoulders.

"Beth, you know if there was anything I could do, I would. But I don't know what Mark is thinking, and to ask is simply unaccept-able. He's very, very private with matters of the heart. And, Beth, to be honest, I don't know if he'd be very good as a husband and father. Seriously."

"Get away from me. It's too hot."

Susan laughed as Beth threw herself back against the pillows, lifting her apron to flap it in front of her face.

"What is with all this apron flapping?"

"It's hot. Don't you ever do that?"

"It takes so much energy flapping like that, you'll just make yourself hotter."

Beth picked up a pillow and flung it in her lap. Susan fell sideways, her wet hair in a long, wavy mane that fell almost to the floor.

"Seriously, Suze, if I could just forget about him, I'd be better off. I try, but then I see him again, and I'm gone. I can't find my voice, my knees turn to rubber, and . . . well . . . it's so bad. He doesn't even know I exist. And every weekend, I'm like this pitiful puppy, hopping around yapping for attention, and he couldn't care less. Does he ever, ever mention my name? I mean, does he ever give any sign that he thinks about me? Ever?"

Susan listened to this outburst with the knowledge there was nothing she could do. Mark was a little younger, Beth's age, but kept to himself with lots of things. He talked about work, horses, his nieces and nephews, the weather, but there was never a word about his friends, his weekends, or any interest in anyone of the opposite sex.

Susan and her brother weren't particularly close. He was their driver, which meant he would wash his buggy, polish his harness, hose down his horse—a Friesian named Chaos—and take the girls wherever the rest of the youth group was gathered. Susan had no idea if he knew of Beth's feelings, as Beth had made her promise never to breathe a word. Knowing Mark's penchant for privacy, she faithfully kept her word, so now she could not confirm or deny anything. Sometimes, when Beth's desperation started to show through and she became a bit silly or too talkative in an attempt to impress him, Susan wanted to shake her. But Beth always caught herself and settled down.

"No, he never does. But he's not the sharing kind. He keeps his feelings to himself, which to me is a brilliant red flag of caution."

"Oh, you're so morose."

"I'm smart. I won't be trapped in a marriage that is anything short of joyful. And there is no such thing."

"So you'll be like the skeleton sitting on the park bench waiting for Mr. Right."

Susan's eyes narrowed. "Not funny."

"Sure it's funny. You'll wait 'til you're dead. There is no such thing as a joyful marriage one hundred percent of the time, and you know it. You're such an old maid in the making."

Time slid by as the girls talked, switching gears to laugh about customers at the deli. Eventually, Susan told Beth how she had yet again been asked about teaching.

"You aren't considering it, are you?" asked Beth.

"Of course not."

"Good. I'd hate working at the deli without you."

There was a knock on the door of Susan's room. Mark poked his head in, his hair tousled with sleep, his eyes half closed. Apparently, he had taken a nap while the girls had been talking. Yes, he was an attractive guy, one any girl would notice, with his tanned skin, his green eyes so much like Susan's. His voice was slightly gravelly as he spoke to Susan.

"I'm going to shower. Do you need the bathroom?"

"No, go ahead."

He said nothing to Beth, closing the door gently. Beth flung herself sideways on the arm of the sofa, putting both hands to her face for a mock howl of despair.

"See that? He didn't even notice I was sitting here. Right here in full view. Any other guy would have said hello. But did you see his sleep eyes?" She groaned into her hands again.

"Beth, really. He's my brother."

"I can't help it. You don't know what a sweet misery love is."

"No, I don't. But I've seen plenty of miserable marriages."

She honestly couldn't imagine being in love. For a moment, she tried to picture herself dating in Lanacaster County, marrying and eventually raising children here in the place of her birth. She loved her home, the hubbub of life among thousands of Amish people and as many Mennonites. But she simply couldn't see herself raising a family here—or anywhere, really. Perhaps the blind spot was merely due to the fact she had never fallen in love, not even close to it.

THE BUGGY WHEELS glistened, the horse's coat shone, and Mark stood at attention like the best groom, waiting for the girls to climb into the buggy and settle themselves before reining up the black Friesian and getting into the driver's seat. They were headed to their supper group, which they had been relieved to learn was being held outdoors in a wooded area due to the heat. Supper group was a chance to meet with other youth and enjoy a meal together, sing hymns, and play games. It was a traditional part of the Amish *rumschpring* years.

The horse pulled the buggy easily, his heavy mane waving in the hot wind. The breeze created by the horse's trotting was refreshing. Both windows were propped open, both doors pushed back, the sun's heat stopped by the roof of the buggy. Small talk made the miles fly by, with Susan and Beth carrying most of the conversation and Mark hardly changing expressions at all as Beth chattered on about anything and everything.

Love could make smart girls be so stupid, Susan thought. Why lower yourself to be a victim of such intensity? Why bother? She would never say a word to Beth, would never want to hurt her, but come on. Beth. Give it up. Mark showed no inclination of being remotely interested in anything she was saying. In fact, he showed more animation at the sight of a goshawk on the telephone wire.

"Hey! I thought they weren't around anymore."

"The statue has spoken," Susan said dryly.

"I'm serious. I thought they were very rare. That was definitely a goshawk."

"Looked like it," Beth said.

Susan stopped herself from snorting. What did Beth know about goshawks?

"I read this book," Beth continued. "*H is for Hawk*. I saw the reviews in one of my magazines. This girl had a goshawk for a pet—she named it Mabel. I learned so much about hawks. Amazing birds."

Susan could only be astounded by what followed. Mark looked at Beth, really looked at her, and she turned pale but kept her blue eyes bravely on his. And she said very intelligent things.

"Goshawks are notoriously hard to train for falconry."

"It was a girl?" Mark asked, incredulous.

"Yeah, she was brilliant. Strong. When I finished the book, I wanted to feel what she felt. I'm a birdwatcher, now. I keep journals and photos."

Mark blinked, speechless. He turned his attention to his horse, reining him in as they neared the home where supper was being served for their group. Other buggies arrived from the opposite direction, filing in the narrow drive to the brick Cape Cod. Susan waved to a friend, and Beth leaned out to wave at some other acquaintance. When the buggy stopped, Mark looked down at Beth and asked if she minded sharing the book. Beth calmly and coolly said he could read it, she was finished with it. Susan turned away so they wouldn't notice her jaw dropping.

EVERY SUPPER AND singing was exactly the same. Same people, same games, different locations. It was enough to curdle your brain. Susan watched as the girls hopped delicately to get the volleyball across the net, their hair and coverings wilting in the heat, their faces red from excitement and exhaustion.

Susan did not play volleyball. She sat on a picnic table with her bare feet on a bench, her dress to her knees, and didn't care. It was too hot to be wearing this lined cape and heavy black apron, too hot to eat the steaming meatloaf and scalloped potatoes. Puddings melted, frosting on cakes became thin and shiny, the fruit salad was warm and mushy. Beth hovered, licking the lukewarm pudding off her spoon.

"He talked to me, Suze. He looked at me," she hissed, dipping her spoon into her pudding for the dozenth time, licking it again.

"Finish your pudding and quit licking that spoon, okay? It grosses me out."

"What's wrong with eating pudding?"

"You're not eating it. You're licking it."

Beth drew herself up, narrowed her eyes, and said quietly but menacingly, "You know what? You really make me mad. Why don't you simply stay at home? Every supper gets worse and worse."

"Sorry," Susan said, turning to Beth with no expression at all.

"You're not sorry. You're bored and hot and mad. You should move to the North Pole for the summer. You'd be happier."

"Sorry."

She didn't sing very much either. The same old songs sung in the same old way. Girls giggling, boys shooting Smarties, girls simpering when they were hit with one. Really? Wasn't there a better way to attract attention than that? Water was spilled, silly girls shrieking.

Susan yawned.

Then she noticed Mark watching Beth, who was speaking animatedly with Nelson King, who sat across from her. Beth glowed like a pale pink flower beneath the light from the lamp, her blond hair shining where it stuck out from her white covering. Susan watched as Mark turned his attention to his songbook, but like a magnetic force, he kept glancing back over at Beth.

Well. Must be the dumb hawk book. Who would have guessed?

Driving home in the dark, Susan was peeved. They had to drive Beth all the way home, which meant she wouldn't get to bed till past midnight, and she had to clean Carol's house in the morning. She wished Beth would be quiet for just one second, then berated herself for being, well . . . for being herself. She really was becoming quite a grump. She had enjoyed having Beth over that afternoon, but other than that, she couldn't remember the last time she had laughed.

"YOU'RE DEPRESSED," BETH told her the next time they were at the deli together. "You're truly and absolutely clinically depressed. You need to see a doctor."

"You know my mother. She'll spend a thousand dollars on herbs before she'll allow me to see a doctor."

"You're twenty-two, which means you make your own choices. Susan, did you think Mark was watching me on the way home Sunday night? What do you think? I thought he seemed a bit more attentive, as if he cared what I was saying. Did you notice?"

"Could be."

She would never tell Beth how she had noticed Mark watching her on Sunday evening. She couldn't deal with the firestorm of hallelujahs sure to follow. And the endless questioning after that.

THE SUMMER WAS long, hot, and predictable. When Susan wasn't at market or cleaning Carol's house, she was helping her mother with the usual frenzy of freezing and canning vegetables from the garden. It was corn, tomatoes, and lima beans in the dog days of August. They had to chop, cook, and strain endless tomatoes for every recipe of salsa, ketchup, chili sauce, pizza sauce, and spaghetti sauce her mother could find. Row after row of colorful jars lined the basement shelves, every jar filled except for the wide-mouth ones for peaches and sausages that would come later in the season.

Cucumbers, red beets, string beans, and peas were all done in June and July, along with the endless rounds of weeding and hoeing, lawn mowing, mulching, and flower planting. So Susan was always busy, always working hard, at home especially, which was normal for summertime.

Beth was convinced Mark was one of the kindest guys she had ever met, the way he drove all that way to take her home every Sunday night. "Every Sunday night," she repeated dreamily to Susan. She would have to take what she could get, she supposed, seeing how he was never going to ask her for a date. He simply did not like her in that way. But at least she got to ride in his buggy every Sunday night, which was a blessing. And they shared the hawk book, that was another thing. Mark had enjoyed it tremendously, had always had a keen interest in birds, keeping pigeons and pheasants as a boy. So Susan had the endless bird conversation to endure as the Friesian trotted slowly through the night, every Sunday night.

Then one Saturday afternoon, when a thunderstorm chased Susan and her family to sit on the front porch, Mark sat beside Susan on the porch swing, looked at her, and asked Susan for her opinion, his voice easily loud enough for her parents and Elmer to hear.

"What do you think, Susan? You think Beth would accept if I asked her out?"

Her parents were shocked into silence. Elmer raised his hands and slapped them on his knees.

Susan grinned mischievously. "I doubt if she would."

"You're serious?"

"Of course not, Mark. You are as blind as a bat. As clueless as most guys usually are. I am sure you won't have a problem."

And he didn't.

Susan told Beth she wasn't going to the supper, saying she had a stomach flu, but that Mark would pick her up Sunday afternoon, which sent Beth into a tailspin.

"But Susan. Seriously, what will we say? I mean, alone. I have never been alone with him. I don't know what to say. Oh well. Why worry. He doesn't want me anyway. He's never going to ask me. Did I tell you about the epiphany I had this week? Any guy that has a good chance to ask a girl after a year, or two, in our case, and he simply doesn't ask, is not interested and never will be. So I'm working on changing my ways. I will return Nelson's attentions and be free of this obsession of Mark. Nelson would make a good husband. It made me sad when I confronted the truth, but it's high time, once and for all, I'm letting him go."

Susan listened without giving Beth a clue.

She dreaded going to work on Thursday morning. Much as she loved Beth, the sheer explosion of feelings would prove exhausting. Mark merely gave her a grin and a thumbs up on Monday evening; his quiet happiness gave her chills.

Beth was surprisingly quiet on her way to work, even quieter when they prepared the mountains of tomatoes, lettuce, onion, the slicer running endlessly. Already the heat was winning, the central air units struggling to keep up. When Susan could no longer take the suspense, she stopped the slicer and asked, "Well?"

Beth put down the block of cooked ham she was holding and replied, "Well what?"

"Did he ask you?"

"He did."

"Did you say yes?"

"I did."

"Aren't you happy? I mean, come on, Beth. You're acting like you're at a funeral when I thought you'd be jumping up and down!"

Beth's eyes filled with tears.

Susan was so shocked she stood speechless, staring at Beth.

"It's just that . . ."

And Beth began to cry in earnest, turning her back as she tried to hide the emotion that had overtaken her. Quickly, Susan went to her, put her arms around her, and told her it was okay, she could tell her everything. She regretted every impatient word or thought she had ever had about her flighty, excitable friend.

"No, Susan. It's nothing sad. I just feel so blessed. I learned a valuable lesson. I gave him up. I truly told God this was it. If Mark was not His will, then it was time to let go. And I did, Susan."

Beth took off her plastic gloves, grabbed a paper towel, and blew her nose, then went to the small sink to wash her hands, dry them, and put on another pair of gloves.

"And then, he asked me. It was so romantic. The warm night, the beautiful Chaos clopping along, the mane and tail rippling, the scent of corn fields and new-mown hay. Oh, I'll never forget it. He reached over and took my hand, Susan. He took my hand. Like this."

And Susan was subjected to her hand being held, turned, her fingers laced with Beth's.

"Like that. It was unbelievably sweet and sincere. Then, he said this. These are his exact words. He said, 'Beth, I have always admired you but would like to take our friendship to the next level. Will you consider being my girlfriend?' And he was still holding my hand. I remember thinking how hard and calloused his hands are, and I also remember that he smelled really good. It took me a while to find my voice. I was in shock."

"Mm-hmm. I imagine you would be."

"It was so unexpected, knowing in my heart I had given him up. And think about this, Susan. Think. He said, 'Will you be my girlfriend?' Not, 'will you go out with me Saturday night?' Girlfriend is a whole new line of security. As if we'll be together forever, and he'll never tell me off. What do you think? He won't, will he?"

Oh boy. Now that the million-dollar question had been asked, Susan realized this would be the new thing. She took a deep breath to steady herself and decided to begin the long journey of assuring Beth every single time she needed it.

"No. He won't break up with you. He's very steady, levelheaded."

"Oh, I know. I know that."

Steve, the boss, came over, his face appearing pinched.

"Girls, I have to ask you to speed up. I know you have important matters to discuss, really, but we need to get this slicing finished."

They apologized and bent to their work.

Good grief, here we go again, thought Susan. *Bossed around as always. I'm just sick of being a servant. Always running on my treadmill, always the boss's voice in my head.* She found her energy waning as she allowed the negative thoughts to enter. Was it the fact that Beth's dream had come true, leaving Susan sitting high and dry while she enjoyed the wonder of romance, the thrill of being a girlfriend?

Well, no. That was not what she wanted. Perhaps it was simply time to find a new job. Check out new horizons. But how wide and how far could an Amish girl's horizons reach? As far as the end of Lancaster County, or perhaps a hundred miles, like the arms of an octopus, to sister communities in outlying counties. There was Dauphin County,

Perry County, oh, there were a bunch of counties. Same kind of people, same dress, or variation of it, same mountains, same jobs.

She decided she was in a funk and simply needed to will herself out of it.

CHAPTER 4

With Beth and Mark officially a couple, Susan was the odd one out, an extra thumb, a third wheel as she rode along to the youth's events. Beth was effusive in her welcome, saying Susan only made it more fun, and that Chaos needed exercise, being so full of energy. But Susan could never forget the vivid description Beth had given her of that first ride alone together. Surely they were both eager to have Susan out of the way so they could return to that kind of romantic bliss. Was she really becoming a tag-along, a charity case? Mark said no, she wasn't, it was fine, not to worry. And so she didn't, for a while.

Summer days cooled into late September, when a chill in the air at night caused her to draw the quilt up over her shoulder, snuggle deeper into the mattress, and smile to herself in pure enjoyment of the cooler temperatures. A great blessing, this turn of the seasons. Her mood lifted and her outlook vastly improved as the days turned chilly enough to produce frost in the morning. Market days were more comfortable and even the air-conditioned house she cleaned for Carol seemed less stifling.

She took to staying home on the weekends, in spite of Beth's protests. She spent Saturday evening with Dan and Kate. Kate was overdue by almost two weeks and Dan had sprained an ankle at work, so they needed a little help with the kids and the housework.

Kate was upbeat, cheerful to the point of being maudlin, till Susan took her aside and mentioned her concern.

"Calm down, Kate. You're driving me crazy."

"What? What are you talking about?"

"You're just so on edge."

"As if I wouldn't have reason to be on edge."

"I know. But just sit on your recliner and rest. I'll put the children to bed."

"Dan . . ."

"I know. I ignore him."

"It's always worse before a baby comes."

"Then stop having them."

"You don't understand, Susan. You're not married."

"No. And thank God."

"I . . . well, you don't understand."

And as the evening progressed, she knew she did not understand at all. Dan lay on the couch, his face to the back, covered with an old cotton throw Susan recognized from Kate's room at home.

Dan turned to face the room and sat up slowly, his head in his hands, a long drawn out groan escaping him.

"Could you please turn the noise down, Kate? My ankle is really hurting."

Instantly Kate was on her feet, bringing a fresh ice pack, putting a hand to the swollen ankle. When he looked at her, she searched his eyes, deeply, then laid a tender hand on his shoulder.

"Lie back, Dan. I'll adjust the ice pack."

"Don't use paper towels. They're too thin."

"Alright, Dan."

It was Dan this and Dan that the whole evening, until Susan could barely stay in the same room. The most maddening scene was the tenderness, the sincere caring for the suffering husband. (If he was actually suffering all that much was anyone's guess.) Kate loved him. Susan could see it in her eyes, the genuine affection, the worry about his pain. It was far beyond her understanding, how Kate could feel anything toward a husband who was lazy, depressed, selfish, and apparently couldn't care less about his wife or children. The children stayed out of his way for the most part, yet he roused himself occasionally to yell at them to keep it down.

Dan's yelling didn't help, but the children did need discipline. All three of them. But Susan felt a certain affection for them after their baths, snuggled into one queen-sized bed in the small bedroom across from their parents', all squeaky clean and adorable after folding their hands in solemn prayer.

"*Müde bin ich, Gae zu ruh* (Tired am I, go to rest)."

And for a fleeting moment, Susan wondered if she'd have children of her own. She closed her eyes, imagining what it would be like, and drifted off to sleep.

She was awakened by rough shaking. It was Dan, in a panic, his sprained ankle evidently miraculously healed.

"It's Kate. The midwife is on her way. I want you to take the children over to your parents' place. Now."

Befuddled, Susan took a moment to remember where she was, then was spurred into action. She fumbled for the light, dressed in a flash, and was out the door, swinging the battery lantern. Throwing the harness across the horse's back, she felt irritation ripple through her, but there was too much at stake to dwell on it. She hitched up the horse, backing him expertly between the shafts, before yelling for Dan to bring out the kids. When there was no answer, she turned the horse, tied him to the post by the barn door, and hurried into the house, where Kate was rousing the children, getting the backpacks ready. Emily started to cry, and Kate told her everything would be alright at Doddy and Mommy's. When she disappeared, Susan knew it was time to go, so she carried one-year-old Micah while the bewildered children trotted along, a hand on her skirt to stay safe in the dark. By this time, Emily was being very brave, holding Micah tightly while Susan unhooked the snap from the horse's bridle.

Now where was Dan? Probably sticking his ankle in cold water. Whatever.

Susan helped the children in and then climbed in herself. She held the reins and chirped, with Duster pulling the buggy smoothly out the drive and down the road.

"Are you cold, Emily?"

"No."

"Here, let me take Micah."

She held the small child easily, driving with one hand. She felt Nathan lay his head against her arm, and a great tenderness welled up for him. For all of them. Would Kate's love be enough to raise them responsibly? Would Dan step up to the plate? Get help to address his issues, whatever they were? She knew she was supposed to have pity on him, but so far, she had found none. What a loser.

She felt mean and offered a quick prayer, but felt just as mean afterward. To love a sister the way Susan loved Kate, to rejoice with her on her wedding day, and then to see this steady decline from the sparkling young woman she had been to this. She hated the way Kate just accepted her fate and accepted Dan, and the way Dan refused to get help for his depression. The whole situation was intensified by her mother and Rose believing Kate was the one who needed help, offering the books, putting an additional load on her already heavily burdened shoulders.

THE CHILDREN WERE happy at their grandparents' place and Susan's parents were glad to have the children. They made a big Sunday morning breakfast, big smiles on their faces. Though Susan sensed the tension in her mother. It had been a while since there were any small children in the house, so it was a bit stressful.

Like most Amish families, they kept their phone out in the shed, so they had to keep running out to check the caller ID. All morning, there were no calls. Her mother grew steadily more nervous. By afternoon, she was fit to be tied, pacing the floor, quick to reprimand the children.

"This is very unusual, for Kate," she muttered to Susan.

When they finally saw there had been a call, it was from Ephrata Hospital. Dan had left a message, his voice calm and smooth, saying they'd had another girl. No weight, no name, no information. Susan seethed, but her mother took up for Dan, saying *ach*, that was men. She knew everything was alright, that was all that mattered. She would have plenty of time to find out the details later.

Emily skipped around the kitchen, waving her arms and announcing that she wanted to go now to see her sister.

"Emma. We'll call her Emma. Emma and Emily," she chortled, which had them all laughing with her. Nathan looked up from his Legos and said nothing, while Micah clapped his little pudgy hands along with his sister's excitement.

So now there would be a hospital bill, Susan thought. There must have been some complication that prevented the birth from happening at home with the midwife. Well, the bill wouldn't bother Dan, thought Susan. He'd just hand it over to the deacon to be paid in full.

It was a blessing for the young couple to have the church to provide for them, but Susan couldn't help feeling like sometimes that safety net was taken advantage of by people like Dan.

Sobering news came soon, though, and Susan felt guilty for even thinking about Dan and the hospital bills. Their sweet baby girl had been born with Down syndrome, Trisomy 21. There would be learning difficulties, delayed motor development. She would need special help, likely even through her adult years.

Susan's mother cried discreet tears at the news, her smile wobbly as she wiped her eyes. Her father went to the barn to deal with the news alone. And Susan was incredulous, questioning why God would do such a thing. With all the trouble dear Kate already had in her life, why send this child who would take extra time and care and expense?

They decided not to tell the children, but instead to allow Dan and Kate to show them the baby and then explain as best they could. Susan called her boss at market to say she needed to take the next two weeks off, knowing Kate would need all the support she could get. Steve was not happy, asking if only one week was possible, but Susan gave him a firm *no*. This was a family crisis. Kate needed her.

ON MONDAY MORNING, Susan drove to Dan and Kate's house to get things in order before they arrived home from the hospital. She put the horse away and herded the children inside, then took a deep breath to steady herself before beginning to clean, giving the children the new coloring books her mother had purchased for them. It was a small home—three children were crowded into one small bedroom, and in the other bedroom a bassinette sat beside the parents' bed, made up with clean blankets and a tiny white sheet. There was one lone teddy bear, a pink one from Emily's babyhood, and a white crocheted blanket that Susan also remembered from those early years of Kate's motherhood. Susan thought wryly of her friends' nurseries—the ample space, new furniture, decorated walls.

Ach, Kate.

Laundry on the line, the house clean, Micah and Nathan down for their naps, Susan sat on the lawn chair on the back porch waiting for Dan and Kate's arrival. Emily chattered away, her excitement palpable.

"She'll be so cute."

"Yes. I bet she'll look a lot like you."

"Why did they go to the hospital?"

"Oh, sometimes a baby needs a doctor to look at her to make sure she's okay."

Emily nodded soberly. She was a perceptive child and seemed to sense something was wrong, but she didn't ask any more questions.

The crunch of tires on gravel announced their arrival, and Emily tore away from the porch and to the car. Dan paid the driver, then went around to lift the baby from the car seat as Kate opened the opposite door and got out, bending to hug Emily, then Susan.

Susan searched her sister's face, but there was no emotion, no tears, only a tired stillness, and a sort of dark heaviness that frightened Susan. *Oh, please let her be alright*, she prayed, without realizing she was actually praying.

Settled on her old, sagging recliner with the broken footrest, Kate reached for the newborn, drew the light blanket away from her face, and motioned Susan over.

"This is our baby, Susan," was all she said.

Susan bent to view her new niece. She had the same thick black hair that all of their babies had, but her small eyes and rounded face gave away her disability.

"She's perfect," Susan whispered, struggling to control her emotions. And she meant it.

"I know," Kate said, her voice level, quiet.

"Does she nurse okay?"

"No. We can't get her started, so I decided to lessen the stress and anxiety and bottle-feed."

"Mam will have a fit."

"She'll just have to, Susan. Dan thought it was best."

Susan nodded, gritted her teeth. *Here we go again.*

Emily ran to the couch and held out her arms, so Susan carefully settled the baby into them, seated close to make sure she would hold her securely.

"We'll name her Emma," Emily announced.

Kate laughed, a tired gasping laugh, but a genuine one.

Dan smiled, too. He sat beside Emily on the opposite side and asked if she didn't think Emma was too close to Emily. She looked up at her father, pursed her lips in thought, and said "Well, maybe."

"Do you like Marie?" he asked softly.

"Marie?" Emily nodded her head very solemnly. "Yes, I do like Marie."

Dan smiled and put his arm around his daughter. "Then Marie it is."

Emily and Dan smiled at each other, the picture of a beautiful father-daughter relationship. Nathan climbed into his father's lap and Dan explained to the two children in simple terms that Marie had Down syndrome. "God made her a little differently," he said without a trace of anger or sadness in his voice. "But I think she's perfect."

Susan was taken aback. She had never seen Dan so calm and tender.

Baby Marie began to squirm and then cry, the wails slight, a bit raspy. Dan set Nathan aside gently and reached for Marie. He held her over his shoulder and started to bounce her slightly.

Kate leaned forward, rising from the couch, but Dan told her to stay where she was, he'd get her bottle.

"But the water . . ." Kate began.

"I know how to do it," he said kindly, still holding the crying baby as he headed to the kitchen.

Susan could hardly believe what she was witnessing. Was this the same Dan?

The feeding was a test of everyone's patience and understanding. Susan watched as milk dripped from the sides of the baby's mouth. She felt helpless as the baby grew more frustrated. Later Kate would explain that the doctor had told them the baby's tongue was wide and thick and weaker than most, due to the Down syndrome. Dan tried different angles with the bottle and shifted Marie this way and that, to no avail. After several minutes he placed her in Kate's arms to let her try and knelt by her chair as she attempted the difficult task of getting her started drawing the milk from the bottle.

Susan sat down with a sigh, watching the two dark heads bent so close, the baby anxiously turning her head from side to side, crying intermittently. Emily went to stand by them, her face puckered with worry.

"You think we should try a different bottle nipple?" Kate asked.

"I don't know. You think it would help?" Dan asked.

By day's end, everyone was exhausted. Nathan and Micah were an unruly mess, getting into forbidden things, crying furiously when Susan reprimanded them. Kate cried when the new bottles made no difference, and baby Marie cried most of the evening, her poor stomach growling with hunger.

It was Dan who sterilized a dropper from the children's Tylenol bottle and inserted it into her mouth, allowing her to taste the formula on her tongue, before letting more trickle down her throat. They all held their breath as the baby swallowed, the crying ceased, and she took one dropperful after another.

Supper, bathing the children and putting them to bed, constantly feeding the baby . . . how in the world did mothers cope without help?

Susan couldn't allow herself to think of two weeks of this, it was too depressing. But she tried not to let her feelings show. The old couch she slept on was lumpy and sagged in the middle, and her lower back ached as she searched for a comfortable position. She heard whispers, footsteps, the baby crying, a shadowy Dan passing through the living room time after time.

Would he actually become a responsible parent?

Tired and already uncomfortably warm at five-thirty in the morning, Susan got up and packed Dan's lunch, made his breakfast, and was glad to see him head off to work at six-fifteen. They would need every hour of his paycheck, what with having to pay for the formula and diapers, not to mention the hospital bills. Susan knew that with his low wages they would easily qualify for state aid, but to accept it would be *ungehorsam* (disobedient) to the Amish way. Each husband was responsible for providing for his family. When hard times fell on someone, they could ask the deacon for help, though if a man did that too often the trustees would make a visit to the home to go over finances and try to get the family back on track.

There were hummingbirds at the feeder and the sun was shining cheerily through the windows by the time the children awoke. Susan lingered at the breakfast table with Kate, cups of coffee between them. Baby Marie slept soundly after her seven o'clock feeding with the dropper, so they talked at length, the children eating their scrambled eggs and toast with jelly. Nathan and Micah were adorable with their sleepy dark eyes, their hair all frizzy in the back. Micah climbed onto Susan's lap and leaned against her chest. He smelled of shampoo and little boy warmth, awakening genuine affection in Susan.

"So, what was it like?" Susan asked. "I mean, did you know right away that something was wrong?"

"It took a few minutes, I guess. At first there's just the relief, you know? Of having labor over and being able to hold her in my arms. But I could tell the midwife was concerned about something, and I did notice that Marie's face looked a little different. It was when she tried to nurse and couldn't that the midwife said we needed to go to the hospital to have her checked out."

Susan shook her head sympathetically. "Sometimes I just don't understand God's ways."

Kate nodded, toyed with her coffee cup, her eyes focused on some unseen point in the distance. Finally, she got up, placed her cup in the sink, poured herself a glass of old water, added a few ice cubes, and sat back down.

"You know, Susan, I thought the same thing. But I'm beginning to wonder." She paused, took a few swallows of water. "I can hardly believe how Dan was in the hospital. Honestly, I'm afraid to even say this, I've been disappointed so often before. But I've never seen him like this. He will hold her for hours, watching her face. He wouldn't put her down when she slept. It's like she touches a soft spot in his heart or something."

"Oh, he'll fall back after the dust settles," Susan said, and then immediately felt badly for being so harsh. But it was the truth, she was sure of it.

"And you may be right."

Dishes washed, house put to order, the washing machine chugging away with a load of towels, Susan stepped outside with a basket of clean bedding to hang on the line. There were weeds in the garden, plenty of them, but it was nearly the end of September, which meant there were only a few rows of lima beans to harvest. The lawn needed mowing and the flower beds needed attention. There would be plenty for her to do, that was for sure.

They made some progress with the bottle, but most of the formula was given with the dropper, which provided enough nourishment to allow Marie to take long naps. Kate slept on the recliner while the children were outside with Susan, chattering as they helped carry weeds to the wheelbarrow. When the heat became unbearable, Susan turned on the sprinkler, got the children into their bathing suits, and allowed them to run through it, shrieking.

Her parents arrived before lunch, followed by Dan's mother and father. They all seemed subdued but congratulatory, bringing bags of diapers, groceries, new blankets and pacifiers, fabric for sewing clothes. Susan did not know Dan's parents well but recognized them both, his mother short, slight, and kind, his father sturdy and soft-spoken.

Kate seemed nervous and was looking pale and exhausted. Mam shooed the men to the back porch and told them to stay there, offering them some molasses cookies she had brought. The two mothers got into a polite discussion about the use of the dropper, seesawing back and forth until they finally admitted they were on opposite sides, before laughing it off, albeit a bit self-consciously.

"I do try the bottle first," Kate assured them. "I'm thinking eventually she'll take it better. It seems as if she has a weak sucking reflex."

"Oh yes. Yes. These babies do," Dan's mother said.

"Not all babies with Down syndrome do, Lydia."

"Oh, I think so. Remember Hausa Sammie's Elam's Jay's wife? She had a baby with Down's, and they said he never learned to suck from a bottle properly."

"Well, how did they feed him? Or was it a girl?" Mam asked.

"I couldn't tell you. But I know they had a *hesslich* (nasty) time of it."

"Is that the one who had heart surgery twice?"

"I think it is."

Kate sad wide-eyed, taking in the news of other families with children like her sweet Marie. She smiled as she listened to the two mothers' exchange. There was no mention of how Dan would provide for the family. Yes, the house was small, the children dressed in hand-me-downs, the food less than ample, but both mothers had lived frugally when they were young. So many newlyweds were downright spoiled these days, they reasoned, never learning to do without. But Mam's lips tightened when she opened the refrigerator door for a drink and found next to nothing in there. What in the world had Dan taken in his lunch? But she said nothing.

Liz and Rose, children in tow, arrived before the parents left. Susan turned into a traffic director, hustling children out of the house and to the sandbox, pouring cold drinks, bringing folding chairs. Her sisters fussed over the sleeping baby, saying she hardly looked like she had Down syndrome.

"She does," Kate assured them sadly. "They're doing tests on her blood, but when she wakes and opens her mouth, you'll see."

And they did see. Both Liz and Rose subtly wiped away tears from their eyes.

After the parents left, the conversation shifted. Liz asked how things had gone at the hospital.

"Dan was amazing," Kate said with an eagerness that made Susan uncomfortable.

"Really?" Liz raised her eyebrows. "I thought surely this would send him into a downward spiral."

"He was so sweet with her, and with me. And he's been such a help since we got home."

Rose nodded confidently. "I knew that book I gave you would help. It takes patience sometimes, but once you really learn how to respect your husband the way God intended it's like everything just shifts and falls into place."

Susan glared at her. So typical. Oh, it upset her, giving Kate all that righteous false hope. Dan was going to sink right back into his old ways whether Kate "respected" him or not, and it was just plain wrong to make Kate feel like it was her fault when it happened.

Liz changed subjects again, rambling on about the new bottles you could get at Walmart. She was going there on her way home, and she'd pick up a couple. Rose said bottles wouldn't make a difference, it was the poor baby's tongue. Liz shrugged and said, "Whatever," but with an extra puff of air, enough to let Rose know she was still getting the bottles.

Kate winked at Susan, and warmth filled her. Sisters. Nobody else like them.

Dan came home before Liz and Rose left. He was clearly tired, but a grin lit up his face at sight of them.

"Hey, the two stooges!" he said.

"Oh, come on, Dan. Give us a break," Rose said, giggling like a young girl.

Liz grabbed his hand, pumped it up and down.

"Congratulations. I love the name."

"Thank you. It was Kate's suggestion."

Kate lowered her eyes, but her cheeks suddenly seemed to glow in a way her sisters hadn't seen in years. Dan washed his hands in the sink and then reached over to take Marie from her.

He held her close to his chest. "They say God gives special children to special parents, and I sure feel like that's true." He looked over to Kate lovingly. "This little girl certainly has one very special mother."

Susan's mouth literally dropped open in surprise.

That evening after supper he pushed the wheelbarrow to the stable door and began to clean the horse's stable, spreading the manure on the pasture. He quit before the sun was sliding behind the horizon, took a shower, and held Baby Marie, patiently trying to bottle feed her. Susan bathed the children, one ear to the living room, listening to the quiet conversation between them.

Next week, he said, when they took Marie back to the doctor, he'd like to stop at Stoltzfus Structures. He had heard their starting wage was much more than he was making now. He thought it was time for a change. Four children, and Marie being special, he needed to face facts and get another job.

She couldn't hear Kate's reply and didn't need to. She could imagine the hope springing up, the fresh outlook. She found herself yearning for the same hope, the hope of a better life for her sister. Was it possible that Marie would be the catalyst for real change in their family? Would her helplessness spur Dan into action? Or was this all a false start, an honest attempt but one that would fall by the wayside, just like all the times before?

CHAPTER 5

THE WEEK WENT BY, A MIXTURE OF FUN TIMES AND TIMES SUSAN wanted to go home so badly she had to restrain herself from hitching her horse to the buggy and driving off. The children quarreled, it was hot, there was an endless march from stove to sink to washing machine. Groceries were so low that she hired a driver, gathered up the children, and went to Walmart, where she bought a hundred and thirty dollars' worth of food. Then she stopped at the Amish bulk food store, where she spent almost as much again. She carried everything into the house, cleaned the pantry shelves, and filled every Tupperware container and every shelf and drawer in the refrigerator. She unloaded laundry soap and fabric softener, soap and toothpaste, a baby gift of softer-than-soft sleepers, and blankets like cashmere.

Kate shook her head. "No, no, Susan, I can't pay for any of this."

Susan popped a doughnut hole into her mouth and said that when she became an old single lady and Kate and Dan were rich, they could take care of her then.

Kate's eyes became very red, but she laughed a strange gasping laugh that was more a sob than anything else, and told her to share those blueberry doughnut holes please. The children had chocolate ice cream and chicken nuggets with ketchup for lunch, a rare and wonderful treat. Dan said they'd repay her, humbled by the refrigerator and pantry containing the food most people enjoyed every day.

"Don't worry about it," Susan assured him.

He straightened his shoulders, his mouth in a straight line, looked at Susan, and said after he got his new job, he'd pay her back.

BETH AND MARK came on Saturday evening, Beth shy and fluttery, keeping all the unspoken words in check. She hardly knew Kate and Dan and was eager to make a good impression. Susan hugged her, told her how much she missed her. She asked how things were going at work.

Beth gave her a wild-eyed stare, which made Susan laugh.

"Don't say anything. I can only imagine."

The children were surprisingly well behaved, and Susan fixed a plate of nachos for everyone. Dan was grateful, quiet as he heaped his plate. Mark and Beth pronounced the baby as cute as a button, for which Susan was, indeed, impressed. That was the perfect description, lifting the hearts and spirits of both Dan and Kate, knowing there would be times in the future when folks were caught off guard, when they stared before moving on.

Only Susan knew the deep admiration Beth had for the unassuming Mark, the sense that she was living in a dream. Her feelings for him fell a bit short of worship, although they were held in check, especially now. When Mark moved his chair close to Beth, she leaned against him ever so slightly before correcting the bold move and sitting with her hands clasped tightly in her lap.

The men discussed Stoltzfus Structures, and what exactly would be expected of Dan. Mark had started off there, cutting plywood. It was in fact very interesting, and Susan told Mark maybe she would apply for a job there, with that kind of hourly wage.

Mark grinned at her. "You should apply. There's this guy named Levi that works in the paint room. I think he's in his late twenties. Not bad looking. He's foreman most of the time. Nice guy. He'd give you a run for your money, Susan."

"Maybe I don't want a run for my money," she answered tartly.

"Yeah, I know. Someday you will."

Kate laughed. "Susan? I highly doubt it. I can't see her with anyone in all of Lancaster County."

"She has never met Levi," Mark insisted. "Would you go on a blind date if Beth and I went? If I got reservations?"

Susan was horrified. "No!"

"Come on, Susan. You don't know what you're missing."

Beth's face lit up when he said that. Happiness did not begin to describe her state of mind these days, and now she had heard affirmation from his own mouth.

Her joy bubbling into speech, she said, "Come on, Susan. Try it. For our sake. We'd really enjoy seeing you with someone."

Susan spread her hands in exasperation.

"What is it about a girl being single? Why does everyone try to marry her off? It's as if I had a strange disease or two heads or something. I do not want to be introduced to Levi, and very likely he doesn't want to be introduced to me, so why would we go sit together in some fancy restaurant just to make you all happy? You two are happy enough, it seems to me."

This tickled Dan immensely. Susan wasn't sure if she had ever heard a laugh like that emerge from him. Kate was as surprised as Susan, allowing her own laugh to join his before meeting his eyes to share the unexpected humor.

"Okay. But I'm going to ask him, see if he's interested," Mark said.

"Don't you dare."

"I probably will."

Beth merely giggled, feeling more relaxed now. She leaned against Mark, who reciprocated by stretching an arm across the back of her folding chair. Ever so slightly, she leaned in a bit farther.

It was sickening, Susan thought. Every person who was enamored, in love, wanted to spread the disease. It was not for her. Why couldn't folks get the hint and leave her alone? Why couldn't they accept that she was content to work hard and save her money without all the unnecessary drama of a relationship with one loser or another?

After the two weeks were finished, Susan went back to her jobs with a renewed sense of purpose. She tried her best in every area, deposited her money, and watched her savings account grow. She visited Kate frequently, a bit apprehensive as she watched the baby's development. But Marie was obviously enveloped in so much love. Now that she had her feeding problems under control, she rarely cried, and if she did, it was a quiet, hoarse little cry that sent Emily and the boys straight to her crib.

As time went on, Kate spoke in hushed tones to her about Dan. The new job was working out surprisingly well. He no longer felt as if his work was a burden, but seemed to look forward to each day.

"Susan, I'm almost afraid to speak of the huge difference in him. He still has his moments, and likely if I said anything to him about making a change, he would deny it. He holds Marie as if she was the best thing ever. He talks to her and loves her twice as much as any of the others. Or as he did when they were newborns."

"That's beautiful," Susan said, because she wasn't sure what else to say.

Kate shook her head. "It is. I'm just afraid to believe it's real, I guess. For years it's been like hanging on to a shred of hope that keeps evaporating."

"You don't want to get your hopes up, only to have them broken again," Susan said, understanding perfectly.

"I mean, his paycheck. Seriously, Susan. I have money to pay the bills and make the house payment. We even got the propane tank filled. Oh, it's a blessing."

"So, which book from Rose brought all this about?" Susan winked.

"Oh, come on. Don't start that whole thing up again."

"I'm joking now, but I'm still upset that she makes it out like it's your job to fix Dan."

"Let it go. My life has definitely taken a turn for the better, so let's give the honor where honor is due. To God alone. How many prayers did I think went unanswered? Too many, till my faith was almost destroyed. And now it's a whole new world."

THE WEDDINGS IN November put a strain on Susan's workplace, with the other employees either getting married themselves, or going to friends' or relatives' weddings, leaving Susan gritting her teeth in frustration. She had plenty of invitations, but she chose not to go, opting to work every Thursday without Beth, putting up with incompetent substitutes that sorely taxed her patience.

Beth, of course, was a frothing well of information—who wore what, who was in the bridal party, who was fancy, who was not, what was served in the afternoon and evening, who took which girl to the table, and on and on and on, until Susan snapped at her.

"Customers are waiting. Can you finish making that sandwich already?"

"You're just bitter, Susan," Beth snapped back, and they spent a long quiet forenoon making subs without further conversation.

Susan felt bad, she really did, but everywhere she turned, there was another marriage or romance shoved in her face. Sometimes she wished she could escape Lancaster County, leave everything she knew. That thought took root in her mind more than once, but her strong sense of duty always compelled her to hoe it out and destroy it. Or maybe it wasn't so much duty, but repetitive motion. Over and over, the scene was the same. How did one go about changing course when everything they'd ever known was built on tradition, rules, responsibility—basically doing the same things over and over again?

Maybe she should have gone on the blind date with Levi, but then again, maybe not. Even the thought of doing such a thing left her numb with despair. It would turn out to be another disappointment and she'd wind up berating herself and the poor hapless guy who was dragged into it. Or maybe he'd fall hard for her and she'd be faced with causing another heartbreak when she turned him down.

But what if Beth was right? *Lord, deliver me from bitterness.*

Was it pride that kept her from considering the possibility of marriage? Was it a lack of trust in God? She wasn't sure, but she knew something had to give.

"Okay," she told Mark finally. "See if Levi will go."

SUSAN FELT A certain excitement as she showered and picked the color of her dress, combed her hair with a bit more attention to detail, using a liberal amount of hairspray before rolling her hair into the usual bun on the back of her head. Levi had agreed to the double date and since then Susan had ping-ponged back and forth between dread and a happy anticipation that surprised her. She put on a new white head covering and her black sweater and she was ready when the driver pulled in with Mark and Beth in the back seat, Levi in the middle row, the minivan driver alone in the front.

It bugged her that no one got out to greet her or hold the door for her, but she tried to brush it off as she seated herself beside Levi.

"Hey Susan," Beth called out, too loudly and too quickly, giving away the bundle of nerves she was.

"Hello, Beth."

What was up with all these *heys* instead of a decent *hello* or a *hi* at the very least.

"Susan, this is Levi Yoder. Levi, my sister Susan."

"Hey."

Oh, for crying out loud.

"Hello, Levi. How are you?"

"Good."

She had a strong urge to ask the driver to turn around and take her home. Didn't anyone have manners anymore? Mark directed the driver to Red Lobster out along Route 30, asking everyone if they were okay with that.

Levi said sure, that was great, and Susan said nothing, trying to get a glimpse of the person beside her without looking straight at him. As far as she could tell he was average, with a haircut in the traditional Amish style, which meant he was a member of the Amish church. She had to admit to herself that his profile was nice.

Red Lobster was crowded, but they were led to a round table with cushioned seats in a semicircle around it. Mark and Beth slid in first, and much to her surprise, Levi stood aside and held out an arm to usher her in, then got in beside her. The lighting was dim and the music just loud enough to be heard through the hum of voices around them. It was surprisingly pleasant.

She dared a sidelong glance at Levi and found him doing exactly the same thing. She quickly looked away.

He wasn't bad at all. Light-colored eyes, a deeply tanned face, a nice jaw and mouth, really quite attractive. He wore a polo shirt the color of pale lemons and neat black trousers.

"So, tell me about you, Susan," he said, evidently at ease.

She turned to face him, found his eyes on hers. She looked away and fiddled with her napkin.

"There's not much to say. I'm an ordinary girl, older than most of my friends. Mine, the ones my age, all got married."

Really? Susan wanted to kick herself. Could her answer have been any more awkward?

"I see. So how old are you?" Levi was smiling a little, but not in a mocking way at all.

"Almost twenty-three."

"Well, I'm twenty-eight," he said, laughing.

After that, conversation between the four of them flowed more freely, with Beth being the biggest contributor, animated beyond her usual talkative self. Levi ordered with careful, unselfconscious deliberation, something Susan realized she found attractive.

She learned that Levi still lived at home, with his aging parents, down close to Coatesville, at least twenty miles from Susan's home. He was the youngest of eight siblings and had always worked for Stoltzfus Structures, loved his job, his home, and had a great time with his siblings. He didn't run around much, the youth infinitely boring at this stage in his life. Susan told him she didn't either.

They talked about their interests and he mentioned he enjoyed snowboarding. "You know what we should do?" he said, suddenly excited. "We should rent a condo in Seven Springs and go snowboarding! Sometime in January, when work slows down."

"Great idea," Mark yelped, and Susan shushed him, embarrassed by his outburst.

Beth said she would never get on a snowboard, ever, but when Mark told her they had beginner slopes or she could go tubing, her adoration was put back in place and she agreed with enthusiasm.

"What do you think, Susan?" Levi asked, and she met his eyes full on for the first time.

For one heart-stopping moment, every coherent thought evaporated. Tongue-tied, she swallowed, choked. A hand went to her mouth.

"I . . . Excuse me. Swallowed wrong there."

She was babbling, fully aware she was babbling, completely mortified. She cleared her throat, picked up her water glass, took a sip.

"I . . . yes. It sounds like fun. Although, I'm with Beth. Never was on a snowboard in my life."

"We'll take you to the easy slopes," Mark said.

Their food arrived, and all thought of snowboarding was let go. It was steaming hot and absolutely delicious, especially the steamed shrimp, a dish both Levi and Susan found was their favorite. She had a fluffy baked potato, a Caesar salad, crab cakes.

She found herself wishing the gap between her and Levi wasn't quite as wide. She knew she was in strange territory when she placed a hand on his arm to ask for the salt shaker, please.

Oh mercy. This was awful.

Susan took a deep breath, steadying herself, and ordered a cup of coffee with all the confidence she could muster. Her voice came out a bit too loud and commanding, but she would not be one of those inarticulate, silly girls who tried to shrink themselves to make the man beside them feel bigger. No, she was strong and independent, facts that so far she had failed miserably to manifest that evening. She resented Levi for the pull of his attraction, the way his presence made her feel weak and muddled.

While the remaining three kept up a lively chatter, she sat back against the vinyl upholstery and drank her coffee, her mind a maelstrom of confusion. She should not have come on this blind date at all. It was amazing how fast an iron resolve could be shot down by a wobbly little arrow straight from Cupid's bow. Now what was this mushy thought? *Cupid? Really?*

"You're too quiet, Susan. What are you thinking?" Beth trilled.

Mark gave her a look, one she had seen many times. The look that told her to snap out of it.

Levi didn't say anything, didn't even turn to look at her. He just dug into his fudge-covered chocolate cake and ignored her.

Yes, he was ignoring her. Now what was that supposed to mean? Didn't he care if she was having a good time or not?

"I'm not thinking anything."

"Oh, fine. Be that way," Beth said, giggling.

"Okay, whoever is in, let me know," Levi continued, and Susan realized he was still talking about the snowboarding trip. "Sometimes it's hard to get one of those houses on short notice. You think we should ask a couple more people? Mary might go. She's good on a snowboard," Levi said, looking animated.

Susan stat straight up, thunked her coffee cup on the table, and asked, "Who's Mary?"

He went right on eating his cake, took a long drink of his coffee, then without giving her the assurance of his light-colored eyes, said, "Oh, someone I know. We've been friends a long time. Do you know Ab's Amos Glicka? From down our way?"

"No."

"She's really cool. She's actually thinking of moving to Wyoming. She loves horses and nature."

Finally, his cake was finished, but instead of looking at her to say something kind, he excused himself to go to the men's room.

Frustrated and unsure how to wrestle with these strange emotions that popped up like land mines, Susan threw herself back against the seat and said she was ready to go. This had been the longest meal of her life. She felt like another person, a different one than the one who walked into the restaurant. When she spied that lemon yellow shirt moving through the crowd, she sat up and put a hand to her hair to make sure there were no weird unwanted puffs.

He slid easily in beside her, a wave of woodsy cologne following. Did he sit closer this time? She wasn't sure.

Good grief. She simply had to get a grip.

"So, Susan, what do you think?"

This time he looked at her, turned the whole way in his seat, and spoke to her alone.

She drank her coffee, which by now was cold and stale, but it gave her a moment to gather her thoughts. Except she couldn't. She set her cup down daintily, turned to meet his eyes, and said the dumbest, most thoughtless thing she had ever said to anyone.

"I don't care. It doesn't matter."

"No, but I meant, will you go with Mark and Beth, Mary, and maybe one of my other buddies?"

"I don't know."

She was lost in those light eyes, completely unmoored. There was no smart comment available, no hope of saying the right thing. Her robotic, monotone replies were the best she could do.

"Well, we'll go ahead and plan it for around the middle of January. I'll book the place and you can let Mark know if you decide to go."

"Okay."

But did that mean she wouldn't see him till the middle of January? She looked at Beth, who caught her bewildered stare and gave her a small smile of reassurance. When Levi picked up the check, placed a card in the plastic holder, and waved it away in spite of Mark's protests, Susan opened her mouth to tell him she would pay, but not one word came out of her mouth. He leaned across her to grab a mint from Beth. Susan was caught up in the woodsy scent of his cologne and could have cried.

And that was, basically, the end of the evening. The driver was talkative on their way home, preventing Susan from having a chance to say something intelligent, and then she was dropped off first. Levi did get out and stand by her side as she stepped out of the van. He thanked her for a fun evening, said it had been great getting to know her. He said all the right things, and the only thing she could manage to say was, "You, too."

It was almost painful rethinking her evening, lying in her cold bed staring at the ceiling, wondering sincerely what on earth had just happened. Well, whatever it was, she was not going to fall victim to the frilly little trap most other airheaded girls did.

Nope. Absolutely not.

Seriously, though, her brother had been working with Levi for three years, probably more. Why hadn't he ever spoken of him? Well, it didn't matter.

There was no *ordnung*, no commandment from God, saying a person had to get married. The smartest thing to do was to stay single, unattached, trouble free. And the best way to accomplish that was to stop going on any stupid blind dates and to stay away from Red Lobster and guys with lemon yellow polo shirts and woodsy cologne.

And what about this Mary? He said she was cool. And just exactly what did he mean by that? *Well, you go for it, Levi, because I am sticking to my guns.*

She had heard plenty about snowboarding, the youth group was full of young people who went, but it never held an appeal for her. For one thing, the clothes were terribly expensive, and not very Amish. Her mother frowned on girls going snowboarding or skiing, saying very firmly it was *opp-schtellt* (forbidden). On the other hand, her father winked at sports activities, saying young people had to do something. She imagined wearing the snowboarding clothes, swooping gracefully down the beginner's slope, the sun sparkling on the pure white snow, impressing Levi. Or falling flat on her face while cool Mary swished by as if she had wings.

She wasn't going. That was it. She would spend the weekend with Dan and Kate. They needed her help. It was the right thing to do.

IT DIDN'T HELP matters at all when Beth leaned close in the market van and whispered, "You like him, right?"

"Sshh!" Susan hissed, effectively stopping all girlish secrets and giggling, something she detested.

There was no more conversation about Levi for a while as they prepared the mountains of sliced meat and cheese, piles of shredded lettuce and tomato. They cried over the onions, joked and laughed as they worked, the easy camaraderie refreshing to Susan. After everything was set up, they filled their coffee cups for a break before the rush began.

"Why can't we talk about it?" Beth lamented.

"About what?"

"You know. Our date. Levi. If you're going snowboarding."

Susan waved a hand. "Sounds boring. Who wants to go sliding down a hill on a board? Besides, where would we get the clothes? And we can't dress in English clothes. You know that."

"Come on, Susan. I don't want to go alone with people I don't know."

"You have Mark."

"But he'll be with Levi. They'll be gone all the time. You know how Mark is about snowboarding."

Susan sniffed, drank her coffee.

"You know what I think? I think you are way more attracted to him than you'll let on, and it really gets your goat. So you're going to sit up there on your pedestal and pretend you don't care. Susan, the untouchable."

"Never. I didn't even think he was all that attractive."

"He is, and you know it."

Susan dismissed Beth with a wave of her hand, told her it was time to get back to work. Beth followed her to the work station with a dozen reprimands held tightly in check.

And Susan got caught up in the rush of the day, so at least for a few hours Levi was forgotten. She had her pride to maintain, and that was very important to her. Being reduced to a simpering, giggling girl who was so obviously besotted by some overconfident young man simply made her skin crawl. She knew her mother would discourage her from going to Seven Springs anyway.

She loathed herself for getting tongue-tied and blushing and acting so stupidly. Well, there would be a stop put to all of that nonsense. How many times had she told herself she was not like other girls?

An irate young man pushed through the line from the opposite direction, shoving an unwrapped hoagie across the counter. The heavy-set woman in line drew herself up to her full height and said, "Excuse me."

Ignoring her, the young man shouted, "No mayo. I said, 'No mayo.'"

"I apologize. My mistake." Susan set to work remedying the situation.

Beth watched Susan, calm, cool, her hands flying, making another hoagie, nodded her head, and thought, *Mmm-hmm.*

If you've lied about something, it will come out in the hoagie.

CHAPTER 6

With Christmas approaching, there was the usual round of social get-togethers, leaving Susan too busy to think much about going to Seven Springs. She tried to forget about the Levi episode, as she dubbed it now, and returned to her cool, calm workdays and weekends. Beth put on an air of martyrdom, realizing she would never get a straight yes or no about the weekend in Seven Springs.

Carol picked her up on Wednesday morning, giving her instructions about pre-Christmas cleaning. She was having overnight guests, so the two bathrooms and bedrooms on the second floor would need special attention. There were crumbs in the pantry and the refrigerator shelves needed to be wiped. Would she stay an extra hour?

Susan agreed to stay longer and Carol left in a frenzy with packages to take to the post office, leaving Susan alone in the house. She gathered all the cleaning supplies from the garage, flipped the switch on the central vac canister, and made her way upstairs. Her starting point was always the main bathroom, the rugs taken up and carried outside to the back patio, shaken and hung on the rail. The air was cold and crisp, the landscape brown and wilted. Birds twittered in the low branches of the neighbor's maple tree, fluttering around the hanging feeders, the birdhouses in the perennial bed emptied for winter.

She grabbed a Diet Pepsi on her way back upstairs, then set to work in earnest, the caffeine in the drink shoring up her energy. As she wiped down the huge mirror, she turned her head to the side, noticed the thinning of her hair. Just the one side, but still. Twenty-three years was coming up fast. But thinning hair was no big deal, unless you were the type to panic about appearances, and only girls desperate for a man did that. So she drew her mouth into a firm line of acceptance, the nonchalance showing in the toss of her head as she finished the mirror.

She got the clean sheets from the hall closet, snapped and tucked them into place, plumped the pillows, shook the rugs. How many times did she run down those stairs and back up?

As she surveyed the spotless guest rooms, a twinge of longing niggled in her heart, but not quite enough to start daydreaming of her own house. Only sometimes, she wondered how it would feel to purchase linens and towels, to decorate a house that was yours and yours alone. Perhaps she could have her own home without a husband if she worked and saved long enough. A husband was a definite risk and could easily ruin the pleasure of owning and caring for a home. Sometimes she wondered if other girls ever had these thoughts, these very rational fears about marriage. She guaranteed Beth had no reservations, not even a smidgen of doubt. Whatever.

She sprayed more Pledge on the dust cloth, wiped down the narrow hall table, the clock in the corner. She heard the garage door open a moment before she turned the sweeper on and sighed. Here Carol was already, following her around as she worked. Susan knew that Carol would sniff, swipe a finger across a tabletop, checking to see if Susan had wiped away every speck of dust. Normally, Susan winked at all Carol's little quirks, knowing she was critical, but never demeaning. Carol was always kind, telling Susan she had no idea how she would manage this big house without her.

Carol came clumping up the stairs, saying town was a mess. She was not going back till Christmas was over.

"So, how's it going?" she asked, glancing along a mirror to see if there were any smudges.

"Good."

Same thing she always said. What else was there to say? If you cleaned the same house in the same way for seven years, it was always good.

By the time she worked her way to the kitchen, her last room, her back was beginning to ache from pushing and pulling the sweeper from one end of the large house to another. As usual, the microwave and toaster oven were a mess, but that went with the job. She wiped and scrubbed racks, removed everything from the refrigerator and wiped the shelves with hot, soapy water, before replacing each item to the exact spot she had taken it from. She knew Carol would be irritated if anything was displaced.

But Carol was elated with the clean scent of her house, gave Susan an extra twenty-dollar bill, and chatted happily on the way home, looking forward to having her guests from Ohio. And Susan felt a bit less like a servant and more appreciated than ever, which made her actually look forward to going the next week.

When she got home, she was surprised to find all her sisters there. They were getting ready to head out, gathering items, putting blankets and pacifiers in diaper bags. Susan had been so busy, she hadn't even realized they were planning a sisters' day. Liz told her maybe if she wasn't always working, they'd get to see her once in a while. Rose said she didn't know how in the world she kept up her energy.

"You forget. Before we had babies, there was never an energy shortage," said Kate.

Susan sat down, gathered little Micah to her lap, and kissed the top of his head. Emily and Nathan looked up from their play, squealed their happiness at seeing Aunt Susan, and rushed over for a hug.

"Mommy didn't give us candy today," Emily announced solemnly.

"We were making date pinwheels, and they ate enough sugar," Rose said sternly. "You know Mam makes the best, and we watched her do it, so we can all go home and make them for our neighbor's trays."

"Well, I'm not sure I'll be able to do that," Kate said, smiling her small smile of humility.

"Of course not, Kate. How would you find the time?" Susan asked. "How is Marie doing for you?"

She held out her arms, and Kate deposited the sleeping baby. Susan looked down into the sweet face, rounded, with the head full of dark hair like the others. She noticed the decidedly smaller eyes and full, thick mouth.

"She's so sweet," Susan said kindly, then felt the prick of unexpected tears.

"She is," Kate agreed. "So *brauf* (good)."

"Is she really?"

"Yes. My goodness, since we have her feeding problems straightened out, she eats and sleeps."

Kate looked around, searching her sisters' faces for approval. Susan noticed, feeling her protective instincts rise up.

"Dan is so good with her. I have never seen him so hands on, so *schlimm* (crazy) about a newborn. He will go into our bedroom and pick her up even when she's asleep, just to gaze at her."

A silence hung over the room for a moment, until Mam spoke up. "That's wonderful, Kate. It shows he has a tender heart."

"It certainly does." Kate was fairly beaming with the newfound pride in her husband.

"How's his new job going?" Rose asked.

"He seems to like it. Says it's nice to be out of the weather."

"Until he decides he doesn't like to be inside, come spring," Rose said sharply.

Kate bent her head to flick something from her apron and had no reply. Susan was furious.

"Why would you say that, Rose? That was plain mean, and you know it."

Rose was astounded by the impact of her sister's honesty. For one second, she felt guilty, but she quickly replaced the feeling with words of self justification.

"I didn't mean it like that. I was just saying . . ."

"No, you weren't. It was mean. If Dan is making better wages and doing well handling his depression, can't we be happy for Kate?"

Mam nodded slightly, but Liz cast a suspicious glance at Kate.

"A man doesn't get depressed if the wife does her *dale* (part)."

"Our driver's here," Rose trilled.

Everyone scrambled for coats and boots, gathering containers of date pinwheel cookies, with Mam picking up missing bottles, shoes, a pair of stockings. And Susan knew Kate would go home from her day spent with family feeling heartsick and alone. Whatever hope she had started to experience had been squashed by Rose and Liz's cruel comments.

The minute the large van was gone, Susan approached her mother and without hesitation opened the subject.

"Mam, where does this come from, this blame placed on Kate's shoulders for Dan's depression? Is there some religious reason, some hidden secret I fail to understand?"

Her mother pursed her lips, put a hand on one hip, and took a deep breath. She proceeded to tell Susan about the latest book circulating among the plain people, the concept being that through a wife's true love and devotion, respect and admiration, a man would slowly be molded into the ideal husband, the woman being the weaker vessel.

Susan took a large bite of a pinwheel cookie, biding her time till her anger simmered down.

She tried to keep her voice calm and level. "If that's true—which it's *not*—shouldn't Liz and Rose be happy that Kate's doing all the 'right things' to make Dan well? Why did they have to go and knock her down again, saying it's not going to last?"

"Oh, it won't last. Kate will be disrespecting Dan again before you know it and then he'll sink right back into his old ways." Her mother went on to say the young generation was spoiled, and the way Dan and Kate spent their *rumschpring* years, well, they were both reaping what they had sowed. Kate would never have given up Dan; now she had made her bed, therefore she needed to lie in it.

"But Dan is not well. I mean, he can't deal with life and ordinary responsibility the way most other men can. You know that. All you and Rose and Liz are doing is adding an additional burden to Kate's shoulders that she shouldn't be carrying. It's not right."

"Kate is ordained to be a submissive helpmeet. Think about it, Susan. God has a special place for women. A helper, a companion, one who bolsters her husband's low moods when they occur. And I have never seen Kate do that."

"What?" Susan shouted, slapping the table with the palm of her hand. "What are you talking about? You have no idea what goes on in that house."

"Susan, I will not allow you to speak to me in this manner. You have not read the book, so don't pass judgment. Kate has a lot to learn. Why do you think God gave them Marie?"

Susan was shocked into silence. It was unthinkable. Her own mother.

"Mam," she said weakly. "Do you realize Kate's phone was turned off because she couldn't pay the bill?"

"What did she do with her money?"

"Dan was hardly working. There was no money. Do you honestly think Dan couldn't work because Kate wasn't stroking his ego enough?"

"She could have paid the phone bill and done without other stuff."

"How can you be so coldhearted toward your own daughter?" Susan asked, giving up on keeping her voice level.

"You don't understand motherhood, Susan. I'm not cold toward Kate. You will learn when you're my age, your children have to be let go. Given wings to fly. Kate was *ungehorsam* (disobedient) as a girl, and not one of us is free from having to reap what we have sown."

"But none of us girls were perfect."

"You three weren't like Kate."

When Susan chose to remain silent, her mother told her the laundry needed to be brought in off the line, the men would soon be home. Susan's mind was reeling. How could her mother think that way about Kate? Kate, who lived her burdened life quietly, without complaint.

Their mother had no idea how selflessly she spent her days in the care of the children, making good meals with a fraction of the money most women spent on groceries, loving Dan in spite of him treating her worse than a shoe rag. How many women suffered like Kate did, all in the name of living up to someone's righteous idea of womanhood?

She thought of Dan, how he sank into vast quagmires of self-pity, yelling at Kate and the children, refusing to harness himself to any financial responsibility, blaming her repeatedly for every single thing that went wrong. Surely that was not fulfilling the role the Bible prescribed for husbands. Why couldn't anyone else see that? And maybe he couldn't help it, maybe his depression was outside his control. But surely it wasn't Kate's fault. If she was to blame for anything, it was for being too submissive and not insisting that he get help. Susan agreed with her mother and sisters that Dan's streak of being kind and responsible probably wouldn't last, but it absolutely wasn't because Kate wasn't being a good enough wife.

Susan brought the basket of clothes to the kitchen table, pulled a chair out, and plopped it on. Taking the clothespin apron from around her waist, she hung it on the hook by the wringer washer before folding towels and washcloths, tablecloths and socks. Her mother moved from sink to stove, her back turned, peeling potatoes, frying meatballs. Susan felt *fa-hoodled* (off) as she struggled to understand her mother's way of thinking.

Were times changing so fast? Were her mother and sisters stuck in an old conservative way of thinking while Susan saw things in a newer, more liberal light? Kate had confided in Susan that sometimes there were days at a time when Dan would not speak to her, cocooned in a thick layer of his disapproval toward her. Kate found herself mentally backtracking, reviewing all her words and actions of the past week or weeks. Having finally pinned down a questionable motive, thought, deed, or misstep, she would ask him fearfully, hesitantly, for his forgiveness, which he might or might not grant.

Only Susan knew how hidden, how devastating his treatment of her actually was. How he messed with her mind. And now, in her mother's words, she had brought it all on herself by her disobedience in her *rumschpring* years and by failing to respect her husband well enough. Where was grace or mercy or forgiveness on God's part? Where was Jesus giving his life on the cross for every mistake man had ever made? And where was that scripture about a man loving his wife like Christ loved the church and *gave himself up for her?*

Well, Susan thought bitterly. *No marriage for me. I'm not going to tangle with my mother on this subject, neither will I ever go on another blind date and act like such an airhead. As frothy as a shaken bottle of Diet Pepsi. Nope.*

THE RESOLVE REMAINED until her brother Mark knocked on the door of her bedroom and then entered with a large grin as he flopped on the small couch by the window.

"Levi wants to know if you're going."

Carefully, Susan dog-eared the page of her book, sighed, and placed it beside her. She swung her legs over the side of the bed, then gave him a withering look.

"I'm not going."

"That's what Beth said you'd say."

"She was right."

"I think Levi really wants you to go."

"Why would he?"

"Are you that clueless? Maybe because he liked you."

"He didn't."

"Of course he did."

"Well . . ."

Susan felt the slow heat rising in her face. She wanted to answer Mark with some witty comeback, but it was buried under a thousand bubbles of confusion and, yes, airheadedness. That dreaded feeling she was determined to control.

"Well, what?"

"No, Mark. I will be much better off at home. He said something about a girl named Mary. She can go with you and Beth."

"You're just using Mary as an excuse. Why do you do this, Susan?"

"Safer?"

"What's that supposed to mean?"

"I could break a leg? Three or four ribs? A head injury?"

"Oh, come on. Since when are you worried about hurting yourself? You've always been athletic."

They were both silent for a moment as she absorbed Mark's words. He hardly ever spoke that much. "You really think I should go?'

"Of course. You have nothing better to do. It's not like a marriage proposal or something. It's just a little adventure."

"That's true."

She was swept right back into the churning waters of indecision. Her mind went back to that lemon-colored polo shirt, the unexpected scent of his cologne, the ease with which he ordered his meal, the confident and gracious way in which he said goodnight, even after her total lack of composure. What girl in her right mind would not enjoy being his girlfriend?

But attraction was just a distraction from reality, wasn't it? Kate had allowed herself to fall, sucked into the abyss of physical attraction, of this thing called love, and it had nearly ruined her. And then there was her sister Rose, who thought she was far above Kate, her husband rolling in money. *Oh indeed, Rose. But what about this tiny problem of your condescending bunch of in-laws, and you becoming—dare I even think it?—fat and lazy as you hold tight to your teddy bear named rebellion?*

But Susan was smart, well-versed in the ways of those less fortunate. If she could depend on her own brilliance and trust herself not to fall into the trap of attraction, why not go for Mark and Beth's sake?

Then she remembered choking on her coffee, the intensity of wishing he would slide over a bit more. What foolish nonsense. Where was her brilliance then?

She told Mark she would think about it.

CHRISTMAS CAME AND went, with its whirl of festive dinners and hymn singings. The whole family gathered in the large basement, Susan's parents presiding over the general hullablaloo with satisfaction and more pride than they would ever admit. Such *an schöene* (nice) family.

Yes, they had *an schöene* family, all the children staying in the faith, staying true to the promise they had made to God and the church on the day they were baptized. They drove their horses and buggies, dressed according to the rules of the church, more or less, showed up at church every two weeks. Here was security, to travel the path of the forefathers, the blueprint laid by those who walked it first. If situations cropped up that rattled the foundation of God and family, they were not to be talked about outside of the family, and eventually, through prayer and a strong faith in God, the problems would vanish.

Her parents played with the grandchildren after the dishes were washed and Christmas carols sung. Presents were exchanged amid squeals of glee, the adults laughing at the little ones' antics. The table was overflowing with ginger cookies, fudge, date balls, raspberry jam strips, and Chex mix. The smell of Old Bay seasoning and vinegar floated in from outside, where Dat was boiling the shrimp, his extended belly forming a circular shape out of his black Sunday coat. Cider, tea, Mountain Dew and Pepsi, endless coffee and cocoa bombs. This was Christmas, so to indulge was acceptable—it only came around once a year.

Mark brought Beth, which was new. She wasn't exactly a stranger to the family, but it was a big deal to bring a girlfriend for Christmas and Susan could tell she was trying to make a good impression.

It was late when Susan's sisters prepared to head home, packing the buggies with leftovers, Christmas presents, sleepy overfed children stoked on far too much sugar. Susan helped her mother clean up, joking that she would always be the old maid servant, which brought a good laugh.

The Christmas singing was actually held on Second Christmas evening. Second Christmas was the day after Christmas, an extension of the holiday. In the western states of Ohio and Indiana, where the Amish lived in huge communities, there was a tradition of Old Christmas which came on January sixth. An old myth had it that when folks ventured into the barn on that evening, the animals were given the gift of speech. But in the East, there was no holiday, no Old Christmas, but instead a Second Christmas.

Susan dressed in her forest green Christmas dress and combed her hair with plenty of attention to detail and liberal amounts of hairspray. She wrinkled her nose at her own appearance, then went with Mark to pick up Beth.

"You look so beautiful," Beth gushed.

"Oh, come on. This green?"

"How many guys will have their hearts completely shattered?" she laughed.

"Stop it, Beth."

Mark didn't laugh but kept his attention on his horse, knowing full well how it was. Yes, she could have anyone of her choosing, both he and Beth knew. She wasn't interested, and that was her charm. Standoffish. Aloof. Too many girls chased after the young men these days. He worried about Susan though, sometimes wishing he could express his feelings better, but the truth was, she intimidated him, same as she did everyone else. And he had not figured Levi out at all. He never mentioned Susan's name, never spoke of the blind date. Mark had sort of fibbed about Levi being attracted to Susan. He didn't have any concrete evidence that it was true, but he figured it must be. Why else would he have brought up the idea of the snowboarding trip? Surely he was just being aloof and Susan had finally met her equal.

As Susan pushed past throngs of people, shaking hands, greeting old and young alike, Mark knew he'd been right. He watched a wave of young men sit up taller, straighten collars, place a hand to their hair with hopeful looks that were met by a blank slate.

The ice queen, Mark thought, annoyed.

No sign of Levi. Whatever. He decided the whole thing was exhausting and turned his attention to Beth, who found his direct gaze and gave him a bright smile. He was so grateful for her guileless, simple heart, her love as easy and as beautiful as a June rose. His love for her grew day by day. He was only waiting the proper length of time before asking her to be his wife.

All evening, though, he watched for Levi. He'd mentioned the Christmas singing, but that, too, was met with indifference. Perhaps they were two of a kind, and if they did begin a relationship, it would only end up as heartbreak.

The singing rolled through the shop where the service was held. Susan sang heartily, enjoying the great swell of sound, a fitting ending for the holidays. And she felt content, surrounded by the people she loved and comforted by the traditions that had held the Amish community together for so many generations.

CHAPTER 7

JANUARY ARRIVED IN A BLITZ OF SNOW AND ICE, TEMPERATURES HOVering a bit above the zero mark. Gas heaters were turned up and parents checked the window latches at night. Where did that cold draft come from? Children were hustled off to school in buggies, too cold to take their scooters. Mothers fussed about the unfairness of children expected to play outside in this weather, the children themselves running around in the cold with no ill effects.

Kate and her four children each put on an extra pair of socks and a light sweater, keeping the house at a comfortable sixty-five degrees. There was coal in the basement, enough for a few more months. This was an unexpected luxury, and Kate took great care to exercise frugality. Dan was still very attentive to Baby Marie and never complained about his job the way he once had. But as the winter wore on, she became apprehensive as he started to display more signs of withdrawal.

When Susan visited on a Monday, she immediately detected signs of former hesitancy, the false starts and stops so typical of Kate's life. Her heart sank as Kate spoke of Dan's reclusive habits returning, though she added quickly that it was only at times.

Susan told her of Seven Springs, bringing a light to Kate's eyes.

"Yes, of course you should go. We went three years in a row. Dan and I were fairly competitive. It's great fun."

Susan's eyes narrowed. "I'm not too sure."

"Who will you go with?"

"Mark and Beth and some other friends," Susan told her, making no mention of Levi.

Kate assured her again it would be a good experience.

Susan drew her sweater tightly around her waist and crossed her arms. She was sick of her own indecision. She would go. For Mark and Beth's sake.

SHE WAS READY and waiting when the van pulled up a half hour late. She was introduced to Mary Glick, a tall, thin girl as blond as Beth with a fair complexion and light green eyes. She looked to be about Susan's age, maybe a little older. There were two young men, friends of Levi named Mervin and Joe, in their twenties, both seemingly well mannered and friendly. Levi was in the front seat, talking to the driver. He didn't get out or offer to help with her luggage, but then, Mark was there to load things into the trunk anyway.

Beth introduced her to everyone, and they were on their way, traveling out of Lancaster County and headed north.

Susan was seated in the second seat from the front, with the girl named Mary, who seemed quite talkative. Actually, she never stopped, except to allow Beth a few moments of speech. Susan found herself in the crossfire, the one young man named Mervin interjecting his thoughts periodically. There was the subject of Wyoming, wild horses and burros, the best way to guide a snowboard, the benefits of new buggy shafts, even the best place to buy a shoofly pie.

Susan found herself enjoying the ride immensely. These were not just ordinary youths—they were smart, had been around, or at least out West. They were more experienced than most Amish youth and more interesting than anyone she'd encountered at the Sunday evening youth gatherings she had attended for years.

When they arrived Susan took in the mountains, snow, chair lift, the beauty of the lodge, apartments, and small houses built among fir trees, surrounded by winding roads. There were gift shops and restaurants, equipment rental shops and winter clothing boutiques. Susan's heart pounded as she saw the size of the ski run and the colorful figures crisscrossing with unbelievable speed down the high mountain. Mary said she'd been coming here since she was eighteen, which was almost ten years, and Susan realized she was in way over her head.

Beth smiled at her sideways, as if to say, "Not to worry, we'll be beginners together."

Susan thought she should have listened to her mother, who warned about worldly places and sports and said no Amish girl should be on the ski slopes, it was *op-schtellt* (forbidden). Her father agreed quite solemnly, but there was a certain sparkle in his eye, the one that said it would be great fun to try it himself.

Their condo was quite large, with gigantic windows overlooking the ski slopes, pines laden with snow at their fingertips. It easily accommodated seven adults, with Beth and Susan in one room, Mary in another, and the guys in bunk beds. Everyone explored, chattered, unpacked ice chests of food and drinks, and settled at the table with a map of the area before deciding on a plan.

And still Levi had not spoken to her at all. It was all Mary this and Mary that. Susan took a deep breath, caught her upper lip in her lower one and told herself to calm down, Levi was nothing to her. Mary had every right to be his best friend.

Just when she thought he'd gone off with Mary—there had been talk of getting supper—she felt a presence behind her as she got down a tall glass to put ice in it.

"Hello, Susan."

She froze. Slowly she turned, forced herself to look up into his face, and found she was blinded by the blue light that sparkled everywhere.

"H . . . Hello, Levi."

He smiled, a slow, relaxed smile, and she smiled back with what she hoped was an imitation of his.

"I'm glad you decided to come."

"Thanks. I think I'll enjoy it. As long as I can stay upright."

"You will. With practice." He smiled again. "You want to come to the restaurant for supper? They have great sandwiches and some kind of chowder."

"Is everyone going?"

"Mary is. Merv said they might, but I think Mark and Beth are staying in."

"I'll go."

"Great. I hoped you would."

And then, he gave her the sweetest, most caring glance, then returned for a deeper, more lasting one, telling her with his eyes how genuine the phrase had been.

I hoped you would.

Darkness had fallen, but nothing was dark at the resort except the navy blue night sky sprinkled with stars directly above them. Mervin and Joe were up ahead and Susan walked with Levi on one side, Mary on the other, listening as Mary described previous visits to Seven Springs.

"Remember, Levi? The time you and I did the half pipe? That was wild. I'm gonna try for the rails this year."

"Are you really?" Levi asked, turning to look at her.

"Sure I will. Will you go with me?"

"Sure."

The booths were deep and wide, so Susan slid in behind Mary, the three men opposite, the lighting dim, the odors from the kitchen mouthwatering. Mary ordered a hot chocolate, which sounded delicious, so Susan repeated it, also asking for a water with lemon. Levi ordered with the same good manners and confidence, and Susan examined the artwork all over the walls. Antiques. A pair of snowshoes, an old pair of skis. She kept her eyes on the walls to hide the swell of pride she felt as she remembered Levi's words back at the condo. Was it so wrong to be wanted? He would be a good friend, she told herself, and she had absolutely no reason to shun him as if she were afraid of a bit of attraction.

She found through the course of the meal that she rather liked Mary. She had no false airs about her, which was refreshing. She was quite comfortable being Mary, and let everyone know this by her unreserved opinions on a wide variety of subjects.

"So, Susan, we rent our gear. It's frightfully expensive. I told Levi he should pay for mine. He has money, you know."

She considered Susan a moment, then blurted out, "You're pretty. Why don't you have a boyfriend? Most Amish girls that look like you have a boyfriend. How old are you? Twenty-three?"

"Twenty-two."

"Whatever. Most girls your age are married and have a kid."

"Well, not I."

"Why not?"

Susan shrugged, felt all eyes on her. "I guess I don't want to get married."

"I'm sure you've had chances."

Thankfully, a waitress arrived with their food, heavy bowls of thick chowder, an array of different sandwiches and salads. They bowed their heads in silent prayer over their food, and the subject was dropped. The food restored everyone's energy, and an entertaining conversation followed, ranging from politics to the raising of Siberian huskies, which was Joe's occupation. When Susan was asked about her line of work, she said she was a servant to the wealthy, in a flat voice that made everyone laugh.

"Come on, Sue," Mervin said.

"I'm serious. I clean a house for a wealthy couple and make sandwiches for Steven Beiler at the Harrisburg Farmer's Market. He owns like three or four properties, likely more."

"Do you like your work?" Levi asked, watching her face intently.

"I do, for the most part. I still daydream about doing something different, maybe having my own business, but that's in the future."

"Enough about work," said Mary quickly, turning the conversation back to snowboarding, a subject she could take the lead on. It was rather abrupt, but Levi didn't seem to notice as he continued sipping coffee comfortably.

At the rental center, Mary took it upon herself to tell Susan which clothes were best, which snowboard would fit. The attendant was a muscular young man who listened patiently to Mary before making his own suggestions, which weren't always the same as Mary's. When he took Mary back to look at boards for herself, Levi hurried over, leaned close, and said quietly, "Listen to what the guy says, but you don't have to do what Mary says. You choose your stuff and she can choose hers, okay?"

Susan nodded, then turned to thank him.

"I hope you have fun this weekend," he said, looking into her eyes with the same heart-stopping light.

Since there were no words to be found, she nodded again, then turned to take a pair of gloves from the rack, trying to still the beating of her heart. It wasn't as unexpected as the last time, merely a slight acceleration of her heart, like a car shifting gears, which seemed harmless enough.

But where do dreams start, and where do they end? She found herself floating along on a rose-scented cloud, a sense of euphoria whenever he was near, a sense of profound loss when he wasn't. She was helpless in the wake of this onslaught, powered along by feelings and emotions as heady as the height of the stars in the navy blue night sky.

She tried not to let on, and by that evening she found herself temporarily forgetting the complicated feelings and just having fun. Seated around the kitchen table, playing game after game of Rook, snacking on homemade coconut candy and hard pretzels, teasing and laughing, she let down her guard and became one of them. Simply herself. She was funny. She shrieked when she lost, yelled triumphantly when she won, spilled her coffee and had to go take a shower, then returned in loose flannel pajamas and her wet hair in a towel.

She pulled off the towel, shook her hair loose, and left it uncombed, not caring how she looked. She felt like she had known Levi, Mervin, Joe, and Mary much longer than she had—already they felt like old friends, buddies. She couldn't remember the last time she had truly had fun. She felt lighter, relaxed in a way she hadn't felt in ages.

They finally went off to bed, overslept, and rushed around with Mary barking orders, the coffeemaker producing a steady flow while they all prepared themselves for the slopes. Susan felt odd wearing her skirt on the outside of her heavy snow pants, but she had promises to keep to her mother. The jacket was light, but puffy and warm; the white beanie felt awkward over her tightly rolled hair.

Levi asked her if she had goggles. She said she hadn't been aware she needed any, then felt idiotic, like a bumbling amateur.

"I have an extra pair," he said, quietly, kindly, then returned with them. She accepted, of course. Could she do any less when he reached out and put them on her face, stretching the elastic behind her head and adjusting the tightness? He stood in front of her and pressed his hands against her cheeks for just a moment, looking straight in her eyes, which were now shielded by the goggles.

He walked away then, and Mary was instantly by his side. Mary didn't bother with the skirt, looking sharp in her navy blue snow pants and white coat. "Race you to the lift," she said playfully, and in a moment they were out of sight.

Once outside, Susan was enthralled with the sounds of swishing snow, the colorful attire of the skiers, tubing children, the boarders, the clear bright air creating a whole new world of excitement and adventure. Susan and Beth took to the small slope, laughing, falling down, trying over and over. Susan had ridden a skateboard growing up, so she had the basic idea of how to balance and turn, but going downhill on hard-packed snow was a completely new challenge. By the time the sun was directly overhead, she was beginning to feel more confident gliding down the gentle grade.

Beth laughed a lot. She shrieked and yelled and waved her arms, fell flat on her backside, and laughed some more. But she was no slacker, and soon was figuring out the basics right alongside Susan.

They sat in the snow and watched more experienced boarders for a while, fascinated by the ease with which they zigzagged down the course.

"Tomorrow Mark wants to attempt the rails," Beth said, awe in her voice.

"Well, he's being snowboarding for years."

"But even so. Isn't he amazing?"

Susan smiled to herself. Mark the Great. In Beth's eyes, he was perfection, and for this, Susan was grateful. Mark deserved an adoring wife. He had never been anything but kind, nor had Beth. They were a good match.

When they all met up outside the lodge before taking a break to warm up, Susan found herself watching Levi and Mary, tamping down any feelings of envy. They came swishing down the slope, practically in sync, grins lighting up both their faces. When they high-fived at the bottom, Susan forced herself to smile, imagining how good Mary must feel to be so confident, so smooth and even elegant on a snowboard. But when he slipped an arm across her shoulders and she looked up into his face, her stomach took a sickening dive.

Hmm. So these were the games he played. Well, she could be quite good at this type of thing, too. Her eyes narrowed as she planned the feminine wiles that would make him miserable, then caught sight of Beth's bright, open face as Mark came to join them and realized her own pettiness. Why did she care what went on between those two? She had even told them she had no desire to get married. If they fell in love, good for them.

By late afternoon, they were all cold and hungry. It was pure pleasure to stomp into their condo, each one drying his or her own clothes, taking long hot showers, and resting sore muscles, snuggled in soft blankets on the huge sectional sofa.

Levi talked a lot, which surprised Susan. Mary corrected him often about anything having to do with snowboarding, and each time he waited, listening to her until she'd had her say. Mervin and Joe made a huge meal, all by themselves, shooing the girls out of the kitchen with their offers of help. Susan laughed outright when Beth rolled her eyes, saying she bet they were going to use every pan in the kitchen and expect the girls to do all the cleanup.

The late supper was superb, with huge slabs of grass-fed steak, baked potatoes, macaroni and cheese done in the oven, coleslaw, and pickled eggs. Mary mentioned the lack of a salad, but the boys laughed, saying who eats a salad on a ski slope? Susan smiled to herself, enjoying all the delicious food immensely. She buttered the baked potato liberally and had a second helping of macaroni and cheese.

Cleanup was left to the girls, but there was a dishwasher, and in fifteen minutes, the kitchen was spotless. Beth plopped down beside Mark, and he shared his blanket as she cuddled against him. Mervin and Joe pretended to be at ease with that, but Susan could tell they were feeling a little awkward. She also noticed Joe's constant awareness of Mary, and how Mary was always tuned in to what Levi was saying or doing.

Did Levi have true feelings for Mary? She knew with startling clarity that he did not. She was pleased to notice Mary's thin, lank hair, the red hue of her wind-burned face, the absence of pleasing curves in her figure. Why did these observations please her? She had no intentions of a romantic involvement, none whatsoever. She had steady control over her feelings, and was planning on keeping it that way. She didn't have any concrete reason to believe that Levi harbored any intentions toward her either. So there was that.

The following day was basically a repeat. Except for Levi. He stayed with Susan and Beth at first, giving them tips and gentle instruction on the easy hill. After a few runs, he asked Susan to come with him on the lift to the top. The sun was already high over head, the snow blinding, and Susan had taken quite a few tumbles, her leg muscles already aching.

"Oh my," she breathed.

"Come on. I'll stay with you. Just to see the view from the top."

Beth went back to the lodge with Mark, her right ankle bothering her.

"I'm really afraid I won't be able to make it down."

"I watched you. You can turn. You'll be fine."

Would she have followed anyone else to the top? She knew she would not. But Levi was . . . well, Levi. To sit beside him, her booted feet dangling, her heartbeats almost choking her as they rose higher than she had imagined possible. Before she knew it, they were approaching the top. She had managed to get off the lift on the beginner slope without falling, but this lift was moving much faster.

"You have to be quick," Levi warned. "If you fall coming down the hill, try to get out of the way quickly so the people behind us don't run into you. Here we go. Ready?" He lifted the bar and she forced herself not to panic.

The lift slowed and she pushed herself off the seat and over the edge down the hill. She staggered, but stayed on her feet. Levi reached for her hand, took it firmly, and helped her to the side.

She stood, exhilarated at having conquered the lift. Then she looked out over the vista before her, taking in the snow-laden evergreens, the bright blue sky, the trails twisting below, the white hills in the distance.

"It's beautiful," she breathed.

"I knew you'd think so," he said, turning to face her. "But there's something else I wanted to say while I have the chance. You are beautiful, Susan."

"But . . ."

"I have a lot of respect for you."

He took her hand, squeezed it, then released it to put an arm around her shoulders.

From behind, a cough.

Mary.

"Uh, how was the lift?" Mary asked, too loudly and too quickly. She didn't wait for an answer, buckling her back foot in as she spoke to Levi. "Race you to the bottom. I'm doing the half pipe."

"Next time. I want to make sure Susan gets down OK."

"Okay, watch me, though. You didn't see my last pipe."

And she was off, her long lean body moving gracefully back and forth as she shot past other skiers and riders. She made it look so easy, so smooth and effortless. They could see the half pipe from where they stood and Susan found herself holding her breath as Mary dropped into it, gliding down a wall so steep it was practically inverted.

Susan could not hold back a "wow" as Mary sailed back and forth, launching off the top of each wall, sometimes doing a full spin as she shot out of the pipe and then landing perfectly to glide back down. At the bottom, she slid to a stop and turned around to wave at them.

"She's amazing," Levi breathed, his eyes alight.

"You go ahead, Levi. Seriously. I'll get down."

"Nah, I'm not going to leave you here."

"Go ahead. I'm going to take my time."

He hesitated and she could sense how badly he wanted to join Mary, so she motioned with her hand. "Go. I'll meet you at the bottom."

He hesitated a moment and then was off, his form as good as Mary's, the half pipe no challenge at all. She could see them high five, but barely, before she adjusted the boots on her board and shoved off. There was nothing else to do, no matter how her heartbeats pounded in her head, no matter how her teeth chattered from sheer dread. The slope was long, steep, the snow packed to nearly ice from the many skiers and boarders. At first she just inched down with her board perpendicular to the hill, as if she were trying to scrape any lingering powder off the hill. But after a few minutes, she took a deep breath and turned the tip of her board downward, immediately going faster than she wished. It was only when she realized her speed could be life threatening if she didn't gather her wits to turn that she put into action what Mark had taught her. She put pressure on her toes, turning to the right, then on her heels, creating a big S. Her speed now under control, she exhaled with relief and a newfound sense of power. She felt the distribution of her weight, felt her knees bent and calves engaged, and was filled with a sense of accomplishment, a thrill of adrenaline she had not experienced before. Her eyes swam from the sting of the cold air, the heady rush of being able to control the frightening descent. Her snowboard, the boots that encased her feet, all seemed a part of her, no different than running or jumping. She was in control.

Before she knew it, she was at the bottom, making a sharp turn and sliding to a stop. Everyone was there, giving her high fives and congratulating her. Mark was clearly impressed and even Mary was generous with her praise.

THEY WERE ON the slopes till the sun sank behind the mountains in a glorious display of color, streaks of navy blue clouds like tossed ribbon mingling with brilliant reds, magenta, orange, yellow, and lavender. Susan took off her goggles, breathless with the wonder of God's creation. She wanted to keep the sensation of being so close to all He had made, the mountains formed by His own hand, the pure beauty of the white snow on dark fir trees, the crisp cold air with life-giving oxygen, and now this blessing of being among friends. She had conquered the slopes and had a sense of being who she was, not caring what Mark thought, not minding that Mary was the more skilled boarder.

The last evening together was bittersweet. Mary was being her gregarious self, her sense of humor bringing plenty of laughs as they cooked another delicious evening meal. Susan was relaxed, much more at ease than she would have though possible, and took it for a good omen.

No more nervous heart palpitations or loss of words when Levi was close, no more wondering if he really did like Mary. He had told her she was beautiful, respected her, and that was enough. She realized the ball was in her court now. She was the one who would have to stop any further advances. Now she knew he was just another admirer, another one she could have had, and she could relax.

Was that so awful?

She thought not. It was a free world, where women could pick and choose, stay perfectly free and unattached. A bit of flirtation never hurt anyone, a bit of spice added to an otherwise tepid existence.

Tepid.

That was the word. Lukewarm. Comfortable. So a weekend away, spent with someone who made her heart race, was quite alright, but now it was time to back away, hold up the palms of her hands, turn a cold shoulder. But she was surprised when Levi mostly ignored her and spent the evening with Mary beside him on the couch in pleasant conversation. Bewildered, she felt a bit unanchored, as if her plan had gone somewhat awry, then struggled to shake off the feeling of being abandoned.

When she made hot chocolate with her own special recipe, he handed his mug to Mary and said he wasn't crazy about hot chocolate, he'd take coffee.

"There's none made," she said briskly, then sat on a reclining chair, reached for a warm throw, and pulled it over her shoulders.

Her thoughts were dark, but level, no highs of euphoria, no lows of hurt. He could say and do whatever he wanted, and so would she. He'd find out not all girls were like Mary, making it obvious how happily she received his attentions.

But just before the van pulled up, when Susan had finished wiping down the countertops and carried her luggage to the porch, she heard her name being called from the hallway. She turned to find Levi, beckoning her to join him. She took a few tentative steps, then stopped, her eyebrows raised in question.

"You intrigue me, Susan. Why are you so different?"

She shrugged, told him she had no idea what he was talking about.

"You don't want a boyfriend, am I right?" he asked.

"Depends."

"What kind of answer is that?" he asked.

And she turned on her heel and walked out the door.

CHAPTER 8

Her mother was outraged at Susan's weekend, listening to her escapades on the slopes with pursed lips. But she couldn't help being pleased when Susan mentioned Levi. She knew his parents, and thought a great deal of that family. She told Susan that if Levi showed an interest, then she should take him. This modern-day acceptance of young women remaining single was not good, this gadding about doing things she would not have dreamed of doing when she was Susan's age.

"Now, Mam," her father chided. "We skated and went bobsledding, you know that. And it wasn't only you and I that stole a few kisses on those hay bales on the back of the bobsled."

He winked at Susan, as her mother snorted, but her cheeks flamed, and she smiled in spite of herself.

"We're all young once, Erma," he drawled, picking up the *Busy Beaver* and riffling through it.

"That's just it. She's no longer young. Snowboarding with the English people, staying in those fancy places—no good can come of it."

Susan knew her mother was disappointed that she wasn't more enthusiastic about Levi. The same letdown her mother always felt when yet another hopeful was shown to the door. Girls had to be married. Safely surrounded by the four walls and a roof the husband provided, settled down and ready to start a family, putting all the learned skills to good use. Bake bread, shoofly pie, a good, honest chocolate cake.

Do the laundry and keep a well-managed house. Be a virtuous woman, content to live her life doing the will of God, a keeper of the home.

"Mam, I understand your concern. I don't plan to go snowboarding again. And as for Levi, he seems great. I'm just not sure I feel he is the one for me, okay?"

Her mother nodded, satisfied with hearing these words. At least her daughter thought about anyone being the right one, meaning there was a future husband on the horizon, even if he was only a small black dot in the distance for now.

Susan's mother couldn't help thinking about how perfect Levi Yoder would be, though. His parents were well-known farmers who still resided on the family farm, kept it in good working condition, produced bumper crops of corn and alfalfa. She'd have to ask Davey, but was pretty sure Elmer Yoder was on the board of the Amish bank, which meant they were fairly well to do. He might own more than one farm. She would have to see what she could do about this situation with Susan. Perhaps a word here or there would be all that was necessary to get things moving. After all, Susan hadn't said she'd turned him down, she'd just said she wasn't *sure*. Sometimes love just needed a little boost, a helping hand.

Susan cleaned Carol's house on Tuesday and went to market on Thursday, Friday, and Saturday with a clear understanding of the word "tepid." She completed her responsibilities well, but felt no enthusiasm. As she stood on the side of Carol's bathtub to wipe down the ceiling and walls of the oversized tub, she caught sight of herself in the mirror, a tall girl dressed in navy blue, black bib apron, ankle socks, white covering. She noticed the raccoon effect on her face, having worn the goggles in the blinding snow and sun. She looked ridiculous but shrugged and turned away to continue swabbing the tub with the thick sponge. The strong smell of Clorox bathroom cleaner brought a cough, then another, a regular occurrence while cleaning Carol's bathroom.

Her mind wandered back to the weekend, which already felt like a dream. Had Levi actually put those goggles on her face, held her face in both hands? She could feel the strength of the calloused palms still. But why did she care? She had brought a swift end to any of these thoughts, had successfully proven to herself she was entirely capable of standing firm in her commitment to staying single.

As she drew the sheets off Carol's king-sized bed, carried them to the washer, and stuffed them in, she thought of Mary's intense gaze on Levi's face, the longing she couldn't conceal. Well, the pitiful burst of jealousy had been put behind her quite efficiently, Susan thought, as she measured laundry detergent, poured, closed the lid, and pressed the button to start the machine. She opened the hall closet door for another set of white Ralph Lauren sheets, Carol's favorite brand.

Jealousy had only proved to be an annoying mosquito, swatted, killed, taken care of. She wondered why Levi told her she was beautiful. What possessed anyone to say that to someone they barely knew? Stupid. She must be beautiful to someone like Levi, old and desperate for a wife. And asking why she didn't want a boyfriend. Really. This is why, Levi. Because I won't be caught in a situation I cannot control.

But my, Levi was a very attractive man. My goodness. She lifted a picture of Carol and her husband, dusted the frame and replaced it, moved on to the middle of the large dresser. The way his hair was piled in thick waves, wet, glossy, healthy after showering, his face even darker from being in the sun. Poor Mary, so besotted. Well, he's all yours, Mary. You would make a wonderful wife for him. She ran the sweeper under the bed, bending low to be positive Carol would find no dust, then moved on to the Persian rug, using the brush attachment for the tops of the baseboard. Satisfied to find everything dusted and swept, she moved on to the guest bathroom, lugging the plastic Rubbermaid bucket filled with Clorox cleaner, Windex, toilet bowl cleaner, rags, sponges, and paper towels.

Mary had talked about going west, with Joe and Mervin chiming in, goading her on. They'd been there the previous summer. They told her that if she wanted to buy a ranch, now was the time. She talked about running cattle on hundreds, sometimes thousands of acres, which meant she couldn't do it alone. Susan could see that Joe would gladly be the husband Mary would need, but Mary seemed to know that and not to care. She didn't want Joe, she wanted Levi. Oh boy. Susan found herself feeling a bit sad as she sprayed Windex all over the enormous mirror, then set about wiping the glass with a large wad of paper towels. She made a wry face, almost laughing at her clownish appearance.

Life couldn't always be figured out.

So, for six hours of housecleaning all these thoughts tumbled around in her head. She tried to disengage herself from the rubble to climb up the ladder of her pedestal, where she could sit, shoulders hunched, arms crossed tightly to be sure she stayed in position. She would keep any romance or unexplained feelings firmly out of sight.

In February, Susan had a firm case of the winter blahs. Frequent snowstorms were followed by a period of elevated temperatures, slush, and mud. Starlings and sparrows squabbled at the feeder, chasing the prettier, more timid cardinals and nuthatches away. A stomach flu made its rounds, so all of Mam's natural remedies were lined up on the counter, like a sentry against all stomach invasions. Susan was sent to help Kate, who was down with the agonizing stomach pains this flu brought on. She called Carol to reschedule her day of cleaning and drove her horse through the slush and wet roads to her sister's house.

She blinked in astonishment when she entered through the back door, finding the house in a deplorable state, piles of clothes drooping from overfull hampers, clothes, food, and toys piled everywhere, the sink heaped with unwashed dishes. Kate was nowhere to be found, but she could hear the sound of retching from the bathroom.

Emily came running, her large dark eyes filled with worry.

"Mam is throwing up," she said, as Susan pulled her into her arms. Nathan waited politely for his own hug, followed by little Micah, who was pale and sickly, a loose diaper hanging haphazardly from his thin hips.

"Poor Micah. Were you sick, too? Come here."

And she held the child against her, feeling genuinely glad to be here, to hold these dear children and help where she was needed.

"Oh, Susan." Kate's weak voice came from the hallway.

"Hi, Kate."

"I'm sorry you had to come over and find us like this."

"It's fine. Absolutely. Don't worry."

"The children have all been so sick."

"And now you."

"Now me." She grinned a tired, lopsided grin, then looked as if she might burst into tears.

"Kate, is everything okay?"

"Yes. Well, no."

A cry from the bedroom interrupted the conversation, a weak mewling cry that sent Kate scurrying. Susan watched her go, sighed, and congratulated herself for her unwillingness to allow this to happen to her.

Kate returned, carrying Marie, her short chubby arms and legs dangling, her tongue protruding from her open mouth. She was so cute. Her black hair had fallen out along the sides, which gave her an appearance of wearing a mohawk.

"Marie, baby!" Susan said, reaching with both hands.

Kate relinquished her gladly, then put a hand to her stomach, wincing.

"I better lay on the recliner," she said weakly.

Susan deposited Marie into her arms, then began gathering soiled clothing, deciding the most pressing duty was taking care of the laundry.

"Susan?"

"Yes?"

"There are a lot of soiled bedclothes and underwear. Just let it go. I'll get it after I feel better."

Susan nodded, then separated the laundry into piles, filling the wringer washer with hot water and laundry soap. Kate still washed with a gas engine attached to the washer, the washer itself barely usable.

She found the red plastic can, shook it, and pressed her mouth into a tight line. No gas. Whatever. She wasn't going to bother Kate with this problem, as sick as she was feeling. But she was determined to find some sort of fuel and get that rusty old Briggs and Stratton engine going. She marched to the shop, found a weed eater with a small blue fuel can with a spout. Yep, about half full. If the old engine didn't work after this, well, then, Dan just might have to purchase a new one. She dumped it into the fuel tank, set it aside, and switched the button from off to on, yanked at the cord ferociously, only to have the engine give a weak gasp. How she deplored the use of a cantankerous, smelly old engine. There were much better ways of running a washer these days. Compressed air, solar power, rechargeable batteries . . . there were lots of options these days. This was maddening. She yanked, adjusted the choke, yanked again, till at least there were enough pops and wheezing noises to get it started. Quickly, she reached down to adjust the choke, and everything stopped.

Dead silence.

Emily and Nathan stood watching, wide-eyed.

"Mam pushes this first," Nathan said calmly, pointing to a white button she had not seen at all. She pushed it, began all over again, and was relieved to hear the steady rattling sound she wanted.

In went the first load of sheets, followed by nightgowns she had rinsed and soaked in Clorox water. Towels, more bedding, a change of wash water. Her fingers were freezing in the stiff February breeze as she pegged row after row of clothes on the sagging line in the backyard. She washed down the chipped cement floor, arranged boots and coats on a clean rug, washed windows in the small laundry, then went back into the kitchen and discovered a terrible stench. Micah had soiled himself and sat crying on the floor, Marie asleep on a corner of the couch, and Kate throwing up in the bathroom.

Good grief. She should have brought Mam.

But by late afternoon, Kate felt decidedly better. The children all had a good long nap on clean sheets, the house was mostly clean, and supper was on the stove. Susan grabbed armfuls of clean, wind-dried laundry and hurried through the snow to fold it quickly, before Dan arrived. He would want his supper, not a table full of unfolded laundry. She had prepared hamburger gravy, mashed potatoes, and green beans, with homemade white bread and jelly.

Dan blew through the back door, his face eager to see his family. He set his lunch on the counter, and turned to pick up Micah.

"How's my little guy? Better?" he asked.

"We're all feeling a lot better," answered Kate. "Susan has been priceless, coming here today. She sure gave me a lift."

Dan smiled at Susan, a genuine welcome she had not received from him in years.

"Good for you. I hardly knew if I should go to work or not this morning, the way Kate was."

The meal was filled with conversation, the children chiming in, telling Dan all about how sick they'd been. He listened attentively, nodded his head, and told them he was glad they were feeling better. Kate ate little, but seemed to appreciate her husband's words.

"So, Susan. Did Kate tell you of our new plans?"

Susan looked from Kate back to Dan, her stomach tumbling, then felt an odd sensation in her chest.

"No," she answered tentatively, as if she was afraid of his answer.

"You want to tell her?"

"No. You go ahead."

"We're moving in a few months." Dan's eyes were triumphant.

"Wh . . . what? Where?"

Dan pushed the palms of his hands against the edge of the table, elevating the two front legs of his chair. He balanced there, crossed his arms, and lifted his shoulders.

"Virginia! Where the land is dirt cheap, houses are even cheaper. A guy I work with is taking us down next week. Well, weekend. We're going to check it out. Kate balked at first, but I think she's getting used to the idea. A whole new adventure will be just what we all need. Plus, the children are still small, don't go to school yet, so I imagine the change won't affect them much."

Imagine away, you loser. Susan couldn't stop this first angry thought from popping into her head. Seriously, what was wrong with this man? Taking his wife so far away from all she had ever known. Lancaster County was a culture, a way of life filled with social gatherings, auctions, family get-togethers. This was truly unthinkable.

And Susan told him so, without holding back.

Dan's eyes narrowed, the color in his face deepened.

"You aren't the one to tell us what to do. If my wife can give herself up to this, then so should you."

Susan turned to Kate, whose face had taken on a porcelain doll façade, her eyes dark and lifeless. Wan from the stomach virus, she merely nodded, her eyelids falling heavily.

"Do you want to go, Kate?" Susan blurted out.

Kate choked out a small laugh, more like a sob. "I don't know. I have never been to Virginia. But if Dan thinks there's an opportunity, I'm sure it will be fine."

"I didn't tell you the best part," said Dan, excitement returning to his voice. "Guess what I'll be doing."

Susan shook her head, not trusting herself to speak.

"We'll be raising dogs. Lots of money in puppies these days."

"But, you'll need to invest in a kennel."

"Of course, I know. This guy I work with is going to finance the whole operation. I'll pay him off fast with puppies."

Susan steadied herself, took a deep breath. She knew who would put in most of the work, and it certainly wasn't him. She knew, too, she had said enough. To keep the peace, and for Kate, she would pretend to show her support.

"But Kate," she breathed, as she bent over the dishwater, after Dan had gone to feed his horse.

"Susan, I know. Don't make it any harder than it already is."

"Are you going?"

Kate shrugged. "What choice do I have?"

"You do have a choice. Have you told him you don't want to go?"

"He'll just slip into another one of his deep depressions."

"Let him."

"No, Susan. You have no idea. I would rather give up everything I have than lose Dan to depression again. It's not worth it. He might do very well, in a new location, away from his family."

Susan looked at her sharply.

"Or he might drown in debt. And you'll have no one nearby to help you."

"Shh. He's coming in."

DRIVING HOME IN the dark, the headlights on the buggy illuminating the roadway and the rump of the fast-trotting horse, Susan allowed tears of anger and frustration to fall. The clopping of hooves, steel rims on the macadam, passing motorists all fell into a kaleidoscope of sounds and sights as her vision was partially obscured by her tears. Angrily, she jerked the glove compartment door open and rummaged around for a Kleenex. Finding none, she brought up a corner of her apron and swiped at her nose. Kate. Oh Kate. Her heart felt as if it had been replaced by a cement block, so heavy she couldn't breathe comfortably.

Her parents sat in silence as she poured our her story, Mark and Elmer coming down from upstairs after they caught snatches of the conversation.

As usual, her mother said the most, while her father pondered the situation before saying much of anything.

"He controls her with that depression. It's a pattern, and it's not fair," Susan burst out.

"But he was doing so much better after Marie was born," her mother answered, always giving Dan the benefit of the doubt.

"Well, wait until he takes Kate away from every support she has and then finds himself unable to climb out of debt."

"Oh now," her mother soothed.

"Making a living with a kennel? Dan? You know exactly who is going to do ninety-five percent of the work." Susan's voice rose, her love for her sister causing rage to take the wheel.

"Susan, you need to calm down," her father said quietly.

Her mother agreed, telling her hundreds, thousands of Amish families relocated for many reasons. Sometimes it was financial, and sometimes they weren't happy with the way things were going in the church, and sometimes there was a pioneer-spirited couple who moved thousands of miles west or east, and lived a very good life. It was allowed, within reason, and if Kate did what the Scriptures asked of her, she would go whithersoever her husband went. It was God's will.

The pious "whithersoever" did Susan in. She told her mother without mincing one word that Dan was not a stable person, he was in no shape to go careening off into the wild blue yonder, his head full of puppies and dollar signs. Her father asked her again to calm down, but Mark and Elmer shook their heads in agreement, telling their father she was right and everyone knew it.

Dat said it didn't hurt for them to go check the area out. Let them go, see what Virginia was like. The few Amish settlements were fairly young, and perhaps they would both decide the whole thing was a bad idea. Nine chances out of ten, this fellow Dan worked with was a smooth talker, and he trusted Dan's judgment.

Susan told everyone a curt goodnight, pushed back her chair, and went upstairs. She cried in the shower, she cried as she brushed her wet hair, she cried in bed as she held her book, trying to read. She gave up, turned off the bedside lamp, and sniffed and snuffled into a wad of toilet tissue. She imagined brave Kate sitting in a van moving slowly along 340, carrying them to Virginia. Why Virginia? Why such an out-of-the-way place?

She felt her prayers hit the ceiling and come back to smack her in the face. She knew why her prayer line was clogged. She detested Dan, couldn't even stand to think of him and his incompetent selfishness. Wooing Kate with his charm as thick as honey, hiding every sign of all the torment in his heart.

She prayed on, asking God to take this outrage, knowing well she was asking to forgive her when she could not forgive Dan. But her honesty helped, and she felt a certain measure of peace.

She woke in the morning with the soft, fluffy feeling between wakefulness and sleep, and then the knowledge of what Dan had said slammed into her. She groaned aloud, rolled over, and covered her head with the sheet and quilt. She eventually dug herself out to hit the alarm button and squinted at the time. Four o'clock. The van driver would be pulling in at four-thirty.

She was ready and waiting, her parents still asleep as she made her way out the door as headlights swept the house. The cold made her shiver, but the van was heated.

The lights of Harrisburg glittered as Susan stared out the window at the distant apartment and office buildings, the bridges across the Susquehanna, miles and miles of highway, busy routes intersecting like a crossword puzzle. Where was everyone going this early in the morning? She thought again of her sister Kate, carried on an interstate highway, against her will, moving to Virginia. The thought ruined her morning, made her coffee taste bitter.

Beth took one look at the crooked, loose roll of hair on one side of Susan's head, the swollen red eyes, and the dent in her head covering, and wisely decided to mind her own business. Steven noticed as he came to fill the tomato pan, took a good look at Susan, and scuttled back to the kitchen. Susan told a customer that they didn't put hard-boiled eggs on ham hoagies. Beth heard her say it and knew she just didn't want to slice them. She decided it was time to brave the frigid winds coming from the scowl on Susan's face.

"What gives, Susan?"

"We're out of eggs."

"I'll get them."

Without a backward glance, loyal Beth was on her way to redeem Susan's ill humor, which seemed to shake Susan's conscience enough so that she smiled weakly. "Thanks, Beth."

At lunchtime, Susan shared the whole miserable story with her best friend, the honest voice of understanding a balm to her battered senses. A true friend was for real everything those sappy greeting cards said they were, and she took solace in the blue eyes of her constant and staunch supporter.

Once Susan was in better spirits, Beth dared ask about Levi, if he'd tried to contact her, or was there nothing going on the weekend at Seven Springs.

"Nothing, Beth. There really wasn't. I think he'd do good to marry Mary, who seems quite smitten."

"She's going out West."

"Well, he can go with her."

Exasperated, Beth looked off across the milling crowd of market goers, willing herself to say the right thing.

"You know you found him attractive," Beth said cautiously.

Absentmindedly, Susan said, soft and low, "Did I?"

"Duh!"

"I might have that first night at the restaurant, but I don't now."

The conversation was left high and dry, with Beth baffled by her dear friend.

Susan decided not to mention her determination to avoid being shackled to misery the way Kate had been. This whole Virginia deal was the absolute limit, and pushed Levi away for good. Perhaps it was selfish, and perhaps she was a coward, but now more than ever, she was taking no chances. Her resolve was set in stone, her mind made up, when Mark cornered her that evening and said Levi would like to spend a weekend taking in the mountain laurel on Skyline Drive in Virginia sometime toward the end of April. Just the four of them.

She was already shaking her head no, till she thought of Virginia. Dan would never manage to buy a property and move in a few months, so perhaps she could scout it out and gain some insight to talk him out of the whole thing.

"I don't know. Why isn't Mary going? Or Mervin and Joe?"

"He didn't say why."

She told Mark her reason for considering going and he rolled his eyes.

"Seriously, Susan. Do you really think that's fair to Levi?"

"What does he care? I told him I'm not interested in dating anyone. If I go, it's because I might get some information that will help me talk Dan and Kate out of this terrible idea of his."

Mark sighed as he left the room.

CHAPTER 9

Rose and Liz were coming to help Mam with her spring housecleaning, a task normally tackled with no qualms by her alone, but a bout of sciatica in her lower back kept her worrying on the couch. Susan's father tried to reason with her, saying one spring without housecleaning wouldn't hurt, but oh no, not Mam. Susan stayed home on a Tuesday, baked oatmeal with peaches, put bacon on jelly roll pans, and turned the oven to four hundred degrees, her mother getting dressed amid many grunts and sighs. Kate would not be able to come, with Dan's sisters coming to help her with her own spring work.

Susan was not excited about spending the day with Rose and Liz, the way they both agreed with Mam about Kate moving to Virginia. Both of them nodded self-righteously, said yes, yes, if a man decided such a thing, there was no choice. You went. It was God's will, the woman being the weaker vessel and blah blah blah.

It made Susan hopping mad. In recent weeks she had taken to swallowing Tylenol PM so she could get a good night's sleep. She'd tried to comfort herself with shoofly whoopee pies and apple cider doughnuts at market until she gained five pounds, and then promptly lived on salads and vitamins for a week, which did nothing for her mood, either.

So Rose and Liz better watch their words, Susan thought, opening the oven door to check the bacon. She used the egg beater to whip up eggs, sliced whole wheat bread, put a clean tablecloth on the table, and set the coffee carafe with mugs and French vanilla creamer in the middle. She was in the pantry looking for paper plates when the front door was flung open and Rose and Liz stepped in on a breath of cold March wind.

"Hey, Susan," Rose trilled.

Susan drew herself up to her full height, said, "Good morning, Rose."

"Boy, we're proper this morning, aren't we?" Liz said.

"When did that stupid 'hey' replace a decent polite hello?" Susan asked, as prickly as a thorn.

"Everybody says it. Get over it."

This came from Rose, shedding her coat, hanging it in the hallway. She was dressed in a tight mango-colored dress, her bib apron made of some stretch fabric, too tight and not wide enough, allowing a very large portion of her mango-colored backside in view.

"How are you this morning?" Liz asked kindly, quietly.

Susan told her she was fine and bent to check the bacon. "No children?" she asked.

"No, Lena Mae is old enough to watch the little ones. Eli's home."

They both turned to fuss over Mam, asking questions, showing concern. No, the chiropractor was not touching this thing, she said, and no, she wasn't going to a massage therapist either. She was putting comfrey packs on it and taking those cure-all supplements her friend recommended. Eye rolls behind her back brought a sense of unity, at least until they all sat down to eat the breakfast Susan had prepared.

Discussions ranged from the weather to local news to hearsay about a child falling on ice at school and getting a serious concussion. Rose mentioned that Leon King had a date with Amos's Martha, which brought one eyebrow up from Susan.

"Leon? She could do better than him."

"There you go again, Susan. Why do you always put down the young men? He is perfectly suitable. I think they make a lovely couple."

Rose sniffed her disapproval, cut herself a second square of baked oatmeal, and liberally added brown sugar and milk. Susan sat back and drank her black coffee, deciding it was best not to reply.

"Nothing ever come of your weekend with those guys?" Liz asked.

"Course not," Rose said, completely out of turn.

"I hope you know you're going to be an old maid."

"You know, Rose, that term is so crude," said Susan. "There are plenty of single girls who are very happy being single. I'm quite happy without a set of imposing in-laws, or having to live a life of deprivation and constant sorrow, like Kate."

"Oh, come off it, Susan. Kate has a nice life with Dan. She may not have all the money in the world, but that's not what's important. His depression is much better since Marie was born. I personally think it's the cutest thing ever, watching him with her. And think how that child will thrive growing up with all those puppies. It's too cute."

Before she could stop herself, she burst out, "You really think he's going to be able to run his own business? You know as well as I do that the responsibility will fall on Kate's shoulders."

Mam held up a hand.

"That's enough now. We aren't in agreement, so let's talk about other things."

They obeyed, with Liz launching into a colorful account of her husband trying a new diet plan and how she found him sneaking a large slice of shoofly pie with his black coffee. Standing on the scales in total despair, wailing how life was unfair, he then went with their neighbor Ralph down to the Bird-in-Hand diner for the breakfast buffet. Out of her sight, it was hard to tell what all the poor man ingested.

Everyone laughed together, bringing a softer note to the table, an easier atmosphere prevailing for the remainder of their breakfast. They discussed the seed catalogues, the new greenhouse on Peony Drive, and suddenly, the conversation came back to Dan and Kate. Susan's eyes narrowed as Rose said she though it would be good for Kate to be away from her family. She would fully depend on Dan, which in turn, would make him feel more responsible and become a better provider. Kate had always been too attached to her family, especially to Susan.

Susan literally bit her tongue to keep from forming sharp words of correction. When Liz nodded in agreement, Mam eyed Susan nervously, giving a small shake of her head. Could it be Mam saw much more than she would ever reveal? But the small motion of her head, the kindness in her eyes, were enough to assuage Susan's outburst.

The remainder of the day went well, with happy chattering and laughing as they worked together, cleaning the upstairs thoroughly.

And Susan was convinced sister relationships were unique. No one could stir up your anger more efficiently, but then no one was easier to forgive, iron things out with, even with no words spoken. Rose and Liz were blood relation with ties like rubber bands, stretching till they threatened to break, but snapping back easily.

When Rose bent over a bucket of water to wring out her microfiber cloth, Susan told her she looked like a weird pumpkin.

Rose swatted her with a wet rag. "You wait until you have children. Every bit of your metabolism goes haywire and every single calorie goes to your hips, so stop thinking you're any better."

But I would never wear those fabrics, Susan thought.

As if reading her mind, Liz chimed in, "Well, Rose, you shouldn't wear those tight dresses."

"Oh, really. Says she of the fat husband," Rose shot back.

"What does he have to do with it?"

"Well."

Rose wiped walls as if her life depended on it, then turned to Liz and asked what she should wear instead. Liz told her it was fine, perhaps a tad tight, especially around the skirt.

The conversation turned to single pleats versus double pleats in dressmaking, single pleats being "fancy," which was frowned upon.

It was all a part of being Amish, what was acceptable and what was not. Bright colors, tight sleeves, and long skirts were all fashionable, and Rose felt a need to be one of the fancy ones.

Eventually, there was quiet, each woman absorbed in her own thoughts as they scrubbed walls. Liz broke the silence.

"So, nothing happened with this Levi? Who is he anyway?"

"What do you mean by nothing happened? What was supposed to happen?"

"Oh, you know. He didn't ask you for a date?"

"No," Susan answered, pausing. "But he did ask why I wasn't interested in having a boyfriend."

Susan reveled in the shock value of her statement, both sisters' mouths open in surprise.

"What?" Rose shrieked. "See, that's your whole problem. Guys pick up on that frosty attitude. They can tell. If you continue on your high and mighty horse, I'm telling you, Susan, it's Loneliness Avenue for you."

"You mean Bored Boulevard," Liz corrected her, and they howled with glee at their own cleverness. Susan couldn't help but laugh with them, their mother giggling in the background.

Susan's heart warmed toward her mother and sisters yet again. There were differences in opinion, of course, but that was only a wrinkle in the fabric of time; the true measure of their relationship was the love between them. Since no one agreed with her about Kate, she had to keep her own view under wraps, for now. And she certainly was not telling them one single thing about going to Skyline Drive in April, or they would be making wedding plans immediately.

In church, there was a visiting minister from Indiana, which brought many families who would have attended services in their own district ordinarily. The shop was filled to capacity, with the couple who hosted services scurrying to provide more seating, asking a row of boys to stand while they brought in more benches.

The air still held the sharp bite of winter winds that morning, but the floor of the buggy shop was heated, so everyone was comfortable, which was a blessing. It was not unusual to have propane heaters hissing in the corners, completely inefficient, the younger ladies scurrying to bring shawls for the elderly women, or rugs for their feet, cement floors being too chilly.

Susan was always the oldest single girl, so she led the long line of teenagers and school-aged girls to be seated on the allotted benches behind the married women. She was glad to have visiting ministers, always interested to hear a fresh voice.

She saw the minister's wife seated in the front row, the bowl-shaped covering so different from the Lancaster *ordnung*. The woman's hair was combed up over her forehead in a sleek upward sweep, something the eastern women would not attempt. Her cape and dress style were also very different, but Susan thought they might be easier to wear, without all the straight pins used in Sunday attire here in the East.

When the singing began, Susan opened the heavy black *Ausbund* and began to sing the slow undulating cadence of German words. She had been part of this singing since she was a very young child, so it was as comforting and as familiar as an old blanket. Today, there was exceptional volume, like a wedding, with almost twice as many in the congregation.

Susan was enthralled with the message of hope and love, the faith to get us through our days. Yes, we are often waylaid by Satan, but the victory is ours through Christ Jesus.

The pronunciation of the words was different, the western dialect so unique, so captivating. There was a special atmosphere of reverence among the congregation.

Susan felt the mellow kindness, the love for the people this minister had in his heart. Moved to tears more than once, she found herself grateful for the handful of Kleenex in her dress pocket.

Life was good. With the Lord above her, His love to cushion the blows of whatever the world might hand out, what was there to fear? She felt replenished, restored. Afterward, she helped with the tables, smiling more frequently and with a greater love than she could have before the sermon.

She felt a hand on her arm, a voice asking if she might have a word with her. She stopped and found herself looking down at the minister's wife, her brown eyes alight with interest.

"I just have to tell you. I keep watching you, wondering who you are, and if I'm right thinking you're a bit older than most single girls. I'm the minister's wife, Jane Mast."

Susan took the proffered hand, shook it warmly.

"It's good to meet you. And yes, I probably am a bit older."

"Here, let's step aside for a minute. There's a lot of foot traffic here," Jane Mast said, smiling as Susan looked around.

"Okay, I know you have no idea what I'm talking about or who I am, but I want to throw this out to you. We're moving to Wyoming, close to the Montana border, where there's a fairly new settlement, and we would certainly be glad to obtain a decent, mature young woman as a teacher for around twenty pupils before September of this year. You know, I'm totally out of my league. It's usually a man's job to hire a teacher, but there's just something about you I keep being drawn to. Have you ever considered stepping off the beaten path and trying something new?"

Susan had been listening, already formulating the words to turn down the offer.

"It's very beautiful there. The mountain ranges are simply magnificent, the weather favorable in the summer. But I'll tell you, you'll need an adventuresome spirit."

"Well, I'm grateful for you thinking I'm mature."

They both laughed easily. Jane put a hand on her arm.

"Please take it as a compliment, the way it was meant."

Susan nodded. She wanted to get away, to disappear into the crowd of people helping to serve the Sunday church dinner.

"Oh, here's Mahlon. Mahlon, come here."

The minister came to join them. He was of average height, with the kindest blue eyes.

"Mahlon, this is . . . oh, I don't know who this is."

Jane's easy laughter pealed out, and Mahlon raised his eyebrows.

Susan smiled, told them her name.

"Yes, well. Susan Lapp, this is Mahlon, my husband. Mahlon, I told her where we're moving and that we need a schoolteacher."

"We certainly do. But Wyoming is not at all like Lancaster. The West might be quite a hardship."

"Maybe. But she might like it out there."

"What do you think, Susan?" Mahlon asked.

"Oh, I have no idea. I don't know anything about Wyoming. I have never been west, not even to Ohio. And I certainly never taught school. Never wanted to."

"What do you do?" Jane asked, as bright-eyed and inquisitive as a chipmunk.

"I clean a house, work at the market three days a week."

"Market?" Mahlon asked.

"A farmer's market in Harrisburg."

"Your capital city, right?"

Susan nodded.

They fired questions at her, Susan politely answering each one, watching as her friends scurried back and forth, serving the crowd of people who all took their turn at the table.

In the end, addresses and telephone numbers were hurriedly exchanged, a small notepad held on a palm, the pen jotting busily. Susan lifted her white apron and inserted the paper carefully into her pocket among the wad of Kleenex, bidding them a hasty goodbye and departing with a sigh of relief.

My word.

She was a bit miffed. They had no right to ask a complete stranger to come to the ends of the earth to teach children. Why couldn't they ask someone from their own community?

She forgot to retrieve the slip of paper from the wad of tissue in her pocket and her mother pitched it in the trash the following morning as she emptied pockets before throwing the colored laundry in the washing machine. When Susan remembered, it was too late—the trash had been taken to the curb and picked up by the large green garbage truck making its Monday afternoon run. She shrugged, said it was fine. There was no chance of her departing for any western state any time soon. Her mother laughed with her, thinking how very unlikely such a thing would be, her daughter happily employed, and now, wonder of wonders, almost dating a young man with great approval ratings.

DAN AND KATE took all the children on their trip to Virginia and returned a few days later, with Kate leaving a message asking Susan to come for a visit if she had any free time. Alarm rose in her chest when she heard her sister's voice, so tired, so quiet and despondent.

She called Carol, said her sister needed her on Tuesday, and drove her horse to her house. They sat in the kitchen with a pot of coffee and a plate of day-old doughnuts, the children climbing all over her, until Kate told them to go play in the living room.

"I'm so scared," Kate breathed softly.

"What is it?" Susan asked, her heart sinking.

"We . . . we signed a contract on an eighty-three acre farm."

Kate looked out the kitchen window to keep from crying, took a deep breath, and faced her sister with heartbreaking courage.

"It's awful, Susan. The buildings are hideous. The farm is in a hollow surrounded by ridges, a high mountain looming to the south. We'll never be able to remodel. We don't even have money for a gallon of paint."

"Don't go, Kate. Stand your ground. Don't do it. Tell Dan you'll never make it. You have the right."

"I'm afraid . . . I'm afraid it's not God's will for me to do that. You know our duty as a wife. 'Whither thou goest' and all that. And Dan is so happy. He's supercharged. He says we'll have a wonderful life living in a secluded area, so close to nature. It's his dream, and how can I refuse him? It wouldn't be right, and we both know it."

"But Kate, you matter too. Dan's feelings are not the only ones that matter."

Kate put her face in her hands, bowed her head, and wept, piteous breaths as light and fluttery as a kitten's. Susan rose from her chair, knelt by her sister, and put both arms around the slight form, holding her silently.

After a few moments, Kate gathered herself together, sat up, and wiped her eyes, squaring her shoulders as she drew up a deep breath.

"I'm a baby, I know. Spineless. Too afraid to go against Dan, and too afraid to go with him. Oh, Susan. The place is disgusting. You can't imagine."

"Do you have pictures?" Susan asked.

"No. Well, a very distant black and white that shows nothing."

Kate stopped, looked into the living room, snapped, "Nathan, don't. Get away from Marie."

She got up, went to the desk, and came back with a sheaf of papers. She thrust them at Susan and shuddered.

"Everything on that piece of paper is a lie."

Susan looked up, amazed at Kate's sharp tone.

"It is."

Susan scanned the papers, handed them back. There was nothing to say, although her head felt stuffed with questions, outraged feelings obliterating any common sense.

"Tell me, Kate. Just tell me everything."

"There's a two-story house with paint peeling off the wooden siding, the front porch sagging in every possible way. There are renters in the house, but they're the kind of people who can't afford a decent place. I can't tell you how bad it is. Weeds, rusted out cars, lawnmowers with flat tires, dogs wandering all over the place."

She got up from her chair to take Nathan by his shoulders and steer him firmly to the couch, telling him Baby Marie's swing was not to be touched.

"The barn is only a tumbledown shell. There are some outbuildings, a corn crib. Dan says it won't take much to get our license and start raising dogs. But we need help, financial and physical. His parents know nothing of this, and when they find out, we'll be disowned. I know they will never offer a penny."

"Surely they will. I thought Dan was everything to them."

"He is, as long as we do what his parents expect of us."

Susan broke a doughnut in half, noticed the dry texture, and laid it back down. She lifted her coffee cup to drink the lukewarm brew, her thoughts churning haphazardly.

"I try, Susan. I tell myself I'm strong, I can do this. And I know Dat and Mam, Rose and Liz will do all they can. But after we're moved and the dust settles, there I'll be, in that awful hollow in that house, with an overwhelming amount of work, a special needs baby, and Dan, well, you know how he is. I want to trust that his good mood will last and he'll be able to work hard to get things up and running, but I just can't."

"It did seem like things were better after Marie was born. Has he gotten depressed again?"

"Things were better for a while. Right now he's on a high, thinking of the riches we'll enjoy with the money the dogs will bring in. He says the few couples who have settled in this valley are progressive thinkers, meaning they won't be very strict about certain things, and he's looking forward to using electricity, which to me is another sign of his unhappiness. He's always going against church rules, and now he'll be even more free of restraint. I just don't know what to think, Susan."

"I have to admit I was skeptical that his new enthusiasm for life would last, but I did hope for your sake that it would. At least he's working more regularly now, right?"

"He makes more money than he used to, but he buys things. He paid over a thousand dollars for a spotting scope, saying it would pay for itself in good deer meat. His trips to the hunting cabin in Lycoming County are not cheap, and he rarely manages to harvest a deer. Anyway, I don't mean to sound bitter. I know he deserves a vacation. It's just hard when we never have enough to go around, no matter what his paycheck is."

Kate picked at the threadbare tablecloth.

"I shouldn't tell you all these things. I don't want to disrespect him. And I think silence, suffering in silence, can bring a blessing. Not really suffering. I'm not really suffering, Susan."

Her sentences ran into each other like traffic congestion as she tried to convey the fact that she was submissive and a good helpmeet, but it was clear that her spirit was in agony.

Susan was thrown into a quandary listening to her sister's voice, the children squabbling in the background. Three under the age of six, and a special needs baby. Should she be supportive of this move, the way her parents and sisters were, or should she speak from the heart? To tell her to give herself up to her husband's wishes in this case was like pushing her off the gangplank of a ship into the raging sea. Kate would be consumed under the unbearable pressure of keeping everything afloat. Or was it weak and faithless to think like that?

The only thing she knew for sure was that she herself must never fall in love.

CHAPTER 10

IN FOUR WEEKS' TIME, THE BUDS BURST THROUGH THE TREE branches, the red-winged blackbirds called their distinctive "Birdy-glee, Birdy-glee," and robins twittered in a mad frenzy as they raced each other to build their nests.

And Dan and Kate were on their way to Virginia, without his parents' blessing, but with Susan's entire family coming along to help them get settled.

The large van traveling south on Route 70 was filled to capacity with the Lapp clan, and a minivan followed behind with Dan and Kate and the children. The sale had been completed with Dat's help, and Dat had given them a little extra money so they could pay to get the barn ready for a horse, have the grass mown, and tend to repairs after the renters left. No one had seen the farm, but everyone was in high spirits, eager to see this home in the lovely hills of Virginia.

"Virginia is for lovers, Suze," Liz quipped, pointing to a billboard as they entered the state. "See that?"

"Yeah, well leave her here. She might catch something in the drinking water," Elmer chortled from the back seat.

Susan slapped at his upended knee propped on the back of the seat. "Get your knee off my back. And get off your phone."

"Old grouch."

He cast a glance at Mark and they howled with laughter.

Susan hid her own smile. She wasn't giving them the satisfaction of making her laugh, but she didn't mind her brothers' good-natured teasing.

When they arrived at their destination, everyone stepped down from the van with expressions of disbelief or astonishment. Dat found his voice first. "It's a real fixer-upper, now, isn't it?"

Susan had felt the potholes in the surface of the drive, the winding muddy dirt lane through the woods off a dirt road without markers of any kind.

To round a bend and be confronted with the buildings took Susan's breath away. It was worse than she'd feared, worse than she'd imagined.

The grass had been mowed, to an extent, and there were a few new yellow pine boards on the barn, a new doorway. That seemed to be the only attempt at improvement, so far as she could tell.

Susan searched her mother's face, the face of her sisters, but all of the were inscrutable. She saw the putty crumbling from old window panes, the paint in curls, peeling off the gray wooden siding, the remaining paint a faint, dirty white. The doorframe was collapsing into the sagging porch. The cement walkway was cracked and broken. There was a rusted tin roof, a block chimney.

"Well, no use standing here. Let's tackle it," Liz chirped in an artificial falsetto that made Susan's skin crawl.

"Right on," Rose echoed, marching up to the formidable porch steps in a hot pink dress with silver swirls in the fabric. She called to the children, who were already dashing about like rabbits, checking doorways, parting patches of weeds, yelling something about turtles.

"Stick around, children. Bears might live on the mountain."

The interior was made up of small dark rooms, paper peeling from the walls, filthy carpeting covering the floor, even in the kitchen, where the once blue carpeting had turned black with dirt and grease. The cabinets were white metal. There was an old-fashioned porcelain sink with a drainboard on each side, which might have been charming if the enamel wasn't peeling so badly. A wooden counter had been provided along the left side, adjoining a filthy, grease-covered electric stove.

Doorknobs were missing, or hanging in disrepair, the narrow staircase showing signs of having been painted many years ago. The only bathroom was upstairs, with a rusted white porcelain commode, a clawfoot bathtub, and a pedestal sink.

When Dan and Kate arrived, a family conference was already being held, but they scattered quickly before Dan could see their concern. Everyone instantly went into high gear, raucously upbeat, saying how cute the house could be made, what a lovely location, and how far to the nearest Amish?

Dat conferred with Dan, walking from room to room, Dat making suggestions. Mark and Elmer did their best, bringing in gallons of paint, plying staple removers as they tore up carpeting. Mam seemed to have the breath knocked out of her body, walking from room to room with a shocked expression, saying nothing. Tomorrow the belongings would arrive, with Liz and Rose's husbands accompanying the drive, but today, they would do their best to make the house more livable.

They removed a partition, went to Lowe's for supplies. They cleaned and scoured, painted walls and floors, ate buckets of Kentucky Fried Chicken with baked beans, coleslaw, and biscuits. They had Mam's whoopee pies for dessert and vanilla pudding with strawberry sauce, all of which she had prepared ahead of time and brought with them.

Dat was the foreman, the one who stayed focused, the one with a plan and the management skills to make it all happen.

By early evening, the transformation was impressive. The scent of Pine-Sol, the whiter porcelain in the bathroom, the cleaner windows and freshly painted walls softly spoke that this unhospitable building just might be able to be turned into a home. And when the sun was lowered into the horizon, the undulating line of ridges turned dark with the blaze of red and orange putting on a wonderful display of God's glory, Susan sat with Kate on the splintering porch steps and put a hand on her knee.

"Think you'll make it?" she asked softly.

"I have to. But yes. Tomorrow our belongings will be here, and we'll see. I cannot believe how much we got done. I just feel bad for Mam. She looks dead tired."

They sat for a few minutes, enjoying the breeze and listening to the crickets.

"You know, Susan, it will grow on me. I'll probably come to appreciate the beauty of the surrounding ridges. We sit on the bottom of a bowl, don't we?"

Susan nodded, noting the underlying sadness in her sister's voice.

"You don't have to pretend for me, Kate. Sure, we've tidied up a bit, but this is no place to live. I mean, do you know any Amish around here? How will you find your way to church? It all just seems like a bad dream." Susan choked on the lump in her throat, looked away across the line of ridges. "I hate this place."

"Susan, don't."

"I hate it. I'm the only honest one who has the nerve to say it. It's a crummy place to live, and you know it. I'd leave him. Let him figure out what he wants from life."

"Susan."

This time there was a note of warning in her voice.

"Dan's face is feverish with excitement. You said it yourself, he's just on a high. And you know what's going to happen in about a month?"

"Maybe not this time."

Susan took a breath, realizing she was about to do more harm than good. There was no changing anyone's mind at this point. All she could do was pray and try to stay in touch.

"Promise you'll call? Promise you'll let us know when things start to go downhill?"

"I will. Call, I mean."

EARLY THE NEXT morning, Dat decided Kate needed decent flooring in the kitchen and living room, found a Home Depot in an old phone book, asked what was in stock, and arranged for a driver to bring over a load of vinyl flooring. He installed it quickly with Mervin and Elmer's help, Dan watching and throwing out instructions. Susan felt a deep respect for her father and brothers, who were going far beyond what anyone would have expected of them, seeming to make the impossible happen.

When the moving trucks arrived and the furniture was put into place, the dresser drawers filled with their clothing, kitchen cabinets stocked with dishes, and Mam's chicken corn soup bubbling on the stove, Susan felt only a bit better. She was beyond weary, having stayed up all night with Mark and Elmer, painting the floor of the downstairs bedroom with a high grade oil-based floor paint. Cups of Folger's coffee helped keep them awake, and at daybreak they cooked a breakfast of canned sausages and pancakes from a box.

"If we ate this at home, we'd think it was the grossest thing," Mark said.

"Is grossest even a word?" Elmer asked.

"I don't know, Professor Schnitzel."

Susan poured more syrup, said it was fine for her, she'd never been so hungry. They laughed and talked until the sun's rays woke the children upstairs and the sound of scurrying feet, excited voices, and running water all promised a day of chaos, children racing around getting underfoot, chasing each other in and out of the house, parents calling names, telling them to be careful, words tossed unheeded.

What was it about a bunch of cousins getting together, instantly increasing the noise level to a deafening cacophony? And yet, for a moment, Susan regretted the fact that none of her children would ever join this happy circle of children. Her own childhood had been filled with cousins from both parents' sides, cousins of every age, size, and description. They had become special friends from the time they crawled on the floor together.

In the afternoon, when the sun was slanting toward the west, Dat clapped his hands and said it was time to get everyone ready to go.

Susan cast a quick look at Kate, whose face had instantly taken on a waxen expression as she stood next to Dan, holding Marie.

Quick hugs, many, many well wishes, thank yous, Dat blinking back tears, Mam trilling bits of advice before pulling herself into the van where she grabbed her handkerchief and buried her face in it so no one could see her tears.

"Goodbye! Goodbye!"

Susan held on to Kate and pressed her thin form to her own, as if the touch could stay with her always, and finally tore herself away, the sobs making breathing impossible.

Rose and Liz rolled their eyes, but Rose wiped a few tears of her own. Emily and Nathan were both crying, and Susan refused to look at them, her chest heaving with raw emotion.

There was talking, of course, bolstering each other's courage, everyone upbeat, hopeful. They'd be alright. Dan was a good guy, Dat said, persuading himself they'd done the right thing by helping them move when Elam Stoltzfus wouldn't give his consent or his help.

Who knew? Sometimes you just had to take the bull by the horns and do the best you could.

Susan closed her eyes, feigned sleep, and allowed a long shudder to move through her. She would never really get over this and felt a deep, abiding sorrow followed by stabs of self-pity. It was one thing to have sisters like Liz and Rose, and quite another to have one like Kate, and no one seemed to understand that. Not even Beth.

She remembered, then, a brief conversation she'd had with Levi. He had seemed to know what she felt for Kate. He had a married brother named Steven with whom he shared his whole life. Steven was the only one who understood, who seemed to care, and she had nodded, told him that was how it was with Kate. She'd watched his profile as he bent his head to search for unpopped kernels of popcorn on the bottom of his bowl, swished them in salt before popping them into his mouth, crunching them between his teeth. The plane of his nose was perfect, heavier at the top than most people's, his eyes set perfectly on either side. She could see him in the firelight now. That fireplace had been perfect, too. Nothing was more comforting after a cold day outside on the slopes than the cracking and popping of a huge fire burning in a fireplace.

"On the slopes." That sounded so English, as in non-Amish. Had she really been there? She had, and was glad of having had the experience. Levi was still waiting for an answer about his trip to Virginia.

A definite no.

And yet. They could stop in at Dan and Kate's, couldn't they?

She would tell Mark that if Levi truly had no intentions of dating and was willing to have her come just as a friend, she'd do it.

She turned around in her seat, but found both of her brothers sound asleep, snoring deeply. She grabbed her own pillow and settled herself for a nap of her own.

The next few days were spent alternating between hope and hidden tears, weeping as she ran the sweeper at Carol's, angrily thumping the bottle of Pledge on the tabletop, before praying for Kate's well-being.

At market, Beth was relentless with her questions. Susan was evasive as always, but she did promise to go to Skyline Drive.

She sewed two new dresses, bought new sneakers, two new black sweaters, and a black hooded jacket, assuring herself these items were long overdue, especially the olive green dress in the patterned fabric. No matter that her closet was stuffed with dresses—this one was a necessity, the color of her eyes, really. She asked Mark if it was hiking or camping or both, or if they'd stay in a hotel, or what were the plans.

He didn't say exactly, so she packed whatever she thought was a sensible choice and left it at that.

But oh my. What was this peculiar unbalanced beating of her heart as the hour of his arrival finally rolled around? It would be entirely different if he were at every hymn singing and youth gathering the way most of the young men she knew were. But he was never there. She wondered what he did on the weekends, but didn't allow herself too much curiosity.

A plain white minivan pulled up. It was the same driver who had taken them to Seven Springs. Mark and Beth were already in the back seat and Levi was in front with the driver.

Good. As it should be. This time he got out, came to the back, and lifted the trunk door. He waited until she approached and smiled that wide smile, making his blue eyes squint, and said, "Hello, Susan."

"Hello, Levi."

He reached for her duffel bag, his knuckles touching hers, stowed it in the back, closed the lid, and asked, "How *are* you, Susan?"

"I'm doing fine. And you?"

"Great. Great."

He opened the door latch but did not slide it open.

"Now that you're here," he added.

Oh boy. Off to a good start there, Levi. She lowered her head and stepped into the van quickly. Better not even to acknowledge that kind of nonsense.

But when they pulled into the parking lot of a car dealership and drove up to a small RV, a perfectly proportioned vehicle for sleeping and eating that would allow them to drive along with all the comforts of home, she squealed and clapped her hands like an excitable teenager. She couldn't help it—she had often thought of traveling the country in an RV. It was kind of a dream of hers, actually.

"Why didn't you tell me?" she asked no one in particular. She didn't mean to include Levi, but he turned in his seat to give her the whole benefit of his warm gaze.

"I wanted to surprise you."

"Oh, okay. Consider your mission accomplished."

Wait. This was flirting. This was being far too friendly. She'd have to put the brakes on.

But really, she couldn't hide her excitement as they explored the interior of this perfectly dreamy RV. It had a table, booths to sit on, cabinets, a tiny stove and tiny fridge, even a shower. Two beds.

The driver's name was Randy, a professional bus driver who had retired three years ago and now made a few dollars hauling the Amish people from place to place. He loved it, he said, and especially enjoyed these pleasure trips. They assured him they were human, same as anyone else, and he laughingly agreed, said he'd found that out. Some

Amish folks were downright disrespectful, throwing chewed gum on the carpeted floor of his van, or waiting at Walmart for two hours then complaining about the price he charged them. There were the loud talkers, the quiet ones, the stop at every fence post ones, but all in all, folks were nice and certainly he loved his job.

So they were off to a good start, with Levi up front with the driver and the rest of them in the back.

She found herself wondering why he hadn't chosen to sit nearer to her, until she caught Beth watching her with knowing eyes. She sniffed, lifted her chin, and stared out the window as Beth went on and on about nothing much in true Beth fashion.

The traffic of congested Lancaster County behind them, they stayed on smaller routes, driving slowly along winding country roads, finding creeks, small ponds, and lakes filled with migratory birds.

For lunch, they found a camping area beside a tumbling creek on state game lands, the pungent scent of pines, the tumbling water and brilliant new growth of grass, purple violets and dandelions creating a sense of gratitude in all of them.

Levi kept a lively conversation going with Randy, Mark, and Beth, who seemingly enjoyed themselves immensely, seemingly unaware of the fact that Susan was strangely quiet. She wasn't really included, so she put mustard on her grilled hotdog, drank her tea, and ate about half a bag of salt and vinegar potato chips without commenting once.

She decided the blue of Levi's shirt was what made his eyes appear blue, because his eyes were not really that color at all. They were green with flecks of yellow. He also had darker hair than she remembered, except for when the sun hit it from between the pine branches. He wore a Columbia vest, in navy, which she admitted was a very good choice.

Well, yes, he was an attractive man. But she knew that already and it didn't change a thing.

She had just decided this when he turned to her, quite unexpectedly.

"Susan, you're so quiet."

"Oh, well, you were talking and I was listening, which is okay. Beth talks enough for both of us. Don't you, Beth?"

Oh please, she thought wildly. The worst kind of babbling.

"Course I do. I always talk. You talk, too, Susan. Just not as much when Levi's around."

What was this? She felt sabotaged from every direction. Mark was grinning like a hyena.

"Do I scare you that badly?" he asked, laughing easily.

She didn't bother answering. If he had so much confidence that he still thought she cared about him, well, he'd find out how wrong he was.

She swung her legs over the bench of the picnic table, said she was going for a walk.

"Don't go too far," said Mark. "We're leaving in about fifteen minutes."

"Can I come?" Beth asked.

"Up to you."

She was not exactly thrilled to hear the pattering of her feet, then felt Beth's hand slide between her elbow and her side.

Susan stopped and stared at her friend, whose serious blue eyes reflected the sky perfectly.

"Levi's eyes are not blue," she said, without thinking.

"Who said they were? Why do you care?" Beth fired back.

Susan shrugged.

"Susan, I'm going to tell Mark to turn this RV around and we are going home if you don't stop acting so strange when you're around Levi. I can't stand it. It's as if you close a spigot and shut everything off."

They were no longer walking, but standing beside the tumbling creek in the spring sunshine. An elderly couple walked into view, tapping their canes for safety, their colorful caps emphasizing the pure white of their hair.

The girls stepped aside to allow them to pass, but they stopped, their wrinkled face showing a keen curiosity.

"Hello, girls."

"Hello."

"Now tell me, are you Mennonite or Amish? I can never tell the difference, and just wish I could, so I wouldn't need to ask," the elderly lady said, giggling like a schoolgirl.

They exchanged a few question and answers before bidding goodbye, the girls watching as they moved off with halting steps.

"See, that's what I want in life. To grow old with Mark by my side. A love that only grows deeper and better as we age. I'm crazy about my boyfriend, Susan. I'm so glad you have a brother named Mark."

And for a moment, Susan considered Beth the lucky one, to be able to unabashedly tell her best friend how much she loved her brother, with no complications involved.

"That's good," she said shortly.

"You don't like to hear that, do you?"

"Why do you say that?"

"You don't."

"Beth, come on, okay? Of course I'm happy for you. It would be nice if I could say the same thing about Levi, since I suspect that is the sole reason for this whole trip despite my efforts to set the record straight ahead of time. Get these two old fogies together, just like the couple we just passed. Doddering into old age together."

Beth was clearly upset, stopping in the middle of the pathway, her fists curled. "Sometimes, Susan, I can hardly stand you."

Susan shrugged, walked on, with Beth following a short distance behind.

When they returned, everyone was ready to leave, watching for them. Mark smiled, and Beth's whole face glowed in return. Susan watched this with annoyance. It was alright for them to be happy, but did they have to make such a display of their affection?

Levi came around the side of the vehicle, unzipping his vest, running a hand through his hair.

"Sun's actually getting warm," he commented.

Everyone started piling into the RV, Levi following to sit with them, sliding into the tiny booth opposite Susan, Mark, and Beth on the cushioned ledge that served for a sofa. Susan was unprepared for Levi's presence. She stilled her accelerating breaths, took off her sweater, crossed her arms, and leaned back without saying anything.

"See? That's what I like about you, Susan. You're quiet. Relaxed. You're so easy to be with."

If he only knew. Men were so clueless. They waltzed their way through life knowing nothing of the thoughts of the women around them.

"Except, it seems like you're even more quiet than normal. Though I haven't been with you that much, so maybe being this quiet is normal for you."

Mark spoke up. "Our sister Kate just moved to Virginia about a week ago. Remember I told you? We were going to try to stop at their place. Anyway, it's tough for her."

"For you or for Kate?" Levi asked, looking directly at Susan, who avoided his frank gaze as long as possible by gazing out the window, watching the green of the forest go by. Taking a deep breath, she shrugged, then looked at the face much too close to her own.

"Both."

"She your age?"

"Older."

"So what brings them to Virginia?"

"It's a new community."

"Amish?"

She nodded, bit her lip. When she looked at Levi the second time, she was deeply touched by the soft expression of sympathy.

"So? I mean, is everything okay with them?"

Susan shook her head, bit down hard on her lower lip.

"It's a hard thing for me to talk about now, okay? I'd rather not."

"But maybe it would be helpful to talk about it," Levi encouraged.

Beth shook her head with a warning look.

"Alright, so we won't talk about your sister Kate. What can we talk about? My family? Everyone in my family is married and gone, and I live with my aging parents. I don't know what they'd do without me."

"It's a good thing, Levi. You need to stay with them," Mark remarked.

"You think? What if I find a girl I like? I mean, really, really like? Do I sacrifice my own desires for my parents' sake, or do I desert them? It's a tough call.

"Everyone needs to figure out what God wants for their life, I guess," Levi finished with a touch of sadness in his voice.

CHAPTER 11

THEY AGREED TO STOP BY DAN AND KATE'S HOME BEFORE THEY traveled on to the long mountain range called the Skyline Drive. They would look for a campground early, relax, play horseshoe, build a campfire, then pay them a surprise visit, which lightened Susan's outlook.

"Let's not do a campfire supper, after hot dogs for lunch," Levi suggested. "There's a little town around here, isn't there, Randy? What is it, five, six miles from here?"

"About that," came from the front seat.

But the town was not very big, or very populated. It resembled an old mill town, with a small river winding through. Most of the stores were closed, other than a Taco Bell and a Sunoco station. But a blinking neon light directed them to J. R.'s Diner, which seemed more inviting.

They sat in a booth, the cracking vinyl a burnt orange color, some bluesy music wailing from a speaker in the corner. There were stares from the locals hunched over the bar. But the waitress was friendly, chatting amiably about the weather, the wreck on the cloverleaf of the interstate, then adjusting her bifocals and asking, "What can I get you to drink?"

After the drinks were served, they all ordered the special, which was a roast turkey sandwich with gravy, stuffing, and mashed potatoes.

Beth groaned at the calories, but Mark assured her she would never gain an ounce, and if she did, small matter. She squeezed his arm and giggled, turning as pink as the curtain behind her, then laid her head on his shoulder.

Susan shifted her weight, cleared her throat, and played with her napkin. Really, Beth. So dramatic.

Levi chuckled, a deep trembling sound in his chest. He turned to Susan, bumped her shoulder with his, and looked at her with a deep twinkle in his eyes.

"Don't you care about calories? If you say what Beth said and I say what Mark said, maybe you'll put your head on my shoulder."

Susan could not speak, she was so taken aback. Then, to make matters even worse than they already were, Levi asked her outright if she had ever had a boyfriend.

She told him no in what she hoped was her crankiest voice, and added that she had no plans of starting to date anyone. Perhaps he had forgotten that she'd already told him that in no uncertain terms.

Annoying, that was the only way to describe him.

But the food was good and the service so commendable. They ordered apple pie and ice cream, two servings with four forks, and Susan was stuck sharing with Levi.

"See, this is almost like dating, Susan. Easy as pie. We could try it sometime," Levi said, teasing her now, watching her face to gauge her reaction.

This time Susan laughed. He wasn't serious—he was just teasing her, almost like a brother. She felt herself relax. Perhaps she was too intense about Dan and Kate, about everything in life. She even laughed when he tried to feed her a bite of ice cream, pushing his arm away and laughing more. She could tell that Mark and Beth were relieved that the tension had lifted.

AT THE CAMPGROUND they hooked up to electricity and water and started to get settled for the night. With the inside illuminated by overhead lights, Susan was hit by the stark reality of how little space they had to maneuver around each other. She became painfully aware of the tiny bedroom, the even smaller bathroom.

She was not happy.

To be plunged into this situation was her own fault, she knew now. Why had she given consent? She was beginning to feel the magnetic pull of Levi, despite her best efforts to ignore it. How could he be so annoying one minute and so charming the next? And actually, his most charming moments were the most annoying, because they made it so hard to keep her feelings in check. What a mess.

The evening was chilly, so the girls dressed in heavy socks and bulky sweaters, grateful for the crackling campfire, the heat in the RV. The driver, Randy, stayed in a cabin by himself, glad for a long night of rest, which left the RV for the four of them.

They made s'mores with graham crackers, squares of Hershey's chocolate, and peanut butter, the burnt marshmallows wedged between. Beth made a pot of coffee in the miniature coffee maker, brought it out on a tray, then pulled her camping chair close to Mark's, spreading a warm blanket across their laps. She leaned into his shoulder.

"Aren't you cold?" Levi asked, sitting too close.

"No. I'm fine."

Nothing more was said. The fire crackled, sending sparks shooting up into the night sky, a small, chilly breeze sending the flames sideways. There were sounds of neighboring campers, doors slamming, children calling out, men laughing. An occasional vehicle wound its way slowly up or down the drive, friends calling out to each other. The silence between the four of them was not uncomfortable. But Susan's mind was full of probing questions without concrete answers.

As desperately as she tried to keep from seeing Levi, her eyes constantly sought after him. When he was building the campfire she couldn't help but notice the length and strength of him, the ease and grace with which he moved. His quick laugh. His ready smile. His wavy, neatly cut hair and light-colored eyes.

What if she responded to his half-hearted attempts at making overtures? But men were all the same. They all wanted a wife, someone to cook, clean, do laundry, and produce children. That wasn't necessarily a bad thing. But sometimes those things were not enough to keep a man happy. Like Dan, who was off on some harebrained wild ride, moving his family to Virginia to start a business he knew nothing about. Nothing Kate could do would make him happy in any kind of lasting way, and so she had to suffer right alongside him.

When Susan allowed herself to think of Kate and Dan's dating, she felt her spirits drop even lower. Kate had been filled with so much joy and excitement in those days. She had no idea of the suffering she was plunging into.

How could Susan be sure this wouldn't happen to her?

The others were talking again now, but Susan became steadily more withdrawn as the evening wore on, her mind filled with catastrophes lined up along the horizon.

"You're not saying much, Susan," Levi said softly.

Mark and Beth watched her, waiting for an answer.

She merely shrugged. Bet Levi would not allow this to be an answer, probing her to tell them how she felt.

"I don't always have something to say. Do I have to talk nonstop?"

"No, of course not. I'm just afraid you're not enjoying this trip."

Levi leaned forward in his chair, his eyes on Susan's face.

"It's fun. I'm having fun."

"You don't look it."

"I'll feel better after some sleep."

Mark nodded, cautiously mentioning again how hard it was for Susan to see her sister move so far away.

"It wouldn't be so bad," Susan blurted out, "but Dan, her husband, is not a stable guy. He has some serious issues and it makes Kate's life really hard."

Levi leaned back in his camping chair, his hands locked across his stomach, his legs thrust in front of him. The campfire played light across his face, creating shadows, illuminating his perfect mouth, then throwing it into the shadows. He nodded slowly, with understanding, his light eyes watching Susan.

"You take her situation really seriously, don't you?"

"I do."

"Which explains a lot."

"About what?"

"About you."

Mark and Beth exchanged a look. He reached for her hand and squeezed.

"Most decent humans care about their siblings, don't they?"

"I think you're afraid of love and marriage."

There was no answer for this, so Susan said nothing, until finally she said too loudly, "Can you blame me? I mean, come on. They were the perfect couple, she was so in love. What happened?"

Levi, wise beyond his years, chose to shake his head, breathe deeply, and ask who was up for a game of Rook. Relieved, Susan lifted a hand and said she was chilly. She was grateful to go inside, grateful to have her mind occupied with something other than Kate and Dan, grateful to have Levi slide into the small booth beside her. There was no denying it.

When he reached across her to pluck a Kleenex from the box, she caught the same scent of his cologne, imagining his arm around her shoulders.

They played partners, the game becoming extremely competitive, all of them quite skilled at the traditional game. More coffee was made, a bag of chocolate chip cookies produced, and Susan was caught up in the fun, forgetting herself as she laughed and yelled.

Levi was pleased she had been drawn out of her morose mood, and was sorry to see the game come to an end. He turned to Susan and wished her a good night. He slid out of the booth, stepped aside for her to slide out, then went outside to extinguish the fire.

Susan had to restrain herself from following him.

She found herself unable to sleep, with Beth snoring softly beside her. She felt hemmed in, as if she were in a trunk and there was no one to lift the lid. Her heart hammered in her chest, her breathing became labored. She rolled from side to side, trying to alleviate the discomfort, but it seemed to steadily worsen.

She sat up, her head pounding. She began to shake. She had to get out.

She grabbed her robe, slid silently off the bed, pushed her feet into sandals, and made her way past the bathroom door, past the booth now made into a bed for Mark and Levi, and slowly opened the door as silently as possible before letting herself out.

She could see a few string lights from the neighboring campsite, a pole light by the building in the center of the campground, and a grand display of twinkling white stars. The trees were stark and black, the budding leaves like frothy lace. Somewhere, music played low and soft. Slowly, she sank into a camping chair, lowered her face into her hands, and let the tears come. She was intensely afraid, anxiety like a swarm of bees, her mouth dry, and the hammering of her heart continued. Was this a full blown panic attack?

The door of the camper opened very slowly. Susan could hear the faint creak, then the knob turning just as slowly, before she heard Levi call softly, "Susan?"

She only knew she had to get away, so in one swift movement, she was out of the chair, knocking it over before she ran blindly into the night. She ran toward the light post, down an incline, across a gravel path, and around a building. She looked from left to right, found no one following her, then sat on the edge of a half wall, grateful for the light. A dizzying array of insects hovered around the light, zooming to their death by electrocution as they succumbed to the intensity of the heated bulb.

Just like me, she thought.

"Susan?"

Levi stepped around the side of the building, his voice pleading.

"Go away."

"I'm not going to."

Her voice was hoarse, her beathing ragged. She felt the wall on which she sat begin to tilt as her dizziness worsened. Her breathing was erratic, her head spun.

"Is anything wrong?"

"Levi, just leave me alone, okay?"

He sat close to her. She got up, moved away, her arms clutched around her waist, drawing her robe tightly.

"You don't seem like yourself."

"You don't know me, Levi. How would you know what I'm like?"

"You seem troubled."

"Oh, so now I'm troubled? So what are you going to do about that? Ship me off to Restful Acres, or Healing Balm, or some other place where they'll decided if I'm a Christian or not?"

"Sarcasm isn't attractive."

"I don't care, Levi. I don't care whether you find me attractive or not. I don't, you know? I'm not on the market for a boyfriend, and certainly not for a husband, some depressed loser who takes my life and shakes it upside down till there's nothing left. Like Kate. I know what you're trying to do by asking me to go on these vacations. Well, guess what? I don't like you, so it's not working."

For a long moment, her words hovered between them. She stood by the half wall, defensive, her hands knotting and untying the waistband of her robe.

Slowly, he came closer. The only sound was the zapping of insects in the pole light, the barely distinct call of spring peepers in a body of water.

He was very close, directly in front of her. He reached out, took her arms, and slowly bent his head, tilted it to the right and found her mouth. The scent of spearmint, his cologne, his nearness.

Then, the touch of his dry mouth.

A shock. She felt an unexpected wave of longing before her mouth softened beneath his. He drew her closer, before her reeling senses straightened. Only another moment of this unbelievable euphoria, before she tore out of his grasp.

The were both breathing unevenly, both staring at each other, before Levi reached out again.

"I'm sorry, Susan."

"Don't be. I could have stopped it."

He reached for her. She stepped aside, turned her back. A hand to her mouth. He moved from behind to take her shoulders in his hands.

She stepped away again.

"Levi." She turned to face him squarely.

"Whatever just happened, it can't happen again. I can't let any man drag me into a marriage in which there is nothing but giving up my own way for his."

"I didn't ask you to marry me, Susan. I kissed you. I kissed you, because at the moment there was no other way to let you know how I felt, and because you don't know how you feel. You're so determined to set Kate and Dan in the middle of every advance, handily throwing off any inkling of romance. Or love. Or mild attraction."

"I don't want a romantic relationship."

Levi cleared his throat, clenched and unclenched his hands.

"OK. Then I will see to it that you never have one with me."

With that, he turned and walked away.

"Levi!"

He stopped but did not turn to face her.

"I didn't . . . I mean . . ."

He turned, the sound of his shoes crunching on the gravel. She felt his anger, felt afraid of her own words.

"Susan, I've been around, okay? I think you know as well as I do, either of us could probably have anyone we chose. I could have had quite a few nice girls in my time, as I'm sure you could have had presentable young men.

"I have never felt about anyone the way I feel about you. The moment I met you, I knew. But if you really are sincere about staying single, I promise to let you do just that. Although I think you *are* attracted to me, if only slightly. Am I right?"

She shook her head. "No. Oh, I don't know. Maybe. But no. A definite no."

"What in the world, Susan?"

She tried to laugh, which soon turned into a watery, throat-clenching giggle, then a sob that caught in her throat.

"Levi, I don't know."

He caught her as she turned, held her against him when he felt no resistance, massaged her back as he would comfort a child. She knew she had never felt this sense of safety, the arms of a man around her, the need to lay her head on strong shoulders and share the burden of her fear.

"It's okay, Susan. You are truly special. But I will let you go. If God wants us to be together someday, we will be. Are you okay with that?"

She looked up into the light in his eyes, shadowed by the pole light behind him.

"Thank you, Levi. You have no idea how much I appreciate your words. I know I'm a mess, really."

"A beautiful mess," he said, smoothing the hair away from her forehead with one hand.

She ignored the gesture, determined to get out what she needed to say.

"Another thing, though. If this isn't too weird. Mary. You know Mary. She . . . she is obviously in love with you. So I think you should consider her. You would have a very good life, her absolute devotion and all."

Levi turned away, paced the length of the wall and back.

"I know," he said finally.

Suddenly, he looked at her with a piercing gaze.

"Why don't we want the ones we can have? Is it human nature to want what we cannot have, or is it merely our own ego? Susan, I know Mary would accept me, but I've never been able to bring myself to ask her. Now that I have met you, I understand why."

"But I just told you I'm not interested."

"Aren't you, Susan?"

When she gave him no reply, he took a deep breath, then asked if she would like to go back. The night was cold, she wasn't dressed adequately, and morning would soon be here. He did not reach for her hand, merely waited for her to join him, before they walked back, side by side, unspoken feelings disturbing the atmosphere around them.

"I won't sleep," she said.

"Neither will I."

"You think we'd wake them if we built a fire?"

"Coffee. We need coffee."

"Bacon and eggs."

"I think this place has a breakfast café. Shall we see if they're open yet?"

"But I'm not dressed."

"Here's your sweater."

He held it for her and she slipped into it, her shoulders beneath his hands, acutely aware of his nearness, his presence so achingly necessary. But he had promised he would not require a relationship, which took so much pressure off.

When he caught her hand in his, she looked up into his face, the profile that made her heart skip a beat, or two, or maybe three, until she felt a bit faint. She wondered if she were his girlfriend, if she could randomly kiss his cheek. She would do that if she was his.

They found more campers, the RV's hulking objects in the darkened campground, occasional pole lights or strings of tiny bulbs attached to tree branches giving off bits of guidance. She let her fingers curl in the palm of his calloused hand, and no conversation was necessary.

She told herself it was OK, he was simply guiding her, holding her hand out of necessity. If he meant it as a romantic overture, it would never be this comfortable.

"Hey, there we go," he said suddenly.

Sure enough, ahead was a log building with windows blazing with light, a neon blinking OPEN sign on the double doors. Once inside, Susan was seated beneath a dim light, her hair in disarray, her sweater hiding the robe beneath it.

Coffee was deliciously life sustaining. Coffee and pancakes with butter and maple syrup, bacon and scrambled eggs.

"So then," she said, "if we don't have a romantic relationship, like, not even think of dating or . . . or the future, can we still be friends and hang out together? I apologize for what I said a while ago. That was awful."

"You were all shook up."

"I think it was a panic attack, or something like it."

"Yes, Susan. We can do stuff together. We'll just skip the romance. That's what you're saying, right?"

"Yes."

"So what would you like to do?" he asked.

"Well, finish this trip first."

They laughed together, and Susan felt the anxiety disappear. If Levi would be her friend, she had a lot to look forward to. Her boring life suddenly seemed exciting. There would be weekends of adventure, exploring surrounding counties, states, or whatever. She could do all kinds of fun things with him without agonizing over whether or not it was a good idea. She felt free for the first time in a long time.

KATE CRIED FROM happiness when she saw Susan and the others step out of the RV. The children clamored around Susan and Beth and then led all four of them outside to see the bunnies, the sheep, the piggies.

Dan appeared from the barn, where he had been repairing doors, a wide smile of welcome on his face. He shook hands, said that was some fancy rig they were getting around in, then showed them all where the kennel would be built. He planned to raise Siberian huskies, standard poodles, white shepherds.

He liked the big dogs. More money.

Mark said he'd heard smaller dogs were less work, but Dan explained away that theory immediately. French bulldogs were where the money was.

He loved this place, he told them. Loved it. He finally had his family where he wanted them. Completely to himself. No parents or in-laws to interfere, no family to mess things up all the time.

Mark cleared his throat and moved his feet self-consciously as Levi gaped at the shorter man, throwing out opinions like a banty rooster strutting his stuff. The more Dan talked, the better Levi understood Susan.

Susan, alone in the house with Kate, fired questions and was dismayed to received evasive answers, her face with that waxen look, the lifeless eyes.

"But Kate, are you alright?" she asked finally, so close to tears she could taste them.

"Of course, Dan is good to me. We have each other. I know the place is a mess, but together, we'll make changes."

No matter how hard Susan tried to convince herself Dan was going to follow through, keep up his dreams, work hard to achieve them, she always returned to negative thoughts.

So much to do. So much money involved. Who was financing this?

Kate did not cry when they left, but stood beside Dan, a small figure of loyalty. She told Susan to write or call soon.

The RV moved slowly away from the farm, bumped over potholes, gravel. Wild rabbits hopped out of the way, and robins chirped from fenceposts before gliding away. Mark and Susan were very quiet, knowing if they opened a conversation about Dan they would regret it later.

"Your sister is very pretty," Levi remarked, perhaps just to break the silence.

"She was always the one with the good looks," Susan said.

When Levi said nothing to this, she was a bit put off. But then, friends weren't required to compliment one another's looks.

The scenery soon became breathtaking, with vast mountain ranges decked in the brilliance of new leaves, dotted with large patches of mountain laurel in the most wonderful shades of pink and lavender. The sky was blue as blue could be, with white puffy clouds floating on the gentle breeze.

They spotted a doe and two fawns, a black bear crossing the road, a family of skunks. Geese honked overhead and ducks winged their frantic way across the sky.

At the new campground, they played horseshoe and grilled steaks. Beth made a chocolate cake in the tiny oven, and they mixed a salad with fresh spinach, tomato, and broccoli.

Susan felt happy and relaxed. Now that she had managed to stand her ground—even after that kiss—she knew she was in control of the situation and had nothing to fear. But that kiss—she blushed just thinking about it.

Chapter 12

That evening, Mark cuddled with Beth by the campfire and Susan and Levi talked well into the night. They discussed new things that came up in the Amish church, the reluctance to accept change, the balance between tradition and the realities of living in the modern world. Mark was very outspoken about the need for good counseling for couples hoping to be married, and how some viewed it as misleading, too liberal.

"Mom says times were simpler, years ago. People were taught to give up their own wills, work hard, bury their feelings, do what was right," Mark said.

"My grandmother remembers living in a house where there was snow on the windowsill. Inside, mind you. They had nothing when they got married. Bought a used kitchen table for fifty cents. Can you imagine?" Beth chimed in.

Levi shook his head, a rueful look on his chiseled face.

"What Mark said is the the truth."

"Yeah, I mean, think about it," Mark said, pointing a finger to the sky. "Our forefathers and mothers all raised families of ten or more children and lived in what we would call poverty now. A woman was subject to the will of her husband, and that was that. But think about it. She was subject to the will of her parents long before that, so she was used to giving up her own will. If she didn't obey, she was taken to the woodshed, likely, and given a good whooping. From a young age, obedience was expected, and if someone didn't listen, there were consequences. And now, well, we've mellowed. Kids run all over their parents."

"You included," Susan said quietly.

"I heard that."

"But think about it," Mark continued. "If a young girl is trained to give up her will, she will naturally be a helpmeet for her husband. A husband who loves his wife more than himself will not present difficult hurdles for her to give in to."

"Ain't no such creature," Susan remarked, sour as green apples.

Levi leveled a look at her, but said nothing.

"Susan, you're so cynical," Beth said, not unkindly.

"Marriage problems are everywhere, even in our plain churches," said Levi. "Now, people talk about their problems, go for counseling. And because it's new, the conservative bishops think it's wrong. But not everything that's new is wrong. Sometimes change is good."

"As long as our marriage problems persist, yes, we need a new approach," Mark said. "I'm hoping Beth and I will be able to receive marriage advice somewhere before that time comes."

And Beth's look of absolute devotion was enough to assure him she was completely agreed. Levi watched the look between them and wondered how God could create two women as different as Beth and Susan.

AT CAROL'S HOUSE, a gloom descended on Susan, an unexplained and unforeseen sadness that shrouded the house in gray. She stepped on a crack in the hardwood floor and received a large splinter on the bottom of her foot, behind the big toe, then had to dig around in it with a straight pin and hobble to the bathroom to look for a pair of tweezers, before extracting it with no small amount of pain. She bumped a shelf with her elbow while vacuuming, then had to tell Carol about the tip of the elf figurine's hat being broken, which brought a scowl, and didn't she know nothing in her house was inexpensive? This left Susan daydreaming about telling her of course not, the only cheap thing in her house were the wages she paid. But of course she did not say that at all.

It was the day after her cleaning day at Carol's when her mother informed her there was a message on the voicemail for her.

"From whom?"

"I don't know. They need a schoolteacher by fall."

Her mother was reading the paper, so her concentration was limited. Susan left her bologna and cheese sandwich and went to listen to the message.

It was the man who had spoken to her in church. She felt a bit breathless as she listened, chewing on her lower lip, then the inside of her cheek. The message said how much they could pay, which was much less than she was currently making. So why couldn't she just say no and move on? She sat in her father's office and thought long and deeply about joining a western group of Amish in Wyoming, on the border of Montana.

With Kate in Virginia, staunchly defending Dan and his dreams, there was nothing much to hold her here. Except Levi.

Oh, Levi. I rue the day I met you.

But she told her mother about the message and was accosted with every effort to keep her from even thinking about it. She must put her family first. Liz and Rose would not be pleased. And she'd be so far from Kate and Dan, she wouldn't even be able to visit them. And what about Mark and Beth?

"What about them, Mother?"

"Stop calling me Mother. I am your Mam," she snapped, her red face a clear sign of rising blood pressure.

"Mam, I am an adult over twenty-one years of age. If I choose to go, you'll have to give your consent."

"You are to honor your parents until the day you die," her mother shot back, her dentures clacking the way they did when she was upset.

"I can honor you by being a good schoolteacher, a help to a fledgling community. I can honor you by doing God's will."

"How do you know what that even means?" her mother asked, on the verge of wailing.

Her father was a bit more sensible, saying she could go if she wanted, but he really wanted her to know she might regret it midterm when the unaccustomed cold and snow might make her life a genuine hardship. He told her to pray about it, see where she would be led.

Susan nodded, much too proud to tell her father she wasn't always sure how to decipher an answer, if there ever was one. How could one be a hundred percent sure of one's calling? How could she let down her friends and Carol and Steve and saunter off to Wyoming with the knowledge she was doing what God wanted her to do? Did He care that much either way? If He was a kind and loving father, He would allow her the choice, and if it was the wrong one, well then, she'd have to suffer the consequences.

A part of her wanted to go. The part that missed Kate horribly, who was sick of dealing with finicky customers at market, kowtowing to Carol and all her meticulous demands. But the whole western dress, the accent, the new and strange area, the thousands of miles between her and all she knew . . .

Before she fell asleep she had decided against going, but the following morning she wondered if Beth, Mark, and Levi might accompany her on the train or the or bus or whichever form of transportation might take you to Wyoming. That would be a long, exciting trip to take. But before they were aware of it, the time would be over and she'd be there by herself, which would be a vast, unending loneliness.

She decided not to call. Then she changed her mind and called, asking for more time come to a decision, which was granted in a voice of good humor and understanding.

She found herself watching school-aged girls and boys in church, wondering how many pupils were in the school, how many families were in the community.

She asked her brother Elmer to Google Wyoming and was amazed at the size and history of the state, then read about Wyoming in the encyclopedia and was amazed even more. She spoke to Beth about it and was promptly given a piece of her mind, which was anything but encouraging.

And then, Levi called her. He left a voicemail with his phone number and she called back as soon as she received it. She spent two hours and fourteen minutes on the phone with him, sitting in her father's dusty office with the shelves crowded with antiques, junk, signs that said stupid things that made her father chuckle.

When she told him about Wyoming, he was quiet for too long, after which he told her she should do what she thought was best, and that he was sure she didn't get much support from her family.

"No," she said. She didn't.

"Why you?" he asked.

She'd been in church, they thought she appeared older, more mature, and sometimes teachers did well in completely new surroundings. When he said nothing, she was afraid she'd offended him, but he told her again she should do what she thought was best. If it didn't work out, she could be back at the end of the term.

They talked about Kate and Dan, and he asked why she couldn't teach in that new community. It was much closer, and she could live with them.

"Dan would never allow it," she told him.

"Why not?"

"He's very possessive of Kate. You heard him. He doesn't want family around."

Finally, he told her the reason for his call was the upcoming farmer's festival in Morgantown. He wondered if she would like to go one evening. The barbequed chicken was great, as was the smoked beef brisket sandwiches. There were rides, games, a rodeo.

"What about Beth and Mark?"

"I thought we could just go by ourselves. I want to take my horse and buggy. You've never seen either one."

"But it sounds exactly like a date."

He laughed. "Susan, I solemnly promise you, it is not a date. Remember, I promised we would be friends. Nothing more."

"Okay. I'll go, for the rides and brisket. That's it."

WHEN SHE WENT to Look's Dry Goods in Intercourse and purchased a new roll of fabric the color of a robin's egg and quickly sewed a dress, she told herself it was for market. And when she bought a new covering, she told herself the market covering had been washed far too many times and was becoming quite limp. She agonized about wearing a sweater, knowing the black would hide too much of the robin's egg blue, and in the end, with favorable warm weather, she left her sweater at home on the hanger in the closet.

When a prancing Dutch harness, Friesian mix horse appeared in the drive at five o'clock, an hour after she arrived home from market, she was waiting eagerly, her blue dress highlighting the tan on her face, her hair glistening with a fresh application of a new hair polishing balm she had bought.

She knew Levi now, knew him well enough to keep her heart from fluttering, and for this, she was grateful. Poise and maturity. A woman of substance, she told herself.

She smiled. He smiled back, widely, easily.

He climbed down, went around to slide the door back, then watched as she stepped up and settled herself on the blue upholstered buggy seat, before coming back to step in on his side, taking up the reins and saying, "Come on."

"Your horse is beautiful."

"His name is Dutch. Can't get more common than that, huh?"

He had on a sky blue polo shirt, with neatly pressed black trousers, so they looked exactly like a dating couple who had planned to wear matching colors.

"Sorry," he said, pointing to his shirt. "Wasn't intentional."

"It's fine. New buggy?"

"Yeah. Just got it. You're my first passenger."

"Very nice."

"I didn't really need it, but my brother Jonas has a bit of a financial struggle right now, and his buggy was in bad shape. So I gave him the old one."

"Gave?"

"He can't afford much right now."

She said nothing but wondered.

"We have a good way to go. You mind? Maybe I should have hired a driver."

"No, no. I love long buggy rides. I always have. And it's a beautiful evening."

It was one of those achingly beautiful spring evenings, when the air seems infused with sweet smells, the trees and blooming flowers almost unnaturally brilliant with colors enhanced by the golden light. They passed women in their gardens, raking driveways, washing buggies, children playing spike ball, men on scooters, cars moving slowly.

"Before we decided to be friends only, I probably would have told you you're beautiful, but now I won't do that."

"Friends can compliment each other."

"Well then, you are beautiful."

"I don't feel like a particularly pretty girl."

"Your face is more mature. More character. There's a certain degree of thought about you."

"Well, that's a nice spin on being old."

They laughed easily, happily.

Then, "Do you find that unsettling, the fact that I find you to be beautiful?"

"No."

"So I didn't overstep my boundaries?"

"No."

After that, the close confines of the buggy seemed too intimate, sitting shoulder to shoulder. Involuntarily, she moved closer to the side, and he to his, as a silence taut with unspoken words settled between them. The horse kept up a steady pace, the easy placement of his feet on macadam like the trained steps of a long-distance runner.

"Hungry yet?"

"Starved. Market was crazy busy."

"You'll miss that if you teach school in Wyoming."

"Don't ruin a perfect evening by bringing that up, okay?"

"Still undecided?"

"Terribly."

"I'll come visit. Never been to Wyoming."

"You'd come that far to see me?"

"I would. Greater love has no man, and all that."

"For his friend."

"That's what I meant."

The evening was perfect. She met some of his friends (who teased them good-naturedly), ate wonderful sandwiches, the barbequed chicken falling off the bone, steaming hot, and washed them down with frosty glasses of lemonade. They shared a seat on the Ferris wheel and got stopped at the very top. Susan was terrified of heights, but Levi put an arm around her shoulder and told her to close her eyes if she felt scared.

"Take a deep breath," he said. "They'll let us down."

She did, then sank against him, grateful for the touch of his strong arm, the softness of the polo shirt, the now familiar scent of him.

But back on the ground, she was her usual self, taking charge of when and where to go next, yelling enthusiastically when a bull rider hit the ground. They ate soft ice cream with dark swirls of coffee flavoring, drank blueberry slushies, listened to an amateur country band play love songs as she and Levi sat side by side on a bale of straw, the lyrics resonating with their hearts, her mind in denial. As the evening came to a close, they were both reluctant to leave.

"I wish we could stretch this evening out. It's barely eleven," he said, after they'd navigated through the worst of the traffic.

"I can't invite you in when you drop me off. Too much like a date." He laughed.

"Sheetz is open all night. We could sit outside, drink coffee."

"I'll never sleep."

"Doesn't matter. I won't either. I'll be reliving this perfect evening."

"Levi," she said, light warning in her voice.

He laughed. "OK. Sheetz? Or home to bed?"

She hesitated a moment. "I'm sure they have decaf."

He smiled as he pulled in the driveway and over to the convenient hitching rack. They got their coffees and wandered around the convenience store a bit. He placed a quarter in a trinket machine and received a ring in a wee plastic container, shaking it a bit before a look of resolve crossed his face. He picked up her hand and looked at it, her long slim fingers lovely in the yellow lights.

"With this ring, I pledge my . . ."

He hesitated. She looked at him, her eyebrows lifted.

"Friendship," he finished. And smiled.

"I can't wear this."

"But you can keep it."

"I will."

"When you go to Wyoming, take it with you, to remember this night."

"But how do you know I'm going?"

"You will. I can tell. You want the adventure of heading into the unknown. And you also need to get away from me."

"Levi."

"I know. But it's true. It will be for the best."

"But . . . don't make it sound so terribly final. I haven't come to a decision at all. I'm still very unsure of anything."

"Susan, in life, things don't always happen the way we want them to. In fact, the opposite of what we want is often true. So I want to tell you how much your friendship means to me, if I don't see you before you go."

"But you will," she burst out. "Even if I go, it's not right away. We'll get together with Mark and Beth or something, right?"

"I doubt it."

"Why?"

He sighed. "Because it's hard for me. After this evening, I know I can't do this. If there is no future with you in it, then I'd rather not see you at all. Is that selfish of me? I don't want to hurt your feelings, but I also have to be honest with you."

"But . . . what do you mean?"

"I thought I could commit to being only friends, but it's destroying my heart. I want to be with you every single day. A weekend isn't sufficient, and an occasional vacation in an RV is a form of torture. So I'm giving you this ring, in the hope you will remember me always. It's your choice. I'll be here when you come back, waiting. I want you, Susan, and you have made very clear that you aren't willing to think about a romantic relationship. You're afraid of living the life your sister does, and I get that, but I think your fear is preventing you from good things, too."

He reached for her hand, slipped the ring on her third finger.

"I love you."

He lifted her hand, brought the fingers to his mouth, and kissed them. Slowly, he raised his head and looked deeply into her eyes.

"Don't say anything, Susan. Go to Wyoming, and we'll see what happens. And may God go with you, keep you, and protect you. I'm going to pray for you every waking hour of every day."

"But I might not go," she whispered.

When he drove her home, there were no words, but at the door, he took her gently into his arms, lifted her face with so much tenderness, a slight question in his eyes. She was the one to bring her lips to his. And she went to bed and cried herself to sleep, without knowing when or if she would ever see him again.

The next day, she left a message for the minister saying she would like to apply for the job. But as time moved on, the days turned into weeks, and there was no word from anyone in that far-off western state. Susan took a firm grip on her thoughts, her heart, and threw herself into her work, taking on a second housecleaning job. She was promoted to manager of the market stand in Harrisburg with a significant raise.

Eventually, a letter arrived, followed by a telephone call, with the time to call back, a full expectation of her acceptance. She spent an entire week soul-searching, being tossed high on the raging sea of doubt, only to fall into despondency.

Why couldn't she accept Levi?

His every intention was honorable, she believed his love to be true. But to give in would be placing herself at great risk. Dan had given Kate no reason to doubt his love, either. She had walked into her life she now shared with this incompetent man with wide-open eyes, the truth hidden from her completely.

The life Susan lived now, here in Lancaster County, was perfectly acceptable—it was just, well, tepid. Lukewarm. Boring.

But still. Two thousand miles. Strangers. Although, in some ways, they wouldn't really be strangers. All Amish people were connected on some level, including east to west, in spite of differences in the way they spoke and dressed. A new community meant there would be hardship, very likely, so why not choose to stay in the safety of the only environment she had ever known?

And what about living her life for someone else, giving her life to the parents and children who needed her in this new settlement out West? Wasn't that a calling? Or was her duty to her parents and family here in Lancaster, and to her friends and employers?

And so she spent time searching, praying more earnestly than she had ever prayed before. The more time she spent in prayer, the more real God became, a Higher Presence who seemed completely real, one who cared and was willing to carry the burden of her doubt.

Through all of this turmoil, the word "calling" never truly left her. It was always there, like a neon sign blinking in the corner of her mind.

What was a calling?

It all sounded high and mighty, really. How could she be certain she didn't have a calling for cleaning Carol's house, working at market in Harrisburg?

But she answered that question very quickly, knowing the only calling she was listening to now was that of building her savings account.

And there was Levi. How was one expected to untangle the vast arena of emotion? Any ordinary young woman would be dancing on clouds of happiness, stars in her eyes, her future certain. A man to love and cherish, her upcoming nuptials as sure as the rising sun.

She spent time weeping, heartbroken, knowing deep inside Levi was not right for her. Not now, perhaps never. Slowly the understanding dawned, first only a slash of light in the darkness of her searching, then a bigger, softer revealing, like a rosy first light of morning.

The only word she received was, "Trust. Trust me."

She would go to Wyoming, away from Levi, her parents, and Dan and Kate. She would be alone in the wide open spaces, a place swept clean of all the things troubling her, and there she would find her calling, one way or another.

CHAPTER 13

Her parents struggled with her decision and Mark was furious. Elmer shrugged, told her she was crazy. Her sisters threw up their hands in defeat, shook their heads, and told her she was officially an old maid.

She went to visit Kate in Virginia one last time before boarding the train for Wyoming. She threw her clothes in a duffle bag, hired a driver, and left on a late June morning, the sun already a pulsing orange ball of heat and discomfort.

The road wound among the beauty of flowering trees, grasses swaying by the side of the road. Deer lifted their heads to stare as the car drove past, their huge brown eyes trusting and unafraid. Dust rolled behind the vehicle as they hit the gravel road that led to the secluded farm where Dan and Kate made their home.

Kate welcomed her with open arms, and Susan felt a slight tremor as she held her sister. When they pulled apart, Susan searched Kate's face, looking for signs of unhappiness or suffering. She drew a sharp breath as she took in the stillness in Kate's dark eyes, the pallor like porcelain, even her mouth clamped into a straight line, a lock and key to all the strife she kept inside.

"Kate?"

With her hands on her shoulders, Kate met her eyes but shrugged away from her touch.

"Kate, are you alright?"

"Yes."

The children came running, laughing, three little bundles of love and joy. They looked healthy, tanned from the spring sunshine. Susan was on her knees, embracing, kissing the pink cheeks, receiving their happiness as she gave them all of hers.

"We have ducks, Susan! Ducks on our pond!" Micah shouted.

"And baby kitties," Emily said proudly.

The children were fine, and that was a relief. Kate took good care of her family, in spite of being awash in her own dark turmoil. Susan looked off toward the barn, noticed the lack of kennels, the half-finished renovation project.

"Where's Dan?"

"He's at work."

Kate met Susan's eyes, but there was no emotion, no sign of tears or pride, sadness or happiness. There was just nothing.

"Work?"

"Yes, he got a job at a pig farm."

"But what about the dogs? The kennel?"

Susan waved an arm toward the barn, her voice rising.

"The man who promised us the startup money? He never came through. We'll be okay, I know. Dan will provide."

"A pig farm? Hogs?"

"Come, Susan. Get your luggage. It's hot here in the sun. Bring your things inside."

She turned abruptly, following the broken sidewalk to the front porch. Susan followed, noticing that the lawn was mowed and how the flower beds sat neatly along the side of the house. The porch was swept clean, the porch swing put in place, hanging from sturdy hooks, a potted plant covered in deep purple blooms. Kate had done what she could, producing a homey atmosphere that was clean and orderly, going bravely ahead with her life.

The interior was cooler, shaded, the house resembling a home. With the partition removed between the living room and kitchen, the living space was open, more welcoming. The furniture was so familiar, the hutch cupboard with the china she'd used on her bridal table, the recliner she'd given Dan for his birthday. The windows contained the old style pull-apart screens, the ones that could be adjusted to fit any window.

"Come, Susan. Let's get a cold drink and you can tell me all about your life. I'm so excited to hear about Levi. Rose said you're dating."

They settled on the porch swing, the children on their laps or squeezed between them. Marie was taking her forenoon nap.

Susan set her straight on Levi and then they talked at length about her plans to leave for Wyoming in three weeks and how Levi was just not what she wanted, which brought raised eyebrows.

"Maybe I should have done what you're doing," Kate said, quietly.

She waved a hand in front of her face to repel a bothersome gnat, then let her hands fall loosely in her lap.

Susan eyed her sharply.

"I've never heard you speak like this."

"Dan has started drinking."

At first, Susan thought she hadn't heard right. Confused, she sat back, said nothing, till an expulsion of air found its way out of her mouth.

"Not drinking. You mean, like beer? Alcohol?"

"Whiskey. Straight up. The hardest liquor he can find. And believe me, Susan, every hillbilly around here makes their own."

Her voice was hard, as if she were coming down on her heels.

"But . . . Kate. He can't do that."

"Can't he? Oh, but he is doing it. Last night he didn't come home till ten, then fell out of the truck and slept in the yard."

The children were chattering among themselves, so Kate told them to go play, that she and Aunt Susan wanted to talk. When they were alone, Kate continued in a hard, clipped voice, her face still showing no emotion.

"His name is Rich Arnold, the hog farm owner. He's an alcoholic, introduced Dan to his magic elixir, the spirits dulling his misery. All

Dan talks about is how the kennels fell through, the dream of raising dogs evaporated, how he's stuck with a retarded daughter.

"'Retarded,' Susan. That's what he calls her. She's a Down syndrome child, created and presented to us by our Heavenly Father, placed in our care while we're here on earth. It's a privilege, not a burden."

"Kate, you can't stay here. You have to move back to Lancaster. He can't be under this hog farmer's influence."

Susan was so upset she raised herself from the swing, walked to the edge of the porch, then came back, sitting down with an expelled breath. She lifted a hand, placed it on Kate's arm, implored her to persuade Dan to move back.

"I can't. He loves it here. If you promise not to tell, I'll tell you more. He hasn't been to church. He wants to leave the Amish. Says there is no spirituality there. He needs a deeper connection to God than what he can find among the Amish."

Susan's shoulders slumped. Her knees turned weak.

"Kate, I don't know what to say. What should I do?"

"What can you do? What can anyone do? He's depressed, maybe even bipolar. I think he often feels awful inside. The drinking helps lessen his fearful lows but then he plunges into a dastardly funk the next day. My life has reached a point of fear and exhaustion that has stretched my limits. At home in Lancaster it was more manageable because there were people to notice, people to help, but here . . ."

Her voice broke off, and a sob, a hoarse croaking sound tore from her throat, and was quickly repressed by a few deep breaths, the waxen composure restored. Her eyes remained dry.

"Kate. Oh, Kate."

"Stop it."

"What are you going to do?"

"It's nothing to you."

"It's everything to me. Of course it is. I'm your sister. I can't walk away from here without trying to help you. Somehow. You can't allow this to continue. You have to try. We have to try."

"How? Tie him down? Cart him off?"

Kate's voice was as brittle as old paint, her eyes as dull as dusty glass, her gaze fixed on the side of the ancient oak tree by the side of the porch.

"Can you honestly say you still love him after he brought you down here, and now this? Why don't Dat and Mam know?"

"I can't tell them."

"Why not?"

"It would be a burden to them. And Susan, you know you are the only person I can confide in honestly. Before we were married, Dat took me aside one evening, asked if I felt sure about marrying Dan. He said he didn't show much of a work ethic at his job. I guess Dat is good friends with Enos King. I wasn't sure what work ethic meant and was too proud to ask. Plus, I thought Dat was being nosy. Of course Dan was perfect. He was, Susan. I was so in love. Now, I can hardly recall the feeling of love anymore."

"Does he treat you well, though? When he's . . . uh . . . okay?"

She couldn't bring herself to use the word "sober." They were Amish. They were a plain conservative group of people who were a light to the world, supposedly the salt of the earth. How incredulous, two sisters on a porch swing in Virginia, talking about a husband being drunk or sober.

It was so preposterous. Unreal.

"Not always."

Susan's head swiveled in alarm, her eyes wide.

"What do you mean?" she cried out.

"If he has too much, he's silly, sloppy. When it's far too much, he turns nasty. I take the quiet approach. The children are in bed. They don't know. And if I do nothing to antagonize him, we're okay. He goes to sleep eventually. I think he often feels like a failure. He didn't get along with his parents. His dad. His older brothers were the favored ones. Oh, I don't know, Susan. I'm no expert on the subject. Dan will snap out of this. He always has."

"But what about leaving the church?"

"He wants to."

"Will you go with him?"

"No."

"But . . ."

"Mm-hmm."

The sun rose higher and the temperature rose. Bees hovered along the perimeter of the porch floor, drunk on the nectar of the climbing clematis.

The air was very still, thick with humidity and the cloying odor of the climbing roses at the opposite end of the porch. Susan's mind tried to unravel the complicated tangle of Kate's life, questions raising their frightening heads.

Who had sinned that this atrocity should have entered their life? Who was reaping what they had sowed? Did every mistake of the fathers have to be visited on the children till the second and third generation, the way God told the prophets of old? What had her parents done wrong, allowing Kate to marry Dan, who had been nothing but a disappointment?

Where was grace? Hadn't Jesus come to bring total forgiveness for everyone's past?

She presented a bombardment of these unsettling thoughts to Kate, who merely shrugged, her face still showing nothing.

"I don't know, Susan. I'm just weary. Done. I'm tired of trying to figure out anything at all. I just survive."

A thin wail came from inside.

"Marie's awake."

Kate rose from the swing. Susan saw the patch on the side of her gray bib apron, noticed the frayed hem of her dress. A sadness so deep and so desperate filled her chest that the pain was almost physical. She sat alone, lost in tumultuous thought. She would speak with Dan herself. She would confront him, tell him the wreckage he had created.

A shrill cry from the yard, and Nathan came running, howling with all his might, his mouth wide open, his face contorted with the effort of his indignity.

He'd stepped on a honeybee, busily collecting nectar on a clover blossom, so Susan tended to the painful sting with a vinegar-infused cloth, while Kate changed Marie and prepared a bottle of formula.

Marie had changed into a roly-poly little bundle of energy. Her thick dark hair had thinned, but she was truly adorable.

Susan held Nathan, comforted him, while Kate fed Marie on the couch. Each one was content to keep the silence as they pondered what had transpired on the porch swing. Kate was amazed at herself, having told Susan so readily everything she had vowed to keep to herself. Susan was struggling to accept this insurmountable hurdle.

Lunch was homemade wheat bread with early garden produce. Spinach, sweet onion, lettuce.

"Sorry, Susan. No lunch meat or cheese."

"This is the best, Kate."

They washed dishes, wiped the table and countertops, then resumed their visit on the front porch. Marie rolled from side to side on a soft blanket, playing with an assortment of toys, and Micah was put down for a nap. Emily and Nathan played with the garden hose, yelling gleefully as they chased each other through the grass.

"So if Dan doesn't go to church, how do you go?" Susan asked, taking a sip of her cold mint tea.

"I don't."

"So . . . aren't you planning on going at all anymore?"

"I have no idea."

A stab of fear shot through Susan. Kate couldn't do this to her. She'd be excommunicated, eventually, after which Susan would be expected to shun her. It was unthinkable, heartrending, being torn apart by one person who simply couldn't get his act together. She was furious at Dan, then furious at Kate, being so gullible.

"How can you live like this?" Susan asked suddenly.

"Like what?"

"Not knowing? Just blindly following Dan, having no vision, no plan?"

"Susan, you don't get it. I promised to care for Dan on the day I married him, in sickness and in health, till death do us part. Right now, God has a plan. I just don't know what it is. Dan is not healthy spiritually or emotionally, but I promised. 'Sickness and in health.' I think that applies to more than physical health, don't you?"

"I suppose."

"I can't see my way through at all. So I plod along, caring for my house, the children, the garden. Every day is a test of my endurance. I often feel numb, dead inside, and I know I am in survival mode. If I felt too much, I couldn't be strong. It's God in me, and me in God, every single day. Dan is becoming someone I don't even know, so I do the best I can."

"But what's going to happen? How can you stop his alcohol consumption? How can you stop his leaving the church? Kate, you made your promise to God and the church the day you were baptized. Being Amish is who you are."

"I know all that. But I don't know if Dan realizes it. He's deeply, truly unhappy right now."

"No wonder. Living in this dump."

Kate smiled. "He loves it."

"That's nice," Susan shot back, her words saturated with sarcasm.

"I know you don't like him."

"I don't. Not right now I don't. What happened? You were so hopeful right after Marie's birth."

"It's always been this way."

"Even when you dated?"

"No, not back then."

This led to Susan telling Kate about Levi, about going out West and forgetting about romance, the way romances often turned out to be terribly disappointing, plunging someone's life into complete misery.

"Is that why you don't want to date?" Kate asked, her eyes wide with her newfound realization.

"Go ahead and make fun of me, but yes, it is."

"You don't get it," Kate said, repeating herself.

"What? What don't I get?"

"Love. Romance. Marriage."

"Obviously, you don't either."

"Meaning?"

"Marrying Dan, a total loser."

For a long moment, Kate was silent, her eyes deep pools of sadness.

"But think about it, Susan. What if I was ordained to this purpose? What if God wants me to be right here between these two lonely ridges in Virginia, to stand by my man when he's obviously not well?

"God never promises us a bed of roses after marriage. We can never predict the future. Do I regret marrying Dan? Of course. Often. Do I love him? Not always. Some days, I'd love to take a baseball bat to his head. But I'm where God wants me to be, this I truly believe."

"But you're suffering, Kate," Susan burst out.

"Sometimes, yes."

"Just leave him. Come home to Dat and Mam. It happens."

Susan began to weep quietly, her mouth wobbling at the thought of her parents, so unaware, so settled in their simple routine-filled life.

Unexpectedly, Kate put her arms around Susan and laid her head on her shoulder. "You won't believe how badly I would love to do just that."

"Well, then, why don't you?"

"Because I am a Christian and I have a cross to carry. I want to kneel at the feet of Jesus first of all, and after that, anything is possible. I can gain strength from His suffering on the cross. We die with Christ, but we rise with Him as well."

"You sound like an evangelist."

"I have to cling to this truth, Susan. I can do this, if God is my strength."

AN OLD RUSTED-OUT pickup truck ground to a halt at the broken sidewalk. Susan watched Dan step down and give the driver a jaunty salute, the driver laughing uproariously as he turned the wheel, put the truck in gear, and rattled off.

"Susan!" Dan yelled as he came into the kitchen. "Good to see you!"

She took his proffered hand and winced as he squeezed it with far too much energy. The odor coming from his clothes was ripe, his hair plastered to his head with perspiration.

"Hello, Dan."

"How was your day, dear?" Kate asked.

"Excellent. Same as always. I love my job."

He dropped clumsily into a chair, reached for his water glass and drained it, then thumped it down on the table. Kate hurried over to refill it with cold water from the refrigerator. The strong smell of alcohol overpowered the smell of hog manure.

Susan narrowed her eyes, allowing the irritation to creep in.

"What's for supper?"

"It's not ready quite yet. Hamburg and rice casserole," Kate said quietly.

"We had the same thing last night, didn't we?"

He reached down to slap Kate's thigh as she passed with Marie in her arms.

"Here, give her here. Come, baby."

Kate stopped to hand her over, and he jostled her on his lap, very nearly dropping her. Susan gasped, a hand to her mouth.

"What's wrong, Susan? I got 'er. I'm not going to drop her, am I, baby?"

Susan left the kitchen and went to find the children, knowing if she stayed in that room another second, she'd be swinging a fist at Dan. She could feel the satisfying clunk. She was so mad, her vision was blurred. She was even mad at Kate. All her high and mighty talk. No, she did not get it. And she never wanted to. The only way out of a situation like this was to never enter it in the first place.

The meal turned into a test of everything Susan knew about being a decent, respectful human being.

"Yeah, Susan. The dog business never happened. Went up the spout before it even began."

He laughed at his own lame joke before starting in on everything that was wrong in the Amish church. Too much tradition, too many rules. He wasn't going to be part of all that stuff anymore. As soon as Kate saw the light they were leaving.

"She's pretty slow on the uptake," he said, laughing at Kate as another puff of whiskey-laden breath fouled the air.

"We haven't had much chance to talk about it," she told him, keeping her eyes on her plate.

"Like I said, you're slow."

"Kate's not slow. She was one of the brightest kids in school. That's just mean, Dan."

If Susan lived to be a hundred, she'd always remember the satisfaction of saying those words. She had never hated anyone, but came dangerously close to it now, and didn't care.

Dan's eyes narrowed. He flopped back in his chair, ran a hand through his hair. He was still handsome, maybe even more than he'd ever been.

"You are not going to sit there and tell me what I don't know, Susan. I guess I know my wife better than you do, and she's slow. Right, sweetheart? Why do you think we have a Down's baby? Because it's in her DNA, that's why."

Susan was honestly afraid she would choke with the effort of biting her tongue. She looked from Kate to Dan and back again, lifted a forkful of rice and hamburger to her mouth, coughed, drank water, watched Kate put a spoonful of rice on Emily's plate, her face showing no emotion at all. When the silence stretched as taut as a pulled rubber band, she cleared her throat and suggested to the kids that they could go to the pond after they cleaned up from supper, which had them clamoring happily in agreement.

While doing dishes, Kate assured Susan he hadn't meant anything by it, really he hadn't. Dan had low self-esteem, maybe a bit to drink before he came home, and if it helped to blame her for Marie, well, did it really matter? She knew that her own intellect had no impact on Marie's Down syndrome.

"Well, tell him then," Susan spat, setting a plate on the countertop much harder than necessary.

"You don't understand. It's not the way to handle him at all."

"Really?"

"Yes, really."

"In other words, he can't be trusted with the truth."

Kate didn't reply, keeping her eyes focused on the water running over her hands and the pot she was holding.

BY THE POND, with the bulrushes in perfect symmetry, the clear water reflecting the evening sky, the iridescent dragonflies hovering effortlessly, God's world seemed fair again. If He could so graciously present all the sinful creatures on earth with the gift of His love and the beauty around them, surely she could forgive Dan, even as he continued to ruin Kate's life. And who was she to judge Kate for staying with Dan if that's what she felt was God's will?

Susan and Kate sat side by side on the grassy bank and watched a frog hop from one lily pad to another and a pair of mallards swim slowly by, as quiet and serene as a dream. Susan felt the bond of closeness to her sister, knowing this might be the last time in a long while they could sit shoulder to shoulder.

Tenderly, Kate reached out and straightened a lock of Susan's hair that had come loose, then fixed her covering.

"Someday, you'll understand. You will, trust me. Life is so much more than what we want for ourselves. And Susan, thank you so much for this visit. It helps to know that far, far away in Wyoming, I have a strong ally. We'll always be together in spirit. You know that."

It was Kate who wiped away the lone tear on Susan's cheek.

CHAPTER 14

COMING HOME FROM VIRGINIA, PREPARING TO LEAVE FOR WYOMING, sewing school dresses, spending time with Mark and Elmer, sisters' day with Rose and Liz—it all seemed like a headlong rush, a kaleidoscope of movement, colors, confusion, emotions ranging from tears of regret to an outright thirst for adventure. Even her mother was supportive in the end, even cautiously optimistic about what lay ahead for Susan. And true to her word, Susan never breathed a word to her parents about Kate's plight.

Her last day of cleaning for Carol was bittersweet, the bonus cash in her pay almost enough to make her change her mind about leaving. Market was not quite as hard, knowing Beth's sister Marilyn would be the perfect replacement. She tried to appreciate every moment, every remembered taste and smell of the market, the clamoring noise of the crowd, the yells of customers greeting each other. Everything was so final. The fact that she was actually going so far away to live among strangers was almost staggering.

The week before her scheduled departure, Levi arrived unexpectedly. He simply arrived at the house and asked if she would like to go on a drive.

He wore that lemon yellow polo shirt again.

His tan was deeper, his wavy hair as perfect as ever. She all but hyperventilated, running upstairs to shower quickly, comb her wet hair, throwing on a light summer dress and a black bib apron. She hardly had time to look in the mirror before dashing out the door, and then tried to look calm and collected as she climbed into his buggy.

"Hello."

"Hello, Levi."

They started down the road and Susan was grateful for the clopping of the horse's feet that occupied the brief silence that settled between them.

"I couldn't let you go without seeing you one more time. I know what I said before, but tonight we can just be friends, okay?"

"Sounds perfect."

And it was. They took a slow drive down back roads, past families in gardens, men baling hay, tractors raking hay, hauling round bales. The cornfields were already ten feet high and growing.

Levi told her he'd miss her, that his life would feel empty without her, but he did not press the issue of a relationship. They stopped at an ice cream stand, then sat at a picnic table by the hitching rack, spooning the vanilla ice cream out of the frothy root beer.

She found herself confiding in him about Dan. She hadn't meant to do it, but probably felt closer to him than she did to her sisters, Rose and Liz, which was an astounding discovery in itself.

They were sitting across from each other, their eyes almost never leaving the gaze of the other. It was as if these were the last moments of their lives, and they both wanted to be assured of the trust and strength they had built.

"You mean, he's actually, like, getting drunk?" Levi asked. "Even around his wife and children?"

"He is. And Kate makes excuses for him. She says he's depressed, he's a product of a father who held him back, and on and on.

"Honestly, he treats her so badly, and she says she's there to help him. I can't take it, Levi. I can't. The best thing for me to do is go to Wyoming and stay there. Oh, and he's talking of leaving the Amish."

"Can't say I'm surprised, given everything else," Levi answered. "Why would he want the accountability that comes with church?"

They talked until the pole lights blinked on and his horse snorted with impatience, tossing his head and pawing at the cement. They ordered burgers and shared fries. The insects sizzled in the heat of the light. Cars came and went, and still they talked. It was only when the small drive-through restaurant closed, the light blinking off, that Levi said they might soon be chased off the property.

The horse was eager to trot home, bringing the night to an end much too soon for both Levi and Susan. When they reached Susan's driveway, she didn't hop out of the buggy but stayed seated next to him, searching for the right words to say and not finding them.

Finally, when the horse no longer wanted to obey Levi's commands to stand still, he told Susan goodbye.

"You still have my ring?"

"I do."

"Where?"

"In a small case in a pocket of my luggage."

"So it's going with you?"

"Of course."

"And I guess with your sister's life going from bad to worse, there is absolutely no chance that you'll change your mind."

For a long moment, Susan was very quiet.

"Levi, she says I don't get it. Whatever that's supposed to mean. But I did gather a few insights when I was with her. You want to hear them?"

"I can't wait."

"I think maybe I'm too selfish to be in love. It's not all about me and whether a person treats me right. My fear of marriage might really be selfishness."

Levi told a long, unsteady breath.

"Wow."

"What does that mean?"

"An answer to one of my prayers."

"You actually pray for me?"

"I do."

"Your horse is going to run away."

"I know. It's just so hard to say goodbye, Susan."

"Goodbye, Levi. You'll write?"

"I wasn't asked to write."

"I'll send you my address after I have one."

The horse took a step, then another. He shook his neck, jangling snaps and rings. The silence in the buggy was deafening, until Levi gave a small laugh.

"Just friends usually means no kissing."

Susan leaned over and held his face in her hands, placed her lips softly on his, and whispered a tender goodbye. Then she climbed off the buggy and hurried away, the power of her emotion causing her to stumble on the steps. And it was only the impatient horse and the power of his willpower that allowed Levi to keep going out the drive toward home.

SHE WAS ON the train, realizing she was dependent on more people that she'd thought possible. She realized she didn't know if seating was assigned or if she could sit anywhere, she needed help getting her heavy bag up on the rack, she wasn't sure whether she'd need her ticket again or could stash it in her bag. She felt humbled by the willingness of strangers, folks genuinely glad to answer questions, but still felt unsettled as the Amtrak hurled toward Ohio. Her mother had packed her small Rubbermaid cooler well with two ice packs, cold drinks, and enough food to feed five people. But when lunchtime rolled around, she was still too anxious to eat.

The departure had not been easy, her mother doing her level best to keep from weeping, even as tears slid down her wrinkled cheeks, her father avoiding her eyes to keep from being reduced to tears himself. He pressed a roll of bills into her hand and made her promise if the homesickness became unbearable, she would come home.

She had promised.

Her mother's soft arms clung to her until the doors of the train had been open too long, and she had to tear herself away. The last picture of her was the big white Sunday handkerchief held to her streaming eyes, one hand flapping wildly up and down in goodbye.

Rose and Liz had refused to come, saying they weren't standing on one-hundred-degree concrete crying like there was a funeral. They had work to do at home, so goodbye, Susan. So long. Try not to be too much of an old maid out there.

And Susan had laughed, then wiped a few tears. She knew exactly how her sisters coped with emotion, inserting pride and humor to replace tears.

She certainly was on her own, much more than she'd thought. She felt small and insignificant, a speck of humanity on the gleaming Amtrak speeding through the countryside.

She tried to relax, adjust her seat, listen to the rhythm and motion of the car, picturing the coupling holding firmly so that one car would not loosen and go flying off into the wild blue yonder.

Eventually, she opened the small cooler, drank some of the Snapple her mother knew she liked, then unwrapped a package of cheese crackers. She realized she really was hungry and ate a whole wheat bread sandwich with sweet bologna and iceberg lettuce.

Yes, she would be alright, she decided, the food in her empty stomach bolstering her courage.

"Ma'am?"

From across the aisle, she saw a florid face, peach-colored hair in tight ringlets, earrings swinging from side to side.

"Yes?"

"Are you Quaker?"

"No. I'm Amish."

"Is that Mennonite, like?"

"Something like it."

"I see. Y'all drive horses and buggies?"

"Yes."

"Why?"

Susan sighed with impatience. That was one of the hardest things to answer. Why did anyone drive a horse and buggy in this day and age? Was it because that was the only way they could get to Heaven? Certainly not. But it was difficult to answer this question without sounding self-righteous or downright condescending. Neither did one want to make it sound as if it was stupid, nonsensical, weird, which to many modern-day people, it was. Born into the Amish world, it was a way of life, a culture you never questioned, content to be part of a group of people who belonged to a church with rules to live conservative lifestyles.

And so she answered that it was the fact of being born into a conservative group who chose to live a Christian life according to the rules of their church.

This resulted in a vague nod of the peach-colored ringlets and another jingling of the hoop earrings.

"Well, honey, God bless you. I sure would not want to drive no horse and buggy in traffic."

Susan smiled and went back to her Snapple.

Whatever.

Being Amish felt normal, but you really had to be born into it to fully understand. She figured it was the same way with any culture. Yes, it was tradition indeed, but the tradition itself was beloved. Some chose to leave it to live lives in the mainstream and thrived, while others would never think of doing that. This life was not chosen by each individual, but there was an expectation of obedience, from parents and the ministry, from the time a child was old enough to understand it.

She thought of the teacher's handbook, then bent to retrieve it from a side pocket and began to read. It was all interesting, and certainly not entirely new. She had a solid eighth grade education, and never had a problem in school, so she figured the curriculum would be basically the same. How hard could it be to teach a handful of students?

The pay wasn't too bad, but then, the matter of her savings account had been settled in her mind a few weeks ago. That was no longer top priority. Since Kate had told her we are not on earth to serve ourselves, Susan had done more serious soul-searching, resulting in the uncomfortable acknowledgement of loving her money, which supposedly was the root of all evil. That's what scripture said. But how could the love of money be the root of all evil, as long as you weren't greedy and selfish and mean? Perhaps you naturally turned into a nasty person without knowing it. That was possible.

At any rate, she checked the roll of bills her father had pressed into her hand and was quite happy to find five one-hundred-dollar bills.

Not that she loved money or anything.

She looked up to find a hurried mother prodding two children ahead of her on their way to the restroom. She smiled at the small blond boy and was shocked when he visibly stuck out his tongue, a mean, disrespectful gesture. Well, she'd try and keep her smiles to herself.

My goodness, she thought.

What if that happened in the classroom? Did she even like children? She then was seized with a fresh spurt of self-doubt and wanted to turn the hurtling Amtrak around and go back home.

She slept, however, the lull of the train in the late afternoon relaxing her, and woke refreshed and more eager to see the great West, eager to begin her new life in an unaccustomed place. She adjusted her seat to a more comfortable position, found her large tote bag, and searched for her book.

She'd brought too many of her favorites, ones she had read and reread, but it was a piece of home, a reminder of her room at home, the long cozy evenings alone, cocooned in her own personal space, her own furniture, her own expression of the things she loved. She would miss her room most of all.

The landscape was nothing much, with ordinary towns, rivers, flat land with boring horizons. She wondered if her journey would prove to be uninteresting, the whole way, without the expected snow-covered peaks, the cowboys on horses, driving great herds of cattle. Another glance out the window was rewarded with a trailer park, patches of weeds complete with an accumulation of vehicles long past the ability to be driven. An automobile graveyard.

They passed a town, with rowhouses standing sentry to a narrow car-lined street, small porches with occupants sitting or lounging against railings, children riding bikes or skateboards, the sun illuminating the scene like a bright painting. It was life in America for millions of folks who loved the city, who were raised in a rowhouse and never missed the wide open spaces of rural living. This was a way of life, working, paying rent, living day to day in close proximity to hundreds of others. And here they were happy, or reasonably so.

As they approached Chicago, she felt her stomach tighten. It was huge. She knew she would have to wait at the Chicago station for four hours and thirty-two minutes and find her way to a different train. What if she got lost? What if she couldn't find the right gate and missed the next train?

When she got off the train with her bag and cooler, she was completely shaken by the number of people, the sea of humanity milling about, all looking so confident, so sure of where they were going.

Susan slung her bag over one shoulder and followed a stream of passengers across an expanse of steel and concrete into an enormous building, a tower of glass and more steel. There was an odor of rust and disinfectant, the sound of voices on intercoms, men and women seated on rows of seats, hunched over the phones in their hands. A baby crying.

Alone, Susan felt isolated, stranded. She could find no available seat, then decided to stay close to where she hoped passengers would be told when and where to embark on the next train. She felt a level of unease she had never before experienced.

"Ma'am?"

Surprised, she turned to find a tall, dark person of perhaps forty.

"Yes?"

"I'll get you to a seat if you'll follow me."

His eyes seemed kind, sincere, his demeanor giving away no indication of ill intent. She was torn between safety and not hurting his feelings by a refusal of mistrust.

She nodded, hitched up the strap on her bag. If the promised seat proved to be too great a distance, she would slip away through the crowd. There were people everywhere and there was safety in numbers.

She watched the rows of shining braids bobbing ahead of her, wondered briefly how long it took to do that to one's hair.

And then the promised seats were in front of her, as well as places to purchase fresh coffee, sandwiches, pizza. She stopped when he stopped, thanked him, and settled into a plastic seat.

"Would you like a coffee?" he asked, his white teeth flashing in a kind smile.

"I was just thinking how wonderful a cup of coffee would be. Here. Wait."

She reached for her wallet.

"I got it."

And he was off into the crowd.

Susan sat, ill at ease, a little frightened, worried. Would she be able to tell from here when her train was leaving? Should she have accepted coffee from a stranger?

When he returned, he handed her a tall, hot coffee, complete with napkins, a stirrer, sugar packets, and a handful of creamers. She smiled at him as he lowered himself beside her.

"Rothby. Herm Rothby," he said.

"Susan Lapp."

"Nice meeting you, Susan."

"And you."

He wore jeans and a white collared shirt that contrasted with his dark brown skin.

She busied herself selecting creamer, stirring, replacing the lid. A sip, a sigh of appreciation.

"So, if you don't mind me asking, what's that thing on your head?"

"My covering."

He nodded. "A covering? And what does it symbolize?"

"We wear it as a sign of subjection to God and the angels."

"And to the husband, am I right?" He said with a smile, and somehow it didn't come across as rude at all.

"Yes. If you have one."

"I take it you don't."

"No."

"Traveling alone?"

"I am."

"I hope I didn't make you nervous, being a stranger and all. No offense, but you looked pretty lost. First time in Chicago?"

"Yes," she answered. "Your eyes looked kind and I decided to take a chance."

He laughed. "I'm a pastor. The International Baptist Church of Chicago. Worship and praise to God above. I know that verse about women covering their heads. The same section where God says the hair is given for covering. Don't matter. I respect the covering. What really matters, honey, is that heart of yours. You accepted Christ?"

"I did."

"Wonderful. You praise God for his salvation?"

"I do."

"Yeah. Yeah, I know you do."

And when he looked at her with all that warmth in his brown eyes, she felt the connection. He took her hand and squeezed. She returned the pressure, warmth flowing between them.

"We're sister and brother in Christ, ma'am. We are believers, you and I. One in Christ."

He stretched out a hand, spread his long, dark fingers that featured three wide gold rings.

"These rings. You'd never wear them, correct?"

"No. It's forbidden."

"Yes. And it's good and right for you. But for me? Every ring is a symbol, every one has a special meaning to me. I love my rings and don't believe God minds. He knows my rings."

Susan smiled, sipped her coffee.

"Now, I'm staying right here, until I got you on the right car, okay? This is part of my ministry, helping folks on to the next leg of wherever they may be going. I meet interesting people, interesting lives.

"You and I, we don't look alike, but inside, our hearts are the same. Washed clean by the blood of the Lamb. The beginning and the end. Ah-men!"

"Amen," Susan said softly.

The remaining hours were spent in astonishing Christian fellowship, the only term that seemed fitting. They compared their ways of worship, their upbringings, their beliefs. She found herself asking questions, answering his, discovering new ways of absorbing chapters in the Bible she had never fully understood.

Tradition was fine in its place, he assured her, but not when it tried to take the place of Christ. There was nothing between him and Christ. A heartbeat away, a living friend whose spirit lived in the center of his thoughts, his mind. Nothing was of any consequence, save Christ alone.

The only thing he could do was spread the love, the love stemming from a grateful heart for the saving grace.

BACK ON THE train bound for Casper, Wyoming, Susan was reeling from the encounter, fully convinced God had sent an angel to protect her, to help her from one train to another, to ease her anxiety at the station. Why had she gone with him to find a place to sit? She knew without question, it was his eyes, the depth of kindness in them.

She slept for a long stretch and woke to find daylight poking at dark night clouds. She longed for a shower, a change of clothes, coffee fresh from the pot on the stove. She made her way to the restroom, washed as best she could, brushed her teeth, and quickly combed her hair.

She was surprised to find the couple across the aisle with cups of steaming coffee and asked without hesitation where she could find a cup.

"The dining car," was the brusque reply.

"And where do I find that?" she asked.

A thumb jerked to the right, with a "two cars down."

She made her way through two more cars, occasionally reaching out a hand to steady herself on the back of a seat. She wondered briefly if this was what it felt like to be drunk.

She found the dining car a delight, with wide windows opening to a vast expanse of grazing lands, a creek winding its sleepy way through the center, brown and black cattle dotting the pasture lands like chocolate chips in an extra-large cookie. She enjoyed scrambled eggs, bacon, and a bagel, endless coffee, and a very friendly waitress who remembered her manners and asked no questions. She lingered gratefully, then began the dubious return, thanking her lucky stars when she landed safely in her own seat.

Eventually, they approached the station in Sheridan, Wyoming. She could see that the town was considerable, more like a city. The Amtrak station was large enough, but a fraction of what she had seen in Chicago. She stood inside the station near what appeared to be the main entrance, waiting, watching. She told herself to stay calm, tried to slow her breathing, ignored the crazy hammering of her heart. They'd be there, as they had promised. If they were late, it was understandable. No one had ever died of waiting on someone in a well-populated train station. At least she was easily recognizable in her Amish clothes—it wouldn't be easy to miss her.

She was getting very weary, shifting her weight from side to side, wishing she'd worn different shoes. She distracted herself with people watching. Wyoming boasted a great outdoors, and by all appearances, most of the travelers lived outside. She saw rugged faces like raisins, wrinkled and browned, crevassed foreheads, eyes underlined with sags and even deeper wrinkles. Women wore jeans and belts with big silver buckles. Men wore black or brown cowboy hats. Everyone wore cowboy boots. Standing there in her blue dress and white head covering, she felt more conspicuous than she ever had in her life.

CHAPTER 15

"SUSAN?"

She whirled around, eyes wide.

"Susan Lapp?"

"Yes! Oh, I'm so glad to see you."

She was clasped in a warm hug from the tall Amish woman with graying hair. Her taller, heavier husband stood at her side. Susan didn't even know their names, but they immediately felt familiar. These were her people and the relief of being with them was almost overwhelming.

"We're so sorry. Our driver made a wrong turn. Too befuddled by his GPS. I dislike all forms of electronic maps and voices."

She learned that they were Roy and Edna Weaver. They were originally from Indiana, transplants to Wyoming. Edna never stopped talking, hardly listened when her husband tried inserting a word occasionally. By the time Susan and her luggage were safely tucked in the small SUV, she had learned that there were eleven families altogether, seven families with school kids.

Roy was the oldest in the community. The patriarch, Edna said stiffly.

"Some of these rowdies think they're turned loose in good old Wyoming, feel their oats. You'll have a few in school. Isaac's kids. Ei-yai-yai."

They lunched at a place called the Wagon Wheel. *What else?* Susan thought. They had passed Wild Horse Saloon, Mountain Dentistry, Top Peak Medical.

Susan found herself drawn in completely. She decided these western folks' accent was so lovely she could listen to Edna all day, which she mostly did. Lunch was delicious, cups of warm chili with cheese melted on top, cornbread, fresh salads. While they ate, she got the history of the Amish community.

It all started when Amsley Mast, in Lagrange, got tired of the crowding, the drift of the church, and went West with Daniel Yoder, where they found what they were looking for in the shadow of the Bighorn Mountains. There were acres and acres of lodgepole pines and the land was cheap. They soon found themselves in a land of snow-storms, cattle farms, and elk hunting.

"And homesick women," Roy added, leaning back in his chair, wiping his mouth with his napkin.

"Homesick is right. The young women are lonely much of the time, you bet they are."

"But do you like it?" Susan asked.

"Well enough, well enough. No one gets rich. Winters are long. I quilt all year, one right after another. It's a good way to make some spending money. If you can get somewhere to spend it. Town's fierce far away."

This was a new expression. Things were "fierce dangerous," "fierce far away," "fierce hot or cold."

Roy paid for lunch and they were on their way to the Amish settle-ment on Crazy Woman Creek in the shadow of the Bighorns.

"My, it sounds wild. So western," Susan laughed.

The mountains loomed before them as they made their way out of town, so much bigger and higher than Susan could have imagined. Snow still crowned the highest peaks. The sky seemed to melt into the highest areas, creating shadows of blue and purple, until she couldn't tell which was more beautiful, the sky or the mountains. The clouds were like cotton balls unraveling into thin, delicate wisps. As they bounced along the dirt roads Susan noticed old barns that winter had grazed with storms, creating weathered boards without a trace of paint. They passed rattling pickup trucks edged with rust and featuring loose bumpers and broken tailgates. She saw trailers loaded with bawling cattle, tobacco juice catapulted from mustached mouths. The air roiled with dust.

Everything was brown and dusty.

"Now Susan, you'll have to get used to the dust. And the dry. You can't expect a decent garden. This isn't Indiana or Lancaster. It's a whole different way of life."

They caught sight of a new set of buildings.

"Rudy Detweiler's," Edna pointed out.

Susan raised her eyebrows.

"Someone has money," she observed.

"He comes from Illinois," Edna said. "He did have money. Don't know if he still does or not."

Susan liked the brown siding, the shape of the barn, all modern angles and heavy post-and-beam construction. Pines made a pretty backdrop for the building and the fenced-in area by the barn contained a variety of horses, some she was sure were riding horses.

She wondered vaguely if she'd be expected to ride a horse. She'd never ridden one in her life. She had hitched them to a buggy plenty of times, and loved her own driving horse, but had never learned how to ride.

"Now, here's our place," Edna pointed out. "This is where you'll stay. Our bunkhouses."

Clearly, Roy and Edna had chosen a good spot to erect their own building, on a rise overlooking vast pastureland ringed by fir trees, rocks, tufts of brown grass, and an almost dry creek bed. The house was a ranch with a deep front porch made of imitation log siding, the barn in perfect symmetry, also long and low, with pine green roofing.

A stonemason had done a terrific job on the front wall of the house, the most authentic stonework Susan had ever seen. The grass was brown, the gravel drive dusty, but there were watered flowers, a few shrubs planted around the house.

The bunkhouse was in back, nestled under a copse of cottonwood trees. It was a small ranch and had a cute porch with a welcoming wooden rocker, a braided rug, and a wooden water barrel that caught the rain water from the spouting.

When she got out of the car in front of the little bunkhouse, she was entranced. It was made of the same logs as the main house and had a stone chimney on the north side and screened windows that were open to allow the fresh air to circulate.

"Go on in," Edna said. "It's not locked."

The sitting room and kitchen were all in one room, with a couch and recliner, end tables, and a coffee table, battery lamps, and a huge braided rug on the hardwood floor.

"I didn't decorate a lot because I thought you might want your own personal touch. The kitchen is equipped, and here is your bedroom and bathroom."

Everything was so cute, so well built and perfectly comfortable. How could she ever miss her room at home? This was so much better than she dared to hope. She remembered to thank Roy and Edna warmly, her eyes shining with eagerness.

"After you're settled in, we'll take you to see the schoolhouse. I imagine you'll want a shower, right? If you need anything, don't hesitate to ask. Oh, there are some basic groceries, but you might want to go to the bulk food store. Amish folks have one out on Route 10. Just about everything you want out there."

The bliss of the hot water raining on her travel-weary body was so soothing. She took her time, luxuriating in the feel of a soft towel, the comfort of clean clothes. The closet in the bedroom was perfect for the dresses she'd brought and the drawers handily held all the other garments. The top shelf was perfect for storing luggage and whatever extra items she might need room for. She couldn't help wondering how long it would be before she got down her suitcase, packed it, and returned home for a visit. She was determined to stay for the school term, but ten months was a long time.

Only for a moment, the distance between her and home seemed frightening, bringing momentary doubt. What if some tragedy struck her family? A death? A terminal illness?

She tied on a clean apron, stepped outside, and took a deep breath of the dusty, pine-scented air. The level of oxygen in the air seemed higher, or of better quality, she wasn't sure which. She just wanted to breathe greedily, breath in, breath out, gulp the goodness of genuine fresh air.

The mountains loomed to her left, their glorious beauty there for her to enjoy every single day. A mockingbird began lilting warbles in the cottonwood tree, which brought a wave of nostalgia as she thought of how her mother chased them off with a broom, whacking it down on the cement floor of the porch over and over until one time she broke the handle.

Suddenly she missed her mother to the point of tears.

THE SCHOOLHOUSE WAS on a windswept knoll, a surprisingly steep grade leading up to it, with the surrounding area relatively flat. Her heart sank at first sight. She took in the rough vertical boards, nondescript tin roof, no porch, only a wooden set of steps leading to an ordinary wooden door. There was a row of two small windows on each side, a hitching rack, an unpainted swing set, and dust. Wind and dust. Dust everywhere, the front steps caked with it, dried clumps of mud turned to crumbling bits of dust.

Roy had to push hard to get the door opened and then they were met with the sound of scurrying feet. Susan saw a floor littered with half-eaten pine cones, pine needles, bits of baler twines, and tiny remnants of tablet paper—all serious indicators of rodent habitation.

The desks were the lift top type, discarded from some public school, the teacher's desk a scratched and dented metal one from a dump, probably.

The walls had been painted off-white by someone who was apparently in a big rush, as evidenced by the uneven surface. The floor was wide pine boards, finished with too many coats of high gloss varnish, which was peeling off where the desks were slid back and forth. There was no alphabet along the top of the black board, no roll-down map, not even a globe.

She was used to schoolrooms being simple, but this was a level of bare bones she hadn't imagined.

Oh my.

"Not much, huh?" Edna said, watching her expression.

"Well, it's . . . not what I expected."

"I guess not. We're planning on improvement. But it seemed as if everyone had their hands full with getting their homes established, and moving takes money, you know?"

For some reason, that "you know" tacked on to the back of her sentence sent a quick shot of irritation through Susan. It didn't look as if anyone spared much cost establishing homes, whereas this school was sadly lacking. She walked around quietly, calming herself as she opened desk drawers and book cabinets, finding nothing. She turned to Roy and asked what the budget was, as far as ordering supplies.

He lifted his straw hat, scratched his head, and drawled, "Well, pretty much zero. Reckon we'll have to take up collection before you can order anything."

"Seriously?" Susan asked, incredulous.

"Pretty much. Our school budget is going to your wages. That was about all we could afford."

She took a deep breath and smiled weakly.

"You don't seem real thrilled."

"I'm not."

"Oh, come on," said Edna. "You're an older girl. Surely you have savings. If you need stuff for the classroom, use your own money and we'll reimburse you at the end of the year."

Roy glanced at Susan's expression and tried to make peace. "Now, Edna. That's pretty harsh. We'll manage to get the supplies paid."

Edna set her mouth in a hard line and made her way out the door and down the steps, where she climbed into the buggy and sat. There wasn't much to do except follow after her, close the door firmly, and return the way they had come. Roy was talkative, but Edna had shut off the endless flow of words, sunk into a full-fledged pout.

The horse was fat and lazy, plodding along at his own pace, the reins dangling from Roy's hands. There was no hurry to go anywhere, given that the dry weather had put a stop to the haying.

They stopped at the grocery store, where Edna met her friend Louise and was pulled out of her funk.

"Louise, this is that Lancaster girl, Susan Lapp. The teacher?"

Louise, short and round, with a thatch of loose blond hair tucked into her bowl-shaped covering, was quite effusive in her welcome, and then ran out to get the girls to meet their new teacher. She returned, pushing two girls ahead of her. They were blond and blue-eyed, wearing small black coverings, the strings flapping down their backs.

"Say hello to your new teacher," Louise said, beaming.

The older of the two said hello while the littlest one merely eyed her, twisting her skirt with her fingers, not smiling.

"This is Patricia and Amelia. We call them Trisha and Millie."

"Hello, girls. How are you?"

"Good."

"Me, too. I just came from the school. I'll spend the month of August getting the school into shape. I think the mice are quite happy with their big home."

There was no answer, only a silent stare from two pairs of very blue eyes. The stare wasn't exactly hostile, but it was certainly not friendly.

"Girls, aren't you going to say something?" Louise prodded.

There was a pause, and then the younger one offered, "*Meyn' masslin kott letch yowa.*" (We had mice last year.)

She spoke in the western dialect with an adorable little girl lisp, and it was so precious that Susan actually had to restrain herself from reaching down and giving her a good squeeze.

"Did you?" she asked, bending to smile at her.

"Mm-hmm." A solemn nod.

"*See sinn ivva da botta chpdunga.*" (They ran across the floor.)

The r's were pronounced with the Ohio burr. It was too endearing.

"We'll take care of them this summer. We can't have mice, can we?"

Solemn head shaking again.

"Susan, you get your groceries now. I have to get supper on the table."

Edna turned to talk to Louise, effectively dismissing Susan, who went to collect a small grocery cart and push it down the narrow aisles.

The store was well stocked with most of the things Susan was used to, except for the abundance of fresh produce she took for granted at home.

She bought homemade granola, some baking items, a bag of potato chips, lunch meat, cheese, bread, and some wrinkled yellow apples. She introduced herself to the storekeeper who ran off to find the boys, returning with three school-aged boys reluctant to have anything to do with her.

Dark-haired and dark-eyed, they shook hands like perfect little gentlemen, but Susan felt pretty sure they were simply putting up with this introduction for their mother's sake.

"This is Harry, Kevin, and Michael."

"Hello, boys. How are you?"

Susan was met with three solemn stares before the oldest one, presumably Harry, said, "Fine."

Kevin looked at Harry, then at Susan, and said, "Fine," which was repeated by Michael.

"Oh, you boys," their mother giggled. "You should hear them when no one's around."

She turned to the boys. "You can go now," which was all they needed to shoot out the door to freedom.

"I'm Marianne. My husband is Darryl. We're from Indiana, same as almost everyone else around here. So you're from Lancaster. That's a place I would love to visit. I've heard so much about it. We surely do welcome you and hope you can make yourself at home."

"Thanks so much."

"It will be a lot different than you're used to, so I'm hoping you can adjust. I'm sure there will be a cleaning day scheduled soon, and we'll be there."

"Thank you."

On the way back, Roy slapped the reins sleepily, looking around for signs of an elk or white tails. He asked Susan if she went hunting.

"No, no. Oh my, why would I do that?"

"We'll get you to go. Showshoes and everything," he chuckled.

"I'll be busy teaching."

"I figured you'd say that."

She detested the idea of shooting a wild animal, the poor creatures perfectly happy in their patch of the forest, doing no harm to anyone. She could never understand the enthusiasm of her brothers when the end of November rolled around and the camouflage came out. She'd have to be literally starving before she'd consider hunting, and she wasn't sure she could do it even then.

She called her mother that evening to tell her of her safe arrival. Susan's voice turned into a squeak of longing while her mother cried openly on the other side of the country. They cried and then laughed and confessed they were like greenhouse flowers coddled and babied, living together in prosperous Lancaster County without hardship of any kind.

"Well, Susan, you know what they say: absence makes the heart grow fonder. We have not been absent very long, but I don't think I ever realized before just how much I love you."

Her voice caught and she was quiet, straining to control her emotions. Susan told her mother of her nice living space, the awful schoolhouse, meeting five of her pupils and their mothers, and finally they said goodbye, both reluctant to hang up the phone.

She slept for twelve hours straight, going to bed at eight and never waking till the sun was high in the sky. Edna had been anxious, wondering if she was alright. She was relieved when she found her up and dressed, sitting on the porch rocker with her coffee. Edna had made raspberry cinnamon rolls, so she brought a plate with four of the gooey treats, then left to bring a lawn chair and a cup of coffee for herself. Her good humor had returned, and she was anxious to fill Susan in on more details of the community.

"You've met some of the folks now, and of course you met Mahlon and Jane when they came out to Lancaster. I'm sure you'll be seeing them at church. You'll have sixteen pupils. That's not bad. You can manage them, can't you? Well, if they all act like Isaac's little wild ones, I don't know. But then, those kids can't help it if their mother died. You know it was our first and only funeral. She didn't know she had cancer till they moved out here four years ago. He offered to move back, but I think she knew then already, knew she wasn't going to make it. She told Isaac she wanted to die here by the mountain. Oh, it gives me chills, just thinking about it."

Edna paused for a moment, making sure Susan was appropriately affected by the tragic story before she continued.

"She was so sweet and pretty, but that cancer went like wildfire into her liver, her blood, just everywhere in so short a time. And I'll tell you right now, Wyoming isn't known for handy medical help, and certainly not the best hospitals or doctors. That's just my opinion, but I know it's not the way it is in the East. Anyway, she died about a year and a half ago, and he has two in school, a boy and a girl. Brats. Doesn't it sound awful, that word? But how else do you describe them? They're a mess. He doesn't have a maid, so we church women go twice a month to clean up around there. It's just so sad. I think he tries to make up for them not having a mother and just spoils them horrible. That's why the last teacher didn't make it. The little boy is something else."

She stopped for a breath while Susan glanced down at the plate.

"Here, eat another one."

"These rolls are the best ever. I heard you Indiana women are outstanding cooks."

"Oh, I like to cook and bake. But some are better than I am."

"Not at making raspberry rolls."

"Well, thanks."

There was a companionable pause while they ate their breakfast pastries, the mockingbird hopping brazenly on the lowest branch of the pine tree. He called out in a "chiree-chiree," then cocked his head and peered at them with beady eyes, as if to ask if he could have a slice of their rolls.

The horses snorted in the dusty pasture, pulling off bunches of hay from the rack. The day would be hot, but without humidity. None of that cloying damp heat in the East.

"So you met five yesterday and heard about two more. That leaves nine of them," Edna rattled on. "Let's see. Oh, there's Ezra. He's in grade eight this year. And his sister Hannah. They're so well-behaved. Make no trouble at all. They say Ezra tried hard to get little Titus to cooperate last year, just a real trooper for his teacher, but it didn't help.

"The thing is, his dad Isaac is no help at all. He just won't accept the fact that his son is a troublemaker. But then, the poor child, having no mother. You just can't understand why God takes a mother, leaving that man with two children. He needs a wife. Now don't think we brought you out here for that. I would never even think it, an eastern girl taking on a whole family. Stepmothers have it rough, I don't care what anyone says. They do. And I'm almost certain he will never love anyone the way he loved Naomi. She was a beauty, and just as sweet as she was pretty. I don't know. Sometimes a man like that never loves again. They just don't."

Edna paused and glanced down at the now empty plate.

"You know, the more sugar I ingest this morning, the more I want. Those rolls were sort of teeny, tiny. I'm going to bring the whole pan. Roy doesn't eat them. Thinks he's too healthy for sweet rolls. Oh, he makes me mad when he goes off on his health rants. Sends for all these pills and oils."

And with that, she was off across the yard.

Susan smiled, shook her head. What a character. She certainly did not mince her words or try to sugarcoat anything.

Edna hurried back from across the lawn.

"You know, it's so dry, the yard crackles under my feet. In case you don't know, don't ever burn anything. Trash or anything. The wildfires can be out of control. Scares me so bad. Anyway, here I am, going on about everybody in Wyoming. Oh, by the way. This is known as the Casper settlement. I guess maybe you knew that. You know what I think when people call it that? When I was a child, my mom bought us these comic books about Casper the good little ghost."

She brought up a hand and flitted with her fingers.

"So I imagine this little, friendly ghost among us. The Holy Ghost. 'Where two or three are assembled in my name, there the Holy Spirit shall be,' Jesus said. Do you agree?"

"Yes, of course."

"Well good. I think our faith is much the same. I love to talk about Jesus. Sometimes He's all I have, living so far away from my relatives. But living here does that, it draws you to God. To Jesus. He seems closer here by the mountain."

Edna jumped from one thing to the next with hardly a pause. "Tell me about yourself. Oh, do you have more coffee? Mind if I fill my cup? Here, take another roll. May as well. Life is short."

She stepped inside to pour herself more coffee. When she returned, she started in on Isaac again.

"You know Isaac, the widower? He's very nice looking, if you like blond hair on a man. He's a logger, big and husky. Nice-looking fellow. But his kids. I'd pity anyone to take them. You know what I mean. There's no one in this community, no single girl or widow. No one. He goes to some of the settlements in Montana sometimes, but I can't imagine there's anyone there for him either. Don't you have a boyfriend? Now, I'm not saying this because of Isaac. I wasn't even thinking about him."

"No, I don't have anyone." Susan said quietly.

"Did you ever?"

"No."

"Really? I guarantee you're keeping them away with a baseball bat. You're attractive. A pretty girl, in a different sort of way. Your hair and covering are so different, too. We should dress you up in our clothes sometime. You'd look nice in this style of covering. Well, you are nice. If you know what I mean."

Susan smiled and nodded. She imagined describing Edna to Levi, telling him about her refreshing honesty and nonstop chatter. Then she wondered what Edna would say if she told her about Levi. And what if she shared about Kate and Dan? Maybe she would eventually share her thoughts and fears with Edna, to get her brutally honest take on it all, if Susan ever had a chance to get two words in.

Buoyed on coffee and the stirrings of new friendship, Susan felt a sense of happy anticipation. Challenges would present themselves, but this morning, she was ready to face them. She felt that anything was possible out here in the wilds of Wyoming.

What would Edna say if she called it the "wilds"? She'd probably say the wildest things out here were Isaac's kids. Were they really as challenging as Edna made them out to be? Well, she guessed she'd find out soon enough.

CHAPTER 16

THE DAY WAS HOT. SUSAN HAD OPENED EVERY WINDOW, BUT THE steel-roofed schoolhouse was like an oven. It sat squarely in the middle of a vast unwooded area, like a prairie, the sun pouring the heat without mercy. There was no humidity, but the dust blanketed everything. It puffed up from books, lay thick on the floor, coated the windowsills. Even inside the cupboard doors, the shelves were brown with dust. Susan swiped a finger across a shelf, examined the smudge, and frowned.

Susan asked Edna after a few weeks if it ever rained, and Edna said a summer storm passed through occasionally, but it didn't amount to much. Irrigation was necessary for gardens and crops to survive.

Susan was getting things in order, a list of pupils at her elbow, taking stock of the few supplies she had on hand, organizing the things she would need. She could not complete her task before the community set the cleaning day, which had tentatively been planned for the third week in August, on a Thursday evening.

She had spoken to more of the parents and children in church, but still didn't have a good sense of whose children belonged to which set of parents. She thought the children were all rather outspoken, asking so many questions.

"Why is your covering so different?"

"How come you're wearing a black apron?"

"Do you ride?"

And she'd been stupid enough to ask, "Ride what?" which brought audible snickers.

"Horses. What else?"

"Oh. No, no." She told them she had never ridden a horse, which brought stares of disbelief and pitying glances.

She'd gone home from church and tried to keep her spirits up, in spite of knowing she'd been placed under a microscope and found lacking.

Well, she had no intention of changing the way she dressed, or of getting on a horse. She was from the East where girls rode in buggies or pedaled scooters or hired a driver if they needed to be conveyed from one place to another. This thing of riding astride a horse was much too *govvrich* (unladylike), and besides, she was scared of sitting on a horse's back. She could handle driving well-trained horses from her perch in a buggy, but the idea of sitting way up on a horse's back with little control over such an unpredictable creature seemed plain foolish.

She had missed her family that afternoon, missed them horribly. She thought fondly of the back patio with the climbing rose bush, the hummingbirds, the bluebirds on the clothes line, twittering anxiously to the fledglings teetering nearby. She even missed the sound of traffic, the flow of engine noise and wheels on macadam, the occasional clip-clop of horse hooves, children on scooters calling out to one another. At home it would soon be time for a shower, getting ready to go to the supper, the gathering of the youth with Beth and Mark. And yes, there was Levi.

Did she miss him? Yes, sometimes when his face appeared in her memory—the slant of his nose, the dimple on his clean-shaven chin, the yellow shirt—she felt a vague sense of longing. He had said he loved her. But did he really know what love was? Did he have any idea the sacrifice expected of him after he actually took a wife? She doubted very much if he did. It was good for her to be away, far away, so she could honestly examine every aspect of their friendship, think through her fears and doubts, remember the luxury of his look, his touch.

Touching before marriage was controversial. Plenty of bundling went on in her parents' day, that practice of sleeping in the same bed while fully clothed. But more and more, the distant courtship prevailed. Most agreed it was better to stay apart without touching at all.

She'd blushed, thinking of the boundaries they had overstepped. But was it so wrong? Those were the times when she'd felt closest to him and it was all out of the desire to know him better, to consider the depth of their commitment, a gauge for the future.

She wiped the back of her hand across her forehead, straightened her back, and groaned. What a mess the previous teacher had left for her. She cleaned, wiped, sorted books, filled a garbage bag with odds and ends, wrinkled her nose at the unmistakable odor of mice. As she reached the back of one desk drawer, her fingers touched the pink, squirming bodies of four baby mice, sleeping in a nest of torn tablet paper. She let out a squeal before composing herself and disposing of them in the most humane manner possible. Then she set the wooden traps with a dab of peanut butter.

It was so hot. She untied her black apron and drew it over her head, flopped down on a desk chair, and sighed. She hadn't slept well the night before, with no respite from the cloying night air. She'd heard rolling thunder, off in the distance, and waited for the approaching storm. She had heard western storms were legendary, and so had not slept, but the storm never came.

Her driver wasn't due till four. She glanced at the clock. Twelve-twenty. She'd eaten her packed lunch, chicken salad on whole wheat, and a sour green apple. Was there any good produce available in Wyoming?

She found a dusty towel, then another. She was so sleepy her head spun, so she rolled the towels into a pillow, laid them on the floor along the wall, and put her head on them, drawing her knees up into a comfortable position. Soon she had drifted off to sleep. When she awoke, she was confused for a moment before she realized where she was.

She spent the afternoon mostly sitting on the steps of the front door, looking off across the endless miles of nothing. She compared the scene to the crowded space in Lancaster County, one farm joining another, business places springing up like mushrooms after a spring rain. Lancaster held a vast number of Amish families, dwelling in unity, or mostly so, raising their children in the pattern of their fore-fathers. There was always drift, the invasion of newer and better ways, but for the most part, the traditions of the elders stayed in place. The way church services were conducted, weddings, funerals, schools—everything according to order. Susan wasn't so sure about this fledgling settlement in Wyoming. No monetary funds for supplies? Who would fix the broken see-saw, the dangling swing seat? And who in their right mind would build a school without a porch?

She gave a small snort as she gazed at the primitive bathrooms, which were more like outhouses. Instead of a proper sink there was a pipe with a spigot on the end. She sincerely hoped it would not freeze up in winter.

The wind that tugged at her thin dress was a hot, dust-laden wind that came up in the west every day and never stopped till evening. It blew the dust in great whirling clouds, tugged the clean laundry on the lines, moaned around eaves and rippled along shingles, bent tall grasses and pine tree tops. It whistled down chimneys, brought bits of straw and hay against window screens, and sometimes, depending on the direction of very strong headwinds, flipped tractors and trailers out on Route 90, Roy said.

Lost in her reverie, she was not aware of any moving creature, until a dark figure to her left caught her eye. She turned her head, following the movement of a large black dog, his head lowered as he sniffed the ground.

When he raised his head, his gaze was wary and he stopped in his tracks. A deep growl came from his throat, followed by a short bark.

Susan didn't feel entirely comfortable, so she made a move to get up and go inside. Immediately, the dog barked again, louder and more forcefully. He took a few steps in her direction.

"Hey!"

A small boy, perhaps seven or eight, appeared from seemingly nowhere, hatless, blond hair tousled by the wind. His shirt was of a nondescript color, the front smudged by what appeared to be mud, his blue denim trousers ripped and torn, too short and much too tight.

"Get back here, Wolf."

The command was obeyed, the dog turning to trot back to his master, small as he was. The boy stood still, a hand on the dog's collar, taking stock of the situation on the steps of the school.

Susan waved a hand, glad to be in the presence of another human being, hoping it would turn out to be one of her pupils. When there was no answering wave, she got up and walked toward the boy and his dog.

"Hi," she called out.

"Watch out. He bites."

"He does?"

"Yeah. Stay back."

"His tail is wagging."

"So?"

"Doesn't that mean he's friendly?"

"Wolf is part wolf. They aren't friendly."

"I see."

"Who're you?"

"The new teacher."

"School's not starting yet."

"I know."

She stepped closer. The dog wagged his tail. His pink tongue came out as he drew back his mouth in a smile. She reached out to pet the top of his head, ran a hand along his ears. So soft and velvety.

"He doesn't like you. Wolves don't like teachers."

"They don't?"

"No."

"Do you go to this school?"

"Course. Ain't no other one."

"Oh, that's right. I forgot. Wyoming is not like Lancaster, is it?"

A shoulder shrug.

Then he said, "I can see through your dress."

"What? What are you talking about?"

Clearly flustered, Susan turned on her heel, went up the steps and into the classroom, and threw on the black bib apron she had left on the desk. She made her way back to the boy, who was inspecting the broken see-saw. She said nothing as his blue eyes bore into hers, as if he'd caught her out and felt clever.

"Somebody broke this last year."

"I can tell."

"My dad's not gonna fix it. He's a logger."

"Mm-hmm. Why are you here alone? Where is your mother?"

"She died and went to Heaven. I guess she did, everyone says so. She was really sick."

A shot of warning went through Susan. So, this was the uncontrollable one with the widower father. What had Edna said his name was?

"I'm sorry."

"No you're not. You didn't know her. You don't care she died."

"But I'm sorry for your sake."

"You don't know me, either."

"No, I don't. What is your name?"

"Titus. But don't say you're sorry, cause you're not."

What he said was true, in a way. She hadn't, until this moment, met any of them, so whatever sympathy she felt was shallow. It was only common etiquette, chosen proper words, to say you were sorry, more to comfort the person from a distance than anything else. But she'd meant well, and he had shot her down.

She felt ill at ease now, flustered. But she knew she could not allow him to see that. She decided to change the topic quickly.

"What grade are you in?"

"Third grade. I'm eight."

"Good, good. I have a lot of interesting learning planned."

"I gotta go. I'm not supposed to be here. I'll get in trouble with Bertha. I hate her."

He chirped to his dog and took off at an easy lope, his bare feet skimming the dry, brown grass, the dog beside him, churning up puffs of dull, gray dust. Susan turned, shaking her head to herself. Teaching Titus would be interesting, that's for sure.

He was quite perceptive for one so young. Why did he hate Bertha, whoever that was? Why had he announced the fact that his father would not fix the swing set? A logger was relieved of his fatherly duties?

The dog situation was funny. The dog was obviously happy to see her, his tail waving like a banner of welcome. It was the boy who did not want to see her. Well, she was here. She'd take one day at a time and hope for the best.

THE DAY OF the proposed school cleaning dawned clear and bright, so Susan did laundry at Edna's house, then cleaned her own small cabin, humming under her breath as she swept, dusted, and mopped. She cleaned windows, then brought her laundry off the line, folded it, and put it away. She called a driver to take her to school, wishing for her own horse and buggy, or scooter. She had never learned to ride a bike and eyed Roy and Edna's bikes with distaste and a certain amount of fear. She thought if she had to make a choice, it might have to be a horse. Bikes were extremely unstable.

When she arrived at the schoolhouse, it seemed especially primitive and dusty. The broken see-saw and lack of a porch were downright depressing. She wondered again why she'd promised to teach this school, what she was doing two thousand miles away from home.

But when she saw the boxes of supplies stacked against the back wall and heard the rattle of carriage wheels as the sets of parents arrived, she felt her spirits begin to lift.

One by one, the women entered the classroom: Louise, Marianne, Annie, Frieda, and Barb. All were outgoing and friendly and more than willing to be put to work. They wiped walls, cleaned windows, polished desks, and mopped the floor, all the while talking, joking, and laughing. Laughing a lot, Susan thought. By the time the schoolhouse was clean, she'd felt as if she'd known these ladies all her life. She was invited for brunch the following Sunday, for a campfire supper that night. She promised to go to both.

The men fixed the see-saw, mowed the grass (or what was left of it), then stacked firewood, repaired the roof, and cleaned the chimney.

They introduced themselves, or were introduced by their wives, and Susan found she felt at home in this strange community far more than she'd thought possible.

Isaac was not there, probably wouldn't be coming, she was told. He logged till dark on most days, traveling forty, fifty miles home, sometimes more.

The men's demeanor saddened, incredulous suddenly, thinking of the children.

"It's a sad thing, losing a wife like that," Darryl remarked.

"Sure is. Wouldn't wish it on my worst enemy," the one called Abe said firmly, shaking his head.

"Tea? Lemonade?" Barb made her rounds, plastic Rubbermaid jug in one hand, a stack of paper cups in another. There suddenly appeared trays of pretzels and cheese and a Tupperware container of chocolate chip and peanut butter cookies. The snacks and conversation lifted their tired spirits.

Susan mentioned that she'd met Titus and his dog. Eyebrows rose and heads shook.

"You know how far that kid walked? Almost three miles. He walks the countryside like a vagabond. Gets away from Bertha, and just like that, he's off down the road. The only thing keeping us from interfering is the dog. That, and Isaac."

The men all laughed together.

Who was this Isaac? For reasons Susan didn't understand, he didn't have to help with the school cleaning, and likely made no apologies for it. Susan wondered about the girl, the one close to Titus's age, but did not bring up the subject. Better to wait and see what occurred on the first day of school.

SINCE ROY AND Edna were also invited to brunch, she could ride in the surrey, free from the responsibility of hiring a driver. The air was still cool as they rattled down the dirt road, the great wide sky above them, the large area of pastureland, patches of cottonwood and lodgepole pines in between.

The pines were a sickly lot, having been ravaged by a beetle that laid its eggs beneath the bark of the tree, ate the tender insides of it, destroyed whole forests. Susan felt a certain sadness over this mutilation of Wyoming's signature tree, but knew other trees would take their place after the beetles died out, or left.

There were cattle and horses everywhere. She admired the sleek brown cows, the black Herefords, and the giant longhorns.

How could they possibly raise cattle in this brittle country? They had to supplement with hay, but how could they grow that if it became this dry every summer? She thought it odd that anyone wanted to make a home in a state quite like this.

But Abe and Louise Mast's home proved to be one of the most welcoming sights Susan had ever seen. They had a house built of logs, real ones, with a deep cozy porch running the length of it, with a hip-roofed barn in dark brown siding, a log fence, flowers in urns and hanging baskets, the trees shading the house.

Louise was clearly flustered, serving up so much food it was bordering on ridiculous. Three different kinds of cinnamon rolls? The breakfast casserole was made of bacon, ham, sausage, mushrooms, peppers, onion, cheese, milk, eggs, and hashbrowns, and then there was sliced ham, sausage gravy, and biscuits. There were crepes filled with a mix of canned peaches and pineapples, cream cheese, and whipped cream. Everything Susan tasted was delicious.

Little Millie and Trisha were delightful, introducing her to their pet parakeet, Joyce. There were new kittens in the barn, which Susan sat and held, and a baby calf in the pen beside the horses.

They drank coffee on the porch as the sun rose high in the sky, but the heat did not seem to reach the heights of the previous week.

Conversation flowed freely, laced with the history of Wyoming, the indigenous tribes that had always inhabited the region, artifacts still being dug up along the Medicine Bow River, which proved very interesting to Susan.

She had planned a lesson for her upper grades—the fascinating history of how the whites took the land from various indigenous tribes—and was glad to be able to practice her knowledge, the book learning she cherished.

Louise wanted to dress her in Wyoming clothes, but Susan said only the hair and covering. Much too hot to change clothes.

Her hair was undone, combed up over her head, and a bowl-shaped covering placed instead of the heart-shaped one. Amid many giggles and plenty of laughter, she was presented to the men who duly admired her, saying she was stunning in western dress.

"Some of the eastern boys need to wake up," Roy said, winking at Abe, who agreed wholeheartedly. It was all in fun, but a refreshing ego boost, leaving a twinkle in her eye as they visited on the porch.

Clearly, Amelia worshipped her by the time they left, which was another spirit lifter, giving her a boost of courage to face opening day of school. Louise gave her a red mug with white lettering, Teacher written on both sides, with a green apple in the center.

They drove to Darryl and Marianne Miller's place, a distance of seven miles. The horse was not feeling very energetic and the miles stretched before them as if there were twenty. Susan felt herself relax, nodded off and had a short nap, the calorie-laden food in her stomach putting her to sleep like a well-fed baby. She awoke with a start, realizing the horse had stopped, with Roy giving the reins to Edna before climbing down and lifting the right forefoot to examine the hoof.

"Looks like he picked up a stone," he remarked.

He bent over the foot and scraped away with his pocket knife until he successfully pried out the offending stone, and they were on their way.

"See, Roy. That's what I miss about Indiana. All macadam. Good old smooth macadam," Edna remarked sourly.

There was no reply from Roy, so she kept up the rant about the pleasures of a macadam road. No mud when it rained, no dust when it was dry. Easier for a horse to pull a carriage, easier on carriage wheels, too.

Still no comment.

"Now, Roy. You know I'm right. You can't deny it. These dirt roads are for the birds. Here I was good enough to move out West with you and you don't even hear me when I talk. The least you could do would be to listen to me. Right?"

A nod.

"Susan, don't ever get married. Don't harness yourself to a man who is not happy unless he lives on dirt roads and takes you thousands of miles away from your hometown."

Roy chuckled, said she was worse than a biddy hen.

And Susan thought a man who loved the West and persuaded his wife to accompany him likely didn't do himself any favors. He might enjoy the novelty of the picturesque mountains, the wide open spaces, the horses and western aura, but he'd always contend with the not-so-well hidden longing of his wife to return to the land of her birth. Unless, of course, he was married to a saint.

Their destination was another interesting property, this time a small two-story house and a shop where shoes, harnesses, handcrafted saddles, saddlebags, and boots were made. Miller's LeatherWorks. A small barn, a few horses and goats, but no sign of cattle on this homestead.

Marianne welcomed them into her home and brought glasses of mint tea as Darryl and Roy went to start the campfire. They cleared away all the dried leaves from the area and had three big buckets of water nearby. Edna reminded Susan that fires were dangerous in such a dry climate, but Roy assured them they were far from the trees and taking all the appropriate precautions. The three boys were nowhere to be found until they caught sight of the campfire smoke and came running out of the barn like flushed rabbits. They lined up in a row and eyed Susan with suspicion until Darryl told them to say hello.

"Remember your manners, boys," he drawled in a soft voice.

They were instructed to bring last year's school work for Susan to examine. She glanced through it and made a mental note to have penmanship classes first thing every morning. Every single morning.

Seated on a wooden porch rocker, the campfire crackling as the sun slid behind the mountains to the west, Susan felt content in the golden glow of evening and the sound of moths flitting from their perch in the grass. She was listening to a vivid account of Rudy Detweiler's bull attack while he was on horseback. The horse, they said soberly, had saved his life.

There wasn't a breeze stirring anything, so why did she suddenly feel as if a strong wind was about to rustle the cottonwoods, build up the fire with a rush?

Suddenly there was the sound of approaching hoofbeats, a rapid staccato, and a giant brown horse appeared, coming fast around the first bend in the road, the rider bent low over his neck.

Roy nodded at Darryl, and they both shook their heads. Whoever was on that crazy horse was someone they knew well.

CHAPTER 17

THE HORSE AND RIDER SHOT ACROSS THE SPACE IN FRONT OF THE hitching rack by the barn, straight down to the campfire, sitting up, hauling back on the reins, calling out a steady series of whoas.

"Whoa. Hold it there. Whoa."

The voice was ringing, commanding, the horse lathered in white foam, wild-eyed, breathing hard. The rider was massive, built like a wrestler, his blond hair disheveled, his hat long gone. Susan watched as he flung himself from his horse and threw the reins up over the ears. He shook both hands as if to resume circulation, then grinned with a lopsided smile of half apology.

"Sorry. Can't hold him. He's a brute."

"So's the rider."

"You'll kill yourself, riding that thing."

"Look at him. Not many horses will do that."

"Isaac, this is Susan Lapp, from Pennsylvania. Susan, Isaac."

Susan wasn't exactly thrilled to meet this brute. Didn't he think about the safety of those around the campfire? For a heart-stopping moment, she'd honestly thought the horse and rider would plunge straight into the fire.

"Hello."

"Hi. Sorry. Didn't know you had company."

"Well, you do now."

"Yeah."

"She's the schoolteacher."

"Oh. So you'll be teaching my kids, I guess."

He gave her his full attention then, and she found herself looking into the saddest brown eyes she'd ever seen. Perhaps it was the shape of them, the way they slanted down at the sides, or perhaps it was the fact that he had lost his wife. He was deeply tanned, but the one side of his face looked a bit different than the other. As if he'd had plastic surgery. He was a good-looking man, huge, powerfully built, but that shock of blond hair was disconcerting. Susan always thought blond hair on a grown man made him appear like an overgrown boy. She thought of Levi's wavy brown locks.

"Yes. I already met Titus. And the dog."

"Wolf."

He smiled at her. She smiled back, and felt absolutely nothing. So much for thinking a lonely widower would win her hand. She felt a sort of relief. Without even realizing it, she'd felt a little nervous about meeting him ever since Edna mentioned that he was a widower. But she needn't have worried. There was no danger of attraction here.

"Do you allow your son to traipse the roads alone?" she asked, raising an eyebrow.

"Why not? Nobody's coming within six feet of Titus if Wolf is around."

"Are you sure? Wolf didn't seem particularly scary to me."

She could tell he didn't like being challenged, saw the heightened color in his cheeks. Well, actually. Only one was colored. Something was off here—that face gave her the creeps.

He opened his mouth to answer, but decided better of it and turned to Darryl and Roy to make small talk. He sat in the stacking chair they provided, dwarfing it entirely. He roasted three hot dogs, ate them all with mustard, then made a s'more.

"Where are the children?" Marianne asked.

"With Bertha."

Before Susan could stop herself, she blurted out, "Who's Bertha?"

"An English girl from town. She rides out every day, then home after I get home. She's good with the children."

Susan almost said "huh" but caught herself.

Isaac added two more marshmallows on the roasting stick and held it near the glowing coals. Eventually, he took them off the stick and added them to the graham cracker with peanut butter, a square of chocolate, and another graham cracker.

He ate it in one alarming bite, a few chews, and a swallow, then reached for another.

"You hear about Monroe?"

"What about him?"

"Broke his nose. Branch smacked him in the face. He's one lucky guy. It could have been as bad as this."

He touched the top of his cheekbone.

Darryl laughed. "Your face is half steel."

"Titanium. It's lighter."

Roy snorted. "You should have been dead, by all accounts, walking out of that woods with a towel around your head, bleeding out like a stuck pig."

Isaac said slowly, "It would be nice to go, some days."

"I suppose, Ike. But the Lord put us here on earth for our allotted time, and we have to do the best we can. Right or wrong, it won't bring her back."

Isaac stared into the fire, his eyes downcast. Susan watched the firelight play on the stone side of his face, and thought he must have been smacked by a tree, somehow. Where did he go to do his logging? For miles around there was no forest, only a few trees scattered throughout the grasslands around them.

She found herself longing for the safety of Pennsylvania, for the Sunday evening supper crowd and the comfort of her own bed, her own dear home. Wyoming seemed raw and untamed. Walking out of a woods with your face open was not a matter she needed to think about just now.

"Yes. Logging is dangerous business. Not for the weak. I can get carried away at times, forget the danger. There's a rush listening to the bite of the chainsaw, the pounding of the wedge, then the ultimate tearing sound and the ground shaking beneath your feet when it goes 'Whomp!'"

His hand came up, smacked his knee with a loud crack, followed by a laugh of boyish pleasure. Susan noticed the one side of his mouth did not turn up as far as the other, giving him an odd look when he laughed. Had she really made him mad, saying that about Titus, or just embarrassed? She couldn't help herself. He was not looking out for his son's welfare.

"How's Sharon?" Marianna asked softly.

"Better. A virus. Bertha said after she got Pedialyte and drank some apple juice, her temperature went down."

"Good. I was so worried about her."

"That's nice of you to care. I appreciate it. Well, I better get on home. Kids are with Bertha."

He bent his head, rubbed his forehead with the tips of his fingers. When he looked up again, his dark eyes shone with unshed tears, his mouth trembling.

"It's tough for the kids."

Roy placed a hand on his knee. "And for you. We'll be praying for you, buddy. Never forget that."

Isaac nodded, and Susan knew he was unable to speak. A big man like him, so strong and rough, yet the loss of his wife was like the emotional felling of a huge pine. She observed it all with curiosity but no emotion. Titus had been right—it really wasn't her concern.

Besides, this thing of allowing that boy of his to wander around with his dog was horrendous. She made a mental note to try and change that.

Suddenly he stood up, saying he'd better be on his way. He was on his horse in one leap, the horse wheeling on his hind legs, coming down already lunging forward.

DARKNESS WHISPERED ACROSS the empty landscape on the way home, the clean night air bringing a pleasant chill. In August.

She leaned forward.

"Is this night air normal?"

"For August, you mean? Oh, yes. It can snow in September," Edna answered.

"Summer's short. You'll get your share of snow, and then some," Roy echoed.

But Susan had pleasant memories of her day, knowing where some of her pupils lived, the environment in which they spent their daily lives like a record for her to picture in her mind. She could see no immediate problem in either home, knew the children had healthy emotional upbringings, with both parents present in a loving atmosphere.

Isaac did the best he knew how, she supposed, but as far as she could tell, he was not especially gifted with a high IQ. That titanium face told her a lot. Well, she'd have to see how this first week with Titus came along.

Then, because she was lonely and she'd slept late that morning, she opened the nightstand drawer, retrieved the small white velvet box, and carefully lifted the ring Levi had given her. It glistened in the glow of the lamp. She turned it around and around, put it on her third finger, then removed it.

Levi, was your declaration of love true?

For one despairing moment, she felt isolated, alone, and that she had done the wrong thing by coming to Wyoming. There were so many girls in Lancaster, ones he could easily have, and here she was on the other side of the country, without his company for the next nine and one half months. Why had she done it?

She knew now that she missed him completely and totally, which amounted to almost loving him. She would do what she set out to do, get through these nine months of school, and then get home to the East as fast as the Amtrak could carry her.

She brought the ring to her lips and kissed it before replacing it in the box. Yes, love was a process for her. Like a young sapling reaching for the sunlight, it would grow and prosper. She felt comforted by this thought and fell into a deep and dreamless sleep.

IN THE MORNING, Edna was a grouch. She'd cut herself slicing bread, a nasty slice into her forefinger, so Susan offered to do laundry, which she gladly accepted. She rocked morosely, admitting she had a bad case of self-pity and homesickness. She plain down needed to go home to Indiana, but Roy said she had to wait till the calves were fatted out, so they'd have money for the trip.

"Sometimes I hate it out here," she whined, holding her cut finger with a paper towel.

"I believe you. No matter how good your intentions are, you are still human, and of course you long to see family. I have in the short time I've been here."

"What did you think of Isaac?"

"He's strange. Just different. It really makes me mad, how he lets that little Titus wander around with that dog. It's not right. I'm going to tell him, too."

That confession only added to Edna's sorrows, having hoped—despite what she'd said—to ignite a spark between them. So many disappointments crashing down on her head were about more than she could take, so she told Susan she'd heard the eastern girls were really particular with their men. Susan looked up from the sorting of clothes, and said honestly, she'd never heard that before.

"Well, you heard it now," Edna snapped.

Later, after the finger was bandaged and the wave of longing dispelled, they hitched up the horse and went to the bulk food store. Edna needed coconut. She was going to make coconut macaroons, something she loved, and had found a wonderful recipe. Susan bought a few items, then bought a book of stamps so she could mail letters to her friends. And to Levi. Better not tell Edna, or she'd be sent straight over the edge, as close as she hovered there these days.

Susan got in her own laundry and then lay down for a restful nap. She awoke feeling refreshed, her spirits bolstered. Her life was so very different here in Wyoming, so peaceful and unhurried, like a slow, meandering stream through a meadow, instead of a rushing waterfall crashing headlong on rocks below. She had time to unwind in the afternoon, time to appreciate the call of a meadowlark from its perch on a post by the pasture. The sky above her was blue and unhurried, the brown grass never in need of mowing. And if the tomatoes shriveled a bit when the drip irrigation went awry, that was okay, they were sweeter that way.

As each day passed, she became more aware of the fact that slowing down was almost a new way of life, an awakening to the small print that showed you the beauty of life, the beauty you'd missed so many times before.

Susan was slowly becoming accustomed to the strange brown, parched beauty of the West. In her mind's eye, the fences, the horses and cattle, the subdued coloring of this land held a restful beauty, one that gave you pause to breathe deeply and allow your version of loveliness to expand. In Lancaster County, the surroundings were in a box: a lovely farm, in perfect symmetry against a backdrop of square green corn or alfalfa fields. A beautifully landscaped lawn, with clipped shrubs, grass like carpeting. An expensive house built of stone or brick in another box. A box containing a winding road through lush cornfields in another.

Here, beauty was scattered, the boxes ripped apart to allow weeds and beetle-infested lodgepole pines and dust to inhabit the grandeur of the Bighorn Mountains, a breathtaking sight no matter how arid the land became as summer wore on. There were unexpected wildflowers, a beauty all their own, thriving against the odds without adequate moisture. Sometimes, when the light was golden toward evening, an old weather-beaten barn against a backdrop of the mountains took her breath away. She even found herself gazing at an abandoned truck, its rounded cab and small window giving away its age like wrinkles on a face, the rust color blending perfectly with the dried yellow brome grass surrounding it.

She asked Edna if anyone had ever taken up painting here. She looked up from her book, blinked, adjusted her glasses and said she didn't think so, but then, how was she supposed to know what other folks did for pastimes? Lord knew the winters were long and boring enough to inspire unusual pursuits.

Susan hid her grin. Edna's bad mood hovered over her head and dipped down occasionally to expel a sharp reply, which Susan accepted with a grain of salt. It was merely Edna being herself, in the honest, unvarnished way she had.

She asked Susan to stay for supper. She'd fried chicken and made dressing.

When Roy got home, his eyes were twinkling with good humor, a ready smile playing around his mouth. "We have company," he said, grinning at Susan.

She responded with a smile, a dip of her head.

"You know, that's one rare quality in a girl," he observed, lowering his tall frame into a chair, reaching out to straighten his knife and fork.

"What?" Susan asked.

"The ability to be quiet."

From the stove came a tremendous snort.

"Really, Roy? I'd like to know how this would go in our house if I wouldn't talk. As quiet as a tomb, that's what. You can never open your mouth to say anything if I don't keep a conversation going."

"Oh now, didn't mean to ruffle your feathers, Edna. You know I enjoy your conversation."

"Then why did you say that?" she asked, joining them at the table.

Roy shook his head and winked broadly at Susan. The answer he chose would be the wrong one, so instead he commented on the perfectly fried chicken.

"Way to change the subject, Roy," said Edna.

Roy paused and looked earnestly at Edna. "Edna, I know you want to go back home. You are homesick, and I can't blame you. We'll try and get you there as soon as possible, okay?"

When Edna gave no reply, but got up and returned with a few tissues, Susan's heart melted toward her. These women who chose to accompany their men to a new settlement might be pioneers alongside their men, but there was a harsh reality attached to the novelty of living out West, and that was the portion of their heart yearning for family.

Susan didn't like to see Edna's suffering but recognized that it was good to experience this firsthand so she'd learn what it was like. She could add Edna's experience of marriage to the list of experiences she did not want for herself. She was glad to see Edna's honesty, the total disregard of pride, the way she didn't try to keep the homesickness to herself.

She knew now that Lancaster County was her home, and more and more, she could imagine Levi being a part of her future. She'd have to confide in Edna about Levi soon to save her from trying to match Susan up with Isaac.

Susan spent the last two days before opening day at the schoolhouse, hiring a driver to take her there, in spite of being offered a bike and a riding horse. Edna didn't offer to take her in the team, either. Instead, she sniffed and turned up her nose to show her disapproval, which, Susan knew, was because her plan to turn Susan into a western girl was going awry.

She had her order of books delivered, sorted out, and piled on neat stacks on every desk. Beside the books were freshly sharpened new yellow pencils and pink erasers. She had brand new lined writing tablets available. Spelling and chore charts were hung on the walls. She found everything cleaned to her satisfaction, though she still disliked the pine flooring, which was varnished to a hideous yellow. She thought longingly of the smooth, waxed tile floors in Lancaster, the homemade desks gleaming smoothly, crafted by an Amish woodworker. These desks had chipped formica tops, the metal bases were gray or green with chipping paint, and some seats were loose.

She'd have sixteen pupils, which felt like a manageable number. It was significantly less than most Lancaster schools, although she had no helper. But she decided that was a good thing; she couldn't imagine getting along with some addlebrained teenager with her head full of boys.

She looked appreciatively at the vase of dried grasses on her desk, a stoneware mug for her red ink pens, the tap bell, books between commercial grade bookends. The drawers were organized and ready to go. She wasn't feeling nervous at all, although she knew she would feel less sure of herself on opening day, with sixteen pairs of eyes staring at her.

She sat on the steps, lamenting the lack of a porch, when she heard the call in a high-pitched voice. "Wolf! Get back here!"

Soon enough, Wolf appeared from a stand of cottonwoods, his mouth wide open, tongue lolling, panting, followed by the scruffy looking boy, Titus. He stopped, watched her warily. The only sound was the sighing of the wind around the eaves of the schoolhouse.

The boy turned on his heel and began to walk away.

"Titus!"

He stopped, turned, threw up a hand.

"What are you doing here?" Susan asked, suddenly eager to talk to another human being, even if a child.

"Chasing stuff."

"Chasing what?"

"Just stuff."

"You mean, animals or what?"

"Yeah, squirrels. Gophers. Whatever."

She frowned at the BB gun on his shoulder.

"You're a bit small to tote a BB gun."

"I'm eight."

"That's not very old."

"Sure it is."

Susan thought his attitude must be from his father, but chose to let him have the last word. Little upstart, really. His clothes were filthy, his pants way too short, and too tight, safety pins taking the place of buttons, one knee torn away completely. His feet were encased in an old pair of Nikes, the laces long gone. His blond hair was matted to his forehead, the back of his head like a metal sponge.

Irritation crept up, mostly at Isaac. Surely he could do better than this. Surely there was someone who could do a better job than this Bertha. How could he go to work with his son in this lamentable position?

"Come sit with me," she said.

His eyebrows lowered. "Why?"

"Oh, just because."

"Do you have anything to eat?"

"Actually, I have a sugar cookie. And some pretzels."

"Okay."

In one swift move, he was beside her, looking up expectantly. Susan smiled into his very brown eyes. He did not smile back. She got up to retrieve the remains of her lunch, handed it to him, and felt a mixture of pity and irritation as he wolfed down the cookie, then handfuls of pretzel, without speaking.

"Didn't you have lunch?"

He shook his head. "I don't stay in the house if Bertha's there."

"Why not?"

"She's fat. Sits around and bosses us. Dat says he can't get anyone else. Our relatives are in Illinois." He took a few more bites, then added, "My mom died."

"I know."

"You know why?"

"She had cancer."

"Yeah. Cancer kills you after chemo doesn't kill all the bad stuff. Dat says it's like weed killer, kills the bad stuff but a lot of the good stuff. Mom was pretty sick, but now she's an angel. Dat said she watches over us, but I never saw her yet. Actually, I don't want to see her, because Dat said I couldn't touch her anyway. Angels are spirits."

Susan nodded, content to hear this small boy's western accent, the lisp, the absolutely endearing pronunciation of ordinary Dutch words.

"How can my mom be in Heaven and be here? I don't think Dat is telling me the truth. He doesn't always. Doesn't come home when he says he will. Bertha doesn't do anything, just sits on her fat behind and looks at her phone."

Susan suppressed a laugh, her mouth twitching. This was getting quite interesting.

"My sister Sharon cries. Bertha smacks her."

Susan looked down at the small boy. He gazed out across the brown landscape, reached down to give the dog a pretzel.

"Did you tell your Dat?"

"Yeah. But he says he doesn't know who else to get. There is no one. We have to behave so she won't smack us."

Susan said nothing.

"I'm going to run away."

"You are?"

"When I'm old enough."

"Where will you go?"

"I don't know. Somewhere."

"Well, first you have to go to school, so you can learn how to get along in the world. How to add and spell and read. Then you can go somewhere to find who you want to be."

He nodded slowly, gave Wolf another pretzel.

"I don't like people. Guess I have to learn that, too, huh?"

"Might be a good idea."

They sat in a companionable silence. Susan reminded herself that every problem child had a root of bitterness or mistreatment, a lack of basic care, of simple love and caring. She felt outright fury at Isaac, whacking around in a forest somewhere, his conscience glossed over with good intentions where his children were concerned. No doubt he deserved a good smack upside his own head. Someone would have to stand up to him, make him see that his children needed him to be a responsible father.

CHAPTER 18

On opening day, Susan decided butterflies in her stomach would be welcome, instead of this dry mouth and pounding heart, feeling slightly sick to her stomach. She regretted waving away Edna's proffered breakfast sandwich, her stomach in an acidic knot.

The children arrived on bikes, with drivers, and one family drove a pony hitched to a small springwagon with two seats. The dusty playground was filled with a colorful array of little people, the girls' white bowl-shaped coverings the cutest thing she had ever seen. In Lancaster, the girls did not wear coverings until they were in eighth grade, but here they all wore them, even the smallest first grader. She recognized the pupils she had met before, but still had some she could not name.

Her heart sank when Titus and Sharon entered, later than any of the others, dropped off from an old green pickup truck, the driver waving at her from the opposite side. Titus was wearing an old short-sleeved shirt, appearing wrinkled and half-washed, as if it had been stuffed in an over-full washer and laid in a dryer too long. He wore an old pair of denims, and his bowl-shaped straw hat was bent entirely out of shape, being too tight and much too old. Sharon's covering was wrinkled and gray, her apron too short, the hem of her dress coming loose in the back. She had no shoes on. Susan watched as she stood alone, her large dark eyes watching her, then the other girls. She was the only girl in the first grade, so she stood alone, twisting her small hands in front of her.

Susan went to her, touched her shoulder.

"Hi, Sharon. I'm Susan, your teacher. I'm so glad you're in first grade."

She stared at Susan, making no effort to acknowledge her words.

"Do you know which desk is yours?"

The strange stare went on, the eyes dark and unblinking.

"Come. I'll show you."

To Susan's horror, she began to cry, a deep, primal sound of despair and hopelessness.

"Sharon, come. Don't cry. Shh."

Susan hunkered down, putting both hands on her shoulders. The little girl twisted away from her, ran to a corner, and turned her back, the crying coming in shaking sobs, uncontrollable sounds of grief.

Susan tried to console her again, noticing she had an audience of concerned faces framed in white coverings.

Suddenly, Titus was there, in all his repressed fury, his fists balled, his dark eyes flashing.

"What did you do to her?" he demanded.

"Nothing. She began to cry, is all. She's frightened, Titus."

He glared at her, but went over to his sister and put an arm around her shoulders, whispered into her ear. She shook her head and continued to cry harder than ever.

So Susan had a acute sense of failure even before she rang the bell. She wasn't going to be late starting the day, so she left Sharon and went to stand behind her desk and say a dry mouthed, "Good morning, boys and girls." She hoped it sounded upbeat, capable, with a certain amount of loving authority, as if she'd hit the right key for respect and cooperation. She was heartened by a ringing "Good morning, teacher."

Little Sharon was still in the corner, her face hidden, her back hunched as she refused to face the classroom. Susan had had to admit defeat, to allow this small child to stay in the only space she knew to be secure. She read a chapter of the Bible and they all stood to say the Lord's Prayer, then made their way to the front of the classroom to form a singing class.

There was a shifting of pupils, the tallest ones in back, the middle row, and the smallest ones in front. Books were passed out, the home-made songbooks with "Bighorn School" stenciled in thick black letters on the cover.

"We'll start in the back row, from left to right, picking a song. Your name?" She raised her eyebrows at a thin, brown face in the back row.

"Norman."

"Yes, Norman. You may pick the first song."

He picked one she had never heard of, but the oldest girl, the one named Hannah, offered to start it, which she did quite efficiently, the others chiming in with surprising harmony. Susan mouthed the words, but could not help very much at all. The second song was a hymn she knew well, "Rescue the Perishing," and she could easily sing along even as she went back to put a hand of Sharon's shoulder, trying to coax her to join the others, all to no avail.

They spent the first period getting acquainted. Susan got all the names straight, did her best to match the names to the faces, printed them all in her composition book, then asked them to fill out the blank spaces for the guest book, which would be a help to her in understanding their hobbies, their goals, and the names of their parents.

When they began, there was a decided sound of water splashing. Susan looked up from her desk and quickly realized a puddle had formed around the bare feet of the little girl in the corner, whose sniffs now turned into wails of shame and terror. Heads turned, eyes wide.

Quietly, Susan went for a roll of paper towels, then to Sharon, who was weeping without constraint. Susan mopped up the puddle, then took Sharon by the shoulders and firmly guided the wailing child outside. She heard the door open behind her and heard the hurried footsteps before she felt a hard blow on her hip, then another.

She whirled to find Titus lashing out with both fists, yelling at her, calling names, completely out of control.

Susan recognized the moment as an emergency and felt the deep inner calm she often experienced in crises.

"Titus, stop. I'm only taking her to the girls' bathroom to clean her up. She couldn't help it. Stop. Don't hit me. I'm not going to spank her. She couldn't help it. She had to go to the bathroom."

Finally he was able to hear her through his rage and stopped, his feet planted on the ground, breathing hard. Susan proceeded to the bathroom and helped Sharon, still sobbing, to get cleaned up.

When she came back, she asked Titus, "Would you mind riding Norman's bike home to get her clean underwear?"

"No, I'm not going. He'll laugh at me."

"Who?"

"Norman."

"Well, I'll ask him."

Of course, Norman said he could take the bike and Titus rode off, with Sharon back in her corner, her face hidden, the crying slowly subsiding. Class was dismissed for recess, with a stern word from Susan not to discuss any of this on the playground.

So it was a subdued group who chose to play the game prisoner's base, with furtive glances over shoulders, watching for Titus to return on Norman's bike. It was only later that Susan thought she should never have allowed him to bike alone, and was much relieved to see him enter the playground, park the bike, and hand her a plastic bread bag containing a pair of tattered girl's underwear.

To pry little Sharon from her corner and get her to go back to the bathroom took plenty of persuasion and the promise of a piece of candy, but the mission was finally accomplished, after an extra half hour of recess.

At lunch time, she was grateful to have the rule of half days the first week, an old rule from the time when children were expected to help with the first harvest on the farm. Susan found herself sighing with relief, her shoulders slumping forward as she sat at her desk.

Did any teacher ever have an opening day such as this? The worst part was not Sharon's unfortunate episode, but Susan's failure to think things through, allowing Titus to bike two miles on his own. Either way, this Isaac was going to face up to his children's needs. The whole community pitied him properly, but that was about as far as it went. She was the teacher and could see no other way except to pay that man a visit.

Dear Levi,

Well, here I am, being a real teacher now, here in the great wild West. I wish you could see the dust and the mountains and the unbelievable expanse of land, the lack of vehicles and places of business, the few homes and even fewer people . . .

She chewed on the tip of her pen, contemplating whether to say how much she actually missed him. Should she write, "Being here allows me to see how much you mean to me?" Or, "I know now you are the one and I realize how selfish I have been?" She decided on a safer approach.

Nine months seems like a long time to be so far away.

Sincerely,

Susan

She had her pen poised to write, "I love you," but could not bring herself to actually do it. "I love you" on paper was too strong a commitment. She felt as unsteady and unsure as wisps of fog on a damp morning.

Yes, definitely though, love was growing, taking root in her heart. She missed seeing him, missed his voice, sitting beside him in the buggy, knowing he loved her. Eventually, she expected, love would grow into a substantial, solid thing, and an "I love you" would be so true and genuine she'd be able to write it with a black permanent marker. But not quite yet.

SHE HIRED THE same driver, for seven o'clock in the evening, to go to Isaac's house. If she was going to be a teacher, she was going to sink her teeth into every responsibility, no matter how uncomfortable. The gentle sympathy that Isaac received from the community was fine, but someone needed to wake him up to the fact that he was neglecting his children and it was unacceptable.

She was shocked when they pulled up to a beautiful home with siding the color of a dusty meadow. It had a gray roof and a stone patio with a post-and-beam roof extending over half, comfortable chairs, and a fire pit. The grass was mowed, the shrubs tended.

"Are you sure this is Isaac Miller's place?" she asked.

"The only one."

She climbed out of the car with her assurance cut in half, wishing she hadn't come. Perhaps she had judged too quickly. Then again, a well-kept home did not automatically mean well-kept children. She approached the front door with a considerable amount of false bravado, knocked, and waited.

She knocked and waited again.

"I'll be right there."

She winced at the invasion of unnecessary volume.

She heard footsteps, then saw the towering form behind the screen door.

"Hey there, teacher. Come on in."

He stepped aside, held the screen door for her, and she felt every bit the unwelcome invader.

"Excuse me, while I help Sharon."

She stood alone, viewing the wreckage of a once beautiful home. Wolf lay on the couch, pillows and blankets beneath him, the floor strewn with clothes and toys, boots and shoes, soiled plates and forks on a coffee table. The smell of a full trash can, un-cleaned bathroom, decay and neglect permeating everything.

Dear Lord, Susan breathed.

"Okay."

He appeared in the doorway of what must have been the bathroom, little Sharon in tow, her hair wet and uncombed, a thin nightie stretched across her small body. Sharon eyed her with suspicion, a hand to her mouth.

"Hi, Sharon."

No answer.

"Say hi," Isaac said, pushing her forward.

She turned away and pulled a lock of wet hair into her mouth.

"So, what brings you? Excuse the mess."

He shook his head, ran a hand through his toweled, unkempt hair, darkened by perspiration. He smelled of diesel fuel, sweat, and dirt. His house smelled even worse.

Susan had no respect for anyone who could not keep themselves or their house decent.

"I have quite a few concerns about your children."

He sighed wearily and nodded his head toward the patio.

"Let's sit outside. I can't see good enough in here. Yeah, well. I'm not surprised."

He led her through the screened patio doors, past a grill, an assortment of junk, a pile of boots. How many boots did these people need?

"Sit down."

She sat, crossed her legs, tried to project confidence. She'd worn her best sneakers, her brightest dress, hoping she'd somehow leave an impression, a figure to be reckoned with.

She interlaced her long, slender fingers the way she imagined an experienced, competent school teacher would do in this situation.

He nodded toward her hands.

"Women's hands. I need a pair of hands like yours."

Caught completely off guard, she released her hands and curled them in her lap, as if they were an offense to them both. Her eyes slid uncomfortably to the right and landed on a plastic hanging basket with the remains of dead petunias hanging over the side. She cleared her throat, buying time till she felt composure returning.

Women's hands could do a lot with this patio, that was sure. She gave a small laugh, felt juvenile.

"These hands have plenty to do."

"I'm sure. So what's wrong with my kids?"

"Look, you're not going to brush this off. I won't let you intimidate me. Your children both have serious issues, and you need to make some changes, or you'll regret it."

His eyes narrowed, his mouth tightened.

"So what are you? Some kind of child psychiatrist, or what?" he asked gruffly, his voice mocking her.

"It doesn't take a psychiatrist to see that there's a problem when an eight-year-old wanders for miles with only his dog because he can't stand the babysitter."

"So what do you suggest?"

"Another caretaker?"

"Where?"

"I have no idea. I know anyone who cares about their children will always place their needs ahead of their own. And seemingly, you go off to work every single day and have no idea what goes on with this Bertha."

"She doesn't do much around the house, but she's good with the kids."

"No, she is not."

"And how would you know?"

"Titus told me."

His eyes met hers again, with a bit of hesitation, the defense a tiny bit evaporated.

"When did you talk to Titus?"

"I spent some time at the school before opening day and he came by. He offered some information."

"Offered? Or you dug around like the nosy school teacher you are?"

A shot of anger coursed through her. She put both feet on the ground and leaned forward, gripping the arm rests of her chair, her eyes blazing.

"You know what? It's men like you that make me thank the good Lord I'm not married. Egotistical, overconfident males make me hopping mad. Your children's emotional well-being is being compromised and you don't care one tiny bit, as long as you can hide in your logging world far away from responsibility you do not want to see."

He laughed. He actually laughed in her face.

Then he said, "I'm glad you're not married, too."

She almost burst into tears of helpless frustration.

She got up from her chair, looked at him in one sizzling glance, and told him if he wasn't going to take her seriously, she was going home. He told her to sit down and smooth her feathers.

She left, slamming the car door so hard the driver jumped.

ALL WEEKEND SHE was tormented, wondering where Titus had been when she was at his house. That great big wonderful house, gone to waste. She was never going back. If there was a problem, she would send a letter in the mail, or leave a message on his answering machine.

Titus continued to misbehave. He whispered, he threw spitballs, he made faces behind her back, and he snapped pencils in two.

She made him stay in for recess, discussed his misbehavior, and always, he promised to do better, without actual results. Sharon sat in her desk, but cried every single day. She stood apart from the other girls and refused to speak to any of them, although they flitted about like bright butterflies, asking her to come play.

The warm weather turned colder, the endless blue sky and astounding sunlight changing to a strong wind with a decided chill in it, the sun often obscured by billowing gray clouds appearing in the northwest.

With no rain, the leaves turned brittle and fell off without much color, the strong wind hurling them away in clouds of dust. Roy said one of these days the snow would come and put an end to this dust, but Edna said as dry as it was, they might not see much snow at all.

This was wishful thinking, Roy said, watching her anticipation build, waiting for the day when she would go home to Indiana.

Edna cleaned the entire house, the clothesline heavy with blankets and rugs, curtains and sheets as she swept and dusted, mopped floors, and organized drawers. In exactly two weeks, they'd be going with a vanload, Roy deciding to go with Edna, if Susan wouldn't be afraid to stay by herself, and if she could handle chores.

Susan could, she said, hiding her trepidation about being alone in this strange land. She would never get used to the open space, the sense of nothingness. The unpredictable weather.

The closest neighbor to the school was Isaac, but she'd go far beyond him if she needed help. It was being alone at home in the evening that unsettled her.

She thought of asking Levi to come for a visit. Levi and Mark and Beth. The thought of the four of them together brought a lump to her throat. The safety, the predictable good humor, the gentle light and good manners surrounding Levi. But it seemed too soon to ask them to come. She'd only just started the school year.

That evening, she was quite sure coming to Wyoming had been a mistake.

ONE DAY SHARON came up to her desk and whispered, "Look."

Susan looked at the small piece of unlined paper, where Sharon had drawn a large purple flower with a smudge of yellow in the center, a truly artistic accomplishment for one so young.

"Sharon, this is beautiful. Really pretty. Is it for me?"

"No, for my Dat," she whispered.

"Can I show the others?"

"No."

"Okay."

But she smiled a tiny smile, and Susan smiled back. When she turned away, she thought she saw the faint outline of a bruise on her cheek, but as thin and pale as the child was, she could not be sure. No use jumping to conclusions. She had to give this Bertha the benefit of the doubt, although she still remained adamant in her opinion of Isaac. She had not seen or spoken to him since that evening on the patio, which she was glad of.

She lost patience with Titus, took away his library book privileges, and gave him projects to improve his arithmetic skills. He glared at her for one whole day, but she chose to ignore him.

They played baseball at recess, intense physical games Susan looked forward to each day. It was good for all of them to have the exercise and she enjoyed the admiration and respect of the upper graders.

When Edna and Roy left for Indiana, she fought back the unsettling sense of isolation, the fear lurking in the corners of her mind. Every evening she read chapters in Psalms and asked the Lord to stay with her and protect her at night and to guide her steps during the day. But every night as darkness fell, she had a serious case of the blues.

She fed the livestock, watered them, and made sure the gates were all secured before going to her small cabin at night. She watched a pair of golden eagles one night, cavorting and tumbling through the air, a backdrop of blues and reds, the sun sliding behind the jagged peaks of the mountain, and thought surely it was a rare sight, even for the West. Mule deer could be seen just before dark, arriving like ghosts at the edge of the hayfield, when the light was barely strong enough to see them. She discussed these scenes with her pupils, asked them to contribute to the beauty of Wyoming with a written composition of two hundred words or more, to which they responded with amazing energy.

And her confidence as a school teacher expanded.

It was with this newfound confidence that she eyed Edna's bike propped in a corner of the barn, cobwebs surrounding it in a telltale display of not being used. She'd actually never seen Edna ride a bike or a horse, come to think of it. Feeling bold, Susan wiped off the dust and the cobwebs, gripped the handlebars, and drew it tentatively from the wall. It seemed to her as if the seat was up too high, but then she was fairly tall, so it should be alright.

She looked around, the quiet of the evening soothing. She was alone, so if she was clumsy, there was no one to see. She wheeled the bike carefully to the most level surface, tilted it toward her, and put one leg across, feeling the seat too high on her back. Her heart was beating hard, but she would overcome her fear in the only honest way possible.

Just get on and ride.

No, she decided. The seat was too high. She drew up her leg to get off and lower the seat, when the heel of her sneaker caught on the middle bar, throwing her on her backside with the bike on top of her.

Instantly, she leaped to her feet, yanked the bike up, and looked around. *For Pete's sake*, she thought. *A wreck before I even get on the thing.*

She looked under the seat, found the lever to adjust the height, pulled back on it and lowered it an inch or two, then tightened it again and prepared to mount the bicycle once more.

She hopped up, pushed down on the right pedal, up with the left, and she was off, the gravel crunching satisfyingly to the rotation of the tires. She tightened her grip on the handlebars, felt in full control, her feet pumping the pedals. For a moment she was amazed at her own ability, but then she tried to navigate around a pothole and lost her balance. Down she went, hard on one knee, the bike crashing into the gravel.

"Whoa, whoa there," a voice called out. A voice much too big and much too loud and thoroughly unwelcome.

CHAPTER 19

H E WAS ON THAT SNORTING MONSTER HE CALLED A HORSE. SHE glared up at him with what she hoped was a venomous stare, but he dismounted, threw the reins, and picked up the bike, then knelt at her side. He smelled. He always smelled offensive. This time it was horse. Horse sweat, that white lather that worked itself from their skin.

"You okay? You landed on your knee. Let me see."

"Get away from me."

He stood up and turned his back, while she struggled to her feet, her knee feeling as if the kneecap had been torn away. She tried to put weight on it, but realized immediately this was simply not possible. Frightened suddenly, she reached out.

"I can't walk," she said quietly.

He turned, looked at her, quiet for once.

"If you were a normal person, I'd carry you to the house, but I doubt you'd appreciate it."

"I wouldn't."

"So?"

"Give me your arm."

He obeyed, which surprised her, and she leaned heavily on his arm, hobbling along, putting a slight bit of weight on her knee. The pain was excruciating, and when she stopped, he looked down to see the blood soak into the gray of her sneaker.

"You're hurt. Look at your shoe."

Without further notice, he bent, put an arm behind her back and one behind her knees and she was being carried along, up way too high, way too tightly, and with far too much horse sweat.

She groaned silently, felt the softness of his black sweatshirt and thought sometimes God just had to place you in positions you found offensive, for your own pride to be eliminated.

Things had been going well, and now she had to put up with this lumbering giant.

Amish girls didn't go around with their knees on display, either. She wasn't about to show him hers. She wasn't going to give him the satisfaction of seeing her faint away like some delicate lady either, but when the world began to spin, then disappeared completely and she woke up on the couch confused and in pain, the last shred of her pride disintegrated like cold gray ashes.

He brought a cool cloth for her forehead, a pillow, then rolled her gently to a reclining position. She moaned with misery, and he found paper towels and a small bucket of soapy water, cleaning everything without saying a word. She closed her eyes and lay still, before she realized her dress was soaked in blood.

When he returned, he said there was no other way, he had to look at the injury. She nodded without opening her eyes, and he examined the wound, then told her he was going to Roy and Edna's, and that he'd be right back.

She propped an arm on her forehead and groaned.

Why him, of all people? Nosy man, snooping around the neighborhood like that. And where were Titus and Sharon? Probably stuck with Bertha.

He returned, finally. Said he had to take care of his horse. *What?* she thought wildly. *He's not planning on spending the night, I hope. Good grief.*

Then she felt his calloused hands, like big meaty hooks, latch on to her leg and twist this way, then that way, which irritated her to no end.

"Hurt?"

"No."

"Not broken. Hold still now. I'm going to clean it with peroxide."

"No. No you're not. That stuff burns."

"That or go to the ER. Fifty-some miles."

She lay back, threw an arm across her eyes, and gritted her teeth.

"We have to get the gravel out, too. Where's your battery lamp?"

"Top of the fridge."

The peroxide burned like fire, the probing and picking like stinging ants. At one point she sat straight up and yelled with the small amount of strength she had left, "Ow! Really, is that the best you can do?"

"Sorry."

Finally, when the light was disappearing fast, he said he'd got everything, and she felt the coolness of the triple antibiotic salve, the light settling of a gauze pad, and the accompanying adhesive tape.

He carried everything to the small kitchen table, then came to stand beside the couch.

"I hate to leave you here by yourself."

"Well, you're not staying."

He laughed.

"You're not staying here alone."

"Yes, I am."

"The only way you're staying alone is if you can show me you're capable of getting up and making yourself dinner and changing out of that bloody dress before bed."

She did not want to do that. She wanted to stay here feeling sick and washed out and for him to go away. Back to his poor children, likely wishing he was at home.

"Why don't you go home?" she asked.

"Nothing there. Children are at Abe and Louise's for tonight. They're taking them to the children's rodeo tomorrow."

"What's that?"

"What?"

"What I said. What is a children's rodeo?"

"A rodeo for children."

She said "Ha-ha," to mock him, but he was laughing at his own joke, so she doubted if he had heard her at all.

"Titus loves the sheep-riding competition. He won last year. I was really proud of him."

Before she could catch herself, she asked if she could go sometime, and he said she could, probably. If horses and bull-riding were interesting to her.

They sat in silence, she determined he would leave before she got off the couch, he determined to stay till she got up. Neither one gave in, so the light steadily diminished as the chill crept over the land, and darkness slowly pushed the light of another day into the west.

Finally, she drifted off to sleep, woke up to find him gone, and was immediately grateful. She swung both legs off the couch and sucked in an astounded breath as pain shot up her leg, but gritted her teeth and made it to the bathroom, gripping furniture, doorframes, and anything she could.

From the kitchen came a deep "You okay?"

Oh mercy. There he still was. *Whatever,* she thought.

"Yes," she ground out.

She heard the whistle of the tea kettle.

She removed the blood-stained dress and washed herself as best as she could. He was not going to see her in her night clothes, but her clean dresses were in the closet in her bedroom. She considered this dilemma, before realizing she was thoroughly stranded in the bathroom, without her dress and with the determined mindset that she would wear one. She put on her robe, crept silently to the dark bedroom, groped for a dress, and slipped it on over her head, before returning slowly and painfully to the couch.

"Tea? Honey or milk, or both?"

"Both."

He brought a steaming mug, grabbed two pillows and arranged them behind her back, then sat in the chair opposite and watched as she reached for the mug.

She sipped it, grateful for the strength she felt.

"You know, you're the first woman I know that sleeps in her dress."

"I sleep in my dress every night."

She tried hard to keep from laughing with him.

"You really do not want me to stay."

"No, I don't."

"If I'd known I'd be here in your place, I'd have showered and shaved before I rode over. I've been working with the horses all day."

"Why did you ride over?"

"I wanted to borrow a bit from Roy. He has a pulley bit."

"What's that?"

"A bit where you control a crazy horse."

"Probably something cruel."

A battery clock makes no noise at all unless a person is completely alone in the dead of night, then the ticking sound is pronounced, as if it needs to make itself known. But it was all they had to listen to, the wind having died down and she wishing he would leave without actually wanting to be rude and asking him, again, to go.

"Don't you ride in the dark?"

"Of course."

He paused, then said, "Okay, look, I'm trying to get up enough courage to ask you what you think I do so wrong with the children. It bugs me, the way you came to my house, and we both got so mad."

"Does it really matter to you what I think?"

She closed her eyes, too weary to think about trying to get any advice through his bad attitude, but when she heard the firm opening and closing of the door, his footsteps across the porch and down the walkway, she was surprised, then miffed.

He was the crankiest, most unpredictable man. But he had been here when she needed someone, although she figured she would have managed alone if she'd really had to. She'd have gotten to the house somehow.

He'd go home, considering himself the handsome knight who had rescued the fair damsel in distress. It just happened that the fair lady had a love of her own living in Pennsylvania, one who seemed much too far away at this lonely hour.

Levi. That fresh, woodsy scent. The cleanliness of a freshly laundered lemon yellow polo shirt. His spotless buggy, the groomed horse and gleaming black harness. His impeccable manners. Most of all, the courage and faith in God to allow her to follow her heart, her mind, her sense of adventure to teach school in Wyoming. Truly, he had given his own self up for her, instructed well in the teachings of the Bible.

As more time went by, she appreciated him more fully, realizing he was the one. If she tried, she could not imagine Levi requiring anything difficult. It was hard to picture him making bad decisions, or hung up with depression, or embarking on some wild goose chase to Virginia. Levi was highly intelligent, a blessing to the community, willingly chipping in with manual labor at the benefit auctions or any social gathering. She could also appreciate the fact she was overcoming her selfishness and fear of marriage. Suddenly, the nine months of teaching seemed a long, long time, and the thought of returning to Pennsylvania, the brilliant light at the end of a long dark winter.

She fell asleep, dreaming of her return to Lancaster. She moved the knee and was pulled into a harsh world filled with throbbing pain, the white gauze pad soaked with fresh blood. She was on the couch, the battery lamp on the table, so she had no choice but to get up and retrieve it, which she accomplished with gritted teeth.

She blinked as the light cast a white glare on her surroundings and groaned to discover there were no extra gauze pads. Typical man. He didn't think farther than the length of his nose.

Well, a tea towel would have to do. She had a light-colored linen one in the drawer. By the time it was applied on top of the bandage, she was quite ready to collapse on the couch, snap off the light, and go back to sleep.

She awoke a few times to hear coyotes howling and yipping in the distance, the dark house so dark it seemed as if a giant sock had been pulled over it. Here in the West, if there was no moon, the dark nights were thick and black. In Lancaster, there were always neighboring lights, traffic, an awareness of fellow human beings inhabiting the same space. Here, she might as well have been the only person on the planet, with no indication of any living soul save for the coyote's primal sounds, which did nothing to comfort her.

In the morning, the light was welcome, the rising of the sun a blessing. Her knee was stiff and sore, the tea towel ruined by a red stain, but mercifully, the bleeding had stopped. She found she couldn't bend her knee without a fresh flow of blood, so she hobbled around, one leg held straight, swinging it out to the side, walking awkwardly.

She glared at the barn, irked at Roy and Edna, to leave her here to do the feeding. How was she ever going to manage?

The air was freezing cold, the wind picking up. She thought of the mare, the new foal. Nothing to do but get out there.

The wind tore at her covering, whipped her skirt. Immediate she felt goose bumps on her spine. The misery of Wyoming was definitely the wind. Always, it blew, moaned around buildings, whipped horses' manes, threw clean laundry into disarray, dancing and cavorting on clotheslines like mad people. It stung through the gauze pad and froze her fingers and face before she reached the safety of the barn.

When the mare nickered, and she found the new foal rocking on her spindly legs, she forgot her woes to take in the sight she loved so much. Horses were a part of her life. Good, dependable, well-trained horses felt familiar. Roy took good care of his driving horses, and one good riding horse, a buckskin with a black mane and tail.

She dumped the oats and corn mixture into the feed boxes, fed blocks of hay, and filled the watering trough before opening gates to allow them to drink, stroking and petting the skittish little colt, smoothing manes, and running a hand along the warm, silky spot beneath it. She talked to them, before putting them back in their space, then went to check the water supply for the cattle.

Cold, her knee throbbing, half sick to her stomach, she made her way back to the house, collapsed into a kitchen chair, and ran a hand across her forehead. Sunday, and she was expected to do chores two more times before going to school in the morning.

She made scrambled eggs, added salt and pepper, ate half before heading for the couch and falling asleep immediately. She awoke to find the gauze pad stuck to her painful knee and that she had a headache and a powerful irritation at Roy and Edna, Isaac, and Wyoming in general.

Why couldn't he have had the common sense to leave fresh gauze and adhesive tape? What was he thinking?

By late afternoon, she realized the gauze would have to come off, and she'd have to use more of the tea towels. She found duct tape in a small drawer with thumb tacks, screwdrivers, and flyhangers, so she set to work applying hot compresses to loosen the gauze. She was shocked to see the gaping wound. She applied the tea towel, slapped duct tape to hold it, and went out to do chores.

She watched the driveway, wondering how he could leave her without checking up on her. Surely he wondered how she was doing, alone with these chores and an obvious wound. But then, he had his children today, and likely never even thought of her, which was fine with her.

She called home, swallowing the lump in her throat to hear her father's voice, then spoke to Mark and Beth, then her mother and Elmer.

All the hometown news made her long to be there, to be a part of the humming beehive of activity that was Lancaster County. Weddings were coming, benefit auctions, get-togethers for the holidays were being planned.

"Susan, Levi misses you terribly. Mark says he's not himself at all."

Susan smiled to herself, a smile of victory, of accomplishment. So she had done exactly the right thing, hadn't she? He was so in love with her, he found it hard to go on without her, which was a good thing.

Before they began a serious relationship, they would have a foundation built of faith in one another, faith in God and His leading.

He had led her to this place to find her heart, and she had found it.

"I miss him too, Beth."

"Oh, good. You're serious, right?"

"Yes, I am."

Susan smiled as she held the receiver away from her ear, the squeal of excitement too shrill to be comfortable.

"Oh, Susan! I can't *wait* for you to come home. We'll spend every weekend together, we four. And after we're married, we'll still do that, make ourselves at home at each other's places. In fact, Susan, we'll grow old together, won't we?"

"We will."

Life seemed suddenly safe and predictable, completely laid out in an understandable sequence. The pattern had been cut by her parents and their parents before them, to get married, raise a family, make a living, live among acquaintances you had known since birth, a way of life holding the promise of a secure future.

DOING CHORES, GETTING dressed, pinning her cape and apron—all of it seemed impossibly hard, her knee red and painful. She set her mouth in a determined line, was ready by the time the driver pulled in, and set about starting her day of teaching.

It was bitterly cold for October, the air holding a puzzling quality. There was the scent of mountains and pines, but something else too, making the hair on her arms tickle. The woodstove at the schoolhouse was cranky, smoking and spewing ashes, which made her long for the turn of a knob on a propane gas stove.

The children were all sympathetic, examining the tea towel and duct tape with serious faces. Titus and Sharon were late again, their coats unbuttoned, faces red from the cold. Sharon's hair was straggly, uncombed, and Titus's shirt was wearing the unmistakable dribbles of cereal and milk. Sharon cried, putting her head in her hands and sobbing, unable to accomplish the addition in her workbook.

Susan comforted her, sitting with her at the table adjoining the desk, but it seemed as if the lesson was overwhelming.

Titus raised his hand.

"I'll help her."

Susan frowned. "You have your own work, Titus."

"I'm done."

Susan knew he wasn't, so she walked over and peered over his shoulder. As she suspected, his arithmetic had barely begun, so she told him firmly he needed to stay busy and finish his own work.

She was shocked when Titus brought a small fist down on his desktop, scattering papers, pens, and pencils, his face a mask of fury.

Without thinking, she brought a hand down to grip his shoulder, which only increased the frenzy. He slid out of his desk and whipped both arms in a furious assault, hitting Susan's legs, her stomach and hip, screaming and crying incoherently. Little Sharon increased her own sobs, with the remaining children sitting in a confused silence.

"Titus, no. Don't."

It was all Susan could think to say, reaching out to subdue the child. One good hard whack to her injured knee, and Susan sank to a desk, half sitting, half standing as she reeled with pain.

Mercifully, Darryl Miller's Harry, the oldest boy in class, subdued Titus by taking him in a stronghold, as he kicked and cried out with rage and childish sobs.

Order was restored slowly. Titus went to his desk, red-faced and disheveled.

Something was way out of line in that house, and she was going to find out what it was. Maybe it was Bertha, but she did not rule out Isaac being an abusive father, taking out his frustration at losing his wife. Unable to accept his loss.

She kept them both in for recess, in spite of fearing another tantrum. Sharon dissolved into another fit of weeping, and Titus glared like a cornered rat.

She faced them both, sitting on a desktop. The wind rattled the roof edging; sounds of children on the playground filled the empty stillness. The sun shone through the east windows, casting rectangles of light on the pine floor.

"Titus, can you tell me what went wrong this morning?" she began, feeling her way as if on thin ice.

A belligerent look, the slight lift of one shoulder.

"Sharon?"

Fresh sobs.

"Sharon, look. We can't have you crying like this every day. Why do you cry?"

"She doesn't know how to add numbers," Titus said, in a flat monotone.

Susan looked at Sharon, who had her face in her hands, shuddering with more sobs. Impatience pounded at her temples.

"Sharon, you can always raise your hand and I'll help you, okay?"

Sharon uncovered her face, her pretty lips in a full pout, and shook her head from side to side.

"She doesn't want to do that," Titus offered.

"Why not?"

"Because."

"Here in school, those are the rules. If you need help with a problem, you need to raise your hand."

Again, the pout and wild head shaking from side to side.

"She doesn't want to."

"Well, I guess that means she'll not be able to finish first grade. Sharon, if you want to continue coming to school, you'll have to learn to obey the rules. If you don't want to do that, you'll have to stay at home."

Indignant, red-faced, Titus blurted out, "But our mother died."

"Which is a very unfortunate thing. But we still have to go on. Sharon, I'm sorry for you that your mother is gone, I really am. But the fact that you had to go through this loss doesn't mean you don't have to do arithmetic. I'm sure if your mother was here, she would want to you to be good in school."

"Not my Dat. He doesn't care. He don't like teachers. He says they're about as irritating as coyotes," Titus said, a touch of pride and a lot of audacity in his voice.

Susan swallowed her outrage. "He said that?"

"Yeah. Last year." Proud of his father.

"Alright. Well, I'll have a talk with him. Now, Titus. I want you to know I am truly sorry for the loss of your mother. But if you ever display another tantrum like this morning, I'll have to call in the school board and they'll have to deal with you."

"Huh. Dat's on the school board."

Susan chose to ignore the statement and turned to Sharon and began to explain addition, bringing out a jar of colorful plastic clothespins for her to sort in numbers, leaving Titus staring at her with a puzzled expression.

Classes resumed without incident, with Susan being more convinced these two motherless children did indeed need love, but a love that set boundaries, a love that could no longer take the death of their mother as an excuse to be allowed special privilege in school. And a very, very absent father, a selfish, self-absorbed giant of a man who handed his children over to a lazy, incompetent caregiver who had no heart for these children at all.

The whole situation would have to be addressed again. Seemingly, her first visit had accomplished nothing. She felt the resolve building, felt the clenching of her fists, and the determination to fight this man until he saw the light.

CHAPTER 20

INFECTION SET INTO HER KNEE, FORCING SUSAN TO CALL ON TWO OF the children's parents, Trisha and Millie's Abe and Louise, who welcomed her gladly. They exclaimed over the horribly swollen and heated knee, called a driver, and accompanied her to the Urgent Care in Wayne.

She was reduced to tears of gratitude, accepted the kindness, swallowed antibiotics, and applied professional bandages and an expensive salve that healed the wound like a miracle.

Roy and Edna returned, weary from days of van traveling, glad to be home to resume their life. Or Roy was. Edna remained in a deep-seated funk, kept to herself, and said very little to anyone.

So Susan kept the trouble at school to herself, sent a note home with Titus that was never delivered, and finally hired a driver in a fit of frustration and went to his house at seven o'clock on a Wednesday evening.

Titus came to the door.

"Hi."

No answer, only a sullen stare.

"How are you, Titus?"

A shrug, another baleful glance.

"Is your father here?"

A slight shake of his head from side to side.

"Where is he?"

Another shrug.

"Is Sharon here?"

Real fear made her voice rise, her breathing accelerate.

"Yeah."

"Bertha?"

"No. She goes home at six."

Speechless, Susan tried to peer inside, but the door was opened only wide enough for Titus to appear.

"Have you been by yourself for long?"

Another shrug.

"Look. I'm coming in. Is that okay with you?"

He stepped aside, an unspoken welcome.

She was confronted with the jumble of misplaced items, the dirty floors and smeared windows, but this time the floor and countertops were even worse.

A sour smell came from the vicinity of the trashcan, and the ripe smell of an unwashed dog hovered over the entire house. None of this was as troubling as the fact that these two small children were completely alone.

Nervous energy compelled her to empty the sink, clattering dishes, scraping pans and caked-on bowls. She fired questions, received sullen answers. She asked Sharon to pick up toys, received a resounding no, a vehement shake of the small blond head.

A dual-wheeled pickup truck roared up to the house, diesel fumes spouting from two smokestacks. It ground to a halt, a door was flung open, and Isaac sprang out. He reached on the back to extract a monstrous chain saw, two five-gallon buckets, and a hard hat.

A hand went up, and the truck roared off.

Titus ran to the door, the expression on his face changing immediately. Isaac put the tools of his trade on the stone patio, came through the side door, and stopped dead in his tracks. Slowly, he hung up his outer jacket, or what remained of it, then turned, letting his shoulders slump.

He said one word. "Caught."

"That's right," she said sharply.

"I'm sorry."

Susan drew herself up to her full height, crossed her arms at the waist, and gave him the full benefit of her green eyes as he sank into a kitchen chair. He saw her thick auburn hair, the white heart shape of her covering, the tiny freckles on her nose that were obvious as her face paled with anger.

"You can't go on this way."

For a long moment, their eyes held and locked, hers with righteous determination, his with defense. In the corner, Wolf thumped his tail on the floor, spreading dust and the odor of dog through the kitchen.

"And who are you to tell me how to live my life?" he asked, his voice thick with bitterness.

"You'll wish you listened to me after one of your children is kidnapped or has a fatal accident."

"I told you before. Wolf will never let anyone in the house."

"I'm going to alert the authorities if you don't change things immediately. You are in danger of having your children taken from you. How would you feel if they were placed in foster homes?"

He snorted, got angrily to his feet.

"They wouldn't be. Look, if you'd be so kind, I'm starved. Did Bertha make something, Titus?"

"We had chicken noodle soup."

He nodded at a Campbell's soup can, the lid still attached by a thin wisp.

"Was it good?" Isaac asked, making a fatherly attempt.

"It was okay. I ate Honey Nut Cheerios."

"Me, too!" Sharon shouted from the living room.

"What's here?" he asked Susan.

"How would I know?"

"Alrighty. I'll get something. I have to wash up. We laid the skidder on its side," he chuckled, as if it was quite the accomplishment. "I'm covered in diesel fuel."

She didn't give him the satisfaction of an answer. He was a walking fuel-covered disaster, smelling to high heaven. His blond hair was

matted and streaked with it, the front of his shirt and trousers slick with
the detestable stuff.

He disappeared into the bedroom, or what she guessed was in that
vicinity. She returned to her dishwashing until she heard the steady
sound of the shower, then opened the refrigerator door, unnerved to
find an alarming collection of rotten vegetables lying in thick gray
slime, packages of cheese left to dry out, a large amount of Pepsi and
Mountain Dew, a gallon of milk past its expiration date, bowls of food
covered in gray fungus. But there were eggs, and a bit of questionable
ham, cheese, and one green pepper with a half of it still firm.

She made an omelet, put bread in the broiler of the gas stove for
toast. She noticed the colorful dishes, the heaviness of the utensils. His
wife must have had expensive taste in her choice of dishes and cutlery.

When the door to the bathroom opened, she set the skillet on the
table, added the plate of toast and jelly, then moved away to join Sharon
in the living room. She was engrossed in a book, pointing a finger,
mumbling to herself, so Susan sat stiffly, wishing she could walk out the
door and never come back, simply wash her hands of this whole needy
mess and go back home to her normal life.

He looked at her. "You made this?"

"Who else?" she answered, with what she hoped was enough
disapproval.

He didn't answer, but bent his head and prayed. She blinked,
surprised.

He lifted his head, upended the whole skillet over his plate, and
wolfed it all down in two minutes, with Titus hanging over the side of
the table for a slice of toast. He pushed back his chair, went to the pantry for a covered cake pan, and proceeded to cut a chunk of cake and
inhale that before drinking a glass of milk, making a face, and lifting
the plastic jug to squint at the date.

"I don't know why she can't keep fresh milk here."

It was the perfect opening, so Susan walked over to the table, pulled
out a chair, and sat down.

He sighed, tilted his chair back, ran a hand through his thick wet hair. He was clean, for the first time she'd ever seen him, and there was a difference. His blond beard was trimmed evenly, his shirt was an unlikely faded brown, but clean. She denied the scent of him, a mixture of soap, laundry detergent, and something powerful.

"Alright. Let me have it."

"You have to get rid of Bertha. She is clearly not capable. You need someone who's going to actually watch the kids and who can do something about . . . this." She spread her hands to indicate the mess around her.

"I know, I know. But who else?"

"I have no idea. I'm new here."

"There are sixteen families, all fairly young, with families. A few fifteen and sixteen-year-olds who wouldn't consider keeping children and running a house. The church women supply an occasional meal or cake or something. We're making do."

"You're in denial."

"Is that what you call it?"

"Yes."

"So tell me what to do. I know things aren't ideal."

"The children need you."

"But I have to go to work."

"I realize that. But when you're home, are you here for them?"

"What's that supposed to mean?"

"Obviously, you're not much of a father."

"Ouch." Then, "Didn't anyone ever teach you manners? Is that the way you Lancaster people operate? Just *blotch* (throw) everything out there? I'm beginning to think there's a reason why you don't have a boyfriend."

That comment was like salt to a wound.

"I'll have you know, I do have a boyfriend. Sort of. It's just not official until I make up my mind, and being here in Wyoming has done just that. I can hardly wait to return to my home and begin the relationship I wasn't sure I wanted before."

For a long moment, a thick silence hung between them, an invisible curtain of protected emotion. Suddenly, his eyes lit up, the dark brown dancing with golden light.

"I know what. I have just the answer we both need. Since you are in love, totally taken, there would be no strange looks if you were to move in as my *maud* (maid), right? The relationship strictly platonic. The widower and his maud. It's done all the time."

"But . . ."

"I know, I know. You can't stand me. That's okay. You don't impress me much either, so it's perfect."

"But I'll be gone in less than nine months."

He sat, lifted one hip to dig in his pocket for his small pen knife, then set to work on cleaning diesel fuel from the rims of his nails.

She grimaced, hating the sound of the blade on the undersides of his nails. She watched the way his large hands gripped the miniature knife, wondering at the thick callouses on his thumb.

"By then, I may have found a wife," he said quietly.

"You . . . have someone in mind?" Susan asked.

"I do."

"Well, then. I'll have to think about it."

Now she knew he was not considering her, or even liked her much, it threw the situation in a whole different light. What would it be like to have free rein with his beautiful home? And the children. These poor children.

But would she be able to handle them? Sharon and her constant sniveling and sobbing, the uncontrollable Titus . . . it seemed like too much. How would she teach school and take on motherly duties in the evening? To love someone else's children was a daunting prospect, plus putting up with a distant and uncaring father.

He nodded, finally. "You think about it."

"I came here to make you promise to replace Bertha, and to get professional help for Titus. I know you can afford it."

One eyebrow went up, a hand through his hair.

"And where, in this great wild West, will you find a counselor for a seven-year-old? Besides, how do you know he needs anything?"

And Susan told him, in detail, and was surprised to find his brown eyes turn liquid with unshed tears.

"These children are hurting," he said, in a strange, choked voice.

"But you can't rectify the death of their mother by allowing them to go undisciplined and unloved," she whispered, glancing toward the living room where Titus had gone to join his sister.

"Why do you keep insisting on me not loving my children?"

"You don't. Your first love is your job."

She could see him wrestling with his anger. He got up, rooted through the remaining dishes until he found the coffee pot, filled it and set it on the stove.

He banged it, banged the lid, and Susan felt strangely calm.

"I don't know how you can come in here and have enough nerve to tell me this stuff. It is actually none of your business. Isn't a man allowed to have an interest in his job?"

"Of course. If he balances it with time with his children."

He looked at the clock.

"When's your driver coming?"

"Nine."

He was relieved to see her go, and she was glad to leave. She thought he'd probably back out of his suggestion that she become his maud, but that was fine with her.

SNOW FELL THE following day, a wet, heavy snow turning the world a dazzling white for one forenoon before the October sun melted it away, leaving the playground a fudge-colored quagmire of sticky, slippery mud clinging to boots and bike tires, embedding horses' hooves in the wettest areas.

Edna was under the weather, and Susan found herself doing laundry and dishes after correcting papers. She listened halfheartedly to Edna's whining about Indiana, rejoicing in her own deliverance of returning to Pennsylvania.

How easy it had all been. How very wise of Levi, to allow her this space. Oh, the wonder of having reached the happy decision, the faith in God's leading. It was nothing short of a miracle.

For one, she could observe firsthand the struggles these women had to endure. Edna's battle to reach contentment was visible every day, the submission she had carried like a flag in the beginning, often flying at half staff or not at all. If Roy felt unloved and unwanted, could it be any different, having gnawed away at his wife's resolve until she gave in?

Yes, none of that would ever be Susan's lot in life. She wouldn't allow it.

She received a long, emotional letter from her sister Kate in Virginia. With disbelief, she read between the lines, the aching heart, the struggle to give in to Dan's wishes, his saying God was leading him to leave the Amish way of life, to embrace the Scriptures more fully. They had been excommunicated swiftly, the conservative bishop wasting no time in expelling the erring ones. Kate found herself cast into a culture in which she had to reinvent herself as a Southern Baptist.

It was a painful, guilt-ridden existence, knowing she inflicted pain and dishonor on her parents and siblings. She'd cut her hair, dressed in worldly clothes, although she clung to skirts. She was studying for her driver's license.

Five pages of deep emotion, swaying from Amish life to unexplored freedom that in the end, probably wouldn't be freedom at all.

"Oh Susan," she wrote, over and over.

To follow Dan wherever he went was right, wasn't it? Or should she have broken the family foundation for her children and stayed Amish if he refused?

Who could know for sure?

Susan wept. She read the letter through eyes blurred with tears, spent days trying to visualize her dearest sister. It seemed like it had happened so fast. She knew Dan had talked about leaving the Amish, but she never imagined it would happen so swiftly. But perhaps he would be content now, his depression lifted, and Kate would have a better life.

She dialed the number Kate had supplied and was relieved to find Kate sounding strong. She drank in the cadence of her words, tried to be reasonable as she justified her decision to join Dan. Yes, she loved him, had always loved him truly, had been a helpmeet to him with his battle with depression and alcohol. He had been saved in the Baptist church, and stood by, staunch in her support.

Her parents were the hardest part, knowing the disappointment they created for them. Rose and Liz were furious.

In the end, Susan pledged her undying love to Kate, said she would never condemn her, ever, and told her the story of her discovered love for Levi, the offer Isaac gave her, his troubled children.

And that night, Susan wept for her sister leaving behind their beloved culture, the upbringing in an Amish home, the heritage.

But she was determined to remain broad-minded, understanding of Dan and his conflict with Amish ways and rules.

She shared all this with Edna over a plate of cream-filled doughnuts on a Saturday morning, taking away her self-pity while she related the story of Kate's life.

Edna slurped her heavily creamed coffee, nodded her head as she listened, and said yes, yes, some men simply couldn't be happy listening and obeying. Or women. They'd have to find contentment in another church, which sometimes proved elusive.

She polished off her second doughnut and wiped her hands on a paper towel before brushing off the spray of confectioner's sugar from her dress front.

"I have enough struggle with myself. It takes me a few weeks to give myself up again when I come back from Indiana. I know Roy loves it here, and would never go back, but it's just not the same for me. I have times when I desperately wish I wouldn't have given in in the first place. But you can't look back. I'll be alright again. It's just these long cold winters. It gets to me. You're lucky, going back home in May."

Yes, she agreed. She was.

She opened the subject of going to live with Isaac as his maud.

"Maud?" Edna shrieked.

Perplexed, Susan looked at her, all innocence and light.

"How can you possibly sit there and say you'll be his maud?"

"What are you talking about?"

"He's a very attractive man who needs a wife."

"He has someone."

"What?"

Her own woes forgotten, Edna lent an understanding ear, especially after Susan confessed about her decision with Levi.

"So call him and tell him," she prodded.

"No, I'm going to wait until May. When I can see him in person. It will be so much better. And I want to be one hundred percent positive."

"I think you are now."

"I am."

"So who in the world is this woman Isaac is thinking of?"

Susan laughed, feeling refreshed and lighthearted after her coffee and doughnuts with Edna. It had taken the edge off her sorrow and disappointment about Dan and Kate, realizing the world went on, Kate was still her sister.

It was the excommunication and shunning that made it so hard. She knew for many, it was serious business, but for others, not so much. The degree of shunning varied hugely from family to family, with most of those who chose a more liberal way of life still welcomed for a visit, the ties never completely severed.

Edna told her that in the western Amish way, the excommunication was lifted after a year or more, as long as the person or couple was an upstanding member of a Christian church. Susan was amazed, never having known that.

"How nice," she mused, and found herself wishing she could have that liberty with her sister Kate. Edna nodded, watched her face closely, but thought Susan could close off any window into her own emotions quite effectively.

As it was, Dan and Kate striking out on their own threw Susan's family into an uproar, with Dat finally speaking with authority, telling Rose and Liz that love would prevail. In spite of keeping the ordnung, they could love one another, keep judgment where it belonged—with God, and God alone. Liz and Rose fizzled out like a small fire with water tossed on it and order was restored. But still Susan received letters from both Liz and Rose, followed by phone calls, with updates on Dan's behavior and shrieks of outrage and frustration.

Only then did Susan allow a smidgen of doubt to enter her mind, wondering if she ever really did want to marry anyone. Here was Kate, being hauled to a new and different culture, bravely copying hairstyles and clothes of which she knew nothing, following her beloved Dan. Here was Isaac, death ripping his beloved away, leaving him searching for something he could not find in his work.

Life was just one big, fat risk.

But school was going well, and for this bit of stability, she was grateful. She found her relationship with her upper graders blossoming, and agreed to have a party for Thanksgiving, which resulted in the hopping up and down and hand clapping of sixteen pupils, requiring quite a bit of bell tapping and admonishing before they settled down.

The weather turned seriously cold, with the cranky woodstove's draft turned on high. She almost burned the schoolhouse down on a windy day when the chimney caught fire. Isaac had to come to the school on a Saturday to make sure the fire liner was fit to use again, but Susan stayed away, knowing he'd tell her a thing or two about wood fires, thinking himself superior.

He forgot about the rodeo, until the week after, and sent a note with Titus to apologize.

Why bother? Susan thought. *I don't care about some dumb rodeo.* But in fact, she sort of did care. She'd looked forward to the event, especially watching Titus and the sheep riding contest.

And she thought how right she was about him. Married to his work.

Titus continued to throw unnecessary fits of anger, but none matched the one where he had hit her when her knee was injured. She made sure Sharon could grasp every lesson, which resulted in a small amount of trust from Titus. She consoled herself after yet another fit was thrown, thinking it wasn't as bad as the one prior.

One day, Titus walked into the classroom, Sharon in tow, holding out a flat, smooth rock almost as black as coal. He told her to hold out her hand, and he laid it gently in her palm.

"I found it in the creek," he said.

Susan shifted it to her opposite hand and turned it over to examine it.

"It's really beautiful."

"I know. You know why it's so smooth? The water rolls these rocks around."

"Really?"

Sharon stood beside her brother, nodding when he nodded, her eyes shining. Their teeth needed brushing, their coats washing, and she found herself hoping Isaac had decided to give her a try. She knew she could make a difference outwardly, but could she really ever feel the right kind of love for these two unkempt, temperamental little ones? They needed a mother, not just a maud. She'd be leaving them in the spring, which seemed unfair. She would wait, stay reined in, especially knowing Isaac had his sights set on a new wife soon.

She prayed for them all and comforted herself with the fact she'd be returning to normal life in a number of months, though she found it puzzling that she cared so much whether Isaac would want her as his maud.

Any normal girl would love to clean up that house. Even live in it. It was the house, she decided, when she felt herself growing anxious.

Seven months wasn't a very long time to see what she could do with restoring it to its former state, so when Isaac sent a note with Titus saying he'd ask Bertha to leave, she immediately accepted the position of housekeeper. She told herself time would go faster if she stayed extremely busy, and she had full intentions of proving her worth to that man and all his superiority.

CHAPTER 21

SHE HAD ONLY A FEW BELONGINGS TO THROW IN THE BACK OF THE Ford Explorer before receiving a big hug from Edna and a meaningful handshake from Roy.

As the couple stood and watched the red vehicle leave in a cloud of dust, Roy said she'd be back. She'd get the woolies of that Isaac in a few weeks. He wouldn't give her a month. And Edna told him to hush, they could at least give the poor girl the benefit of the doubt. He put his arm around her ample waist and she leaned into him and was glad for the comfortable stability of a long marriage, living in Wyoming or not. Life had its ups and downs, and Susan had already experienced more than her share, so she'd stay strong, she felt pretty sure.

The little cabin seemed dark and empty, but Susan said she'd invite Edna over as soon as the house was decent, so that was a comfort. That, and the fact that she had her own personal little soap opera playing out in her mind. This would all prove interesting indeed.

SUSAN FOUND MOVING in quite awkward, with Isaac taking her upstairs to show her the room and bathroom she would be occupying, then showing her a framed photograph of his wife, a short, plump woman with a pretty face, eyes as blue as the sky. Pale skin, so womanly, so unlike her own tanned, freckled face.

She hardly knew how to find the proper words and just mumbled something about her beauty, and Isaac choked up and went down the stairs, leaving her to distribute her clothes in drawers and on hangers.

The room was pretty enough, in a roughrider, western sort of way.

She didn't like the print of the quilt but was grateful to feel the good solidness of an expensive mattress. Everything was coated with dust.

Titus and Sharon came up the stairs, shy, uncertain what needed to be said. She smiled at them, told them to come in, that they were allowed to watch.

It was hard to grasp, the fact she was unpacking again so soon after having moved into the small cabin. She felt she had disappointed Edna, but there was a need here, and a genuine one. Her upbringing had taught her well in the way of freely offering to help, especially where children were concerned. She'd have to do the best she could with Isaac, which for now would likely be staying out of his way as he wallowed in extended grief and self-pity, throwing himself into logging and basically ignoring his children.

"How come you wear those black things?" Sharon asked, as Susan hung her bib aprons on hangers alongside her dresses.

"They're our aprons we wear in Lancaster."

"Mam never wore one of those."

"No, I guess not."

"Dat is working today," Titus said suddenly.

"Yes. He left after I arrived, right?"

"Yup."

Susan felt a sense of encouragement after her belongings were unpacked and put into place. The house was large, intimidating, so very much in need of a thorough housecleaning, which seemed to slap her in the face with reality. Now she was both a teacher and responsible for a home and children. She went to the kitchen, made a mental note of devising a schedule, somehow. She'd have to leave school as quickly as possible in order to have a hot meal on the table when he came home, then grade papers, plus cleaning, laundry, and the children's needs. Isaac could take care of himself apart from family meals.

She stood at a window, allowing herself the pleasure of appreciating the view before her. Fences, the barn, the sun brightening the Bighorn Mountains, the shadows creating layers of light and dark, the snow on the peaks like frosting applied sparingly. A line of fir trees like jagged teeth on a broken comb. Horses grazing, manes and tails moving in the eternal wind, the brown, yellow, and green grass rippling in the same direction.

She wondered who had designed and built the barn. It was an immense building, with a gray steel roof, weathered board siding, cupolas, fancy doors, a post-and-beam porch. How could he possibly have an area that size occupied by animals? He'd have to own at least forty or fifty horses.

She tore herself away from the few moments of luxury, the moments of taking in her new surroundings, allowing herself to ask the questions likely to go unanswered. Either the man was chest-deep in debt, or he'd had the means to build a home this size.

She wrinkled her nose as she lifted a smelly dishcloth, emptied the sink before filling it with hot water and dish soap. She frowned at cast iron skillets with burnt remains of something, eggshells and spilled milk, caked-on cereal in bowls, soggy paper towels and burnt matches.

Really. Burnt matches. It was the year 2021. What was wrong with using a small BIC lighter? She snorted softly.

From her elbow came a soft lisp. "You have a booger."

She sniffed, looked around for a box of Kleenex, found there were none, and resorted to paper towels. She smiled wryly at Sharon.

"Sorry."

Sharon shrugged, before asking if it was alright if she dried dishes, then pushed a chair to the sink and climbed up on it. Susan cut off the irritation that rose to the surface, needing the space Sharon had taken, or in general terms, simply wishing she'd go play and leave her to get the work done. When Susan did not start a conversation, Sharon looked up and asked if she couldn't wash dishes and talk at the same time.

"Yes, of course," Susan said, smiling.

"Don't you have anything to say?" Sharon persisted.

"What do you want to talk about?"

"Titus kills rabbits."

"He does?"

"Yes. Him and Wolf."

"Where are they now?" Susan asked, suddenly aware of the boy's disappearance.

"Who knows? They come and go. We hardly ever know where he is. Bertha watches stuff on her phone. She lets me watch stuff."

"What kind of stuff?" Susan asked.

"Cartoons. I like Paw Patrol. And Baby Shark."

"Mmm."

"I'll miss Bertha and her phone. No more shows. I loved to watch them. Bertha was nice. She brought red licorice and M&Ms."

"Okay. Dishes done," Susan said, without extending the Bertha conversation. She had no phone to entertain the child, and had no intention of plying her with candy.

She was alarmed at the lack of affection she felt for Sharon. If she wanted to replace the questionable nanny skills of Bertha, she'd better come up with a plan that included more than cleaning the house. She didn't need to pretend to love them like a mother, but she needed to make the children feel that she genuinely cared. Which she did, didn't she?

She worked hard, all afternoon, starting in his bedroom and bathroom, appalled at the condition of his king-sized bed sheets, the mounds of soiled clothes thrown into corners and on chairs, the dust and cobwebs, the amazing amount of soap buildup in the shower-tub combination.

She enjoyed stuffing soiled clothes into hampers, dusting, wiping down cobwebs, putting clean sheets on the enormous bed. Obviously, his wife had loved the color purple, with a large amount of artificial flowers of that color in vases, on wreaths. Purple towels, purple rugs, sprays of purple flowers above the sink.

She sniffed, grimaced. She really couldn't stand all this purple, or the flowers, but then, none of it was her business, thank the good Lord. She couldn't imagine sleeping in that disgusting bed. Isaac was likely the type of man who slept without a shower, then got up and washed all that diesel fuel off in the morning, something her mother never allowed. Mark and Elmer showered before going to bed, as it should be.

She would have to talk to him.

He came stomping across the porch and into the kitchen at six o'clock, leaving a trail of dried mud and sawdust, smelling of diesel fuel and something she couldn't place. He didn't speak, simply walked through the kitchen and hung his filthy straw hat on a hook, shrugged off his heavy outer shirt, and hung it up.

"I just washed the kitchen floor, so I'd appreciate it if you left your shoes in the mudroom."

A grunt. Then, "I hate taking off my shoes before I do chores."

"Is that right?"

Her eyes flashed green anger.

"That's right."

"If you want a clean floor, you're going to take off those boots."

He came closer, his dark eyes black with his own resentment.

"I don't give a hoot about this floor. And if you think you're going to sail in here in your high and mighty Lancaster way, then you can just pack up and leave."

Susan blinked her disbelief. How could this man say this to her? She couldn't let him get away with it.

"As long as I am your maud, you will do as I say."

"And as long as I am your employer, you will do as I say."

With that, he slapped his hat on his head, shrugged back into the coat, and slammed out of the house, calling for Titus as he went.

Titus. She had gotten so into cleaning and preparing dinner that she had completely forgotten about the boy and his dog.

Well, everyone was used to him meandering through the countryside, so evidently he'd appear in the usual way. She opened the oven door, poked a fork into the beef roast, added more beef broth, and set to work putting plates, knives, and forks on the table. From time to time, she glanced at the encroaching darkness, the light fading fast after the sun set behind the mountains.

Her heart sank when the mudroom door opened and Isaac bellowed, "Titus here?"

"No."

"Well, where's he at?"

Susan cringed at his grammar. "I have no idea."

"You were in charge. Why did you let him wander off?"

She felt the color drain from her face, felt her hands curl into fists. "Well, you're home now and the children are your responsibility." She stomped up the stairs and into her room, had the gratifying luxury of slamming the door as hard as possible. She stayed there all evening, marveling at the man's stupidity, the audacity of blaming her for Titus, when that boy knew nothing but meandering anywhere he pleased. It wasn't like this was a new thing, and Isaac hadn't seemed to care much when Bertha was in charge.

But as darkness enveloped the house, she found herself standing at her door, her ear pressed to the woodwork, listening for sounds of Titus below her. She was torn between real fear of Titus being lost and the pride of her own ability to stand her ground.

When she couldn't decide if she heard anyone's voice, she opened the door, very slowly and quietly, before tiptoeing to the landing.

"Titus, you can't continue to do this, I guess. Not if Susan's here."

There was a small boy's unintelligible reply, Sharon's lisp.

"She's upstairs."

Another jumble of children's voices, then a round of real laughter from Isaac. Her face burning, she backtracked, slipped into her room, and sat down hard on the edge of her bed, an expulsion of breath leaving her throat.

Oh, he was a despicable man. Pity the woman who would ever consent to be his wife.

Seven months unfurled like a thick scroll ahead of her.

ON SUNDAY MORNING she awoke, tilted the small clock, and found it to be only 6:45. There was not a sound from below. She was thoroughly awake, longed for the first cup of coffee. She threw on her robe, belted it at the waist, fixed the elastic in her hair, and went slowly downstairs to the kitchen and put the kettle on.

The light in the east drew her to the porch, the magnificent patio off the kitchen with the spectacular view of the mountain.

She almost gasped with the sheer beauty of the first rays of sunlight playing across the curved ridges, throwing a golden, pink light across it, as pristine as if God had only introduced this sight for the very first time. She opened the door, let herself out, breathed deeply, the frosty air filling her throat, her lungs, invigorating.

She found the first two lines of her favorite hymn crowding out her thoughts, music filling her heart and soul.

Oh Lord my God, when I in awesome wonder.
Consider all the world Thy hands have made.

And when the golden light turned into a rosy glow, she felt her throat tightening as tears pricked her eyes. She felt her heart yearning toward the beauty of God, the wonder of His creation, the great and perfect exquisiteness of His design. She worshipped him in the only way she knew how, in quiet yearning toward a Higher Being.

"Do you always wake up a house with a tea kettle?"

She jumped, instinctively drawing her arms around her waist. She turned slowly.

Isaac stood, his blond hair tousled, sleep in his swollen eyes, a mocking smile lifting the corners of his mouth.

"Oh. Sorry. I . . . I've never seen anything like this." She waved a hand in the direction of the mountain.

He said nothing, and when she looked at him, she was unnerved to find his eyes on her.

"I mean, I never saw the sun shine on the mountain at this time in the morning."

Still he said nothing.

Then, gruffly, "You want your coffee?"

"Um, well, yes. I guess so."

"I'll get it."

The mugs were brown ironstone, with logging emblems, the coffee steaming hot, the air filled with a sparkling frost. The world had turned into a rosy, diamond-filled wonder. She could do no more than perch on the edge of the stone bench, cross her legs, and lean forward to catch the best view of the rose-colored mountain. There were no words necessary for quite some time, and none were offered.

Then, "I thought you were an angel in that white bathrobe."

"Huh. Not much of an angel."

"No. Not last night. I apologize. I was in a mood. Remember, we put the skidder on its side. Lots of damage, as it turns out."

"Wasn't my fault."

He looked at her. She looked back, unflinching. Green eyes clashed with dark brown ones.

"You Lancaster girls must be from a different mold."

"Mh-hmm."

"Look, if you're going to be my maud, we have to come to an understanding, okay? I won't boss you around, and you don't boss me."

"You think?"

"Stop it, Susan. You make me feel like a kid. I won't take it."

"By the way, where was Titus last night?"

"Out somewhere. He usually shows up before dark. Said he had a skunk trapped under the woodpile, but he makes stuff up."

He slurped from his coffee cup, squinted his eyes at the mountain.

"Don't you worry?"

"Not really."

Susan shook her head.

"Don't start. He needs space. He's no scholar. He hates school, never did well there. He's an outdoorsman like me. I never liked school, never got along with my teachers. So give him a chance."

"But he'll fail third grade if he doesn't try harder. He doesn't apply himself at all."

Isaac shrugged. "You're the teacher."

"Really? That's all you have to say?"

She picked up her coffee cup and went into the house, got dressed, and sat on her bed. She read her Bible for a while, then asked God to please give her strength to carry on for these remaining seven months. Somehow, dear God, they seemed like seven years.

"Just let me go home to Levi and announce my love, be married to him in safety on the rock solid foundation of Jesus Christ, my first love."

So Susan found herself in a much better frame of mind as she made breakfast and greeted the sleepy, tousle-headed children.

The kitchen island was bathed in sunlight as they sat on barstools enjoying the crispy bacon, the eggs scrambled to perfection, the pancakes made from scratch. Isaac wolfed his food, spoke little, then left for the barn, Titus in tow. Sharon helped with dishes, talked in her lisping voice, then sat down on the mudroom floor. She pulled on a pair of pink and brown cowboy boots and a coat and scarf, before telling Susan she was going to the barn.

That was when Susan discovered the children's riding ability, both of them galloping past the house on full-grown horses. Her breath caught in her throat as they flew past, appearing so small and vulnerable on the large horses. How could he allow this? These children should be on ponies, animals their size. Evidently, the man had no fear, not for himself or for his children.

She sighed, swept the floor, sat on the couch, picked up a magazine and tried to concentrate on an article about conservation in the state of Wyoming.

Why didn't they come back from the barn? What kept them out there most of a Sunday forenoon? She decided to write letters, pushed back the urge to see the interior of the immense building for herself.

She wrote to her family, describing her new surrounding in detail, then wrote another, shorter version to Levi. She found herself missing him much more than she thought possible and wondered if she could go home for Christmas.

To ride in his buggy, attend the Christmas hymn singing, to feel loved and adored by him, to be by her parents and siblings—thinking of it brought a fresh wave of longing so forceful it was almost physical. She missed the bustle of market, the scent of the sandwiches, Beth's constant chatter. She wanted to go home, the only pace in the world she could truly be herself, to relax and grow in love and returned kindness. Another moment of regret, followed by despair, and she'd be awash in self-pity, unable to face the eternity of seven months.

She isolated herself from Isaac and the children when they returned from the barn, feeling like an outsider, and was glad of it. They made ham sandwiches, chocolate milk, then asked her to accompany them when they went back out.

She frowned, looked up from her book, and shook her head.

"What do you do out there?"

"Play with the horses."

"I don't ride."

"You can learn," Titus shouted from the mudroom as he stepped into his boots.

"I don't think so."

Isaac gave her a look and a shrug and went out the door, with Sharon on his heels. Well, this was strange. A distant father who didn't seem so distant on a Sunday. These children stuck to him like glue.

She decided to see what this barn was all about. She put on her coat and sneakers, let herself out, walked across the porch and the gravel drive and into the door of the barn, discovering a whole different world she had never imagined.

There was an indoor riding arena, complete with sawdust, a huge roof over everything, gates, barrels, ropes, and Isaac standing in the middle, a young horse on a long rope, trotting, lowering and raising its head with impatience.

Titus and Sharon sat cross-legged on the sawdust, observing every move their father made, eyes bright with interest. When Isaac caught sight of her, he stopped the horse, gave him to Titus to put away, and came over to Susan.

"I'll show you around."

There were ten horses, part Friesian, part quarter horse. There was a gypsy vanner cross, a wild mustang bought at a rodeo. There was a Shetland pony and a Hackney, a donkey named Brighty.

The donkey made her stop, look up at Isaac.

"You read that book?"

Sheepishly, he nodded. "I still have it."

"Me too."

"Marguerite Henry."

"*King of the Wind.*"

"*Justin Morgan Had a Horse.*"

"*Brighty of the Grand Canyon.*"

They laughed, became ill at ease, embarrassed to be caught with the same childhood interest. She was intimidated by the beauty of the horse barn, the rows of clean box stalls with metal grating, the saddles and bridles, blankets and colorful halters and lead ropes.

It was almost unbelievable that the unkempt children, pitied in school, motherless and in the care of the slovenly Bertha, had a part in this barn filled with horses and costly tack. Just went to show, you could never tell, unless you spent time in a home. Susan started to understand Titus's disinterest and unwillingness to learn. He had much bigger and more important things on his mind than being boxed up in a classroom. The great rolling vista where he lived, the horses, the heavy equipment and chainsaws—it was all far more exciting to him than math and spelling.

No excuse, though. She was the teacher hired to give them *all* an education, not just the ones who wanted to be at school.

She watched Sharon saddle up the Shetland pony, her father patiently instructing her on how to tighten the girth, how to slide the leather straps beneath the silver ring to tighten it. She slipped the bit in the pony's mouth expertly, then looked to her father for approval and was rewarded with a wide smile and the crinkling of his eyes.

"Way to go, Sharon."

She sparkled as she rode the pony in a gallop, around and around, sitting straight, one arm holding the reins, the other at her side, relaxed.

"She's amazing," Susan observed.

"She'll be competitive once she's older."

They watched in silence until Sharon drew in on the reins, stopped the pony, and leaped off the saddle. Titus took a turn, but was not impressed with riding a pony. Susan could tell he felt himself far superior to that little animal, almost embarrassed to be riding at such a low level.

"Do you ride?" Isaac asked.

Quickly, Susan shook her head. "No. I have my own driving horse and buggy, but where or how would I ever have learned? Have you ever been to Lancaster?"

"No. But I've heard a lot about it."

"It's a lot different than here."

"I imagine. Do you want to learn?"

"To ride? No."

"Why not?"

"For one, I don't own a pair of trousers, for another, there's no way I'll get on a horse with you and the children watching."

"Everyone's a beginner when they start."

"According to this family, I'm about fifteen years too late."

"How old are you?"

"I just turned twenty-three."

He said nothing.

The evening was uneventful, the children quiet with their play, Isaac falling asleep in the recliner before bedtime. Susan read her book, turned the battery lamps on when it was time, then wrote another letter to Kate while sitting at the dining room table, her glance going out to the brown pastures, the line of fir trees beyond.

CHAPTER 22

Monday morning was a rush. Isaac left at six and then Susan did laundry, made breakfast, and had the children ready and out the door before eight. In those first few weeks, she often felt more than a little panic, wondering how she would ever manage her schedule, but by the time Thanksgiving arrived, she had acquired a semblance of order. Every mother with children in her classroom brought pies or cookies, an occasional casserole or pizza, which made her cooking in the evening much easier. There was a general show of support from everyone, so by the day the Thanksgiving dinner was held at school, Susan felt that she was truly a part of the community.

She had come to look forward to church services, sitting beside Isaac as they drove the surrey across the dusty gravel roads, winding in and out of copses of trees, on high pastureland, and always in the view of the mountains. The manner of speaking in the western dialect grew on her, and before she was aware of it, she found herself rolling her r's in the same way. She sat with the single girls, who were all much younger—fifteen- and sixteen-year-olds who wore the bowl-shaped coverings and combed their hair up over their heads. Sometimes she felt like a goose in a duck pond, but everyone accepted her with so much kindness, appreciating her efforts as a teacher.

Then, like a descending storm, Titus threw a major fit about washing his hair before attending the Thanksgiving dinner at school. He refused to open the bathroom door no matter how they pleaded and cajoled. Isaac was finally summoned and Titus gave in to his rebuke. When Titus opened the door, he was escorted outside to the barn for a firm talk, or whatever form of discipline was carried out. Paddlings were still perfectly acceptable in the Amish culture, but everything within reason, so when Isaac returned with a chastened Titus in tow, Susan asked no questions.

The dinner went well, with a few skits bringing laughter, and an atmosphere of gaiety keeping smiles on faces as the children sang the songs they'd practiced.

Compliments were genuine and frequent, with Susan's face glowing as the turkey and mashed potatoes were passed.

Isaac visited with the various fathers. He was dressed in a navy blue shirt, vest, and Sunday trousers. Susan was unaware of whispers behind her back, the titters and silent shaking of hidden giggles, as the more romance-minded mothers already had poor Isaac married off to the school teacher.

Roy Edna, as wives were dubbed in western culture (the husband's name preceding the wife's), put a quick stop to any matchmaking, telling them in clipped tones that Susan was spoken for and so was he. Edna rolled her eyes in a superior manner, said she'd heard he was certainly a looker, that Levi in Lancaster. And no, one couldn't say who Isaac had in mind, but he was writing to someone.

So the matchmakers' dreams were dashed to the ground, resulting in some not-so-well-hidden disappointment, James Frieda snapping at Roy Edna for having made too small an amount of macaroni salad, and Roy Edna putting on a royal pout for everyone's benefit. Frieda justified her admonishment by thinking she'd said it for Edna's own good. Edna was always so tight, bringing those small Tupperware bowls of whatever when there was a potluck—someone had to tell her.

Titus refused to sing. He never opened his mouth to join in. This was not lost on the audience, but what was to be done? He missed his mother, poor boy. Susan felt that Isaac addressed the problem in a good way, pulling Titus aside after and gently asking him why he hadn't sung and then reminding him firmly but kindly that it was disrespectful not to participate.

Susan's approval of Isaac was apparent, which brought a fresh wave of surmising from the ladies, but not one soul mentioned it, with Roy Edna sitting in a corner with her ruffled feathers and terrific pout.

THAT EVENING AT home, Susan basked in the approval of the community. She expected that Isaac was waiting until after the children were out of earshot to tell her what a good job she'd been doing at school, but he brought the mail in and handed two letters to her without a word. She looked at him, questioning, but he didn't favor her with as much as a glance before disappearing into his bedroom.

She shrugged and ran upstairs to tear at the envelope with eager fingers, unfolding the large sheet of notebook paper and proceeding to read the letter from Levi. His writing was so good, his spelling perfect. Her heart raced as she read of his longing to see her, his offer to pay her way home for Christmas. She held the letter to her heart and thought, *Yes, oh yes, Levi, I will be home for Christmas.* And again, she was reassured that she really did love him now.

She ran back down the stairs to find Isaac in the recliner, reading.

"Isaac."

He put his book down, looked at her with tired eyes.

"Yes?"

"I . . . um . . . just received this letter. Levi asks if I can go home for Christmas."

For a long moment, there was no answer. The footrest of the recliner banged down, and he laid the book aside, rubbed his eyes, ran a hand through his hair and looked at her, taking in the sparkling eyes and flushed face.

"I don't know why not."

"Really?"

"I'm sure someone will be able to handle things for a week."

"Thank you. Oh, thank you so much."

"Another thing. You many not have to travel by train. We'll call around, there might be someone visiting in a neighboring community that can take you along back."

"I'd be so grateful. I miss my parents. And Levi, of course."

"Of course."

There was an awkward silence as thick as molasses before Isaac cleared his throat.

"I remember dating Naomi. It was a time you can never replace. I think in each life, there is one great love, and only one."

He stopped and rested his elbows on his knees, his gaze on the wide boards of the hardwood floor. The silence was broken by the sound of Sharon rocking her baby doll, singing a Dutch lullaby.

"That is why I'm so hesitant, suddenly, with Mary Amstutz, the widow I have been corresponding with. She's a lovely lady, in every way, but I just can't grasp what I had with Naomi. Should I accept this as normal, or should I let her go? The last thing on earth I want to do is hurt her, but I'm still a young man. I'm hesitant to enter a union where it's more my duty to provide a mother for my children than a wife, a lover, for myself."

Susan blinked, surprised to find him sharing his thoughts. She had no idea what she should say, so she remained quiet and sat down on the couch opposite him. She was uncomfortable with the word "lover" and wished he had not spoken as freely.

"I feel relieved, Susan, when I think of ending it. Pure relief. Is that so awful?"

"I don't know."

"Smart words."

"I don't."

He nodded. Suddenly, he sat up, pierced her with his gaze.

"Do you ever feel this way about this Levi?"

She met his eyes, saw the dark brooding of his sadness. She meant to shake her head no, but something stopped her, an unseen force.

"I have, often, in the past. But sometimes even when a couple feels sure about each other, things go wrong. I have a sister, Kate . . ."

And she told him the whole story of Kate's life, now living in Virginia as an English person. Sometimes, she swallowed her tears, sometimes vented her anger and frustration at Dan, but mostly she portrayed the disbelief of Kate's steadfast love and devotion, no matter what Dan chose to do next. She finished with a spreading of her hands.

"I mean, come on, he'll have her practicing to be a clown, or a nun, whatever pops into his head."

They laughed together.

"So that's partly why I'm not married yet. It seems like a huge risk."

"Smart girl."

"Thank you. But since coming here to Wyoming, I feel much clearer about what I want."

Another silence.

"And what is that?" he asked.

"Levi. To return to my home, get married, and live with my old friends and family. It's all I know. And I trust Levi. He's very loyal to his job, his boss. He works with my brother Mark, and is a foreman at a shed building place. He seems rock solid."

"Good. So how long have you dated?"

"We didn't really date formally. Just did three mini vacations. Snowboarding. RVing."

"So he's not your steady boyfriend?"

"It's up to me, when I'm ready to start."

"Which is in May?"

"Yes."

"No boyfriend before this?"

"No."

He shook his head. "Hard to believe."

"That's what everyone says. Why is that so hard to believe?"

He gave her a hard stare, a mocking grin.

"You know why. You can't be blind when you look in the mirror."

"But . . . looks should not have anything to do with it."

He laughed a little. "Would you be interested in Levi if he weren't good looking?"

She shrugged, feeling her cheeks begin to blush.

He sighed and moved to a more comfortable position on the recliner.

Sharon came over, rested an elbow on Isaac's knee, crossed one foot over the other, and clutched her doll to her chest. She fixed her dark eyes on Susan, then lisped, "I hope you never come back."

"Sharon!" said Isaac.

"I hope she doesn't. Bertha is better."

"Sharon, I wouldn't want my teacher living with me either, but Susan has done a lot around here and you're being pretty rude."

Sharon marched back to her perch on the child's rocker to resume her lullaby.

"Sorry," Isaac said.

Susan waved a hand in dismissal.

SUSAN COUNTED THE days till departure, while Isaac made the necessary phone calls, finally concluding the date of her return to be on the twenty-second of December. She would have only three days in Lancaster before coming back to Wyoming, by Amtrak. Susan swallowed her disappointment and nodded her head at the arrangements. She had plenty to do to prepare the school children for their Christmas program, so she made herself focus on that before allowing herself time to revel in the joy of heading home.

Isaac took her to Sheridan for shopping. She was in bewilderment, amazed at how he could so easily buy gifts, ticking them off one by one with no doubt about his purchases, while she wavered, hemmed and hawed until he walked off and told her he was leaving if she didn't make up her mind. He made her so mad she wished he'd go on home without her, except she needed the ride.

How did he manage to make her feel inferior? Some of the gifts he'd bought were plain dumb. Giving his mother a set of cookie sheets? Really? Any mother had her own favorite set. Titus, the one who disliked any schoolwork, especially reading, would be getting a set of books about horses. He'd never be able to read them. Let him find all that out by himself. He wouldn't listen to her.

He told her he wanted to eat at a steakhouse, a nice sit-down type of meal. Did she want to join him? She did, but what about the children, at Harvey and Barb's? She was assured they'd be fine. They adored Norman and Marvin, who were both little blisters.

And Susan burst out laughing.

SHE COULDN'T HELP comparing him with Levi. His manners were rough around the edges, his table manners even worse. He was so huge and ungainly, the titanium plates in his cheekbone evident in the yellow lamplight. He mispronounced the cheese for the salad, didn't put his napkin on his lap, and ordered Mountain Dew to drink.

She winced at all of this, wishing for a bit of refinement.

She supposed all loggers were too big and too fearless, barging through life with a gasoline can in one hand and a chainsaw in the other.

He ate his steak and potatoes in the same way he ate at home and was finished long before she was, then sat back and watched her eat while drinking another glass of Mountain Dew, which made five total.

The waitress, a deeply tanned woman with false eyelashes, allowed him the luxury of her appreciation, and he left her a fifty-dollar tip, which absolutely infuriated Susan.

"Why'd you do that?" she blurted out.

"What?"

"Leave her that tip."

"She was a good waitress. Sort of cute, too."

"Puh. False eyelashes."

"How do you know?"

He was laughing as she got up, shrugged into her coat, and marched out of the restaurant ahead of him, her head held high.

"Wait. Not so fast. I want to see if your eyelashes are false."

She walked faster. He grinned.

Life was interesting, he decided at that moment.

On December twenty-second, two feet of snow kept all travel at a standstill. In the previous days, a winter storm advisory went largely unheeded by Susan who was accustomed to eastern weather, which often was blown out of proportion by overly anxious newscasters heady with drama. So when the storm actually hit on the night after the school program, she cried herself to sleep, alone in her cold room, allowing the homesickness and self-pity to wash over her.

She called home, crying, then called Levi and accepted his sincere condolences. He said it was better not to take chances during the winter, with the weather so unpredictable, and said it would be spring before they knew it. He was more concerned about her safety than having her back in Lancaster, which she found comforting. So much unselfish love. What a true harbinger of things to come.

She awoke on the twenty-third in the middle of a howling blizzard. She hated the West, Isaac, and every stupid decision she'd ever made.

Her hair was dry and frizzy, every split end split again, she decided, her eyes red and swollen, her lips parched and cracked from the dry cold. She was thoroughly stuck in this house, kept like a prisoner by the elements. No school, nothing to occupy her mind except trying to avoid Isaac and put up with the children. She was mature enough to recognize that none of this was their fault, so she had to try not to ruin their Christmas with her bad mood.

Then the doubts fired up like a well-fed woodstove. Levi surely didn't seem to mind very much about her having to stay in Wyoming. In fact, he seemed to be certain she'd stay here all winter. How was she supposed to deal with that?

She put all her angst into baking, mixing five different kinds of cookies. She made chocolate fudge and peanut butter fudge, decorated the stair railing with fir branches she clipped from trees in the yard, getting freezing cold and very wet in the process. The children were delighted. They hopped up and down, squealed, and clapped their hands until she made them stop, then began jumping on the couch and sliding off headfirst.

After the children were in bed, she talked to Isaac about Levi, trying to sort out the fears that raged in her mind. The house was clean and quiet, the only sound the crackling of logs in the fireplace. He listened quietly, watched her face as the parade of emotion marched across her eyes, the set of her hands, intertwined in her lap, the way the firelight played across the contours of her cheekbones.

"What do you think?" she concluded.

He didn't know, although, like she'd said, it was certainly chivalrous of him, the way he worried about her safety. Did trains derail in a storm? It could happen, he supposed, although he was sure the weather was monitored closely.

"Do you think I could go in February? For Valentine's Day?"

She blushed, wishing she hadn't asked such a silly question, then wondered why she always felt like that around him.

"I'm guessing you could do that," he said slowly. "As long as there's good weather."

"So that will give me something to look forward to, right?"

"Sure. Yeah."

It was warm and cozy on the couch. She was reluctant to go to her room, which was always much colder. Here in Wyoming, she was always cold, from one bitter windstorm to the next. The ceaseless wind howled around the corners, sending great billows of snow whirling away across pasturelands with blinding ferocity. Trees bent and swayed, branches snapped. Creatures left outside would freeze if untended. Weather was not to be taken lightly here, where in the East, a forecast of two to five inches halted school bus travel.

"I'm always cold," she complained.

"Are you? I'm sorry. You can sleep in my bed and I'll sleep on the couch."

"Thank you, but that's OK. I'll throw an extra blanket on my bed."

She did not want to sleep in that diesel fuel-infused bed, the mattress and pillow never free of the lingering odor. Besides, it was too intimate, inhabiting his sleeping place.

"We'll have to do something about that cold upstairs, though, if you're uncomfortable."

"I'm alright. I'm cold everywhere. It's just cold, cold, cold in Wyoming."

She shivered, then got to her feet.

"Well, goodnight."

"Goodnight, Susan."

She stopped. "I just want to say thank you."

"For what?"

"For listening. For letting me go home in February."

"Levi will want to see you."

"Yes."

He heard her footsteps all the way up the stairs and to her room before he sighed, got up, and walked slowly to his own bedroom.

The day before Christmas, Susan fully realized the extent of her homesickness, struggling to maintain her composure as she read the story of Jesus's birth to her pupils that morning. The children fidgeted, threw bits of eraser, grinned, shuffled papers, and clicked pens until she stopped reading, glanced up, and frowned, putting a stop to the noise.

They were all wound up, having been conveyed to school with horses straining to pull carriages through snowdrifts, the wind slamming into the team with serious strength, visibility obscured time after time.

The day would be shortened to one o'clock, with Christmas upon them, and a few spelling and arithmetic lessons were followed by a gift exchange before the holiday began at home. But Susan was struggling to feel festive. She snapped at unruly students charged with adrenaline at the thought of a gift exchange, then felt like weeping. There were seven more weeks before she could even think of seeing her parents, her siblings, Lancaster County with its gentle snowstorms, the state trucks rattling by with chained wheels, spreading calcium and salt, traffic moving, secure in the knowledge of safety.

To be honest, she had never been quite as scared in all her life as she had been that morning, conveyed to school against her wishes, telling

Isaac it wasn't safe, going to school with the wind whipping up the snow like that. He'd laughed at her. Laughed in her face.

The horse he drove was a monster, a huge reckless animal complete with flaring nostrils and wild eyes. The children clambered into the back, their wrapped Christmas packages clutched in their hands, chattering the whole way without fear. When the blinding walls of wind-driven snow hit them, Susan huddled against the side of the surrey and closed her eyes to keep from crying out, while Isaac sat as calm and dumb as a boulder.

He was so big and so wide, she barely had any room at all, and had no intention of sitting shoulder to shoulder, covered in that fur lap robe. He never said much of anything, but she could tell by the gleam in his brown eyes, the way he sat up straight and leaned forward, how much he enjoyed this perilous trek. Didn't he realize he was putting their lives on a full collision course?

Then, to make matters worse, he tied that gigantic horse to a wooden pole and insisted on starting her fire at the school, saying it was tricky in this wind, while she busied herself with the day's lessons and wished him gone.

When he finally did heave himself out the door, leaving a trail of woodchips and melted snow, the irritation was replaced by an impending homesickness like a runaway train. And when the children sang a glorious rendition of "Hark the Herald Angels Sing," she felt the sting of tears, felt her lips go wobbly, her nose burn with emotion. She turned her back and allowed a few warm tears to drop on her cheeks before brushing them away with the back of her hand.

It was only sheer determination that shoved her along all day, pronouncing spelling words, handing out assignments for arithmetic.

Some of the excitement rubbed off on her as the children exchanged gifts, gasping and squealing in pure delight at which person had the other person's name, giggling and tittering on about the presents.

Titus accidentally broke Caitlyn's snow globe, and she stood in disbelief as the water and flakes of artificial snow spread in the aisle by her desk. She lifted her chin and glared at him, and he retaliated by saying it was her own dumb fault, then stomped off in a huff. Susan hauled him back, handed him a roll of paper towels, and told him briskly to start cleaning up the mess, while Caitlyn put on quite an elaborate show of sorrow.

When one o'clock finally came and the buggies showed up to take their children home, Susan was physically and emotionally exhausted. She swept the floor, drew the curtains, and was ready to go when Isaac showed up a half hour late.

"How was your day?" he asked, as he stepped aside to let her in the surrey.

"I've had better," she said crisply.

He didn't bother answering, but merely climbed in beside her, filling up the entire carriage, leaving no space for her with his arms working the reins as he tried to keep the carriage on the road in spite of the poor visibility.

She complained about the constant wind, wondering aloud how the horse was going to get them safely home, pulling this carriage straight into its teeth.

"Trevor? He's powerful, believe me. The best."

Everything he had was the best. His confidence bloomed like a hot air balloon all the time. He had had the best wife, owned the best horses, had the best view from his house. She felt sure he had the supreme assurance he was the best logger, with the best equipment, the best record of felling trees.

When they finally came in sight of his homestead, she had never been more relieved, the dark brown house and barn jutting from the snow like a haven. Smoke curled up from the wide stone chimney, the fir trees like soft ice cream cones, laden with snow, the wind chopping away at them until the deep green needles emerged.

It was beautiful, the great swells of windswept snow rolling like ghosts, creating a sense of movement with light and shadow.

This land seemingly had no boundaries. Here, your soul could expand and enjoy the immense power of wind and sky and sculptured mountains. In this wild place, human beings were not subject to certain boxes, or stacked neatly into structured spaces. Weather was unpredictable, timelines were not always neat, and people learned to laugh at danger.

And yet her heart longed for home. Longed with an intense physical ache.

"Here we are, home again," Isaac shouted as he drew back on the reins, and she thought there was no way this isolated place could ever be her home, no matter how beautiful and wild and free it was.

CHAPTER 23

ON CHRISTMAS MORNING, SUSAN WAS RUDELY AWAKENED BY squeals and shrieks from the children, stentorian yells from who else but that exhilarated Isaac. What was wrong with him? She rolled over, reached blindly for the battery alarm clock, and groaned to find the red 4:30 glaring at her.

She was awake now, and knew the noise below would not subside. She pulled the heavy covers over her head, found herself unable to breathe properly, and removed them before trying to cover only her ears, leaving room for her nose and mouth. The air was freezing cold, as usual, and chills raced up her spine at the thought of getting dressed in the upstairs bathroom.

Another yell.

She grimaced and squeezed her eyes shut. She had no intention of going down those stairs at this indecent hour. She wouldn't be part of their gift exchange anyway. She was only the teacher and the maud.

She could hear the wind against the window, but it was still pitch black outside. She lamented her state, being two thousand miles away from her family on Christmas morning. It simply wasn't right.

Nothing could have prepared her for this. She swallowed the rising lump in her throat.

She dozed on and off until a weak light appeared at the window. She drew a deep breath and threw back the covers. She pushed her feet into sheepskin moccasins, the only thing she'd bought for herself in

Sheridan, and the smartest. She washed her face, brushed her teeth, and combed her wavy tresses into submission, rolling them expertly along the side. She noticed the tanning of her skin, the smattering of freckles faded, the green of her eyes accentuated by the dark lashes.

Normal. Her face was normal. An average person's. She was no fair-haired beauty like Beth. Or Naomi. No porcelain skin or bright blue eyes.

If anything, beauty was a liability. Wasn't that what drew Dan to Kate and she to him? Susan again thought of Kate, glowing, in love, riding in fast cars with the handsome Dan, blinded to all his faults, all admonition of things to come. Surely, he didn't care about who she was beyond her looks. To have your own identity removed, and your husband's version inserted, would be a living nightmare. Yet Kate had been so sure that love would conquer all.

How did one go about keeping a sense of self, a healthy well-being, emotionally and spiritually, when she was completely overridden by an insufficient husband who exercised a ridiculous sense of power? He saddled Kate with his pouts, depression, fits of anger, then drank to medicate his undiagnosed mental illness, finally taking her away from her culture, away from family and all she had ever known.

In that one moment, as Susan looked in the mirror, she realized that if she was ever going to commit to marriage, she would have to overcome her fear of winding up in Kate's shoes. The pain of her empathy had become a disease in her heart, slowing the beat.

Perhaps it would be different if Kate had a barbed tongue more like her own, an iron will and a sense of self, but she was a sweet, trusting, simple soul, who allowed her boundless adoration to one man to control her life.

Susan swiped a hand across the steamed mirror, as if with one wipe she could erase the past.

She dressed in the red dress she'd brought for Christmas, threw on the black bib apron, then the white covering, and made her way downstairs.

Isaac looked up from his place on the floor, a set of directions spread before him, the beginning of a plastic tower emerging. Titus looked up, waved a hand, and yelled, Sharon hopping up and down beside him.

"A marble tower, Susan!"

"Good morning, Susan!" Isaac rang out.

She replied more gruffly than she intended, praising the tower out of necessity, before moving through the living room, past the kitchen island to the stove, putting both hands around the Lifetime drip coffeepot to see if it was hot. She turned the gas burner on before getting a mug.

Sharon tugged her into the living room, proudly producing the pile of toys her father had given her, then showed her all the Legos, skateboards, new bridles for the ponies, currycombs. It was overwhelming and completely unnecessary, this vast amount of gifts. Isaac was merely trying to compensate for his lack of time spent with these children, and a quick flare of irritation made her grip the handle of her mug.

She'd have to have a talk with him.

But she made a special Christmas breakfast, the waffles fluffy and crispy on the outside, with melted butter and maple syrup. She made scrambled eggs and bacon, toast from the loaf of homemade bread Edna had given her. There were glasses of orange juice and cups of hot chocolate with marshmallow and crushed peppermint candies.

Susan did her best to hide her bad mood, but when Isaac offered to wash dishes while she read the Christmas story of Jesus's birth to the children, she snapped her refusal, then set about washing dishes and scrubbing the stove, the countertops, the refrigerator door, everything, as if somehow she could scour away the ill humor.

When she slammed drawers and rubbed plates until they shone, he got the Bible story book and began to flip pages. Titus acted strangely, refusing to sit by his father's side, saying it wasn't his job. He kicked at the marble tower, then slammed a fist into the arm of the couch. Sharon began to wail, rubbing her fists into the streaming eyes, while Isaac sat, looking helplessly from one to the other, then at Susan, who quickly turned away.

"Mom always reads the story," Titus shouted, then burst into a volley of accusations against his father, who sat large and helpless.

"Your mother is in Heaven," he said finally.

"And it's your fault!" Titus screamed, butting his father with his head, pounding his arms with his fists, until Isaac overpowered him by restraining the pummeling hands. Susan pretended not to notice the whole episode as she continued to work in the kitchen.

Eventually, Titus calmed down, with the promise that no Bible story would be read since it was so upsetting not to have their mother there to read it. Sharon sat beside her father, sniffling, and he brought out a handkerchief and wiped her nose, then drew her onto his lap and held her quietly.

Susan busied herself with mixing bread cubes, cutting celery and onion, preparing the heavy Christmas roasting chicken for the oven. She watched the desperate birds at the feeder, kicking their inadequate feet through the snow like harried matchsticks, searching for sunflower seeds.

"Didn't you fill the birdfeeder?" she asked, her back turned. When there was no answer, she turned to show him her disapproval and found the most astonishing sight of her life.

He had his face against the top of his daughter's head, the tears a baptism of his sorrow, her blond hair becoming wet. Beside him, Titus's face was a thundercloud as he stared ahead as if to capture and punish the cancer that had taken his mother away from him.

Suddenly, Susan knew and recognized her own selfishness, her own unwillingness to care for others with a heartbreak much greater than her own. She would see her home in Lancaster again in a matter of weeks, but Isaac and the children would never see their wife and mother again in this lifetime. She was stung with guilt and shame, but still could not bring herself to enter their sorrow. Pride presented itself, and she hurried to the mudroom to find the container of seeds, to push the door open and flounder across the patio in the deepening drifts, anything to disengage herself from the scene in the living room.

When she returned from that duty, she swept the kitchen floor and moved quickly through the living room and up to her room, where she grabbed a book, randomly opened it, and began to read, telling herself she was only the maud and none of them wanted her interfering anyway.

But the book would not hold her interest, and neither did the chapter in Luke, the story of Elizabeth and Mary, on up to the three wise men's visit to the Christ Child. She read on out of duty, then finally admitted to herself she could not stay holed up in her room and went downstairs to find Isaac with the children asleep in his arms, the recliner's footrest up, the back comfortably positioned for a much needed rest.

Edna had supplied a box of homemade candy, so she set about arranging it on a plate, along with one of pretzels and cheese, a plate of cookies. All the school parents had given cookies, many of them going the extra mile with all kinds of Christmas treats, which had been more than generous. She was arranging all of them on plates when she heard the clunk of the footrest, Isaac disengaging himself from the sleeping children, carrying Sharon to the couch and covering her with a soft throw. Titus was curled up on the recliner, the palm of his hand tucked against his cheek.

Isaac sat on a barstool, his eyes thick with sleep. Blond stubbles sprouted from his cheeks, the uneven distribution of them evident in the brilliant glare of the sun on snow.

"Christmas, huh?" he said in a mocking tone.

She avoided his eyes, put the finishing touches on a plate of cookies.

He reached for a piece of fudge, then another, without bothering to bite it in half. A whole piece into his mouth, barely chewed, and down the hatch.

"This is really good."

"Roy Edna."

"Really? She a good cook?"

"You should taste her strawberry rolls."

"Well, I better shower. The kids got me up at four."

"Why don't you do gifts on Christmas Eve?"

He shrugged. "I don't know. I guess Naomi liked Christmas morning. Didn't matter to me. Women have a way of getting what they want, I guess."

She didn't smile, or bother to reply, wishing he'd go get a shower and do something about that hair and the lingering diesel scent.

"You're in some mood," he observed.

"You think?"

"You know, that's the most irritating answer anyone can come up with."

She didn't favor him with a glance, or a reply.

"Guess I'll have to drum up a bit of Christmas spirit by myself. Hey, look there."

He pointed to the birdfeeder, to show her the rare sight of a brilliant red cardinal, the feathers in bright display against the pure white backdrop. She turned to watch the birds busily gorging themselves on fresh sunflower seeds, found the little pine siskins amazing. She was caught up in the moment when she sensed his nearness, realized he was directly behind her. Her breathing caught in her throat, and she held perfectly still.

He moved away, and was gone.

THEY ALL DID chores together, navigating their way to the barn through the path he had shoveled, the cold seeping through the heaviest outerwear.

The children saddled and bridled the ponies with the new gear, then galloped their little animals around and around, their faces shining with a new happiness. As always, they begged Susan to ride, which she refused.

But the barn was warm, the smell of wood shavings and molasses mixed with corn and oats comforting. When she sensed the children becoming excited, she realized something was in the air, but she was not ready for what came next.

"Come here! Come here!" Titus sang out, with Sharon hopping up and down.

She noticed that Isaac was unusually self-conscious, not like himself at all, as he drew back a door on one of the box stalls.

She began shaking her head, thinking, *no*.

Her eyes adjusted to the dim light and she saw a horse as black as night, a mare with a long flowing tail, a forelock hiding the intelligent eyes, a red ribbon woven into the mane, a giant bow attached to the beige halter.

"Merry Christmas!" Titus shouted, and Sharon hopped up and down harder than ever.

"She's yours. She's yours!" she lisped, her words bouncing along.

"*No, no*," Susan said, realizing in full what was happening. "I can't take her. I'm going home in May."

"You'll take her along," Isaac said gruffly.

"But . . . not a horse," she protested.

"Go ahead. Go on. See if you like her."

She felt his hand at her waist, giving her a little shove, and found herself unable to resist. The silkiness of her! The warm, gentle brown eyes were placed perfectly in a perfectly shaped head. The thick neck was hidden by the luxurious, rippling mane.

She held on to the halter, brought a hand to her forehead, cupped the velvety nose, and fell in love. She brought her face to the beautiful face of the black horse, and felt that she understood all of Susan's homesickness and confusion. She found herself crying and sniffling and coughing because the horse was so beautiful and the connection she felt to her so unexpected.

Titus tapped his father's coat.

"She bawling," he whispered. "Why doesn't she like her?"

Isaac held a finger to his lips.

Susan led her out into the riding arena, walked her around, then stepped back to look at her. She was by far the best horse she had ever encountered, and she'd seen more than a few.

"Now you'll ride?" Sharon asked.

Susan's eyes were red-rimmed, but shining with a new light. She laughed ruefully, shook her head, shrugged.

"How can I say no?"

"You can't, you can't!" Titus yelled, and Sharon echoed his words, clapping her hands as she began the usual bouncing.

He had remembered, and presented her with a wrapped box, containing a pair of black leggings. She blushed, but excused herself to put them on, then returned to find Isaac saddling the mare with a black saddle studded with silver ornaments.

"I'll bridle her. I'm used to that part," she said quietly.

So he stepped back, and she spoke softly to the mare, slipping the bit easily into her mouth, then sliding the leather up over her ears and attaching the chin strap. She stepped back, eyed the stirrup, the height of the saddle, and realized there was no way on earth she could ever hope to insert a foot into that stirrup, let alone swing herself up over the back of that horse. Besides, the horse had begun to prance, step sideways.

She looked up at Isaac, pleading.

"Don't make me do this."

"I'm not. If you don't want to, it's okay. We'll unsaddle her."

"Well . . ." Then, "How in the world am I supposed to get my foot in there?"

"Just step up. Here, stand on my hands."

He bent over, cupped his hands, and waited.

"No. I'll get it."

She would never step on those hands. If she was going to learn how to ride, she might as well do it right. She wished there was no one to see.

She lifted one leg as high as possible, failed to hit the stirrup, and tried again. On the third try, she got it right and felt the satisfying piece of wood under the sole of her sneaker, grasped the saddle horn, and pulled herself up with the aid of one foot in the stirrup.

She was shaking, her teeth practically chattering.

Now that she was up there, her opposite foot could not find the stirrup. She fumbled. The horse side stepped. She had to bend over and hold the stirrup with one hand before she was able to insert her foot.

She was still way too high up off the ground. The horse's mane and ears were much too close, her dress and bib apron way too far out of the line perceived as decency.

"Sit straight. Reins tight, but not too tight. Heels down."

She obeyed, desperately hoping she wouldn't fall off.

"Now tell her to go."

"How?"

"Loosen the reins. Make the sound you would to your driving horse."

"Will you lead her? What if she gallops?"

So Isaac led the mare and Susan found herself carried by a smooth gait, the ears bobbing a soothing rhythm. She found a laugh beginning deep in her chest and felt on top of the world.

"Okay, let her go."

Confident now, she wanted the freedom of being able to ride on her own. She walked her horse around the perimeter of the horse barn. Isaac stopped her to explain neck reining, the opposite of driving a horse, learning to lay the reins against the neck on the opposite side.

She trotted, then galloped, a smooth rocking gait, her confidence building faster than anyone would have imagined. Isaac and the children were impressed, telling her she was a natural. She laughed out loud, not wanting to dismount. Riding a horse was the most unbelievable sensation, like a queen being conveyed through the air by some fairy tale magic no one had ever experienced before.

When she finally consented to dismounting, she miscalculated, her foot slipped, and she sat down hard, surprised to find the ground quite so far away.

They all laughed as she scrambled to her feet.

BACK IN THE house, Susan finished making supper, the good roast chicken and filling, the mashed potatoes and gravy. As usual, Isaac lowered his head and wolfed down his food, the amount he shoved into his mouth in a short amount of time completely staggering.

He leaned back, sighed, wiped his mouth with his napkin, and said it was a long time since he'd eaten roast chicken. He hadn't been aware they'd had one in the freezer. She said it was underneath the hamburger on the right side, and he nodded, a faraway look in his eyes.

After they played with the marble tower, Susan got the children's baths ready and put them to bed. Afterward, she cleared the table, scraped leftovers, and filled the sink with hot water and dish detergent.

He joined her, picking up a tea towel.

"Mind if I dry?"

"Not at all. I'm ready to call it a day. I'm too old for all this excitement."

He made no comment. She washed a plate, then another.

He cleared his throat. "Mind telling me why you were so grouchy this morning?"

"Homesick, I guess."

He nodded. "It seems to be the cross most of the women carry out here in Wyoming. I don't know. Sometimes I wonder if Naomi didn't suffer a lot more than I'll ever know. I've heard stress can cause cancer. Perhaps her death was my fault, moving her out here."

"Did she want to move?"

"She said she did."

He lifted a pile of plates, set them on the cupboard shelf, then reached for a lid.

"But how many women just say things out of a sense of duty? Or the submission they have been taught?"

Susan shook her head.

"That subject sets me off, every single time."

He lifted an eyebrow, but didn't comment, allowing her time to go on.

"I told you about my sister Kate."

He nodded.

"How can someone be so in love and so disappointed in later years? She acts like everything's OK, but it's not. She's miserable, and she once told me she doesn't know if she loves him anymore."

"Marriage is never easy," he said unexpectedly.

"Never?"

"Never. There are variants, of course, but you have to work at any relationship. I wonder if you're being unrealistic. Like you have to have a better marriage than anyone else, a perfect one, or else you're not going to bother."

"My sisters' marriages give me reason to be cautious."

"Every one of them?"

"Yep."

She wiped the counter, telling him about Rose and Liz, and he threw back his head and laughed, then said she'd convinced him she was the most negative person in the world. He told it sounded like those two sisters lived perfectly normal lives and were actually in pretty good marriages.

"Well, you can talk like that, but if I can't do better than they have, forget it."

And she meant every word.

"So you're planning on giving this Levi a fair chance?"

She hesitated, then stepped back to look up at him.

"You think I should?"

"By all means, give the chap a chance."

He smiled down at her.

"I'm sort of relieved I'm not in his shoes."

"What is that supposed to mean?"

"I'd hate to have my girl living with a widower. A young widower, without seeing her for nine months."

"Ten months. Almost eleven," she answered, then said quickly, "Well, you're different. I mean, I never think of you in that way."

"Never?"

"Of course not."

"That's probably a good thing. It makes it easier for you to be my maud till spring, right? And you'll be going home in May?"

"Yes. And I'm glad."

"Of course you are."

She hesitated, then looked up at him, meaning to tell him how much she appreciated the horse, but there was an intensity in his eyes that scattered the words from her thoughts. He did not touch her, did not say anything at all, and yet the kitchen disappeared for a moment, a poignant reminder that he was a man and she was a woman, alone together.

She stepped back and held the back of a kitchen chair as the house came back into focus.

"Thank you," she whispered, and fled to her room.

THE NIGHT WAS calm, the cold creeping like an invisible hand across the house, enveloping it with its power. Wood siding creaked, branches heavy with snowfall cracked and fell, and deer nesting in underbrush nearby lifted their heads to hear. Far away, where the ground dropped away to rocky outcrops and sheer cliff walls, a lone wolf lifted his shaggy face to the receding quarter moon and opened his mouth to send the spine-tingling primal howl of his species ricocheting among the crevices. And even farther away, as far as the base of the Bighorn Mountains, came an answering, undulating howl.

The gray wolf stopped, sniffed the large boulder on which he stood, then turned and trotted away, instinct guiding him as he set off to find his destiny.

ABOUT THE AUTHOR

LINDA BYLER WAS RAISED IN AN AMISH FAMILY AND IS AN ACTIVE member of the Amish church today. Growing up, Linda loved to read and write. In fact, she still does. Linda is well known within the Amish community as a columnist for a weekly Amish newspaper. She writes all her novels by hand in notebooks.

Linda is the author of several series of novels, all set among the Amish communities of North America: Lizzie Searches for Love, Sadie's Montana, Lancaster Burning, Hester's Hunt for Home, the Dakota Series, The Long Road Home, New Directions, and the Buggy Spoke Series for younger readers. Linda has also written several Christmas romances set among the Amish: *Mary's Christmas Goodbye*, *The Christmas Visitor*, *The Little Amish Matchmaker*, *Becky Meets Her Match*, *A Dog for Christmas*, *A Horse for Elsie*, *The More the Merrier*, *A Christmas Engagement*, and *Love Conquers All*. Linda has coauthored *Lizzie's Amish Cookbook: Favorite Recipes from Three Generations of Amish Cooks!*, *Amish Christmas Cookbook*, and *Amish Soups & Casseroles*.

OTHER BOOKS BY

LINDA BYLER

LIZZIE SEARCHES FOR LOVE SERIES

BOOK ONE   BOOK TWO   BOOK THREE

TRILOGY

COOKBOOK

Sadie's Montana Series

BOOK ONE

BOOK TWO

BOOK THREE

TRILOGY

LANCASTER BURNING SERIES

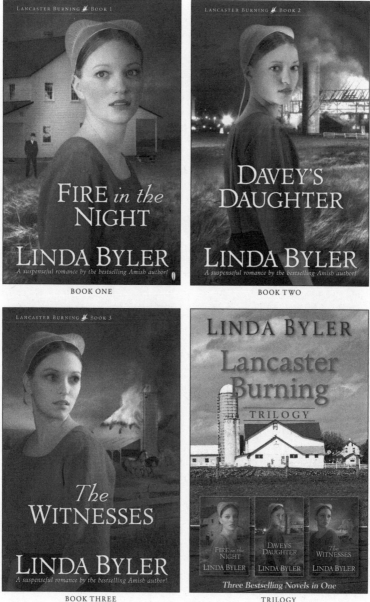

LANCASTER BURNING 🔥 BOOK 1

FIRE *in the* NIGHT

LINDA BYLER

A suspenseful romance by the bestselling Amish author!

BOOK ONE

LANCASTER BURNING 🔥 BOOK 2

DAVEY'S DAUGHTER

LINDA BYLER

A suspenseful romance by the bestselling Amish author!

BOOK TWO

LANCASTER BURNING 🔥 BOOK 3

The WITNESSES

LINDA BYLER

A suspenseful romance by the bestselling Amish author!

BOOK THREE

LINDA BYLER

Lancaster Burning

TRILOGY

FIRE *in the* NIGHT
LINDA BYLER

DAVEY'S DAUGHTER
LINDA BYLER

The WITNESSES
LINDA BYLER

Three Bestselling Novels in One

TRILOGY

HESTER'S HUNT FOR HOME SERIES

BOOK ONE

BOOK TWO

BOOK THREE

TRILOGY

The Dakota Series

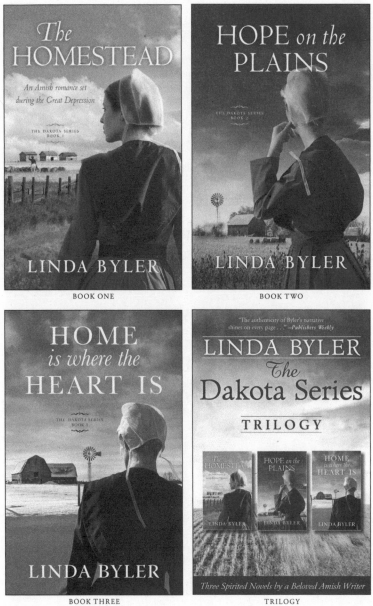

The Homestead
An Amish romance set during the Great Depression
THE DAKOTA SERIES BOOK 1
LINDA BYLER
BOOK ONE

HOPE on the PLAINS
THE DAKOTA SERIES BOOK 2
LINDA BYLER
BOOK TWO

HOME is where the HEART IS
THE DAKOTA SERIES BOOK 3
LINDA BYLER
BOOK THREE

"The authenticity of Byler's narrative shines on every page . . ." —*Publishers Weekly*
LINDA BYLER
The Dakota Series
TRILOGY
Three Spirited Novels by a Beloved Amish Writer
TRILOGY

Long Road Home Series

BOOK ONE

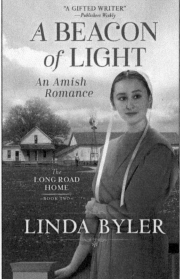

BOOK TWO

BOOK THREE

BUGGY SPOKE SERIES FOR YOUNG READERS

BOOK ONE

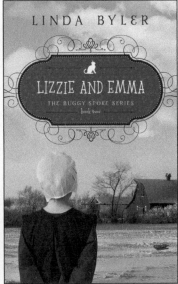

BOOK TWO

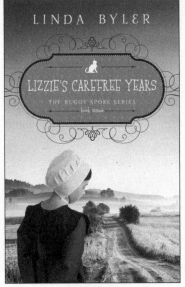

BOOK THREE

CHRISTMAS NOVELLAS

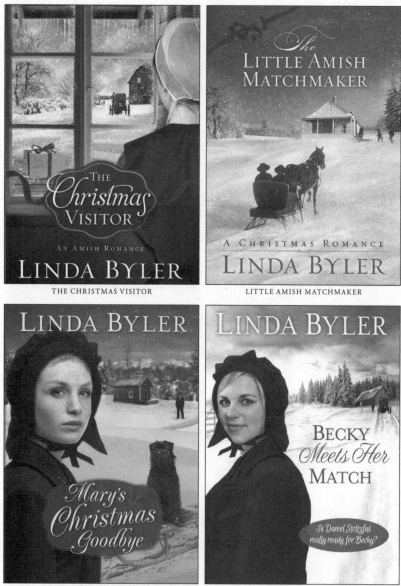

THE CHRISTMAS VISITOR

LITTLE AMISH MATCHMAKER

MARY'S CHRISTMAS GOODBYE

BECKY MEETS HER MATCH

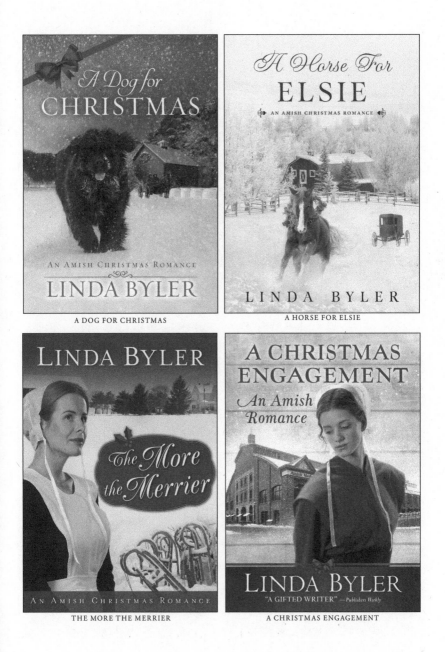

A DOG FOR CHRISTMAS

A HORSE FOR ELSIE

THE MORE THE MERRIER

A CHRISTMAS ENGAGEMENT

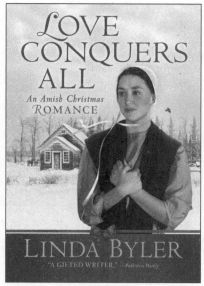

LOVE CONQUERS ALL

Christmas Collections

AMISH CHRISTMAS ROMANCE COLLECTION

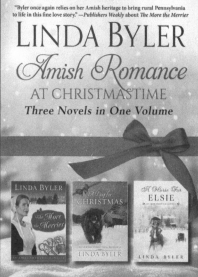

AMISH ROMANCE AT CHRISTMASTIME

Standalone Novels

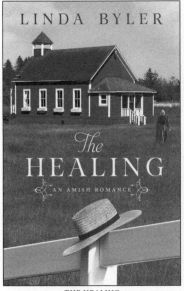

THE HEALING

A SECOND CHANCE

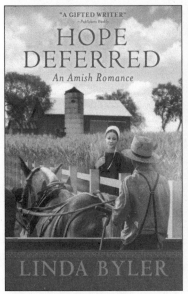

HOPE DEFERRED

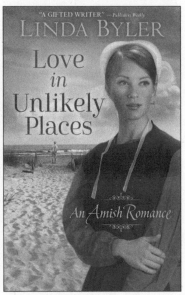

LOVE IN UNLIKELY PLACES